SWIFT and The Falcon

ISBN – 979-8-218-45477-7 SWIFT and The Falcon

SWIFT and The Falcon

The first Maximillion Moore International Crime Mystery story

By

Tony Moore

Dedication

SWIFT and The Falcon is dedicated to my many police, military, special forces and government agency friends in the UK and here in the US. My character, *"Nozzer the Cozzer the High Flying Rozzer,"* (London slang), Norwell Roberts QPM, is based on the real person, Norwell Roberts and the description is a true likeness of my long-time friend.

Norwell was in fact London's first black police officer as part of London's Metropolitan Police. On his retirement, Norwell was awarded the prestigious Queens Police Medal (QPM), by King Charles III, for his dedicated service to London's Metropolitan Police. He became the "Poster boy" for a campaign to bring in more ethnic minority police officers representing the cosmopolitan nature of today's British police force. Norwell wrote his own story in his book, "I Am Norwell Roberts."

Other characters are also based on real-life people, though the roles they play here in my book are entirely fictional.

Charlene Willoughby is based on my own "Aunty" Mrs. Bleby who I was placed with, from age 1 year to 8 years old, because my own mother had TB and died when I was 5 years old. Aunty' as we all called her opened her large home to many children who, like me, could not live at home. She became my mentor and my surrogate mother advising me ever since those days.

Aunty drove a white MGB convertible sports car which she bought (for cash) at age 75 and drove until she was 87. She was my real-life mentor and she, like my character Charlene Willoughby, loved her garden, with a passion.

Chapter 1

Leicester Square

Typical London weather, bloody pissing down, cats and dogs, with rain as if it knew I had to walk the distance from my office to the pub. I rushed through the busy street trying, in vain, to avoid the puddles and the spray coming up from the road traffic. It was mainly black cabs who always think they own the roads, as I made my way on this dismal grey Wednesday to the Piccadilly line station at Leicester Square and home.

Who am I? I'm Maximilian Moore, (Max to those who know me and filth to those I've put away). I was on my way back after a late lunch meeting that took the usual amount of time at the "Tom Cribb" pub a short distance from Leicester Square tube station close to where my office was. But the meeting with my friend always led to us both drinking a few too many pints keeping each other up to date with our busy lives.

My office location was more for the London Street address than being a practical location as I wanted a Leicester Square address. Anyway, my tube ride to and from my office when I was working from there was always a hoot, seeing the things people do when they think they are not being watched. I have always been an observer of people simply because people fascinate me and after all, it is the things they get up to which has earned me a great living since I began on the "Job" 20 years ago.

In the words of a recent pop song by Lorde, I was on a "Zipcode envy" with my WC2 street address which I hoped would make my business seem more prestigious. Truth is my office was not too big but it separated my work from my home and I didn't mind the commute as it was always so entertaining.

However, my main work took me out and about travelling all over the place so my assistant, Jeannie, was usually the only one manning my office phone. I was meeting my friend and former colleague, Keith, who was now at the ICC (International Criminal Court) in the Hague.

The International Criminal Court ICC is an intergovernmental organisation and international tribunal located in The Hague, which is in The Netherlands. It is the first permanent international court with jurisdiction to prosecute individuals for the international crimes of genocide, crimes against humanity, war crimes and the crime of aggression. The ICC is distinct from the International Court of Justice, an organ of the United Nations that hears disputes between states.

It was established in 2002 and is considered by its proponents to be a major step toward international justice, international law and human rights. Several governments have refused to recognise the court's assertion of jurisdiction, while other civil groups accuse the court of bias.

We were both in the Metropolitan Police stationed at Acton in West London. I had retired from the "Job" but Richard, "Keith" had moved on to better things and was now involved with international criminals together with Interpol. One could never miss Keith, whose full name was Keith Davies he was a tall 6'3" with red hair, a strong Welsh accent and a dry sense of humour. And, by the way, Davies, according to Keith, is the second most popular name in Wales!

I suspected he was with 6 (MI6) but never asked him as I knew he would never tell me. But he was well connected internationally within Interpol and other law enforcement agencies and told me he would always help me if I needed it. I knew he would and there was one time when I needed his help, but that story is for another time.

One time when Keith came over to meet me in Ealing, from The Hague, for a drink and some catching up, my daughter who had known Keith all her life, drove us around as we were planning on doing what we always did when we met up, have several pints in one or more of our many local pubs.

We seldom got to meet these days as we were both busy, Keith with the big stuff and me chasing deadbeat husbands while tracking down a slew of affairs of married men and women.

Yep, that was me moving on from crimes and misdemeanours, for the local nick to eventually branching out on my own. Yeah right, I'm right in West London's den of iniquity. But as my reputation grew, I was now a super sleuth as one London newspaper referred to me. After several years of success, I was solving the unsolvable and now I was working with high-profile clients often with big business, corporate clients and multinationals that needed a quiet solution to their problems.

I like what I do now because I am protecting businesses from fraud, corporate espionage and theft of patented materials. You might think so what? What's important about that but as I see it companies employ people and people need to work and as such their intellectual property, what makes them a success, should be protected in order for them to remain in business and employ people.

My secret? Apart from being a brilliant sleuth, which of course I am, I am also the epitome of discretion and never revealed who or what case I was working on except with my assistant, Jeannie. Jeannie was well named as she was a real whizz, a "Genie" with high-tech equipment and could find anyone anywhere in the world. I teased her sometimes saying she could find a stray flea on a camel's arse in the Sahara Desert if she looked. She also had a sing-song Welsh accent. If she had chosen a different path, she could have been a master criminal involved with international finance fraud or similar.

Why she wanted to work with me was still a mystery but I'm happy she does. Maybe it's just my unabashed brilliance, but I doubt it. I think it's the fact that our business is fast moving and now I'm outside the Met, I don't have to work under such strict conditions as I had to as a CID officer working with the Met, which leaves us free to do all we can to solve the cases we work on and are well paid to do so.

Jeannie is not the typical Millennial, she had a master's degree in IT and another in math, of all things and was damn good at just about every facet of this technological miracle that we call information technology.

Jeannie could break into any surveillance system and had proved her skills many times in our previous cases. I have no bloody idea how she did it but she did. I used to hate all those cameras all over London and other places around big cities. But now based on our line of work, they were a valuable source of information.

Many of the systems were considered to be "Secure" whatever that meant, but were never secure from Jeannie, who had a method of breaking into any and all of them.

One thing for damn sure, what I was making working cases freelance as a private eye was far better than what I was making as a DS with the Met. My clients started out as cheating husbands and wives but my breakthrough came from a case involving a high-flying corporate CEO who thought his wife was straying. Turned out she was telling company secrets to her boyfriend working for the competition and she was making a fortune from selling company information.

Now my clients range from medium-sized companies to mega-corporations. I know they see me as a street-smart gumshoe and it is what it is, but I was always blessed with an intuitive brain that I use 100%. Even in the Met, I managed to have a high close rate but the money was not so good.

Some may call my ability to think coupled with a good intuition while others call it a gift, but whatever we call it, it works for me and helps me solve cases I work on. I had the uncanny ability to connect the dots as they say. Anyway, it's fun placing all the pieces of the puzzle together and winning.

Anyway, I was on my way home and was catching the tube from Leicester Square to Boston Manor a 20-minute ride on the Piccadilly line. I descended the stairs onto the crowded westbound platform at the beginning of the usual rush hour in London.

To call it rush hour would be like calling a blue whale a large fish. Rush hour in London starts at 4 am till midday with people heading into the city. Then after midday, the entire crowd heads out of the city back to the suburbs. This lemming-like rush lasts until after 8 pm then it starts all over again 5 days each week.

As I arrived on the platform and was waiting the usual 3 or 4 minutes for the tube to arrive, a train heading to Heathrow and not Uxbridge. As I was waiting there was a commotion at the other end of the platform I was waiting on. I looked over to see several people now gathered around a man lying on the platform. So naturally I made my way over to see what the problem appeared to be.

When I got there, I could see a well-dressed man, wearing a suit, lying on the floor but he was not moving. His shoes were clean (always the details with me) and had been polished.

My aunt always said, "You can tell a man by his shoes" and believe it or not that has always stayed with me. His skin was blueish white and a young lady who was kneeling next to him said, "I think He's dead" which caused a collective gasp from the small crowd gathered around the body lying motionless on the platform.

The young woman who was bent down close to the body, told anyone listening that she was a nurse and was going through a routine to see if the man was alive.

I knelt down to join her and went through his pockets to find anything that might tell us who he was. I was surprised to find he had no identifying documents in his pockets, no wallet, no driver's license, nothing at all, which is unusual these days when most people have some form of ID. But he did have around a grand in cash in his inside jacket pocket.

Someone had called the police and the local station security, had finally arrived probably after seeing the small crowd gathered on the platform and asking us all to move back. I had already taken a couple of photos of the man's face and demeanour on my phone.

I asked the young nurse her name and she told me it was Brianna, or Bree for short. I asked her where she worked and she told me she was an ICU nurse at Kings Cross hospital close by.

The body was finally removed and I hung around to find out where it would be taken to. One of the two ambulance people, a man and a woman, who were placing the body into a body bag told me they were taking him to St Thomas' University College Hospital which was close to the tube station. After the commotion had died down and the body had been removed, I awaited the next train and made my way home, but I kept thinking back to the events that took place on the platform as something didn't add up but I couldn't put my finger on what it was.

I called Jeannie on my way home; she had left the office already as it was now well after 7 pm. I sent her the photos I had taken to see if she could work her miracles to find out who he was, adding that tomorrow would be fine there was no hurry. She got my message and called me, asking what it was all about.

My instincts told me there was something more than just a man collapsing on a train platform especially as Jeannie was to find out later that all the station cameras went out at the time this happened.

She found him entering the station at 6.35 pm. I was thinking, he had no idea this would be the last journey he would take in this life, as none of us ever do. Oh, the mystery of our lives, who knows what the great puppet master has in store for any of us? I know for damn certain I don't want to know when my number's up. In the words from a great movie, *"Smite me O mighty smiter!"*

What didn't add up was the lack of any identifying documents, no ID, no driver's license, no credit cards nothing at all. This and the way he just collapsed and died so suddenly was what made me, as an experienced private eye and former cop, know that there was more to his story. Well, do I or don't I proceed with this?

As far as I could estimate this would only take a few days of work to find out who he was but I would check with the local Nick to see if they had anything on our man. I can tell you this though, Jeannie would find out much more and far sooner than any cop shop would ever do.

She shared my passion for solving each case. Where my former colleagues had a "Job" to do. We had a case to work on. I had worked with the best but there's a difference between passion and just doing a job and by the way the pay was considerably more.

Anyway, I had to decide whether to find out more or not. I knew that both Jeannie and I once we got started would always be caught up in the case at hand and this so far, was not one we may get paid to solve. But the more I thought about this the more my instincts told me this would end up far bigger than it seemed at the onset. Well, time will tell.

Anyway, the decision was mine to make and I decided to pursue this wherever it led us. We were both on board so let the games begin! I thought we had a multi-pronged search, finding out who the deceased was; why was he now dead, who cut the CCTV cameras off and why did our man have no identifying documents on him?

I headed home and when I arrived at my station, Boston Manor, I stopped off at my local, which was the Royal Hotel. There were, as usual, several friends there already so I joined them for a drink.

One of them was also a cop attached to Ealing Nick. We had worked on several cases together. I had a pub sandwich for dinner. I had no specific time to get home as I was divorced. My ex and I were good friends and we both realised our marriage would never work, unfortunately. My passion was for my job and it took me into long hours and a lot of travelling all over the globe, following cases of corporate espionage.

This John Doe bothered me, not so much his death, suddenly becoming brown bread, (dead), as we Londoners say. I knew this would eventually happen to us all but like this. Of course, I felt sorry that his family were probably unaware he had passed and may have been waiting for his return after work which forever more would never happen again.

It had more to do with his anonymity, who the hell travels with no identification unless they have something to hide? The other possibility was that perhaps he was hiding from someone. So, one way or another this John Doe had my attention.

He had gone to great lengths to remain anonymous and how did he just drop down dead? My mind was, as usual, racing ahead to many different scenarios that Jeannie and I would go through as we were between cases at that moment.

This case was for free and if the only result was to inform his parents of his demise, then so be it, that would be the outcome which by itself would be a result.

I can't tell you how many times I have had to pass on information about a deceased family member and that part of my former work, as a London cop, was never fun. Well, tomorrow was another day and I would see what unfolded with Johhny Doe, now brown bread.

I knew from experience that what seems strange at first becomes unbelievable as we uncover the facts around an incident like our John Doe.

Chapter 2

The Man Who Never Was

The following day I went to my office to find Jeannie already there, as usual, working on the photos I sent her. I went around her desk to see what she had found but nothing was showing to link the face with a name. Usually, we get a hit on our software which is a clone of the police software (and others we can't name to protect the guilty) for facial recognition, which we always use.

I asked Jeannie if she could tap into the station's CCTV software to see if there was anything leading up to the death of the stranger. I was busy writing a report on my latest case about the theft of sensitive information from a global pharmaceutical company who were about to launch a new breakthrough drug for Alzheimer's.

They were all launching a breakthrough drug of one sort or another and if I watched TV which I seldom did I would believe I was on death's doorstep and needed an unpronounceable new drug. What made me smile was all the side effects that seemed far worse than the disease (they were all diseases) itself.

In my previous case, I found out who it was, selling her corporate espionage, to the highest bidder, through telephone records and surveillance footage but it took me months of gumshoe work to eventually uncover the culprit who was none other than a board member who wanted to make a few million for herself on the side.

The thing is that now the overseas Chinese competitor, who paid her a few million quid, had the stolen research data and they would go ahead and use it regardless of international law. So, although I had caught her, permanent damage had been done to my client.

Still, that was something those overpaid corporate execs would have to deal with, not me, I was well paid for the job and it took months of careful work and I understood the cost and the damage done. But I had little concern for my client since their bottom line was in the billions and the cost of their meds was prohibitive to most of us especially their Insulin drugs which were free in the UK but charged at over $300 per month in the US. if you didn't have insurance or were self-employed and couldn't afford insurance. Anyway, it paid my bills.

I finished my report for the client and went over to see how Jeannie had progressed, but nothing was shown on his name with any of our facial recognition software. She was reviewing the CCTV recordings and we both went through several camera angles but although we saw him enter the station, the cameras went offline so we couldn't see what occurred.

Hmm, strange coincidence, but with all I have learned there are no coincidences linked to a sudden death. She knew what to do and went to the street cameras slowly going through them where they covered the entrance to the tube station.

After searching for a while, she found a couple of images of what looked like our John Doe walking down Cranborne Street which was a very busy pedestrian and vehicle road with thousands of people and vehicles moving along it at nearly all times of day and night. So much for a rush, "Hour" went on all day merging from coming into London in the mornings, from 4 am to the afternoon, then switching back the other way as people headed home. There was a non-stop ebb and flow of human traffic at that time of the day.

I seldom had to tell her what to do she already knew and began to do facial recognition on people entering the station in close proximity to our man to see if anyone showed up as a villain or known to the "Job" (the cops). At this point, I thought to pay a visit to the hospital to see what I could find out. I knew where the morgue was and had a great relationship with the physicians there. So, I decided to go there to find out what I could.

Chapter 3

Forensics - The Science of Ghosts

I arrived at the hospital and made my way down to the morgue and, luckily for me my friend Olivia was there, after I knocked and looked through the round window, she let me in. Olivia was an old friend of mine and we had worked together on several cases when I was with Met at West London's Acton CID unit.

Although I was not allowed to go into the morgue the staff knew me since we had worked together on several cases a few years before with a good outcome, and if Olivia was working, great she was a gem!

Olivia was a slim attractive studious-looking, intelligent young woman. She sometimes wore glasses, though not the normal glasses that a professional scientist would wear. Hers were bright blue and were "Dolce and Gabbana" designer frames, (from the obvious gold logo on the temple) bloody expensive from the look of them and they suited her.

Olivia had cascading dark wavy hair, often tied back in a ponytail and with her pale complexion probably from working in a basement morgue for a living she seldom ever got out in the open-air sun. She looked like your typical Irish girl. But there was more to Olivia than meets the eye, she was a gamer. She played online video games and apparently according to her colleagues was a damn good player.

These games were not your usual arcade-type games, pinball, space invaders, War Zone and the like. She played individually created games with others on a private website where a games master created and set up the characters and the game rules and objectives. Not my scene at all but she loves it and that's fine by me. It probably keeps her mind off dead bodies.

Boy, whenever I asked her about her out-of-work activities, she came alive explaining the roles she played and how many times she won. everyone needs an out-of-work activity to take their mind off work. Other countries have got that right and provide plenty of vacation time for their staff. As for me, I loved my work and my work was my passion.

Olivia and I were friends and she knew I was there to see the latest John Doe. She smiled her knowing smile and went across to open the cooler drawer for me to see the body. She had seen the police report and remarked that there were no tell-tale signs on the body to show signs of foul play. I told her I was there when he collapsed and what I had seen. I told her there was not one single identifying document on him and the CCTV cameras all went off which was why I became interested.

Olivia said as she was bent over the body scrutinising some molecule or other, "As it looks to me, unless you or the investigating officer can find a reason to show foul play, I have to report it as death by natural causes." "Does it look like a heart attack?" I asked, and she told me. "At this point in time, it could be since there isn't any other incidental evidence. There are no contusions, bruises, scratches dents or anything at all." She said still scrutinising the body.

There had to be a full autopsy and I knew I had only a few cards to play at this stage since it was in the hands of the local police. I told her how unusual it was for the series of coincidences surrounding this death, I paused saying nothing more knowing she would fill in the gap to ask me what those coincidences were and she did. I'm that bloody good! I thought to myself.

I told her about the station CCTV cameras all suddenly going down just before he collapsed on the platform. She already knew he had not one single identifying document on his person which was unusual for someone so well dressed. I added that he did not appear on any facial recognition software, so far. She confirmed that too adding they could only name him John Doe with the date and TOD added unless the case officer wanted a DNA sample.

I asked her if she could do me a solid and get a blood tox screen to show if it was a death by natural causes or something else, she thought for a moment about what I had just told her, who cut the CCTV cameras off? She asked. I mentioned again the list of negatives surrounding his sudden death and she agreed adding that there were several inconsistencies with our John Doe.

That was another drink I owed her. I told her how quickly, according to those present, he had collapsed with not one symptom, no visible chest pains, no arm aching movements according to those standing next to him told me, he just fell down, collapsed, seemingly, dead before he hit the ground.

We were both looking at the dead man, our John Doe and I hate that name. To me, these were once children, now grown up. Their mothers and fathers wanted nothing more for them than to enjoy life and be happy. Perhaps get married and have children.

But now this man, probably heading back home never expected to die on that platform, right next to an exit sign, always the details with me! I stood there watching Olivia do her work carefully, meticulously, following her standard procedure she would go through every inch of our deceased to ensure her final statement was correct as it pertained to this man.

I could do no more at the morgue so after a careful once over of his clothes, noting the names on foreign labels inside. I asked Olivia if she would let me photograph the labels. She said, "Wait a moment I'll check with John." Then she went over and looked at his face bent forward and said leaning close to his ear, "My friend Max here wants to take photos of your clothes, do you mind?"

She bent forward as if listening carefully to what our dead friend was saying, nodding her head and commenting, "Oh, of course I see, yes, I'll have to check," Then smiling at her obvious humour she said, "He wants

a copy of the photos," It meant she did so I told her, looking at our John Doe, "Oh ok, I'll bring them for your records, colour or black and white?" I said adding to her humour. I took closeups of the jacket and the label which was Zegner made in Italy. His shoes were hand-made by Berluti apparently, according to the label, which said "Fait main en Paris," meaning hand-made in Paris. This was no common bloke or dude as my American friends would say.

I took another set of photos of his suit, the cloth, the label and his shoes, checking the quality as I may not get another opportunity. I showed Olivia the photos. "See these labels, our man here was wealthy and could afford expensive, bespoke, clothing made in Italy and Paris. He came from good stock," I said.

"Why do you think that?" she asked. "Because these are not your more common Ralph Loren or Johnson and Murphy gear available in most high street shops, he would have travelled to Paris and Rome for this gear," I told her. We shared the same humour and as I left, I called out to the body, "Hey thanks John, I'll send you my shots hope you like them," I said as I headed for the door.

"That's why you, mister Maxamillion Moore get the big bucks," she said smiling. I thanked her with a smile and a kiss on her cheek and left. She had my number for the results of a tox screen. Olivia was a gem and had a soft spot for me, the feeling was mutual.

Chapter 4

Curiouser and Curiouser

On my way back from the morgue. I went over to the cop shop, on Agar Street in Covent Garden not far from Leicester Square. I wanted to see who was running the case. I went to the front desk to see someone new there, a larger lady (to put it nicely) she occupied all the space behind the desk and looked over the rim of her multi-coloured thick-rimmed glasses at me. "Can I help you sir?" she asked, never stopping chewing her gum, in a bored scene and doing it all before voice while tapping her pen, annoyingly on her desk.

I fixed her with my best, most authoritative "Hello gorgeous, I'm here on official business, so don't fuck with me look," but it fell somewhere on the desk in front of her large fat arm and her ample breasts, that were struggling to remain confined in her far too tight, but thankfully infinitely stretchable miraculously made top. Brrr, reframe my thinking I thought. It was images like hers that had a way of reemerging just at the wrong time when I was with a drop-dead gorgeous woman, in my past, bonking or similar.

I asked her who was the officer dealing with the dead man on the Piccadilly line station case yesterday evening. "And what has that to do with you?" she asked. "Absolutely nothing," I said, "I just came in off the street to see what was up at this cop shop!" and I looked at her waiting for the next gem uttering from her puffy lips, still chewing her gum. "But since you ask, I was there on the platform when this went down," I replied. "So what? Are you a witness or what?" she said somewhat caustically. I'm thinking, "Who the fuck is this fat bitch at the front desk and where is Darcy?" "I'm not in the habit of discussing ongoing police business with the front desk," I answered. "So again, respectfully, who is running this case."

"I'm here to see whoever is leading the Leicester Square station John Doe sudden death case, yesterday afternoon," I said as if I had a natural right to know this. Just as I said, Chief Barlow came through.

She looked up at her boss showing new respect on her chubby face. "Mornin Cheryl," he said. Then looking over to me he said, "Max! And what do we owe the pleasure of your company today? Slumming it are we?" he said picking up a folder and looking over to me.

"I was there on the Leicester Square station platform when the John Doe collapsed." I told him, "I see! Did you leave your contact info with the officers there?" he asked. I told him I was already late and couldn't stop but thought to come by today.

"What's your interest in this?" He asked and I told him a little white lie when I answered, "He looked like someone from a case I worked on a few years back," I answered, not knowing at the time how right I was. "Hmmm," he said, fixing me with thoughtful a stare. "Just wait here and I'll send someone out." So far so good. I knew I could wing it from here.

I never understood what it was with the subtle animosity between the Met and people like me who were doing exactly the same job covering different areas that in all honestly were not cases they would handle. Maybe they were jealous of the money, but as a private eye, I had no guarantee of work, unlike my previous colleagues at the Met.

I dealt with crimes in secret dark places, not yet too visible and needing a careful hand and mind to uncover the perps. Theirs were crimes, in the public arena often black and white guilty or not guilty crimes, with a villain to be tracked down from a crime that had been proved. These were in the dark corridors of the business world, subtle, with big rewards unless these perps were caught. Enter Moi, Maximillion Moore and be prepared to be caught! It made me smile thinking about my last case.

After a short while, a slim, young very attractive woman with blonde hair tied back in a ponytail, a CID officer came out. She couldn't have been more than 16 years old, ah Tempus Fugit, how time flies, I thought.

She was older than she looked I thought, but then they all looked much too young to me. I was the only Joe public in the sparse waiting area. She came over and introduced herself as D.C. Angel Borowa (pronounced Borova) and as I found out later, she was apparently Polish.

Now I'm not too shabby myself as a 45-year-old rugged-looking ex-cop divorcee with a thousand years of experience behind me and the reputation of being a "Don't fuck with me ex-London cop." Anyway, she never made my connection as a former London Met officer, so I left that gem out of the conversation. I knew she would find out later adding the intrigue, the enigma that was moi! (yeah right, I'm now just a gumshoe).

She took me back to her desk which was in a typical large office with around 10 other desks around hers. All the other desks were loaded with case files and hers was no different except for far fewer files I've always thought you can tell a lot about a professional person by how they manage their desk space, though mine would have embarrassed a worker at the garbage tip. Anyway, I digress.

Angel's desk was stacked neatly with just a few files (not even close to those I had on my desk) of what I suppose are a few current cases. On her partition wall behind her desk was an A4-sized poster decorated with posies, which read, "A fun thing to do in the mornings is don't fucking talk to me!" I had to smile that she was probably not a morning person, but I get that, neither was my ex, in fact, she was not a day person either, but more of her later.

Me? I'm the opposite, I'm at my best in the mornings I hit the ground running ready to go and luckily, I don't need much sleep. I never have, I'm good to go with only two and a half hours of sleep, which used to piss my ex off, mainly because I always managed to wake her up when I got out of bed. But to me, being pissed off every day because she didn't like me getting up early was pointless.

Anyway, I sat at her desk and she offered me coffee. I declined knowing how bad cop shop coffee was. She got her notepad out and opened yet another desk folder for this case. "So, tell me what you saw," she said.

I went through all I saw, which wasn't that much except as I told her all the station cameras went offline for 30 minutes at the time John Doe collapsed. "How do you know this?" she asked. She apparently didn't know my police background and I didn't volunteer it at this time. I thought to wait until she found out for herself if she was even interested in doing so. Test number one, for her assessment skills to see if she was meticulous or not. I answered that I overheard station staff talking.

I didn't want to be combative at this point as I was interested to see how this apparent rookie cop would handle this case. To be honest though, on the face of it, it was seemingly a "Death by natural causes," open and shut case. Except for those pesky CCTV cameras all going off at the time of death. So, there was that.

I added that there seemed nothing wrong with him, no visible signs of a heart attack, or a stroke, no blue lips, no pallor, no skin discolouration at all according to those standing next to me. It was as if he just died of nothing at all. "The nurse who was at the scene confirmed him to be deceased at the time" I offered helpfully.

She nodded and made some notes. She didn't bother to ask the nurse's name so I didn't offer it. "And how did you know she was a nurse?" asked the obvious! "She was wearing a uniform," I answered her. I could tell she was really not that interested, so neither was I interested in helping her and knew I was wasting my time at that cop shop. This was not the same as my posse at Acton Nick who would be all over this like flies around, never mind.

I told her to call me if she needed to and gave her my phone number but I didn't give her my card. I did get her card though and told her, "If I think of something else, I'll call you." I said knowing I probably wouldn't make that call.

It's funny, how things have changed when I was a cop, I especially took notes on anyone who volunteered to take the time to come into the office to give me information on any case. You never know when piecing together a case, how every detail forms a picture of what occurred. Angel's desk was nothing like mine, stacked up with a current caseload all of which I was working on at any one time, ten times her caseload!

Chapter 5

Working Outside the Lines

I did my civic duty and gave my info to an uninterested police department. But I just couldn't let this go and I knew there was something else to this story. So I went back to my office and sat down with Jeannie, who was busy researching our John Doe. I filled her in on the meeting I had with Angel and gave Jeannie Angel's card to add it to our database, knowing Jeannie would add her own description, some of which were hilarious, but that, as they say, is for another day.

I learned a long time ago to bounce a case I was working on, off others, to listen to their perception and get their input. Many of my peers thought this was a sign of weakness in seemingly not managing the case personally, but I knew with 100% certainty it was always worthwhile.

Jeannie was a very perceptive woman and this Pow wow was what we did in every case. I had called her to let her know I was on my way back and when I arrived, she already had a coffee waiting for us both.

We sat down and started going over the very sparse information we had. "I dunno, I said, there's something about this John Doe that doesn't add up." Jeannie finished what she was doing and looked thoughtful, thinking about this case. "Let's put our ideas on the warboard and see what comes up," I said wheeling our large whiteboard over. It was, as usual blank but would soon, (I hope) be filled with connections and information.

Jeannie placed the photos I took of John Doe in the middle of the board then on the far right we added what sparse details we had. CCTV off, no credit cards, no ID, database zero, facial recognition zero, then she added suit, Italy, shoes Paris, tie, Sally Army, (Salvation Army to see if I was taking notice, Expensive shirt, well educated?

Then she placed a comment, CCTV cameras turned off. Next on the left side, we both added possibilities of who he could be. Diplomat? Corporate executive? Agency? She placed me in a circle with MI5, MI6, and CIA, as all were, to us, related as possibilities which we would explore later, then I added "Whistleblower?"

It was everything we had, but it was nothing much yet it was a start and I knew it was far more than the police had. Angel needed new wings! "So where do we start?" I said rhetorically. Jeannie was, as usual, busy on her keyboard and looked up, with a pencil in her mouth, as she was adding notes on her computer.

"Where do you want to start?" she said. "I think we should start on two pieces of this puzzle that we know as facts," I said looking at our whiteboard. "We have two things worth following up on, one is the street CCTV cameras to see if we can trace his movements before he entered the station," I said. "And what's the other?" she asked. I told her we should follow up on the designer labels of his expensive-looking suit and shoes to maybe get a name.

Jeannie immediately started looking into the Zegner bespoke suite and in no time found locations in London and Italy.

I had left it that when Angel or Olivia found anything out they should let me know. Now I'm not stupid and I knew Angel would find nothing as she was seemingly uninterested in looking into the case of a dead John Doe. But I knew there was more to this. How? Well-dressed, well-groomed people just don't drop down dead with no symptoms on a busy tube platform.

Often, I found that when the answer is not apparent, we have to stand back and look over everything from 30,000 feet up to see what is unusual which then stands out. Burying ourselves in the details, down in the weeds, at the early stage of a case is a waste of time and my methods worked as my cases were largely resolved.

Chapter 6

The Italian Connection!

When I was a cop, I wanted to report only when I had a significant piece of intel that was leading me closer to solving a case, not all the way through step by step (as my chief wanted) but with a significant piece of the puzzle. I estimated that I wasted 20% of my time on nothing that took me further to solving the case I was working on, simply complying by making pointless reports just to appease a boss.

My hit rate working outside the lines was even higher than when I was a DS with the Met. It suited my style to be a free bird working at my own pace and not having to do daily verbal reports to a boss who micromanaged his operation.

Although I loved what I was doing as a cop, there was so much wasted time and I only wanted to focus on facts using my brain power to take a blank sheet and solve a case. But I knew I was part of a big law enforcement machine and could not work alone as a maverick.

But, after a long service, I had reached the point at which all I was doing was repetitive, boring even, so it was time to move on to do what I wanted to do, which was running my own business uncovering and solving all those cases that my previous job as a cop was unable and under-resourced to do.

Jeannie checked out the photos I took of the clothing labels. The label that intrigued me was his suit which was Ermenegildo Zegna. This was no ordinary fashion designer this was one of the top 10 designer labels in the world. The so the suit was bespoke, measured for our John Doe and from Zegner a made-to-measure suit was always a one-of-a-kind item.

We started following up on the designer suit. Unfortunately, Ermenegildo Zegna's bespoke clothing items were sold in many upmarket stores. We found a store on Oxford Street and another on New Bond Street, both upmarket locations selling Zegner clothing.

I went to both Zegner shops while Jeannie was doing what she did best, clicking the keys on her computer, breaking into databases with the uncanny stealth of a crafty cat searching for an elusive mouse. Initially, the assistants, at Zegner were reluctant to give me any information but when I told them I was trying to find a name to inform the family of the death of a family member wearing one of their bespoke suites, they became more helpful.

I showed them the photo of the label but in both stores, they informed me that the label was not theirs but probably came from Italy. "How do you know that?" I asked. I was told that the label was an Italian label theirs were English. "Are all your suites bespoke?" I asked and was told no but they also have a ready-to-wear range available in the "Lesser" locations but not with the label I showed them.

In both stores, they told me the suit did not come from either of their stores. The label was printed in Italian and all I could find out was it probably came from one of their Italian locations, maybe from Rome.

But one of them gave me a vital clue in telling me that if the suit was genuine and not a knockoff, then on the inside of the jacket, between the lining and the outer cloth, there would be a label with a serial number not visible but used to ensure the item was genuine and not a knock off. If there was no inner serial number, it was a knockoff. I asked them where that label would be, hoping it was the real thing and not a knockoff.

The salesman, who prefers to be called a tailor, told me it was inside the jacket on the right-side seam under the arm, adding we would have to cut the seam between the outer coat and the inner silk lining as it was sewn in and deliberately hidden. I thanked him for the information and asked him if I gave him the serial number could he tell where the suit was bought off the peg or bespoke?

He told me yes there were sequences and a code of manufacture, relating to the location and the date of purchase. But he could not give me details only a location. Well, it was a start and left the Bond Steet shop.

I called Olivia and asked if she had any news on the tox screen but again, nothing yet. I then asked her if the case officer from Agar Street Nick had been back in touch with her yet about the body. She told me no, not yet but added, "There's nothing to tell the police yet as we have no name no ID no DNA result nothing!"

I told Olivia of my lame meeting with the case officer, "Fallen" Angel, adding that I doubted they were remotely interested in finding out who he was. I told her what I had learned about the jacket and asked her to open the seam to look for the serial number on the inside.

"Max," she said, "Where on earth did you find that out?" so, I told her of my meeting in the Ermenegildo Zegna shop on Bond Street. She chuckled and said, "Only you would think of that!" "Yep," I answered, "A lifetime pounding the streets as a seriously under-paid London cop!"

But at the end of the day, I was only doing what any case officer should do, grafting at the puzzle, putting the pieces together. I understand the police mentality that since there was no apparent crime, only an unfortunate death why would they be interested?

I headed back to my office to see Jeannie working on the inner label that Olivia had photographed and sent to her. The label said Rome, Italy. At last, we were getting somewhere I hoped and prayed this lead would give me a name.

I sat down at my desk and looked up the Ermenegildo Zegna website searching for their Rome number. I called the number, placing it on the speaker and asked if I could speak to the manager there. The person on the other end replied, *"Scusa non ti capisco, parli italiano?"* Now normally, if I was interviewing at the cop shop, I would have an interpreter with me.

Jeannie was listening to my conversation and came over, "Want some help?" she asked. I covered the phone and replied, "Not unless you speak Italian." Well fuck my old boots, she did! She spoke Italian fluently! She took the phone and started a rapid-fire conversation in, what seemed to me, perfect Double-Dutch. I just sat and stared at her in awe. She turned to me as if this was a normal everyday thing that speaking Italian is what we always did before lunch!

She knew I was asking about the label. After a seemingly very friendly conversation, I could hear a lot of "No, *capisco*," which I knew she was saying I understood. But she continued saying, "*Chiamo da Londra, puoi almeno dirmi in quale negozio è stato comprato questo vestito?*" which was "At least can you tell me which of your shops the suit was sold from?"

I could tell Jeannie was putting on her best English Italian accent as we both know Italian men are suckers for an English girl speaking Italian. Or better still, Italian men are always after women, no matter where they are from as long as they are still breathing! But that's just me.

After she put the phone down with many, "*Grazie mille per il vostro aiuto.*" She turned to me and said, he told us which shop in Italy the suit was bought from. "It's in Rome," she said casually.

Me? I looked at her dumbfounded at her new skill. "So how do you know Italian?" I asked her as she was walking back to her desk. "Sorry I thought you knew" she answered over her shoulder, seemingly enjoying the moment and carrying on working as if this was a normal everyday conversation. But I did see a slight, almost imperceptible smirk on her face.

"One of us will have to go over there to meet the shop staff face to face." she said, "Because according to that assistant, they are not allowed to give out confidential client information, especially over the phone, ever!" I was not surprised at this because obviously selling designer clothing to the rich and famous was, after all, a secret.

Chapter 7

Connecting The Dots

Jeannie deserved to come with me to Italy after all she had done so much to help my small but very effective PI business to succeed and without her help, I couldn't have solved as many cases. We were a good team. So, it was settled, although I had no idea where this would lead us, more than finding a name which we could, hopefully, follow up on.

I thought about Jeannie's conversation in perfect Italian and knew I would be useless at any conversation. "So how do you know Italian?" I asked, "I learned it in school," she said, "That was no high school Italian," I said, "Well I spent a year in Rome and travelled around Italy," she added. I didn't know this but then again, she was full of surprises.

"What other languages do you speak?" "Conversational French and German," She told me, "Oh and Spanish." Wow! I was blown away by my assistant's hidden talents. So, I told her she had to come with me to Rome. "What," she said, so I repeated it. We would both be going on a short trip.

She booked our flight to Rome leaving the next day, I could see that she was happy to be included and I told her, "Jeannie, I had no idea you spoke Italian," "There's a lot about me you don't know boss!" she said with a smile.

I thought about her comment and realised she was right we had only ever talked about the work on hand and never about ourselves. I hid behind the thought that I was always focused on the case and never the emotional personal stuff. But I knew she was probably telling me to notice her as a person and not just as my assistant.

So, a lesson was learned and she deserved more than just "Business as usual" from me. After all, she had skills I did not possess and we did make a great team.

I caught the tube from Boston Manor, on the Piccadilly line to Heathrow and as Jeannie lived south of the river we agreed to meet at the airport, at the United flight desk. We travelled on a Wednesday at midday as flights seemed cheaper midweek.

On the flight over Jeannie started to talk about the case and said, "There's something we're missing, something doesn't make sense in this, I'm going to go over those CCTV street cameras again but now we are across the pond I'll do it on the dark web, just in case," she said.

"A man as well dressed as he appears to be, doesn't just suddenly drop dead on the underground platform, with no visible signs of the usual heart attack or stroke according to your conversations with those who were there. So according to what you always say," she said turning to look at me, "In the absence of any other information, the obvious answer is usually the right one, Occam's Razor" she said. "OK go on" I replied, wanting to hear her train of thought. "Someone must have given him something and whatever it may have been it acted very fast." She added.

I already knew this which was why we were on our way to Rome to investigate, but I asked her, "What makes you think that?" "Everything else could have seemed normal, maybe a stroke or a heart attack, except for the cameras," she offered. "Why were all station cameras turned off and not, according to the station workers, for any routine maintenance." We were both bouncing ideas off each other, on the flight from Heathrow.

We arrived mid-afternoon and caught a taxi to the hotel. I have to add here, don't look out the window when you are inside a taxicab in Italy, especially in Rome. They are crazy drivers and we had so many near misses along the way, with our operatic taxi driver who thought he was Pavarotti, singing a very loud rendition of Nessun Dorma.

It was a miracle and I was surprised his cab had no dents or broken bits. I just closed my eyes otherwise I would have had a damn heart attack. Jeannie, however, loved it and was laughing at the way he was driving and all the near accidents we missed on the trip. Maybe she was a taxi driver in a past life. We were both jerking back and forth and from side to side with his evasive manoeuvres as we sped along.

Jeannie had booked us into the Hotel Michaelangelo in Downtown Rome very close to the Vatican. In fact, we could see the dome of St. Peter's Basilica at the Vatican from our hotel rooms. I checked us both in with adjoining rooms so we could work on the case. The Rome, Zegna Boutique, was on the Via Borgognona and only a few clicks from the hotel Michaelangelo where we were staying. We could, if we chose to, walk there.

I decided we would go to the Zegner boutique first thing in the morning as it was now late afternoon. I checked the opening hours of Zegna and they opened at 9 am.

That evening we went out to a local restaurant; it was a family-owned pizzeria and I had never eaten an Italian Pizza so I was interested to compare theirs to a Chicago or London-style Pizza.

The restaurant and the staff, probably all the family, were very friendly and welcoming, probably thinking we were a couple. Yeah right me at 45 and Jeannie at 28, to an Italian, anything is possible. Anyway, we were both sitting outside on an elevated level overlooking the street. I was thinking about how beautiful the setting was and how much I loved Rome.

After we had ordered, Jeannie excused herself to go to the bathroom while I was miles away wondering where this case would lead. If I was an attorney this would be a pro bono case, but to me, we were flush and our finances, after several high-profile, high-reward cases, were very good. Anyway, this was, for me, a case worth delving into.

I looked at my watch realising that Jeannie had not returned and had been gone for 40 minutes. I got up to see if she was ok and made my way to the restroom.

As I passed the kitchen, the door was open and there was a lot of laughter inside so I looked in to see Jeannie sitting at a long table with what I imagined were the owners and their family. There were 8 people sitting around the kitchen table. Jeannie was sitting on a chair placed there for her at the head of the table, next to the Patron. She was speaking in rapid Italian and they were all laughing.

I just stood there watching until she eventually looked up and noticed me. She waved and called me over; well great I thought so I went over to her feeling like an idiot as she was introducing me in Italian. The look those women gave me said it all, a boss and his assistant here in Rome in the springtime, yeah right!

No matter how it looked I was fine that we were there on business. Jeannie, however, was playing it right to the line enjoying my discomfort and obviously knowing what they were thinking and probably saying, after all, innuendo belonged to the French and the Italians. Anyway, we thanked them all and went back to our table just as our pizza arrived.

Our real Italian Pizza was very different from what we were used to in London. This Pizza was thin crust and not nearly as loaded as those we had at home. But this was made with real mozzarella cheese and Italian Pepperoni, not the plastic version as in a London Pizza. It was really good but so filling. We chased it down with a bottle of local house wine which was excellent.

After we had finished, Jeannie went back to the kitchen to thank the staff still very noisy, still laughing and happy to have made a new London friend who actually spoke like an Italian. I could see she was happy to be in Rome on business. Once back at the hotel, I said, "Can you go into the CCTV cameras without showing anyone looking, to see if they may have been caught or are being watched? IP addresses and access points are not visible on the dark web," she added. "If they had planned to take out the CCTV cameras they may be looking to see if anyone noticed," I said. "Not if I use the dark web" Jeannie answered.

The following morning, we caught a taxi to the Zegner Boutique and as we had discussed it over breakfast we made up a story to tell them why we needed the owner of the suit. We were to tell them we had found a jacket left by mistake on a train and wanted to contact the owner and since we were in Rome on business, we thought we would check in with the shop.

The Zegner boutique was on a narrow cobblestone street with tall stone buildings on either side of the road. There was barely room for our taxi but being as we had Mario Andretti's dad for our taxi driver, he raced his little turbo Fiat down the road and came to a screeching stop outside the boutique as if he was in a Formula 1 race at Monza.

I paid him and we exited the taxi. "Never again," I said not enjoying this ride and Jeannie laughed. "Welcome to Rome," I said where drivers have a lead foot on the accelerator pedal believing the roads in Rome are a trial run for the Monza Grand Prix. Either that, or they think they play football for Inter Milan.

The Zegna boutique was in a narrow street with all old grey stone buildings. The front of the boutique was rather understated and quite plain and as we say in England, "Sometimes less is more." And this storefront was deffo quite understated.

We entered the boutique, it was around 10 am since I knew Italians had to have their espresso before 9 am and we wanted his full attention. The assistant at the Zegna store was helpful and we had found the serial number thanks to Olivia at the morgue, who sent me a photo of it.

But Jeannie would take the lead as she spoke the lingo. We entered the store and I kept quiet, watching what would take place there while I was pretending to be interested in the clothes on show. Yeah like I could afford the millions of Lire just for a bloody tie!

We had a photo which Olivia of the coat at the morgue showing the outer coat and the inner label so we could verify to Zegna we had the real coat. I continued looking while Jeannie began talking.

I was casually watching their body language to see how their conversation was going. So far, all smiles on both sides but then the conversation changed and there was a lot of "Non, non," going on.

I heard him tell Jeannie what, with my limited knowledge of Italian, "Mi *dispiace, non mi è consentito fornire tali informazioni sui nostri clienti.* Then as expressionately as all Italians do, he threw his hands up and said, *"I nostri clienti sono confidenziali."* I understood the last part to mean their exclusive clients were always confidential.

But Jeannie was really turning it on and was standing close to him talking quietly. We discussed this beforehand and agreed a bribe in hundred Euro banknotes might do the trick if needed. Jeannie leaned in closer to the handsome (probably gay) assistant and placed a hundred in his hand.

He looked shocked but flicked his head off to one side as if saying, really, I can't, but if you insist, keep it coming, smoothing his hair, while he tossed his head feigning shock. But Jeannie just smiled and pressed the C note into his hand.

We know that regardless of how exclusive the shop is, a shop assistant will readily accept free money, especially in cash, readies, gelt, and buckaroos and it always opened doors.

She showed him the serial number we needed to be searched, then peeled another 100 Euro note and waved it in front of him adding another and another after the 5th "C note" he waved his hand at her and turned to his computer, after carefully taking the money and sliding it into his pocket. Jeannie stood behind him and was carefully videoing and photographing his screen noting his access code, while he was focused on finding the coat serial number, on his computer.

He looked up smiling, yeah damn right at five hundred Euros he damn well should be smiling from ear to ear! He turned the screen, clicked a few times and showed her the name and address of the customer

linked to the serial number. Jeannie pretended to be on the phone but was taking screenshots of the software on his sales computer. She had made a mental note of his log-on codes, which she made to look like she was entering a phone number.

"Can you remember what he looked like?" Jeannie asked, "So we can check the person who claims the jacket, to ensure it is the right one?" He thought for a moment then answered giving her a vague description of the client. I mean honestly, average size, average looks, no distinguishing anything! What the fuck do we do with that? How did he pay I asked Jeannie to interpret, which she did. All I heard was *"Contanti"* which I knew was Italian for cash. He added that the suit was mohair and silk a very expensive blend, exclusive to their store and it was made with a silk lining.

As for me? Looking at those beautiful clothes made me feel really shabby! Which I probably was. I knew one didn't ask the cost of the clothes in such an exclusive store like this, as it gave away the fact that one probably couldn't afford to shop there.

I got that little gem from a Rolls Royce car salesman friend of mine working in a dealership in Hanwell, West London. He told me when the first thing a customer asks is the price, we know he can't afford a Roller (Rolls Royce) and we usually just leave them to window shop, that is unless the customer is a rock and roller.

On the way back to the hotel Jeannie was saying, "Pity he was gay, he was a real hunk." Tall, slim, with dark wavy hair, chiselled face, and impeccably dressed. To me, he looked more like one of the Chippendales, but that was just me.

The entry was dated 8 months prior on September 8th at 11 am, so the suit was fairly new. We thanked the assistant and headed for the hotel. When we got back to the hotel we began to search for the name, Richard Whitehead, with an address, on a road named Memlingdreef, in a town called Overijse just on the outskirts of Brussels.

As Jeannie said, "He had to have a complete address otherwise the assistant could not have completed their warranty details and as long as it was a real address no one would bother to check further and honestly,

I doubt they even bothered once the sale was complete." I thought about this and wondered if he had produced a driver's license or maybe a passport, but since he paid cash that was all they would have been interested in, after all, cash is king! "How much was the suit" I asked out of curiosity, she replied, "Are you ready for this? It was six thousand Euros, bespoke, (made to measure) suit!" "That is a very expensive suit," I replied, "So he obviously had an expensive taste which was funded from the money he had ready access to," I said. "And he paid in cash," Jeannie said, so once again our man, now moved from a "John Doe," to becoming a "Richard Whitehead," which was the name the assistant gave us, leaving no trail behind for us to follow. But that was moot since he was dead now and anyway, we were going back into history on someone we had no idea who he was.

But this intrigue made me more curious as to why he was so meticulous about not leaving any credit card trail even for such an expensive suit and now I was even more curious since he was really good at hiding in plain sight which was a conscious effort to remain anonymous, so what was the reason?

We could do no more in Rome but we had at least another lead. Back at the hotel, Jeannie had gotten into the street TV cameras but too much time had passed and they had no feed now some 8 months later unless we went to the location where these camera feeds were located and there was no reason to believe they had saved any feed going back that far. We then left Rome and headed back to London.

We hopped on the tube at Heathrow's terminal 2, me just 8 stops to Boston Manor and Jeannie stayed on to south London making her connection at Piccadilly Circus. It was Friday so we agreed we would pick this up in the office after the weekend.

I arrived on Monday morning and added the latest information onto our whiteboard about the label and the name. But I added a question mark next to the name in case this too, given all he had done to hide in plain sight. Was his name merely a misnomer leading to another blind lead?

Chapter 8

Rocks in a pond

Back at the office, we looked up the name, Richard Whitehead but once again nothing showed up. "So, did we pay 500 euros for nothing?" I asked Jeannie, "Well we'll soon find out," she said. "Something about this is too easy, we arrive at the boutique as complete strangers and the assistant holds us for 500 Euros and just hands over the name, just like that, it was too bloody easy," I said and again I was thinking something still just didn't add up. But Jeannie didn't agree, she said, "To be honest I had to give him the readies (cash) one note at a time and then he finally showed me his screen."

I went over to Jeannie's desk and asked, "Has anything shown up yet on the Facial recognition for our John Doe?" She shook her head, "Is there another search we can do to find similar faces to his, maybe we can work that angle to see how many faces we would have to search out?" Jeannie replied, "We could try adding a similarity factor with a percentage accuracy, but that may give us thousands of similar faces," she said.

"OK but what if we start wide and then begin to narrow the result to say 90% similarity to see where we go with this? Well as it happened this was something Jeannie had been working on several months earlier, building an algorithm to do this and just for names that didn't appear on our first search. The reason was that when searching for those perps involved in corporate crimes, seldom did we ever find a match."

Anyway, there was nothing found on that name in any database, Interpol, the FBI database, our own Met database and even 5 (MI5) not even facial recognition either so this was so far another dead end. I decided I would call a friend of mine working at the ICC (International

Criminal Court) in The Hague to see if there was anything on the highly secure program they had. This rock had successfully hidden itself right at the bottom of a very deep lake and I was determined to get to the truth.

So she gave it a try focusing on Richard's ear in the photograph which I knew was unique to everyone like a fingerprint, the latter of which showed no match. She carried on while I called Angel's office number to see if she had any more news. Once again, she wasn't in her office so I left a message for her to call me back.

Keith had called me earlier to tell me a former colleague of ours, Martin Ade, had been killed the previous weekend on the ski slopes in the French Alps skiing at a resort called Val d'Isere. But I had seen Martin ski as part of the British Olympic team.

I asked him if it was the same Martin Ade. He told me yes it was and he was killed in a tragic accident when he was "Off Piste" (not on a regular run) and hit a tree. Martin used to work with Keith and me at Acton Nick. He was now working at the ICC where Keith was working also.

I had many questions; did he have family, what was his past and what was he doing at the time of his sudden death? Who was this Richard Whitehead? I knew we would eventually get to the truth and the intrigue was, for me, why I love what I do.

Was my work dangerous? Well yeah sometimes especially in the big game when I finally caught up with the perp. The reason big corporations and drug companies used me, to solve their problems, often led to a conspiracy of people not just a loner. So, I could never move forward on what I found until I had all the pieces of the puzzle.

Sometimes my cases involved calling for backup even though I was no longer part of the Met, while other times I would pass the file back to the corporation that hired me, for them to do the honours and make the call. One thing for sure, whenever I got to that final stage all my ducks were in a row and there was absolutely no wiggle room for the perp.

But the thing is with corporate crime the victim is the company so dealing within the law for a result through the criminal justice system was not always a possible outcome for a win in court.

These people, men and women, were crafty and left very few identifiable clues that could get a result in court. Now sometimes I was asked to get enough on the case to force a trial but not often.

Once these white-collar criminals were caught, as the end result of my investigations, all roads back for them were now blocked and the strange thing is that many of these companies leave it at that or deal with the matter in ways I don't need to know.

What I do know is that there are three parts to every event in our lives; there's the decision, the action to do something about it and then that last little part, the consequence of that action.

Everyone is fine with parts one and two, but then there's part three and the consequences for those involved in the high crimes of corporate theft and espionage were right at the top of the heap.

When one leaves a message for Keith at 6 (MI6) one doesn't say, "Hey man it's me call me back ok bro!" All incoming and outgoing calls and messages are always monitored. So knowing this I left a somewhat cryptic message saying, "Keith it's Max," a name "Richard Whitehead," and left it at that knowing he would do a name search for me to see if there was anything they had at the ICC or even 6 attached to the name.

Meanwhile, Jeannie was busy checking and the Belgian address, he gave Zegner turned out to be a real address, but whether it was his or someone he knew was something we would have to follow up on.

Later, Keith left a message for me, all it said was Red Lion 8. This meant I should meet him in our usual meeting place, the Red Lion pub, opposite Ealing Film Studios, at 8 pm.

The pub was fairly small and had the nickname Stage 5 since Ealing Studios only had 4 stages throughout its vast history going back as far as 1902. It was the oldest working studio in the world and stage 5 was the name given to the pub as that was where they went at the end of a day's shoot.

We both loved the pub as it had a long history associated with Ealing Film Studio which was just the opposite. In the main bar were caricatures of some of the famous old Ealing film and Ealing Comedy stars, from its past glory making films like Colditz, The Eagle Has Landed, The Blue Lamp and comedies including, The Lady Killers, and many of the "Carry On" comedies created at the Ealing Film Studios.

I arrived at the pub at 7.45 pm and spotted him sitting, as he usually does in the darkest part of the bar right in the corner facing out. With his red hair and 6'3" height, he was tall even sitting down. I had to smile at his ingrained, careful, no one's going to sneak up behind me, a position as I expected him to be. I guess old habits are hard to break!

He had his pint of Fullers ESB (Extra Special Bitter) and my usual pint of Guinness waiting for me as I sat down to join him. After we were greeted with the usual, "Fuck off nice to see you," I began to fill him in on why I was interested in our John Doe, now named Richard Whitehead. Keith sat there and listened until I had finished. I showed him the photos I took on the underground platform a week earlier.

"What bothers me is why and how a well-dressed man, in his mid-40s, apparently in chipper health, then goes and kicks the bucket dropping down brown bread, (dead) with absolutely no ID, no credit cards nothing at all to say who he was."

One minute he's "All fine over here thanks for asking, nothing to see here, all tickety boo, then the next minute he's just brown bread, he just drops dead on a busy Piccadilly line platform at the beginning of the rush hour," I said.

"Why does it bother you Max, some John Doe kicks the bucket and you're all over it?" he said, "I dunno" I replied, "But everything tells me something isn't right with this scenario and since we're between jobs, I thought I'd see what's up with this," I answered. "By the way how's

Jeannie" he said adding. "Are you being paid for this?" "Nope, it's pro bono at the moment," I replied.

"Then why are you bothering with it Max?" he said taking another sip of his London Pride. "Look Keith, have I ever been wrong when my gut tells me something ain't right?" I said. "Well, as a matter of fact, all the fucking time" he said smiling and I knew he was joking. But then he thought for a moment and asked, "So what have you got so far?"

I told him about the Zegner designer suit costing six G's and I told him what we had checked out from the label, "500 bloody Euro's that little gem cost me!" I said. "Pity you didn't have your old warrant badge with you," he chuckled. "Wouldn't have helped me in Rome," I answered, "Anyway since I don't speak Hi Ti (Italian) Jeannie came with me."

"Did you know she's fluent in several languages?" I said, "And maybe a few more I don't know about!" "Hmm she is one smart sort (woman)," he said. "And not too shabby looking, which is why I don't understand why she's working for a reprobate like you," he said, smiling as he raised his glass in a "Cheers mate."

"So anyway, I looked up the name you gave me, "Richard Whitehead" and nothing much came up except there was a reference to that name as a possible witness in a crime ring we were looking into. But not as a suspect only a POI, (person of interest), he said. But like you, nothing else showed up." "What does that mean?" I asked, "When you have a name someone bothered to enter into your huge database, then nothing else about the name?" "Hmm, well there is something else," he added. "Really, and what is that?" I asked.

"I can't say too much for obvious reasons, but since it's an old, closed case and since there was nothing more about the name, I thought it was worth checking into, just for you mate." "And?" I asked. "Well, the case was an old case but the agent, was Martin Ade, who was working on it and placed that name, Richard Whitehead, in the file, but he died before any concluding info was put into the system." He said. "Died how?" I asked, "According to the report, he was on a skiing trip with friends and hit a tree coming down a black slope, in Val d'Isere in the French Alps." "I thought there were not supposed to be trees on a black slope for high-speed skiing," I said. "Yeah right" he answered, "Well there are always a few trees there along the edges and skiers on a black slope are usually good enough not to hit them because they ski in the middle of the runs but he, unfortunately, hit one at full speed."

"Did anyone go to check?" I asked. "Look mate I know where you're coming from but no, there were eyewitness reports, from friends he went there with. They said the same thing, flying down the slope at full tilt and then veering off to the tree line. According to the report that came back and the body came back under diplomatic immunity and that was really all there was."

Now I should add here, that this was his way of getting whatever information someone had, by playing the "Aww come on, nothing to see here, you're imagining things," ploy to get another person to open up. But in my case there really was clearly more to this.

I had seen Martin skiing in the Olympics with the British team, where he won a silver medal and was surprised at his tragic accident. I remember him saying Val d'Isère was his favourite place to ski. Keith looked deep in thought. "I suppose it was kind of interesting now we have another dead body. But the thing is, there's no connection." He said. "Let's have another, my shout, same again?" I asked. "Damn right he said" and I went up to the bar.

Now whenever Keith and I got together it was always in a pub and often we involved other former colleagues from the Met who we had worked with, in our previous lives as London cops. Every such evening it ended singing Welsh rugby songs, led by our Welsh friend and drunk choir master leading a bunch of misfit drunks trying to remember the words!

When I sat back down, Keith was still in deep thought, so I asked him, "What about the case Martin was working on, how was it left? Unresolved or what?" I asked. "Last time he and I met he said he was on to something but no leads and nothing to follow up on and that's all I can tell you. Official secrets and all that crap!"

"So, take a step back," I said, "We now have two seemingly unrelated deaths in two countries, one a former cop and former Olympic skier, who apparently is killed on a slope, while the other drops dead on a tube platform and when we find out who our John Doe was, it's the same name in both cases, so we have a link," I said stating the obvious trying to get Keith to see what I was talking about.

"Honestly Max," he said, I think you're making connections that don't exist. "But Keith, there is a connection. Who is this Richard Whitehead who went to great lengths to remain anonymous? He even paid six grand for a suit in cash! Who the fuck does that?" I asked rhetorically. "And where did his money come from?"

I changed the subject, letting my comments sink in. I knew I had struck a chord with my friend and I was thinking about how to proceed. I needed his help but there were protocols and lines neither of us could cross those lines in the sand, things never said but understood. I would tell Jeannie for her to check out to see if there was any more information on Martin Ade's skiing accident in Val d'Isère. Maybe there was a news article or similar I thought.

"How's things at The Hague?" I asked him, though not too subtly, changing the subject. "Same old same old," he said, "But it's always interesting, same as with you when we get deep into a case there's nothing like it and that's what brings us back every time."

"Yeah I know," I said "And I'm on one right now. Look, Keith, at least look into your man and I'll do some digging too." "What will you look at?" he said. "Maybe who he was travelling with and see what I can dig up," I said adding, "It's interesting that two people both dead linked to the same name. Do you believe in coincidences?" I asked and I knew he didn't because we had this conversation several times before.

Martin and I worked together for a time, at Acton Nick, before he moved on, so I asked, "What was Martin like to work with since he worked alongside you longer than he did with me?" "What do you want me to say, Max?" he replied. "I only ever worked one case with him, a few years ago, though we did interface on the rare occasions when we were both in the office and we got on well." He added

"But as you know our work is outside not in an office and in answer to your question, he was a stand-up guy, brilliant mind, good at his job. He was a bit like you, focused, a no Bull shit kind of guy. But now I think of it, he mentioned Val d'Isere several times. So yes, that was his "Brighton Beach," his favourite holiday location where he often went skiing."

"Anything else?" I asked him, "Like what?" he said. "Well for a starter, anything else about Martin Ade?" "He worked with us for around four years and before that, he was with you and I at Acton for a while. I had moved to the ICC before he joined me there too. We don't bother to check out our colleagues because once they have been thoroughly vetted, we know they are good to go,"

I was thinking, Martin was an "Off-Piste, black slope skier and could handle himself very well, after all, he was an Olympic Downhill silver medalist, second best in the world! Though the press and many pundits thought he was in fact the best skier in the world. So how does someone like Martin end up dead I was thinking?"

After another couple of rounds, we parted and I left it at that for the moment to be added to our war board when I got back to the office. The following day I went to meet Angel unannounced at the Agar Street cop shop. I didn't want to find her in the office as that would confirm she was ignoring my calls and part of me hoped she was not deliberately ignoring me, but I would find out when I got there.

I checked her name, as I always did, nothing outstanding in the way of success, in fact, a perfectly ordinary background. Well, I would go to see her as my civic duty as a "stand-up bloke" to tell her what I saw.

But what did I see, a man who collapsed with no signs of anything wrong, who just dropped down dead? But who was he and why not one item to say who he was but ten grands in his pocket? Many of the corporate cases I now worked on began with a question. Someone had an inkling or a few facts about something they were aware of but didn't have the time to investigate. In these cases, it was my job to find out the details, as I was in this case. But as of the present moment I was clutching at straws with very little to go on.

But in this case, there was a very strong link from a highly trained ex-cop, now in the International Criminal Court, who had taken the time to add the very name that I was researching of another person who had simply died.

No, I knew I was on the right track but I was a little surprised that Keith, my longtime friend, was seemingly uninterested after all what we did often began with unrelated information just like this. Maybe he was busy on other cases and was not happy to be drawn into this especially as there was so little to go on at this point. Whatever the issue Keith clearly didn't want to be involved or didn't think should waste my time pursuing this. Time will tell.

Chapter 9

The Puzzle Starts Here

I arrived at the Agar Street cop shop, around 10 am and thankfully Cheryl was not at the front desk. She had been replaced by a middle-aged woman with a pleasant attitude. "May I help you?" she said, "Good morning miss, er, Chambers," I said looking at her name tag. "Please call me Josey," she said. "I'm here to see Angel Borowa," I said in my best

"I'm a good guy voice. "I'll check to see if she's in, though I haven't seen her today," the woman said, looking at a large open visitor book in front of her.

she gets it." Josey my new best friend replied. Well, at least this one was more helpful than chubby Cheryl at the front desk. So I wrote the message saying, *"I dropped in to see you, I have news about your John Doe, Leicester Square tube platform, call me,* signed just Max" and left it at that with no number since she already had it from our meeting the previous week. Another test was to see if Angel bothered to follow up.

I decided to swing by Leicester Square tube station to check in with the staff as it was close by, just to check on any details as to how all the cameras were off. I had my Oyster Card with me topped up so I could go through the barrier and maybe come across a station worker as the two in the entrance were busy watching passengers come in and out of the station.

I was in luck seeing a guard standing on the platform and I recognised him as being one of the guards who came when Richard collapsed. "Hey, how ya doin'?" I said smiling. He looked blankly at me so I added,

"I remember you when you were here last week when that man died on the west bound platform." "Oh yeah, I remember you and that nurse lady," he said remembering the event. We chatted for a while about how often this ever happens and apparently, this was his first after working at the station for 10 years.

"I heard the cameras were off when it happened," I said. "Yeah, they were. It happens very rarely, maybe one or two go offline but not all of them!" he said. I kept the conversation going without drawing attention to the questions. "I work locally and always catch the westbound tube to Boston Manor where I live and for me this was a first, I felt sad for that guy," I said and waited for his response.

"Me too," he said, I've never seen a "Brown bread" (cockney for dead) in this station before. "Is it weird that all the cameras were off at the time?" I asked. "Yeah very," he said, "But there's a master camera on a separate feed that wasn't off," he replied. "We did that after the IRA were bombing our trains and buses, but we didn't tell people about it. But now that trouble is over, I suppose it doesn't matter too much," he said. I was thinking "Loose lips sink ships" something my dad who was in the Navy told me years ago.

"Look, I know it's a strange thing to ask, but did you watch that feed after they took the body away?" No, he replied, "Hmm maybe I'll take a look," he said. Ok now for the 64-million-dollar question, I thought. "Could I take a look with you, as I'm helping the police to identify him and so far, they have no leads? Maybe there's something there that might help," I told him. "No, we are not allowed to show anyone who's not station staff what's on that camera," he said. "OK I completely understand, but I'll let the cops know in case they want to review that video."

"At least could you do me a solid and show me where that camera is located?" I asked him. So, he took me to the entrance and, without pointing he said, "Look up behind me in the corner, that's the camera."

I casually looked up to see the camera and noticed there was a number under it, maybe that was its reference. I made a mental note of it and thanked him, slipping him a score (twenty quid) which he took and thanked me. At least this one was a good bloke on London Transport and

I found his name was Erik McGivern. I'd keep that name for future reference. I headed back to the office and passed on the info to Jeannie. She immediately went to work to see if she could find that particular camera feed and hack into it and as I went back to my desk, I could hear her clicking away at her usual lighting speed.

She was on a mission and doing what she does best working her keys to search for the undefinable. She called me over, "Do you think this could be him?" she said showing me a slightly blurred image of a man walking towards the station. "Can you enhance this image?" "Your wish is my command," she responded adding her magic image-enhancing software and voila! We now had a clear photo of our man.

I'm going to backtrack to see where he came from and if there is anyone else appearing close to or following him or popping up near him. She was off on her new mission and was busy tracking the cameras to see where our man had come from. London is flooded with CCTV cameras and in fact, there are 691,000 cameras all over London.

So following a person or a vehicle meant they could be tracked very easily. To this point, Jeannie had her own facial recognition software she had developed which would track someone as long as they were on the street. She could even find which station, bus stop or vehicle they entered and got off from without the need to hack into any of the more official channels.

"YES!" I heard her shout out as she finally got a hit on our man, "There he is and guess where he comes out from?" I was busy uploading more information to our war board. She told me to come over to see, so I did.

He came out onto the street, from none other than Thames House. Well, well, well, this is MI5's headquarters, known as Thames House, located in Millbank, on the north bank of the river Thames, adjacent to Lambeth Bridge.

So now at least we had a beginning for Richard Whitehead's last trip on this earth. "OK so far so good," she said, "And now I'll check on anyone close to him or following him." "If he is an operative, he'll know if he's being followed," I said, "Maybe, but if this killer or killers could bring down someone like Richard Whitehead then they probably will use more than one tail," I added. But I didn't need to as Jeannie knew all the angles and would be looking for anyone and everyone, she worked best alone!

It made more sense now since we knew he had come out of Thames House meaning he had business with MI5. Was that the reason he was so secretive? But if he was working with 5, then how come he could afford such expensive clothes and who carries six grands around to pay for a suit?

Each answer led to more questions but I knew we were moving forward even if we thought we were not. Thinking back Keith's demeanour on this obvious link was puzzling. But I knew with his line of work he was often seemingly vague if not for obvious reasons then for the fact that he was not allowed to share information outside of his agency.

Chapter 10

A Cocktail with a Kick

We had looked up the name, Richard Whitehead, on several databases, but once again nothing showed up. "So, did we pay 500 euros for nothing?" I asked Jeannie, "Well we'll soon find out," she said. "Something about this is too easy, we arrive at the boutique, complete strangers and the assistant holds us for 500 Euros and just hands over the name!" I said, "Just like that, it was too bloody easy." and again I was thinking something still just didn't add up.

But Jeannie didn't agree, she said, "To be honest I had to give him the readies (cash) one note at a time and then he showed me his screen." I left the conversation at that but my gut told me that episode was a little too easy. I'd save that for later and follow up on who that assistant was as we already had his card, showing his name as Guiseppe Donatelli.

Anyway, there was nothing found on that name in any database we had access to, Interpol, the FBI database, our own Met database and even 5 (MI5). There was not even facial recognition either so this was so far another dead end. I decided I would call my friend Keith at the ICC (International Criminal Court) in The Hague to see if there was anything on the highly secure program they had.

The next day as soon as I got to my office, I checked my voicemail to find that Olivia had left me a message, maybe she had found something about our man. Jeannie was in her office already, busily striking the keys with lightning speed, 100% focused on her screens. I was at my desk making notes on our visit to the Zegner boutique with our adjoining door as usual open never closed. I returned Olivia's call, "Oh hi Max," she said sounding pleased with herself, then casually said, "Can you maybe swing by later?"

Now one thing about Olivia was that I had spent many hours with her on prior cases and told her never to trust a phone call as being safe and secure. So I said I could but gave her no specific time making it seem we were just going to spend some time together.

I entered the details of the additional camera at Leicester Square station and the helpful guard's name. Then, after checking with Jeannie I found she had 1000 similar faces to go through as she went from 85% similarity to 90% then 95%. "Maybe focus on the ear as well," I said, "As eye distance and other features may be false leads," I added looking over her shoulder.

Jeannie turned and looked at me with such a look and said, "Really Max! I never thought of that, I'll try it now. Wow thanks so much! Oh, look there's an ear better take a better look as I've never seen one like this" she said sarcastically as she zoomed in to make our man's ear the size of the two screens. "Ok, I should have known, I'll leave you to it, I'm going to see Olivia maybe she found something," "Yeah you do that," she said laughing at the zing she had thrown my way!

I headed back out to see what Olivia had found and made my way straight down to her morgue. I learned long ago never to hesitate or look lost when entering an official building and to always hold a piece of paper or a file in my hand making it look like I was part of the scene there. A con? Yeah damn right but it saved so much time as I nodded to the front desk on my way straight down to the dingy depths of Olivia's domain working with the deceased.

"Hi Max," she said as I entered her morgue, "Take a look at this," she said excitedly knowing she had found something. I immediately went over to her and gave her a hug and a big bar of her favourite dark chocolate I picked up on the way. Olivia loved Cadbury's dark chocolate and I was always happy to pick up a treat for my second-most favourite girl.

She slipped it into her fridge alongside all those nasty bits she had placed there to study at some other time. Boy, I would never ever do her job! Anyway, she started showing me the results of the tox screen, though I had no bloody idea what I was looking at.

To me, it was just a jumble of seemingly random images on several slides. She looked at me in triumph, "See?" She said. I looked blankly at her, "See what?" I said. "Right there on the slide," she said as if I should understand microbiology.

"Ok, I can see the slide but what's all that stuff on it?" "It's obvious" she said, "It's poison and it's from a Pufferfish but not just that, it's been concentrated to be even more deadly and it's been mixed with a neurotoxin, "Curare," see those dots around the edges those pink dots? Those are bound to the Pufferfish venom."

"Now we were getting somewhere, so how deadly is this cocktail?" I asked. "It's the deadliest poison I've ever seen and it has been developed specifically to interact together killing anyone who touches it, within mere minutes. It can be absorbed through the skin or by injection and doesn't even need to be subcutaneously involved. In other words, just touching the skin with this stuff will be enough to kill anyone in seconds. The lab called me to tell me they had to place this upstairs to the chief coroner to warn him of this deadly toxin."

This news proved what I had been thinking all along our John Doe, now Richard Whitehead, had been murdered and by a very deadly neurotoxin. Olivia was happy to have found what had killed our man. "If it wasn't for you Max, I would never have bothered to look into a tox screen. So, with this, I should tell the case officer and the coroner to change the COD (cause of death)." I agreed and mentioned that Angel, was the CID officer who had the case, but she had not returned my calls.

But by law, Olivia was compelled to inform the cops and I knew that this would now muddy the water for our own investigation. But having been in the Met myself I had to go along with it and I didn't really mind as long as our Angel would not try to block my own investigation. Time will tell.

I thanked Olivia and told her this was a breakthrough and I owed her several pounds of Cadbury's dark chocolate. "No" she said, it was you who got me to check and you know how I love to have the deceased all buttoned up.

I would want the same for myself and my loved ones if anything had happened. It's what separates us from the beautiful animals we share this planet with and that's why I love what I do.

I have to add here that my lovely Olivia was a real scientist, it was often her information that led to a murderer being caught. Her science included biology, material technology and biological science, toxicology and human behaviour, even knowing if a person was right or left-handed just from minute evidence.

Her skill was amazing and I was so happy to call her my close friend. We both shared a mutual admiration, me for her incredible scientific knowledge and her for me, as she told me many times, for my uncanny deductive powers to connect the dots that most would never be able to connect.

"Ok, where could something like this be created, what should I look for?" I asked her. "That's your department Max, but I can help a little. Whoever did this has a deep knowledge of neurotoxin science and probably had, or has, government or a sophisticated science operation's funding and a chem-bio lab." This was helpful but not really, where do I start? I thought. "One thing though, Olivia said, this neurotoxin has a marker that I think will lead back to a bio lab that specialises in this research." I could work with that and follow through to see who was suspect.

"What about ingredients to make this, is there such a list?" I asked her, "If there is can you send it to me and maybe we can look at who or what company has bought these chemicals. At least that would steer me in the right direction." I added. "Hmm, I'll think about what might help and send you what I can," she said.

I told her that was another dinner I owed her. "Just doin' my humble work, anything to help the boys in grey" she said smiling, proud that she had found something real. I was now one of the boys in grey, not blue! "Keep me posted, as I want to add whatever you can find into my 'nefarious people' database," I told her I would keep her in the loop, as anyway, it may help with future cases.

Chapter 11

Names and Databases

I didn't need to make another trip to Angel's cop shop, as she finally returned one of my three calls and boy was, she pissed! "Good morning Angel," I said but was cut off before I could finish my innocent and happy morning greeting (I'm a morning person).

"Good morning my arse! Well Max, why the fuck didn't you tell me you were formerly job?" She hit me immediately I answered. "And if you fucking tell me, I didn't fucking ask, I will be fucking scream!" she added. Such a potty mouth from such an attractive woman!

She appeared to be somewhat pissed, can't think why! After all, I went to her and called her several times, to follow up. She was her problem, not me. "And, by the way, if you do have anything to add to this case then let's have it otherwise, I'll have you for obstruction of justice!" she added.

"Yeah, really, good luck with that, you've just blown any info I may have been prepared to share with you, so you do your thing, whatever the fuck that is, and I'll do mine. As I said before I don't work for you and neither am I obliged to share my findings which are confidential between me and my employer," I said, "I don't need your help to do what I do," she yelled down the phone.

I let her rant, then decided it was time to level with her, well kind of, "Look I don't know you, Angel, I came to see you when I was under no obligation to do so. I gave you what I had from being there, I also gave you my gut feeling and I have no idea how you work or really who you

are, but there's one thing for damn certain, you took your sweet time responding to my three messages and my note and by the way, I came to you not the other way around and to be honest you looked bored in what I, as a seasoned ex-cop was telling you. You took very few notes and despite my many more years' experience than you have, I have to tell you, you appeared uninterested in John Doe, or what I was telling you. So, despite giving you my valuable time and my observations on the unfolding case, I thought I would follow up with you, not once but three times, because you never responded" I told her.

I was on a roll and continued my own tirade. "With what I saw, why would I bother to tell you anything about myself? So, I kept our conversation on the matter at hand" I said. "And, if you were even half a cop and by the way I don't work for you, you are not my boss," I said.

She broke in again saying "I have other cases I'm working on and to be frank, there's nothing here on this John Doe. He's just someone who dropped dead on my watch." She said still fuming. "That was enough for me I had it with her attitude."

"Ok," I said calmly, "If that's all you got after finding out who the fuck I am, I've learned all I need from you Angel, which is nothing of interest because there's nothing there to see. So, whatever, see ya someday soon, but I won't hold my breath," I said as I ended this call with Angel still fuming. But fuming over what exactly? I didn't tell her who I was and anyway, why would I especially with an attitude like hers?

I thought it would be even more amusing when Olivia told her what she had found and why she even sent for a tox screen at my request. Anyway, I had other things to delve into and continued back to my office thinking why a Pufferfish poison? Why make a cocktail? Why did it need to be administered in public, and who had the ability to turn off those cameras? My phone rang again, it was Angel but I was in no mood to continue listening to her petulant rant and ignored her call.

I entered my office to hear Jeannie in a heated call with who I deduced to be Angel who had probably called her after I refused to answer. Jeannie looked up and looked up to the ceiling as if saying, who the fuck is this? I slid my hand over my throat telling her to cut the conversation which she did. "What the hell?" she said so I filled her in on my conversation with Angel and moved over to our war board. "Anyway, let's focus, I have more to update." "And so have I," she said.

I relayed the poison information on our whiteboard adding we were to receive a list of ingredients from which we could check further, compliments of Olivia. Jeannie turned her screen around to show me 11 images that were a 90% match.

I went over to take a look. Each of them could have been our man as each was a very close match to the photo I took, but we needed more background knowledge. Once again Jeannie was one step ahead and had prepared a list of questions, she had researched the answers to adding this to each of the names now on our war board.

"So which ones do we follow up with?" I was thinking out loud. There were 3 names with a question mark next to them. "But suppose our man who appears to have been so meticulous about never leaving a money trail, had created a false legend," I said looking at our board. "Well then any of these 11 could be our man," she said. "Ok we'll assume all of these names are a created legend, so let's go through each of these in detail where they were born, school, work, and if any had been in military service.

We'll need to eliminate them one by one. If we can't reach any one of them place them on a separate list. There's one thing for damn sure if any of these is our man, then legend or no legend that one is not around now that is unless someone somewhere knows or planned his demise and if there are more people involved someone may have updated his legend."

I took a closer look at the information and then homed in on one name, Olivier Nicholas. He had very little information added and was in the database with the word "Restricted, NTKO" next to it. Meaning "Need to Know Only" next to that name.

"What database did you find this one?" I asked Jeannie. "It was on an Interpol database but nothing showed more than that comment," she said. Why stick a restricted notice on it when the database is only used by those who already have clearance to have access?

Maybe I could ask Keith to check it for me, but I couldn't send the name in any message, not even WhatsApp which is encrypted peer-to-peer, (yeah right). If some public media platform or corporation encrypted their software for public use then they were deffo also reading the messages and this would be flagged to both of us. It was nothing more than a scam to make us feel good. Anyway, Jeannie used her own version of VPN which did in fact inform us if we were being tracked.

I damn well didn't need any spooks knocking on my door so I decided, rather than wait for Keith to come over to meet me again in London where his trip may be monitored, I would fly to Brussels then get the train to Amsterdam then drive on to The Hague. It was a 13-hour drive but no problem it would only leave a connection with me as a tourist visiting Europe travelling with my female companion. It would not lead to me or where I was headed.

I decided to take Jeannie so she could share the driving and register as the driver when we rented the car, less info to raise any red flags, not that we were anything special but my gut told me to proceed with maximum caution. I was of course thinking of that poisonous cocktail used to kill our man.

We caught the train at St. Pancras on the Eurostar to Paris through the "Chunnel" which went under the English Channel then caught another going on to Amsterdam. From there we would drive to The Hague and rent a car at the station. I remained in the background while Jeannie concluded the hire contract, once again speaking perfect Dutch. She had already set it up from our office. She rented an Audi Sport, a very fast V8 gas guzzler and I had to smile knowing she had often talked about owning one, one day.

I asked Jeannie to call Keith on his apartment number and left a message saying she and I were taking some much-needed time off to go sightseeing in Europe. I didn't mention that we would meet him, but I knew he would get the fact that I was not that sight-seeing type. I also said we were going to be away for a week in case he needed to reach me. That would tell him to expect to see me within a few days.

We set off on what was a long shot, could we find out more about our top-secret name or was this a red tape "Blind stop" leading nowhere? On the journey, we were both discussing the case and the more we found out the more questions we had.

My instincts told me we had our man, appearing on a top-secret list with nothing more. I really hoped Keith could at least point us in the right direction but if not, this resourceful sleuth would try another route to travel to update my friend. The cost was not that much and far less visible than using a flight. We planned to fly back from Schiphol International Airport in the Netherlands.

I explained to Jeannie along the way that if Keith couldn't help, I had another contact I could try over at 5 (MI5) so there was a chance this would get us to the right name. But I owed it to my Welsh Red-headed friend to update him, just in case we might need his help later on. Well, really, I wanted to let him know our John Doe, now Richard Whitehead was a real case and not some wild goose chase.

We sat together in a seat not too far from the dining car. One thing about these Euro trains is they were damn fast at 125mph and smooth as silk. We grabbed a sandwich and a coffee from the restaurant car so we could relax and go through what we had.

The coffee was surprisingly good as were the sandwiches. How things had improved since I last travelled by train and never had I travelled on the Eurostar or the European rail system. Anyway, we wanted our trip to be as incognito as we could manage and rail was actually often faster overall than air travel with all the waiting taxying and flight times.

We were eating our lunch which, as I said was surprisingly good and I was thinking back to that time when Egon Ronay, a famous chef, ripped into those motorway restaurants, what was it he said? Coffee that smelt

of washing-up water, tough bacon, ridiculous chips and a host of other comments but one thing for sure, he turned it around and made the owners a fortune from selling average food which was a step up from the disgusting food they sold before!

I snapped back to matters at hand, "We'll see if he can help now we know there's a link to 5 (MI5) if not it's back to basics and good old surveillance looking through all that footage leading to the station which we will end up doing anyway to find our murderer. We recapped our findings, looking out the large window at the scenery flashing past." So he came out of Thames House, and you can't do that unless you're either part of 5 or involved with them, so he must have been followed.

"What was it that Olivia said? That the poison works almost immediately so whoever shut down those cameras knew he was headed to the station. Anyway, who on earth uses Curare and Pufferfish venom?" I was thinking out loud, with a jumble of thoughts about Pufferfish and the remote tribal venom that was used.

I jumped, "Oh my God!" I said too loud, turning to a shocked Jeannie, "Think about it, if he was so damn careful, meticulous even, about not leaving a trace of his movements or whereabouts even when he bought his suit, then a meeting set up with MI5 at Thames House would, for damn sure, have been set up in secret, wouldn't it? So, if he was murdered half an hour later someone knew of that meeting. Maybe we have to look at 5 for the murderer. If not then someone who knew of that meeting."

"Agreed," she said, "I'll check for who entered or left after him or around that time. He must have been followed. We'll get nowhere if they used text or phone calls to set this hit up." I hoped this would not be the case here, but a bad feeling was looming that if MI5 were involved then tracking this down, just became ten times more of a problem. Well, one step at a time as we had always done and it had always worked as it could, eventually, here.

"What do we tell him when we see him? He'll shut down on us if we don't handle this with Kidd gloves and this will be a wasted journey. I decided it would be best to tell Keith the truth and see how the chips fall.

Chapter 12

Once That Door is Opened

I decided I would tell Keith exactly what we had found and gauge his reaction. After all, this information was now fact and facts are, after all, what we always try to find and they lead to the truth. I didn't tell Keith we were heading there to see him as I knew from our many conversations where he would be after work on the occasions when he was in his office and not out and about. I had found out he was in all week, from a prior conversation.

We checked in to the Babylon Hotel, in Den Haag on Bezuidenhoutsweg, a main road just 1.6 miles from the ICC. Opposite there was a bar and restaurant where he often hung out after work. We booked 2 rooms, very inexpensive on a special deal and the location overlooking the street, was perfect so we could see the "Stations Huiskamer" bar restaurant from our hotel window. We took turns to watch the street waiting for him to enter the bar. We didn't have to wait long; he went in at 7.35 that evening.

I went down to the lobby, while Jeannie had decided to stay, to do more research on who came out of Thames House close to when our man left the building. She would go back and forth from there to the station searching for anyone who was in both places. A long shot I know since professional surveillance usually involved more than one person following the "Mark" But as usual she was on a mission to follow up.

I told her if she got a hit to call or text me immediately so I could decide how to handle it depending on my friend's reaction to my evidence. Either we would keep that back for the time being or we would show him who came out. I was undecided as I left the hotel for the bar opposite. Good thing Keith was a creature of habit, at least where his local drinking haunts were concerned!

I went over the road and entered the bar restaurant, which was a large modern place, not like the Red Lion one of our local watering holes. I Knew he would be sitting in a corner facing outwards as I entered, and sure enough, there was my red-headed friend with a beer. He looked up masking his surprise as I sat down to join him.

He leaned forward with his arm outstretched waving me to a set next to him. "Joining me for dinner?" he said smiling. "I thought I would" I replied, "After all, I heard somewhere the food is good here so I thought I would at least check it out. Anyway, my local bars don't have what I fancy to eat today," I replied as I sat down.

"I wondered when I would hear from you again, so what do I owe this impromptu I visit?" he said as I sat down to join him. A waitress came over as I sat down and I ordered a beer, the same as him I told her as she went off to get it.

I paused before speaking, thinking where do I start? I asked him if he had done any more research into our deceased. "You mean your newest theory with that bloke who died at Leicester Square station?" I nodded, "Yup that chap." He told me no he was working on a new case and as he said, "To be honest Max, there was nothing much to go on. But seeing you here unannounced, which by the way is a pleasant surprise, I'm guessing you have something to share." "Yes, as a matter of fact, I do," I said as the waitress arrived with a large stein of beer.

"Where are you staying?" He asked and I pointed to the street. He nodded, "Figures," he said. I asked him if we could talk here or if it would be better to go to my hotel. "Better meet over the road," he said and we began drinking our beers. "Look," I said, "I can't do our usual as I have a long drive when we are done and this is a business trip for me." "Me either," he said, "As I too have a busy day tomorrow."

We made small talk while finishing our beer. If Keith didn't think we should talk here, that was good enough for me.

Just then another man came into the bar, I didn't see him enter but Keith who was facing outwards just flicked his eyes over in his direction. He sat a few tables away from us and started looking over the menu.

Keith was also studying the menu and said quietly, "What's your room number," I told him, pretending to be on my phone, he said, "You leave now and I'll follow in a bit," as if he was talking about the menu. I nodded and said out loud, "Well sorry mate but I've got to go we have plans tonight. Thanks for the beer," I said smiling knowing I had left him to pay my tab.

I texted Jeannie as I left telling her to watch the restaurant and left to head back to the hotel. But I walked off down the street and crossed over further down the street in case I was being followed. I caught a cab at the end of the street and asked him to drive around the block and drop me off at the side of the Hotel telling the driver I left my phone in the bar. Two can play at the surveillance game and I learned a long time ago just how.

I paid cash and exited the cab quickly entering the hotel through a side door keeping my head down as if looking for something in my pockets. I was being overly cautious I know but as they say, "An ounce of caution now, saves a ton of sorrow later" (actually that's my saying, and you're welcome). I went over to the elevator and pressed the floor below mine so I could walk up the stairs one flight to my floor. Again, I was being careful but the thought of having that deadly cocktail that was used on the victim was, for me, a serious warning telling me to be damn careful.

Jeannie was looking out the hotel room window with her phone camera pointed to the bar entrance as I entered and I went over to her. "What's going on?" she said, "You were very quick," I told her about the warning Keith gave me. "Well I suppose he's on board then," she said still looking out the window. "Maybe, he is and maybe not but we'll find out soon as he's coming up here shortly," I answered. "Do you want me to stay out of the way when he gets here?" she said. I turned and gave her my best "What on earth are you saying," look. "No" I said, "I brought you here as my assistant not as a secretary!" She smiled at the obvious recognition I gave for her valuable contribution to our company. We both knew I couldn't do what I did without her help.

Around half an hour later there was a quiet knock on the door, Jeannie opened it and Keith came in quickly. He went straight over to the window looking out at the entrance of the bar. Jeannie told him she had been watching the entrance the whole time and had photographed everyone entering and leaving the bar.

We sat down to tell Keith about our findings, the results of the tox screen that Olivia had told us and the poison used to kill him. Jeannie showed him a photo taken from the CCTV camera feed of the man following our mark coming out of MI5 headquarters at Thames House. We were both filling him in with the details but as I told Jeannie before he arrived, keep it impartial and only tell him the facts, of which there was plenty of new information to discuss.

Keith listened impassively as we laid out where we were going to try to find out who our Richard Whitehead really was. When we had finished giving him the update, he told me he recognised the man who entered the bar and sat near us. "He's a trained operative who I've seen lurking around over this past week," he said. "Seems one way or another we've opened a door and something bad has come through," he added. "No" I said, "The bad was already here with the sudden death on the platform, all we're doing is connecting the dots trying to find out the truth wherever it leads us."

He looked thoughtful and said the words I was dreading to hear, "The fact that the operative followed me, or maybe you, into the bar was no coincidence. We may have a leak," he said. I answered, "We've been very careful not to leave a trace of what we are doing, we came by rail and road with Jeannie here doing the tickets and the car hire, so as not to link anything directly. That was why we didn't alert you to our visit."

"So where and how could a leak have connected anything to us?" "Dunno yet he said but we'll find out hopefully soon and when we do we can lead a false trail. I've done this before and it's no biggie," he added.

"Are you on board with us in that this may be a bigger issue than a John Doe dropping dead on the platform?" I asked.

"Well, you found the poison which is very rare and maybe they thought his murder would be seen as simply a John Doe. So, any triggers that may have been flagged, if your friendly coroner did online research, or maybe got the tox screen back, would alert them. Or perhaps the lab she used may have been part of a large-scale search by whoever these perps are who may have been looking for any tox screen search result that would come up with the poison used. You can check that out with her to see what she did online. You're good at tradecraft and can go underground to get the information needed."

"I use my own VPN," Jeannie added, and no one can trace any of my searches as I only use the dark web," she said looking at Keith. "I'm always careful because of the cases we've worked on," she said. "But a leak may not have come from you but through any of these third-party operations you may inadvertently trigger," Keith said.

The room went quiet, "OK do you want to work with us on this or are we running two separate operations looking for the same people," I asked and waited for him to consider this, if he hadn't already. "The two of you can do things that I can't, things that are done outside of the local police and outside of either 5 or 6," he said, "And anyway everything I do is monitored for obvious reasons. So, I think we see where this goes but if we do work together then we have to have a means of communicating our findings and that means us both using tradecraft," he said.

I'm ok with that and so is Jeannie as she is already doing it for any case we work on. But we need a link between you here in The Hague and us in London, without direct communication, so how do you want to do this? I asked thinking of the many ways we could communicate. "We need several methods so we can spread our communications without having it from only one. Maybe trade press and ads in local news or a dead drop if you have someone you trust." I said, "I think both of those are needed after all we're working at the moment against 3 or more agencies, one or more of which has already linked you or me, or both to finding out what is behind this murder." He said. "Is there someone you trust over here that you can use over the dark web who can link up with Jeannie?" I asked. Yep, I have a very good person and I think you, Jeannie, will like working with her." "How good is she at our dark arts, Jeannie said, "Does she have good cred's is she street smart?" She asked. "She's the best and that's all I can tell you, for obvious reasons, but also she is 100% reliable and has worked with me in the past, far above my pay grade." He said.

I knew he would not tell me more with Jeannie present but that was his decision to make and I trusted his judgement. "Where is she based?" I asked. "For the present, you don't need to know that, but as I said we can absolutely trust her and anyway with today's technology we can work in separate locations. She has an incredible knowledge base, and she is English that's all you need for now." "OK I said Jeannie can be the conduit with her can you give us her contact?" "Leave that for now as I need to speak with her before we set this up and I'll send you a link with all protocols for communicating with her," he said.

"Good enough for now, so let's divide up the work. Can you find out who the operative is both here and the one Jeannie found following our mark in London and we can begin to search the names Jeannie found to see who this Richard Whitehead really is?" "Ok and I'll work on the leak," he said.

"We have tried and tested ways of discovering a leak and when I know who it is we can use that knowledge to spread disinformation for a while. But eventually, he or she will have to be exposed as we will not be able to keep this as a disinformation source for too long," Keith said.

"I know I don't have to tell you but I think this is going to be far bigger than either of us realise at this moment so absolute caution from here on and any info we find, keep it strictly within our communication methods." We both knew this but his warning reinforced how we would work from here on.

Chapter 13

Let the Games Begin!

We now had four people involved and I hoped we would not need anyone else as four was enough and adding more would only add to the possibility of increased risk. Keith left us and disappeared into the night. Jeannie and I had dinner in the room so we could work through dinner.

"When we get back, I'll go and see Olivia to find out which lab and what if any info she placed publicly so we can see if there's a leak possible there. After all, if these people are as sophisticated as I think they are then they may have been looking for anything where those poisons were named on any private or public domain. But I want you to search further into each of the names you had on your database for our Richard Whitehead?"

The following morning, we left for Schiphol airport which was a 10-hour journey north from The Hague. The more I thought of the journey the more I knew we were now being very careful with good reason. We had agreed that I would get a bus from the hotel to Mauritshuis where there was an art museum while Jeannie would drive from the hotel's underground car park and meet me at the museum. We paid for our rooms separately and we had not been seen together at the hotel so we were confident no connection had been made.

The art museum, at Mauritshuis, looked a little like a smaller version of Buckingham Palace with similar architecture at the front. I got there before Jeannie and had a look at the art there. Most of it was old masters which, to be honest, I never found interesting except for the amazing detail. But then again without TV, Facebook and other distractions, they could spend a damn site more time than people have today. But that's just me!

Were we being over-cautious? My gut feeling said no, especially with the tail that arrived at the bar which was too damn much of a coincidence along with the fact that Keith knew of that man and warned me to leave separately. Although we didn't have unlimited funds we had not spent much so far and I was determined to get to the bottom of this case.

After we met at the museum, we stopped for a coffee in the beautiful town of Mauritshuis before setting off for Schiphol International Airport. "So, what do you think of Keith?" I asked Jeannie once we were on our way. "I think he's the real deal and he obviously trusts you otherwise we would not have had the meeting last night," she said. "Yeah, we go back a long way, kicking in doors, arrests, bringing gang bangers to justice and it was always fun we were a good team," I said.

Changing the subject, we discussed the case so far and homed in on possible leaks. The obvious leak would, I think, come from the lab Olivia used but we couldn't jump to conclusions yet, and anyway that would only get to Olivia's name. We'll check with her to see if there were any questions back from the lab and who was doing the search.

"How far away from our office is the lab?" I asked her. "It's in Leatherhead in Surrey," she answered, which is around 15 miles outside London. Depending on what we find out from Olivia I may have to pay them a visit. "You don't need to," Jeannie said, "With the name of that lab I can hack into their database to see if they sent the tox report to anyone else and if we can get a phone number I can look into that as well" she said.

I knew we were moving forward but at the same time, it seemed we were one step forward two steps back, as each time we gained ground there was something else going on. I told Jeannie the spook in the bar in the Hague really concerned me and I don't easily get spooked.

One thing though, is I can handle myself and learned to do so in many multi-skills classes, plus I spent several years in the army, an infantry unit, deployed in various parts of the world. The funny thing is I had been going to self-defence classes since I was a kid and had become really good at taking people down.

It was because of my skills with being able to handle myself as well as being a damn good shot, was why I was placed into a small special operations unit of 10 men. We were still an infantry unit but we were never talked about and never as a unit did, we talk about what we did. I kept in touch with my unit after I left and we met occasionally. As part of our training, we were sent to Hereford to train with the Special Air Service boys.

That training was intense and some of the stealth techniques of surveillance were drilled into us. I loved the training but didn't want to continue with the military life. However, the skills I developed with them helped me enormously. Training with the SAS taught me that you don't have to be a hulk, which is good because I'm not a hulk. But being agile, which I am and having the intelligence to connect the dots, assess a situation and think fast in a tough situation is what I am good at.

Some would say I'm paranoid, but to me, I have always had a "Heightened sense of awareness" (which is what I call it). I am acutely aware of my surroundings and whenever I enter any building, I automatically look for exit choke points, ceilings, windows, and stairways as all may come in handy in case there's an emergency. By the way, during my time in the military, there was always an emergency on each and every call we went out as a unit, that was why we were deployed.

But I didn't like others to do my planning and thinking, that was for me to do which was why I joined the police. I gained a reputation as a "Don't fuck with me," cop which I accepted but which was only one side of my skills. What my colleagues never got was how and why I had such a high close rate and I was fine with that. I made it look easy plodding through each case sometimes with my partner and sometimes alone.

Back to the case at hand, what I'm explaining is why and how I connected the dots with our John Doe and why I wanted to continue to find out why and who was behind his extreme murder.

I drove while Jeannie was working on her laptop which by the way had full military-grade encryption and had the fastest processing unit available. Jeannie had modified it to suit her own needs.

She was going through an encrypted facial recognition software to see who it was at the bar. She had managed to get a good photo from a video feed she took and at one point he had looked around and that was the frame she was working on. She was on her own version of the dark web and, as she constantly informed me, she was invisible.

We were heading to Schiphol with me driving so Jeannie could do her thing on her laptop. Just as we were passing through Wassenaar, Jeannie let out a yell, "Ha! Gotcha" she exclaimed looking over at me and grinning from ear to ear. She turned her screen around to show me. I glanced at it but was driving fast so I didn't take a close gander (look) at it.

"I thought we agreed to let Keith handle that part," I said. "Yeah, we did but I want to see the bloke who spooked you both in the bar." She replied. "So, who is he," I asked. "Well according to his profile, he was with the French Security Services, the DGCE, but that was 5 years ago," she said. "What about Interpol?" I asked. "Not directly, but there's always a link there," she said.

I recapped thinking out loud, "So this ex-French-security operative was tracking us here in The Hague while another in London who we think had something to do with MI5 was coming out of Thames House to follow our man just before he was murdered. This is beginning to look like our government may be involved and if we find that link this game just got a whole lot worse."

Jeannie was focused on her screen. "I'm checking our London operative out on another of my search engines which links the CCTV cameras to search for his face. We can backtrack to see his movements but it may take a while," she said. "So what's his name, not that it makes much difference at this point," I asked. The London man is "Michele Debusse," she said, "If that's his real name. But his name is not as important as his facial recognition." I had a feeling that we were finding out a lot more than we were supposed to and I was going to focus on how a leak had occurred and from where.

"Got him," Jeannie said sounding pleased with herself, "Our man leaving Thames House is working for French Security. Actually he works for The Directorate-General for French External Security or direction générale de la Sécurité extérieure," she said in perfect French, or DGSE for short. The DGSE is France's foreign intelligence agency, equivalent to our MI6 and the American CIA.

The DGSE operates under the direction of the French Ministry of Armed Forces and works alongside its domestic counterpart, the DGSI (General Directorate for Internal Security). As with most other intelligence agencies, details of their operations and organisation are highly classified and not made public.

The agency goes back to the 1940s, when a central external intelligence agency, known as the DGSS (Direction générale des services spéciaux), was founded by politician Jacques Soustelle. The name of the agency was changed in 1944, to DGER (Direction générale des études et recherches).

The DGSE safeguards French national security through intelligence gathering as well as conducting paramilitary and counterintelligence operations abroad. It also covers economic espionage and is headquartered in the 20th arrondissement of Paris. So now we know who Michele Debusse was and who he worked for. We couldn't determine if Michele was a friend or foe yet, that would come later.

Anyway, we left for home and our drive north to Schiphol Airport was uneventful. The last few miles were a straight run. She dropped me off at the South side of the airport and we would travel separately on the flight which was just around an hour to Heathrow.

When we arrived, it was now evening so we both went home. I decided I would head to the morgue at the hospital to meet with Olivia to see how the information may have got out. I got off the tube at my usual stop, Boston Manor, just seven stops from terminal 2 at Heathrow. I was tired more from what we were up against than from the travel which I was well used to. I ordered a carry-out from my local Chinese and added notes on my laptop before calling it a day.

The following morning, I went uptown to Leicester Square and headed to St Thomas' University College Hospital to see my bestie, Olivia.

I knocked on her locked door and she came over to see me. I immediately put my fingers to my lips to tell her to be quiet. We hugged and I asked her if there was somewhere we could talk. She said quietly "The supply room" and I followed her down the corridor to the supply room.

"What's going on?" she asked. So, I told her about the possible leak around her poisonous findings. "It's possible that someone was listening in on my phone call with the lab," she said, "But how and why?" She was now growing concerned as this had never happened before. "We think it was an algorithm looking for anything over the web that came up on those named poisons and when or if your lab had searched for the poison online that may have been a red flag.

How was this information relayed to you?" I asked. "By phone as usual as soon as the lab technician, who by the way is a longtime friend, found it. Look I trust the lab 100% and I've worked with them for years!" she said. "That's not the issue here, it was the search online for two unusual poisons that was probably what triggered the red flag to whoever was looking for it. By the way, has Angel Borowa from Agar Street called you yet?"

Apparently, she had not, so my angry, now lazy friend who was the case officer was too busy to follow up on a murder case despite our heated conversation. I knew I could confide in Olivia as we went back so far. I told her this was a case of collusion to commit a murder and although we don't know yet where it would lead, I had to caution my friend to be careful with the information. "Have you called Angel yet to tell her your findings?" I asked her. "Yes, twice I left a message to call me

back but I said nothing more than for her to return my call. I don't know her and anyway, I never volunteer findings over the phone unless it's you." I had to smile as she fluttered her eyelashes at me pretending to flirt "Good!" I said, "Don't offer anything over the phone, even if she asks you. Tell her, when she calls, if she calls, that you are going to be offsite and can meet her, choose a public place where you can give her your file and make it seem normal. Look I know I'm asking a lot but believe me, we are caught up in something and until we know who is involved, I'm asking that you be very careful. Take the file with you in your bag so it doesn't show and remove all information off your computer and save it on a thumb drive." I was scaring Olivia, so I qualified why.

I gave her a burner phone which I had bought on the way from one of those small 'hole in the wall' shops selling everything from ciggies, sweets, newspapers and magazines and now mobile phones. I gave Jeannie the number and had her set it up on my way, I didn't want anything to happen to my friend who through no fault of her own was now caught up in this, whatever it may turn out to be. I placed my number and Jeannie's number on the phone but not any names which I explained to her.

"When you use this phone don't use names just start talking, any calls on this have been screened by Jeannie and cannot be traced," I told her and made the call from outside not in here. "There's a spot at the back of the hospital which is not covered by the CCTV cameras I'll show you on the way out. I know I'm being cautious and it may end up being nothing but just in case, an ounce of caution now," "I know I know" she said smiling "You've told me this before."

We walked out together and I stood letting her know where she could call us where the CCTV cameras did not cover the area. "One last thing, make your report on the COD (cause of death) seem routine a heart attack or stroke don't put the poison on the report," I said. "I can't do that," she said.

"My report as the coroner for this case is a specific document which must be a true statement. But I can make a reference to another document and place the real information on that." She said.

"Great, look, these people are serious so please be very careful you can call me or Jeannie anytime," I told her. I don't want this information to get into the wrong hands which it seems to have done already. But no matter, what's done is done and we are closer to finding the leak.

I was worried about my friend and even more concerned about what may happen once Detective Angel Borowa got her hands on the information. I knew exactly how the police worked and this would bust our case wide open if it got into the wrong hands.

But as in the Kennedy assassination, once the information was out, there was little danger to Olivia. But regardless I wanted to do what I could to prevent a third unnecessary death. I would alert Jeannie to be extra careful if or when Olivia made contact and not to use her name on the call.

We would find the leak either through Jeannie and me or through Keith and his operation.

Chapter 14

One Step Forward

I waited around for 20 minutes after Olivia went back to her office before, I walked back to my office. As usual, my paranoia was with me, like a shadow on a sunny day. I stopped several times looking at the reflection in shop windows to see if I was being tailed. I wasn't but I made several stops and went into a newspaper stall on the pavement taking my time to pick up a magazine while looking to see if anyone stopped as well. They didn't so all was OK for the time being.

Jeannie was, as usual, focused on her screens as I entered my office and filled her in with my meeting with Olivia telling her I was worried that Olivia had been caught up in this, but nothing to do except help her play it down. I went to my desk and added the latest information, saving it onto my 2-terabyte thumb drive before removing it and placing it in my pocket. She was busy with her new algorithm searching through facial recognition to see which of our "Face fit" finalists had won the prize. I knew not to ask as she would tell me when she had something.

It was now a week since we had our meeting in The Hague and I hoped Keith would have more news on who the operative was and if there was a leak. I told Jeannie to focus on the face recognition of Richard Whitehead only, as we had to find him. After all, he was the key and all the other stuff was just, at this point, a distraction.

I was looking at the name Richard Whitehead on a search engine Jeannie had set up, which was not traceable. The only name I could find was a World War Two reference so I started to look into it. It Turns out this Richard Whitehead was killed in action during a raid when he was a British Commando Sargeant in what some considered the forerunner of the SAS.

Not sure if that is correct but I was only interested in who he was. I looked at what had occurred but there was not much detail only that it had occurred in Burma now called Myanmar. I should go to the Imperial War Museum on the Lambeth Road in Kensington to see if their records could tell me more. I could also try the Churchill War Rooms at King Charles Street, London, SW1.

I told Jeannie I was heading out and left for the museum catching a cab outside our office. The museum was located on Lambeth Road, London, SE1. If I couldn't find much there, I could take a look at the Churchill Rooms which I may do anyway. I caught the cab went into the building and asked one of the curators how I could search out a name. He told me they had 11 million photos all catalogued there covering all aspects of World War 1 and 2 plus more information on our military campaigns elsewhere. He showed me a series of books telling me this is the Burma Section and if you can't find what you need let me know. I know this place inside out he told me, good to know I thought!

I looked through the books but it was like shooting at a flock of pigeons so much to see but where do I look? After an hour or so he came over, "Find what you're looking for?" he asked. "No, I said, I'm looking for an uncle of mine who was in Burma is there another way I can search? Yes, he said, we have Microfiche records as well," he told me. I had used microfiche before when looking through old news archives and I knew these may not help. "Can I do a name search," I asked him. "Oh yes, of course, that will be on our computer, Sorry, I thought you just wanted to see photos. I didn't know you were searching for specifics," he said.

He took me over to a couple of public workstations and showed me how to do a search. Just out of interest, are these online, could I do a search from home? "Oh no not at all this information is, privately public, if you know what I mean, you can only search while you are here. May I ask what you are looking for specifically?" he asked.

I had thought of this question on my way and told him I was writing a book and wanted to do a chapter on my uncle. He showed me how to search several different ways, by country, by campaign, or even by military unit and date.

I thanked him and began my search for Richard Whitehead. I only put the surname and bingo after a few minutes I saw a faded photo of a small military unit of 10 men, lounging around in the middle of what looked like a clearing in the jungle. There were tents in the background meaning it was a small ops encampment they had cut into a dense forest.

I had been there and done that in my previous life and had empathy for this unit. At the bottom of the photo, someone had typed the names of these 10 men. I saw his name, Richard Whitehead with the letters "KIA," next to it. I marked that photo to get a print and continued to search for more photos. I found several with his name taken earlier also in a group but there were several with just him and another man. The other man who appeared in several photos was named William Standford Smith, with a bracket naming him (Wild Bill).

They were part of what was known as the "Burma campaign" which was a series of battles fought in what was back then, the British colony of Burma. It was part of the Southeast Asian theatre of World War II and primarily involved forces of the Allies (mainly from the now-former British Empire and the Republic of China, with support from the United States).

During the Burmese Campaign, they were fighting against the invading forces of the Empire of Japan. Imperial Japan, as it was then, was supported by the Thai Phayap Army, as well as two independence movements and armies. In 1942 and 1943, the international Allied forces in British India launched several failed offensives to retake lost territories. Fighting intensified in 1944, and British Empire forces peaked at around 1 million land and air forces. These forces were drawn primarily from British India, with British Army forces (equivalent to eight regular infantry divisions and six tank regiments). I thought back to my own military deployment and knew some of what they were up against.

I found some details about their unit which had been deployed by airdrop into Burma on July 15th, 1942. I bought the photos, 11 in all showing the unit and our Richard Whitehead along with "Wild Bill." So, one step forward two steps back, why was our man named the same as a KIA Richard Whitehead? Had he become a ghost? Was he a dead man walking? I would get to the bottom of this and decided to go on to the Churchill War Rooms to see if there was anything else.

I thought back to when and where those photos were taken, thinking they were a real snapshot in the life of those 10 men, taken by maybe someone in their unit or perhaps a photographer there for the purpose. Either way, those brave men lived for the day and as none of us do, they had no idea what tomorrow may hold for them. For me, looking at these old photos, made me sad, not one of these brave men would be alive now. These were ghosts of the past that most nowadays had no idea who they were or what they did.

The Churchill War Rooms were just that and it was more for me to see where Sir Winston Churchill had his underground nerve centre, while he was running his military operations at a level below the River Thames, where his office and war rooms were based. This was where a considerable portion of World War Two was planned, complete with the large map of Europe and the Far East used for strategic military operations. I was deep in thought trying to place the pieces we had uncovered in this maze of detail.

Maybe I was looking at this all wrong, maybe there was a good reason why a deceased Burma war vet's name had been used. Maybe the original man didn't die back then but even so, he would certainly be dead by now. I could go on with the what-ifs and maybes till the cows came home but I had to follow the facts. I was on the right track and I knew we were getting closer to who he was.

I headed back hoping Jeannie had found something and if she did it could wait till I arrived. I did the usual looking in the shop window reflections to see if I was being tailed, I wasn't.

I got back around 4 pm and brought back a sarni for Jeannie and a cup of tea. The sarni was ham and Swiss on rye from the deli at the corner of our road. It was her favourite, knowing she probably hadn't eaten since yesterday. "I'm fucking starving!" she said grabbing the huge 3-inch-thick deli specialty.

"You're the bffft," she said, talking as she took a huge bite and crammed a huge mouthful holding the entire sarnie between her teeth as she pointed to her screen with the Styrofoam cup in her other hand. "Yeah, I know," I said, "I really am."

I waited for the three and a half seconds it took till she demolished half the huge three-inch-thick sarnie in just two bites and could talk. She gulped down a mouthful of tea before I could warn her, "Son of a bitch!" she shouted, "That was fucking red hot," "Well you didn't give me a chance to warn you," I replied as she rushed over to our small sink and with her mouth under the cold tap.

She pointed again to her screen, then doing a little dance she sat on her desk and started in a rush of words. So, you think you're the biz she said as I filled her in on who Richard Whitehead was and laying out the photos on the desk I pointed him out. "Hmm, interesting, who were those others," she asked. I pointed to her their names printed at the bottom of the group photo and pointed out several photos with just him and another man. "Seems these two were very close," I said.

"William Stanford Smith known as Wild Bill, to his mates, that's his friend's name and maybe we can see what happened to him after the war. Anyway, what did you find out?" I asked her. "Well since you insist," she started before taking another huge bite.

"Here's what I found," On the facial recognition program set at ninety per cent accuracy we had a lot of names, fifty in all. So, I ran them through increasing the accuracy by one per cent, then half a per cent, more accuracy. I got down to five names we can look at and these are them," she said. "Good work, now we have the real person we can start to home in to see who he is."

I looked at the 5 names and compared them to our man they all had similarities but I had photographed a deceased face, so as far as I could see they were each close but not exactly. "OK, add more accuracy and see what we get," I said. We were both watching to see which names disappeared. She got us down to 1.5% and we were left with two names.

"Can you focus on his ear and overlay the original?" I asked, and she did, she overlayed my photo cropped with each of her finalists adding a transparency so that each ear was visible but none were the same. "Damn, I said out loud, what's going on?" I said out loud. "Would a weight gain or weight loss make a difference?" I asked her. "Nope, my app works on ratios and the nose, eye mouth measurements and ratios are always unchanged," she said. Can you imagine someone's eyes being changed in the width of each? she said and we started laughing.

"Hmm, ok let's look back at the 10 you found at 95% recognition to see if we get a hit on one of them focused on the ear instead." I'll leave you with this as it's now 10 pm Euro time and I want to call The Hague. I left her to find a match while I messaged Keith on an encrypted link hoping he was available. My message said only one thing 10? (10 minutes) In the meantime, I went over to our board and added the war photos adding a red circle around William Standford Smitha and began a name search to see what I could find.

My phone rang, it was Keith and he began by telling me what he had found. "Our Spook (our name for the tail) came up blank which can only mean one thing, he's a contractor a "Clean skin." But no worries I'll find him." "So, who's he working for is it 5 or 6 or who else could it be," I asked. "I don't know yet. What did you find?" he asked in his sing-song Welsh accent. I told him what I found out at the War Museum and said I'd send him the relevant pics knowing he would know what to do.

I told him I had found the name of the close friend seen with him in the photos at that time and that maybe there was a lead there. "See if you have anything on the name William Standford Smith. We kept the conversation short and I had Jeannie send him the photos using her encrypted peer-to-peer software. I had placed a red circle around William Standford Smith's name and image. He would look into it from his end as I would too."

Chapter 15

Old Records New Names

I went back to searching for the names on the photos but found nothing there. I looked in the births and deaths register now. The original Registrar of all births, marriages and deaths were set up in Somerset House, where they had been for over 130 years. Somerset House held all birth, marriage and death certificates in England and Wales until 1970 when the Registry and its associated archives were moved to nearby St Catherine's House at Aldwych. They were then moved to Batley, part of Kirklees, in West Yorkshire, south-west of Leeds. Batley in the north of England was too far so a visit would not now have been worthwhile.

I looked online, though I preferred to go there and seek the help of those archivists who knew how to find the names, but the current location at Batley was too far and I could seek help directly, faster and probably more accurately. The other reason for a phone call was that despite all our encryptions, it was always possible for someone to set a red flag for a particular name leading them to us.

I called the number and told the girl on the other end I was looking for relatives and asked if she could help. I gave her the name thinking I could start there. There was also one other name of a person who was with our Richard and William, his name was Nigel Hargreaves. I told her I wasn't sure which of these names was my ancestor, but I knew the regiment and she was fine with that. She asked for my number and email so she could get back to me.

I gave her our side email which would not lead directly to our office. With that, I asked her to search the names of Nigel Hargreaves and William Standford Smith to see if either of them had relatives I could follow up with. She told me it would take a few days as they were inundated with searches. "Can you see if anyone else has searched for these names, so I could reach out to tell them we may be related?" I asked her. "Yes, there is a link next to some names but not all searches are possible. You could try a DNA search with Ancestry or 23 and Me," She offered helpfully. I thanked her but I knew that wouldn't be linked to me as a relative. After all the DNA searches that Olivia used showed nothing. Our man, Richard, was a ghost!

"Pow wow" I called over to Jeannie, which meant we would stop what we were doing and go over what we had so far. I found that sometimes we have to take a step back to redirect or to check our progress making sure we were on point. In this case, we were not being paid, so we had to ensure we stayed on target.

"So, what have we got so far? We have 2 names linked with Richard Whitehead in the military who were on active duty in Burma, he is marked as KIA, but is he? So that is one search we can do to see if any relatives may know more, where was he buried did he have a military honours burial? I have someone in the births and deaths registry office looking at 2 of the three names. I kept Richard's name out of that search for the moment." I told her.

Jeannie was still looking at a match from the database and had now found 2 names that were very close to our man. "I'm sure we are missing something, why is this so difficult?" I said, "One murder, a suspicious death of an expert, silver medalist skier, a tail who followed us at The Hague and a series of blind alleys leading us nowhere. What are we missing?"

"OK, what did you get from the names of those travelling with Martin Ade?" I asked Jeannie. "There were four of them, two women and two men including Martin." "OK give me what you have I'll do two and you do two," "What are we looking for," she asked. "Anything out of the ordinary, was he feeling sick, was anything unusual and did they think it could have been something else because, after all, he was a damn silver medalist who knew those slopes. Was one of the girls his girlfriend?"

Yes, she said, "Hillary Courtauld Blake, who seems to have travelled with Martin several times," "OK, I'll check into her and Martin you search the other two," I said. "Just get an impression of how close they were at that time, had they been on these slopes before and where was his body taken. Oh and did he have an autopsy?" You cover that and I'll check out Hillary."

"Keith is checking into our spook who he believed was tailing us at The Hague," I added "But you never really know with him, he never reveals all his cards," I added. So we both had assignments to focus on and I started looking into Hillary to see who she was.

It turned out that Hillary was an aristocrat coming from the original Courtauld family who were multi-millionaires from the Courtauld group of companies. Courtauld was a UK-based manufacturer of fabric, clothing, artificial fibres, and chemicals. It went back to its establishment in 1794 becoming the world's leading man-made fibre production company, before being broken up in 1990 into Courtaulds plc. and Courtaulds Textiles Ltd.

Our Hillary was a wealthy heiress. I found that she lived in Gerrards Cross, to the west of London. I had her address and phone number and since it was just 30 minutes away from Boston Manor I would pay her a visit tomorrow morning. I assumed she was not a working girl since her family were worth billions.

I decided to do a cold call on Hillary, the following morning, as I didn't want her making phone calls or text messages to any of her friends before I could ask her about the accident or perhaps warn her to be careful. I drove to Gerrards Cross and her home was a beautiful, gated mansion set back from the road and it was huge. I stopped at the tall steel automated gate and rang the buzzer. I told them I was looking into Martin Ade's accident and needed Hillary's help.

The gate opened and I drove up the graveled drive ending in a large circular area with a fountain in the middle. The landscaping was stunning, with a manicured lawn, shrubs and trees.

Her home was a large, sprawling, beautiful Tudor-style home with a myriad of diamond-shaped leaded windows. I drove around the circular gravelled drive to the front of the mansion I must have been seen as the front door opened and a young, attractive woman was there looking at me. "Are you with the police?" she asked waving me into a large kitchen.

"No," I said, "I'm a private investigator looking into Martin Ade's death at Val d'Isere and I gave her my card." "And why is that?" she asked somewhat caustically. "May I call you Hillary?" I asked her.

"Well that's my name, what else would you call me?" she said looking at me coolly. "I would like to know some details of your vacation with Martin especially since he had that fatal accident. Can I ask you how many times you both have been to Val d'Isere?" "We went there many times," she answered. "And on those particular slopes?" I asked her.

"That slope was his favourite and now I think about it he must have skied it dozens of times," she answered. I told her that I knew Martin was a silver medalist and had been on those "Off-Piste,' slopes many times in the past while taking part in professional contests."

"How long were you and he friends?" I asked her just as a pot of tea was brought in. She did the honours, "Milk, sugar?" she asked, "Just a little milk is fine," I answered. I noticed she drank hers with no milk or sugar.

"Martin and I go way back more than 15 years. He was a very dear friend and we often spent time together," she told me. "Can I ask why you are looking into this and not the police?" I put my cup down, "Martin's death may not have been an accident, I have reason to believe he was too good a skier to have simply hit a tree and since you were there with him I naturally want to find out if there was something, anything untoward that may have occurred to cause the accident," I told her.

With that, she looked deep in thought before responding. "I'm not sure what you are looking for but yes I was there with another girl further up the slope and yes, he was a damn good downhill skier, probably the best in the world despite only winning a silver at the Olympics," she said. I thought, "He only won silver?" I thought!

"Did he tell you what his job was?" I asked. "No but I knew he was in some government department or other and he travelled a lot," she said. Adding, "You understand I have to be careful who I hang around with."

"I understand that of course, but we are both on the same side here," I said. "When I heard about Martin's accident as part of another case I am working on, I started to look into it. I believe there may be more to this incident than just a skiing accident and I need to find out if this is true, then what is it," I said, hoping she would open up a little to tell me more.

"There were four of you travelling together, did you know the other couple?" I asked. "No, we never met them before. I thought they were friends of Martin's but he told me they only met at the airport and as they were carrying skiing equipment we found out they were going to the same place we were headed. I was recording my conversation with Hillary so I wouldn't miss any details."

"What were the other two like?" I asked, "And do you, by any chance, have a photo of them?" She got up and retrieved a phone from a desk drawer as she was answering my question.

"As a matter of fact I have a photo of the four of us, but they made it clear they didn't like being photographed," she said looking through her phone for the photos. "Here this is one and these are them," she said pointing them out. "Did you see the accident?" I asked her. "I did better than that, I was videoing his descent as he was so cool to watch," she said looking at her phone.

"May I see it?" I asked her as she gave me her phone. I had a small camera on my lapel and was holding the camera to show the video feed to Jeannie as I knew she would be watching. I watched it in morbid interest to see Martin zipping down the slope, in a giant slalom with ease.

He really was a fantastic skier, but just as he was about to slalom away from the trees something made him lose his track.

I rewound and watched it again and asked her if she had seen the video. "No, I was too distraught," she said, "And actually I have never seen the video as it is too awful to watch the death of a good friend as it happened"

"I totally understand but I think you need to see this," I handed over the phone to watch her reaction. It was clear how she felt as she jumped, holding her free hand to her mouth as she saw him hit the tree at what must have been faster than 80 mph just as he reached the fastest part of the slope.

She watched it again in horror, as she saw what I saw, that something had spooked Martin causing him to lose control and hit the tree. She gasped and started shaking with tears in her eyes. "I'm sorry to hit you with this but now you can see why I'm looking into this. Where were your companions when this happened?"

"Umm, she was with me higher up the slope but I don't know where he was. Thinking back now he had gone down before Martin, but although he was a good skier, he was nowhere near as good as Martin was. Oh My God! she exclaimed, with tears forming in her eyes, I knew this was a strange thing to have happened but never thought to watch that horrid video. I never thought past the fact that four of us went there and only three of us came back," she said clearly distraught.

Hillary was in shock at what had happened and although she was nodding I could see that it wasn't sinking in yet. "Let me get you a glass of water," I said and went over to the sink. "Water is in the fridge," she said which by the way was huge almost a walk-in fridge.

I came back and handed a bottle of Perrier to her. She was shaking as she went through the details in her mind and processed what she had just seen apparently for the first time on her phone.

I watched the video again noticing another couple on the opposite side of the slope filming Martin's descent. "Did you know those two on the other side of the slope, who was, what seemed to be, filming Martin's descent?" I asked her. "No not those two, but the couple who joined us at the airport and at the bar for a few nights was Niel and she was Bridgett. They told us they were from Dorset." "Did they say where they were staying," I asked.

"Let's see," she was thinking, "We were staying at the Hotel Val d'Isere where we always stay and they were at umm, oh yes, Le Refuge de Solaise Hotel, we met them there for drinks one night."

"Thanks," I said and asked her, "What were they like?" "They were very pleasant and he was constantly on his phone almost the entire time," she added. "Did you swap phone numbers?" I asked, "Yes with both of them and she gave me the two numbers."

"Did they call you after you returned?" Yes just once, a couple of weeks after we got back, Bridgett asked me if the local police were looking into Martin's death. But I had no idea then what I know now and told her it was deemed "Death by misadventure, which it was," she added. She said she was so sorry and to keep in touch.

"Were they both together when the accident occurred?" "No, he was down the slope and now I come to think of it she was with me up the slope, talking as we were watching his descent." She was thinking back, "Yes he was down the slope somewhere, I thought he was just waiting for Martin."

"Did Martin and Neil talk together before that particular run?" I asked. She thought for a moment. "Yes, as a matter of fact, they were discussing the fastest lines down and now you ask, Neil was saying it would be fun to try out a new run down the slope. He was pointing to the right showing a run very close to the tree line they could try rather than the standard line in the middle of the run. Neil said he would try it first. He was good, but not close to Martin's skill," she was in deep thought about the time just before that last run. "Did Martin often ski so close to the tree line?" I asked.

She thought for a minute and said, "Actually no, never, it was too dangerous, but then again he was always game to try something new. That was what I loved about him, his sense of adventure. He was such fun to be around and very fit he could ski for hours and still not be tired." She said.

"What was their reaction to his sudden demise?" "Umm, she seemed devastated, but he was, how do I put it, he showed concern but not like Bridgett. But I just thought since they had only met us before the holiday it seemed a normal reaction."

"Can I borrow your phone to download the video and copy your photos of the holiday?" "Of course," she said, "Take it, I only use this one for holiday stuff, please take it and let me have it back when you're done." "Is Bridgett's number in here?" I asked. "Yes it is just under Bridgett, she never gave me a second name neither did Neil. They gave me their numbers while we were on the slope and I only put in their first names," she said.

"It's ok we'll do some checking on our end, I'm sure we can find them," I told her to make her feel better but part of me doubted this would lead somewhere. "I hope you understand that this is potentially a dangerous situation with a lot more that I can't tell you about just yet and I must ask you not to tell a soul about this, not anyone not even your closest friend" I paused to let this sink in. "And you must do what I ask as your own life may now be in danger if you don't. You must never ever mention your phone or the fact that you were filming Martin's descent."

"Did Bridgett see you filming?" I asked her. "No, she was in front of me watching Martin's run. I was standing back from her a little further up the slope." "Good," I said.

I took the phone knowing Jeannie would be able to do far more than just watch the video. We were getting somewhere at last and at least I had connected the dots with Martin's so-called accident.

This meant these deaths were probably connected. I learned a long time ago not to come up with a scenario and then try to make it so and right now I have to remain as objective as I could. But the dots were connecting however I saw these events.

I was right about Martin Ade's death. I asked her who she may have told about what happened. She said she told her mother and referred to it as an accident, even with her best friend only. I warned Hillary once again, on my way out telling her not to talk about this to anyone or write anything down anywhere and if she told

anyone about it I asked her what she said. She said it was a terrible accident on one of the black slopes and that the coroner had called it death by misadventure and that was all.

She had my number and she thanked me for filling her in as I left. Her cool demeanour towards me when we met was now very different. I told her that if she needed to contact me just text the number I gave her using an App I placed on her "Other" phone and told her to only call me using that App.

She was obviously very close to Martin and did not seem like someone who would call all her friends to tell them about the events of her short vacation in Val d'Isere but I thought even if she did, what could she say? I said I would return her phone and then left for home.

On my way back from Gerrards Cross I was thinking how cold and calculating Neil and Bridgett were. Knowingly befriending two complete strangers knowing they were looking for a way to kill one of them.

They were obviously a professional hit team and had planned their hit on Martin very carefully making it look like an accident. I called Jeannie to fill her in, while driving back, telling her I would bring the phone in tomorrow so she could look at the video. The App was one that Jeannie had created and was safe with no number, times or possible data collection from it. Well, in reality, anything we put onto any phone could in fact be hacked but this was as secure as it could possibly be.

I hoped for Hillary's sake she had told me the truth and if I am a good judge of character (which I am brilliant at) I believed her. But, if she did say more it may cost her dearly maybe even her life as whoever these people were they were closing all the loops. These people had seemingly vast resources to strike wherever they wanted.

There was a lot to go through now and I needed to prioritise what to focus on first, as there was only Jeannie and I involved. I gave her Hillary's phone as I got to the office and she immediately downloaded all the data on it. We were watching the feed on our big screen with the attack or whatever we could call it.

Jeannie let it run through a couple of times then ran it in slow motion. "Freeze it right there," I said and right there we could see what looked like a ski pole shoot out from behind a tree tripping Martin. It happened so fast it was almost imperceptible, but we were looking for something immediately before he struck the tree and this was it.

It was a perfect hit at the fastest part of the slope right by the tree line. So our man Neil, if that's his real name, convinced Martin to run close to the tree line knowing that would be the perfect spot to hit. These two were a piece of work but no matter what, we would find them'

Chapter 16

Connecting The Dots

Jeannie had uploaded all the phone data and was looking through the photos of their vacation. In one short video of the beautiful Alpine mountains, shot from what looked like an open-air bar or restaurant there was a group of skiers talking and laughing. "Hold it there," I said looking at a couple who were sitting a few tables away from Martin's group.

In the shot was a couple, sitting and drinking together. He was wearing very distinctive bright red and white ski gear and his companion wearing bright blue and red gear. "I'm certain those were the two who were filming Martin's descent on the opposite side of the slope. Go back to the incident and we can see if it's them," I told Jeannie.

"If it is them and we can track them down they have something showing who it was standing, hidden from view in the tree line where Martin went down. A long shot I know but worth following up."

I messaged Keith to call me when he could and went back to research the army names I now had from Richard Whitehead's Green Beret unit. It was later in the day when he called me back and I filled him in on what I had found. "Damn!" He said in his strong Welsh accent, "You may be right and if you are we can place more resources onto this from here."

"No," I said, we don't want that until you find the leak at your end. "Do you have anything yet?" "No," he said "But I'm on the right track and should have something very soon. Things like this have a special protocol we follow and we are quite successful at it," he said confidently.

"Ok, let's just compare notes, we now have two deaths neither of which are natural and not accidental as we were initially led to believe. Both were made to look like normal events and were well planned, these people are pros" I added.

"We have the army records showing a tight military unit related to the origin of someone named Richard Whitehead; we also have a video which, by the way, I'll share with you in person as soon as I have one more piece to add which, I hope will show us who this assassin was."

"Ok," Keith said, "I'm following up on something else here around Martin's last case and maybe we'll have an answer from what he was working on. I'm chasing down our spook also, but nothing showing yet."

We left it at that for the time being and I went over to see what Jeannie had come up with on her search through Hillary's phone. "One thing I can tell you about our Martin Ade," she said as I walked over to her desk, "He was a superb skier and there's more footage here of previous runs including his Olympic Silver and a couple of videos of who was there at Val d'Isere the same time as our two." "Are the two at the open restaurant the same as the two filming his run?" I asked her. "Yep they are and I'm trying to find their names."

Try the airport CCTV cameras a few days around their vacation, to see if you can check what airline they flew in with or maybe from where they came from. Hell, they may even be wearing the same gear as many others do to show they are "Cool skiers," I said. I shouldn't have bothered. "Already on it," she said.

I went back to the military records on my search into Richard Whitehead and his small company. I found a website for Killed in Action, KIA, servicemen from various campaigns and entered his name I got a result showing the date and location of his death which was in Burma but no details were shown. But the record said MIA, assumed KIA. I photographed the record and then did a search for William Stanford Smith.

His name didn't appear in the KIA records. Other KIA's were shown in detail, showing when, where and the company that person was in at the time of death. But this detail was missing from Richard Whitehead's entry. Bloody hell, this was so frustrating! I was going around in damn circles and every lead ended in a dead end. Was Richard Whitehead actually KIA as it showed on the old photo, or was he missing in action? I needed to find out. I next checked the registry of births and deaths online and searched for his name.

His birth certificate was there along with an address in Kings Lynn along with his date of birth, April 8th, 1922, making him around 20 when he was deployed to Burma. Under his friend, William Standford Smith though, there was an honour with a discharge date some 10 years later. Apparently, according to the records he was assigned to a special operations unit but nothing more than that. So at least I had something we could follow up on.

Meanwhile, Jeannie was busy doing what she does best, looking for the two other skiers, Neil and Bridgett, though we both knew those were not their real names, as well as the two in their colourful gear on the other side of the slope. I asked her to check out any calls from Bridgett or Neil coming in around two to three weeks after the incident on the slope on Hillary's phone. "We have their numbers and there was a call from Bridgett three weeks after they returned as Hillary said. Jeannie pinged the number but it had been disconnected, of course."

She checked the cell towers to triangulate the call and find where the call came from and found it came from a location in Central London on the Embankment. Bloody perfect! I thought, of course, it did! But Jeannie smiled, as she was working the keyboard fast as lighting, and said, with a pen in her mouth, "They just made their first mistake!" "Ah yes, of course, the Embankment full of CCTV cameras," I said.

We had the date and the precise time of that call and with that, I knew she could home in on who made the call. Of course, there were many people using mobile phones at the same time but we had a photo of whoever our Brigitt was and that would help locate her. It didn't take her too long to find some Bridgett possibilities.

She checked the actual call time down to the second, to see which women were making calls on the embankment at that very moment and which women were a possible match. There were 12 of them in total. "Seems women like to make calls when strolling along the Embankment," she said laughingly.

After checking the precise time of that call, only one of the women remained as the only Bridgitt possibility who finished the call at exactly the time Hillary's call ended. "Gotcha," she said out loud," as she began the process of loading the woman's face and clothing onto the CCTV feed to follow her automatically. We saw, on the CCTV feed, that she made another call after her call to Hillary "They just made their first mistake!"

"Ah yes! The Embankment call Bridgett made had now terminated, so we traced where that second call went. But it didn't go to the number we had for Niel's phone, instead, it went to a phone located in Horsham in Surrey."

This was either Neil, whoever he really was, or it was someone else who she had contact with hopefully to report the news that an accidental death verdict had been determined by the coroner.

The timing, immediately after her call with Hillary was, we hoped, another link in the chain. We watched as she tossed her phone into some bushes, another mistake and maybe one luckily for us that would tell us more of Bridgett's story.

I was already on my way out the door to find that phone when Jeannie was following up, using her magic, to locate who was on the other side of her call. I was heading to do some hedgehog impressions, rummaging under that bush to see if I could retrieve that phone. A long shot I know but since it had only been ten days since that call was made maybe I would get lucky.

I would have to ensure that whatever leads Keith was working on, nothing could lead to Hillary. I knew he was the ultimate pro and decided to wait till he called me to make damn sure there was nothing connecting our new findings with the official coroner's report. He had to find out if there was a leak and if where was who it was that led to Martin's murder on that fateful slope. I hoped the second call Bridgett made would connect the dots between Brigitte and whoever the hell Neil really was. I hoped to find that phone and if I did we could get fingerprints and maybe even DNA from it if it hadn't been washed off by our wonderful London weather.

Anyway, I got close to where the call was made from and called Jeannie. "Am I close?" I asked her, she was watching me on a live CCTV feed. "No walk a little forward to where that streetlamp is, where the hedgerow and trees are on your left," she said. So I walked forward and began a search for the phone. I was just south of Tower Bridge and it was like looking for a fucking needle in a haystack full of needles, but it was worth the try.

I made several passes and started very carefully rummaging in the leaves and debris under the hedgerow. On my third pass and nearly an hour later I found it! At last a break, I thought and held the phone up to the camera for Jeannie to see as I knew she was still watching the live feed, so I held up the phone using tissue from my pocket as I didn't want to disturb any prints or DNA on it and headed back to the office.

On my way back I was thinking how the hell do I search the DNA database and the AFIS fingerprint database without creating a red flag to whoever was involved? I was worried that since Martin Ade had made a connection to Richard Whitehead, in his notes, it had cost him his life so we had to be extremely careful not to end up the same way and we had to include Hillary in our group. She had already lost her close friend and I didn't want her to join him on that big ski slope in the sky.

We needed help and I thought back to my former colleague Noz Roberts, at Acton Nick, who was always using the AFID database so maybe he would know how to do it incognito. His real name was originally Norwell Gumbs but his name was changed to Norwell Roberts or to his colleagues he had the nickname "Nozzer the Cozzer, the High Flying Rozzer." But we always called him Noz. Noz was a big black man, six foot three built, as we say in London, 'like a "Brick shit house door," but probably more like a linebacker to my American friends.

He had a great sense of humour which he needed to do his job and never let us forget it. He was also London's first black cop which led to an incredible spate of prejudice against him. But that's for another day as they say.

I called Noz at home, on his landline, not wanting to leave any official pathways leading back to what we were doing, or what names we may reveal in any search. I asked if we could meet up at one of our former local haunts but I needed to talk with him. He mentioned a bar in North Ealing called The Village Wine Bar which we all used to go to when we were off duty. I knew it from my police days in Acton and I agreed to meet him there around 7 pm. We had spent many great times there and the owners were discreet, it was an excellent location for a quiet meeting.

The weather was warm so we sat at a table outside at one of the tables set up on the wide pavement to talk. I had a beer and Noz had a glass of wine. "So, wassup mate, long time no see. How's your new life as a high-flying private eye going?" he asked. "Going great and that's why I wanted to meet up with you to go through something sensitive," I answered.

"OK, fire away, I'm all ears," he said and he waited for me to go on. I needed his help and I knew I could trust Noz as he and I had been involved in some sensitive stuff when we worked together. One case was the robbery of a few million quid in silver bullion from Heathrow Airport. The suspects apparently got away in an ambulance, which we thought was loaded with the stolen silver bullion.

I told him my problem with searching both AFID and the facial recognition databases without raising any red flags with the names. "So Martin Ade is brown bread (dead)?" He said. "He was a damn good cop, back in the day and I see now why the secrecy," he said thinking. "So all he did was to make a note with the name and that was enough to top him?"

I told him how we got the information through the WWII records from the Imperial War Museum. "Good work," he said. "How on earth did you connect those dots?" He said. "Because I'm that brilliant!" I told him.

"Yeah right!" He answered laughing. I told him of the facial recognition Jeannie was doing and how the only reference we had was a military record in World War Two so I followed it up. I told him I needed to use the AFIS and facial recognition databases but not leave a trace.

"Well, the truth is whenever you go onto either of those databases, facial recognition or the AFIS database, an automatic tracker is placed but this has more to do with opening up your search in case anyone else, in the Met or elsewhere on the job, or in an official capacity, can feedback on your search." "But, and this is a big but, I get that you need secrecy in this. I know someone in the central records who owes me a favour," he offered. "Central records, what is that?" I asked him.

He explained that it was in central records where these databases were managed and if anyone can find a way to keep your search off the tracking system, my friend there can, as she actually manages their operation and had a hand at building the database. Anyway, I want to help you and Martin's memory as well. He was a mate and a damn good cop and whatever help you need, if I can, I'll help and mum's the word.

I thought for a moment, I know I shouldn't ask you this but," He interrupted me, "Then don't!" he said smiling, "And before you ask, yes she is 100% legit and as we say in the biz, she would take it to her grave," "Hmm," I said, thinking that Martin had done just that and had taken whatever it was to his untimely grave.

We agreed that Noz would give me her details after he had cleared it with her, so he was not directly involved with this in any way. That worked for me and he told me her name was Isabelle Rodriguez and he told me to wait a few days to give him the chance to explain the situation.

I told him everything we do from my office goes through several stages of encryption and that we used both a VPM and the dark web to do our research. "Who the fuck set that little gem up for you then?" he asked and I told him about Jeannie. He was not surprised and had followed some of the cases we had unravelled.

"So it's her not you that is the brains of the operation," he said, jokingly. I laughed and agreed with him adding I'm just the runaround boy. I bought Noz another large glass of the bar's house red which was pretty good and I had a Belgian beer which was their specialty as we sat outside talking.

Noz was a stand-up guy and a good friend who, earlier in his career had been a poster boy for the Met who was trying to recruit more of an ethnic mix of new recruits reflecting the current mix of Londoners, from India and the Caribbean and he had often been seen on posters around town. He was even on the London underground in his uniform doing this or that. One advert showed him directing traffic, I had to smile at that.

It was a warm and beautiful early summer evening when the owner of the bar came out to join us and greeted us both. Her name was Jane, a petite redhead who had been in the film business before opening the wine bar. I bought her a glass of wine and as the special on the menu that day was her famous chilli, we decided to eat there as the business part of our meeting was concluded.

A few of my old friends arrived around 9 pm, I looked over at Noz "You set this up didn't you?" "Me? Nah would I do that?" It was just like old times me and my friends at The Village Wine Bar. We didn't discuss our business again and instead enjoyed the bar, the company and the food. John Done, Pete Miles, Robin Perry and Bob Lewis were all still working in Ealing and Acton nick and I knew then it would be a session, so no more business was possible at all.

We went inside after a couple of local patrol cars came by flipping on their lights to say hi. God, how I missed those days working at the local Nick. Things seemed so straightforward back then, but it also became time for me to move on.

Anyway, we stayed till closing time and then Jane offered us to stay after so we did what we often used to do when I worked the beat there. We had a whip round and each put a score (twenty quid) in a hat, used for just that purpose to spend after hours. Jane closed the bar and since it had a tinted window onto the street it was difficult to see inside.

The Village was one of our favourite haunts though, to be honest, there were a considerable number of other places we also went to. I started thinking about them all back when I was on the beat.

Ealing had a lot of great pubs; The North Star, The Haven Arms, The Queen Vic (Victoria) The Red Lion, The Three Pigeons, The Bell, The Feathers and these were by no means all of them. I smiled to myself thinking of the great times we had when we all worked on the Job together. They lived in a section house, converted into apartments where they were all living at the time!

There was the story Robin told us when his girlfriend who was staying at his flat in Hanwell Broadway was having a blazing argument with him. She was standing in front of the window, as Robin's gaze focused behind her on the back of the shops opposite. He wasn't listening to her but was now watching a man climbing up the drainpipe opposite, shining his way, 2nd floor up to get to an open window a few yards away. Anyway, Robin's girlfriend became furious as he wasn't listening to her rant.

As he ran past a very surprised and angry girlfriend heading out the door, he shouted, "Call the police, there's a robbery taking place!" He ran down the stairs and crossed the road. He climbed up the drainpipe to catch the villain. He managed to grab his ankle, with one hand, while hanging on to the drainpipe with the other. He turned to look back at his still angry girlfriend standing at the window watching him. He shouted across to her, "Call the cops, I need backup!" to which she placed her hands on her hips, before drawing the curtains on him.

He got the villain and had to hold him down while calling for backup. We were all cracking up. Later, feeling no pain, we parted company around 1 am.

Me? I was legless as we say, pissed as a parrot, drunk as a skunk and made my way home in a minicab. It was often like that back in those days. All working the beat in Ealing and Acton then heading off to one of the many local bars.

The strange thing was that several of the villains we had put away were often drinking at the same places we were at, but the local pub was off limits and we all needed somewhere safe to drink at. Although I missed the old days, I loved what I now did and was well paid for my work. I also like not having the constraints of having to report to my seniors and having to write up the numerous reports that took up so much of my time.

But meeting my old beat friends was a great reality check, I was listening to their stories of cases they were currently working on and it was a reminder to me as to why I left the job.

They were telling me of changes that were now making their way into the Met. More report writing, and training on treating all people with kid gloves, more for political correctness than for results. My friends and I considered everyone we were tracking for crimes the same and we always had. We certainly didn't need bloody training to tell us that!

Chapter 17

Phones and Maps

I was hung over the following morning, thanks guys, same old same old, as I made my way to the office. Fuck these noisy tube trains I thought as I made my way to the office. I grabbed a black coffee on the way, from a stall at the station entrance, when Keith called me to tell me he was on the trail of the leak and that they were moving upstream to find who was her controller. "Good," I said, "Anything else?" He said no, so I started to fill him in on what Jeannie and I were checking the phone our accomplice tossed into a hedge on the Embankment.

"Wow that was a piece of luck, how did you find that out," he said. So I told him of the phone call Bridgett made to Hillary a few weeks after she returned and how we found her making the call on the CCTV feed at the exact time the call was received on Hillary's phone. "Do you have a photo of this woman?" he asked. I told him no not yet but I would get it to him on our secure link when we find her.

I was on the tube to my office at Leicester Square so we finished our conversation and I started thinking, going over all we had got so far. My head was exploding with the noise of the tube. Call it intuition or gut feeling, I call it stunning brilliance, but I've always been one to understate my abilities, but that's just me.

Anyway, whatever, something didn't add up with this. It was very unusual to get nowhere on what should have been a straightforward murder investigation. What was I missing here how did a hit team know where Martin was who hired them and why? How did that spook know Keith and I were meeting at that bar in the Hague? Jeannie and I needed a Pow wow as soon as I got back to my office. When I got there Jeannie was, as usual, there already.

"Pow wow!" I said as soon as I went in and we both sat in front of our war board. "So? What's been happening on your end?" she said, "And by the way, you look like shit this morning! Have a good night with the boys in blue did we?" she said smiling as she went over to the coffee. "Please pour me a cup of black coffee while you're over there," I asked her.

I filled her in with my meeting last night with Noz and told her of my thought process and it was beginning to look like the leak in Richard's office at the ICC was always one step ahead. I told Jeannie not to do any more name or fingerprint searches on the phone or on AFIS or anything yet until Noz messaged me with Isabelle Rodriguez's contact details.

"If whoever it is we are up against, can set up a hit in France, just based on a handwritten note, drop someone else in the middle of London's rush hour, then send a spook to clock (watch) us in a bar at the Hague, their resources are vast. They are also able to tap into what is going on in Keith's office, and that is supposed to be highly secure" I said. "You still do regular sweeps here don't you?" I asked Jeannie and she gave me that look that says what the fuck! "Of course I do!" She answered.

She thought for a while, as we both did, then asked me if I told Keith about my conversation with Noz. "Actually no I didn't because I was getting on the tube and it's always so noisy." I answered, "Then maybe don't until he finds the leak because one thing is for certain, all these spooks, hit squads and poisoners are not coming from this office!" she said. "This stuff was in play before we got involved and to be honest, if you weren't there on the same platform when our man was knocked off, then we wouldn't be stuck in the middle of this, whatever this is," she said stating the obvious.

It was then that I realised I had not been contacted by Keith's old lady friend who he thought might be able to help us. But perhaps this was a good thing because these people would not stop at just two murders. We had to find the link, whatever it was that Martin working on.

We needed eyes on Martin's file to make our own assessment, not that Keith's office can't do the same, but since we agreed to keep

Martin's murder secret, MI6 were only aware that he died as the result of an accident. I wanted to keep it that way for the time being.

I have to look at that file and maybe a different view might reveal something that we're all missing. I sent a message to Keith to get us the original file I didn't need to say more. We had a PO box set up under a different name and he knew this.

"What have you got from Hillary's phone, was there anything else there?" I asked her. "Yes, I looked at the locations where Neil and Brigett made calls from. It's interesting because their phones were in use right up until Brigitt made her last call to Hillary." With that, she put a map on our big screen showing where calls had been connected.

The map showed the locations where both phones made calls from and to and the phones were live 3 days before they all arrived in France. They had been opened in Basel in Switzerland, then located in London, in Russel Square, the day before their flights to France. Jeannie would follow up looking for CCTV camera footage to see if they were visible there. I made a timeline showing Neil and Bridgett's movements before and after they arrived and left France.

Very few calls had been made using their, what we assumed were burner phones, but the calls were enough to provide more information and where the locations were. A call was made from Neil's phone to a number in Switzerland from Heathrow Airport, at 11.02 am probably to tell whoever, they had established contact with. That call went to a location in Basel, Switzerland. That location rang a bell with me but I couldn't place it yet.

We could check these locations out from the CCTV footage at the airport, which was a breeze for Jeannie, so we could cross reference these two with the locations. It was a short call but we now had a connection hopefully to whoever was on the other end of that call in Switzerland.

We now had another link in our chain of information, gradually connecting those dots, but where this would lead we had no idea yet. We were slowly building up our war board. The two-person hit team that took Martin Ade out were good but not even close to our devious abilities and what was even better was that neither they, the folks nor the folks at The Hague knew we were on to this group whoever they turned out to be. We had the advantage for sure and I intended to play that advantage until I was damn well good and ready to reveal all we knew.

Jeannie showed one more call made from Neil's phone to a location in The Hague and what was interesting was that the call was the same afternoon as my meeting with Keith. So Neil somehow knew of our meeting which was why he was there, in the bar, when we met.

The number he called was still in service and this would provide a new link to who the spook was that had arrived at the bar where Keith and I met. He probably had another communication method, maybe via a program with peer-to-peer encryption, but his mistake was in using his burner phone which we had now which we used to track his calls.

Two days later I had a package at my PO box number with the name associated which was under the name Anthony Smock which was my alternative ID. I went to retrieve it and didn't open it until I was back at my office. It was what I hoped it would be, it was Martin Ade's original file. I called Jeannie over so it would save time for us both. We put on some rubber gloves since we weren't sure who may have touched it.

Keith had told me about Martin's tradecraft which was top notch so he knew all the tricks. There were a lot of handwritten notes, with numbers and strange wording which we thought were perhaps codes.

There were a couple of typed sheets also but these seemed to be completing what was required to cover himself with a bona fide open project file the name of which was a delineated series of numbers. On a couple of the hand-written notes was the reference to Richard Whitehead but he had not put more than just the name. We looked through the file searching for, we didn't know what yet, then we placed the notes on our large ops desk.

Jeannie went over to her desk and brought back her hand-held black light which she used to go over the file and the documents, checking for any invisible messages Martin may have left. Old school I know but sometimes old school sometimes works the s best.

There was one message handwritten in invisible ink comprising two sets of 10 numbers which looked like a map reference. We entered the map coordinates to see that it was the Bank of International Settlements, or, BIS Tower, located in Basel, Switzerland.

Voila! We made a connection to the phone call made from Neil's phone to the location in Basel Switzerland and now we had reached what Martin had seen. But Martin unfortunately got no further.

Well, I would for damn sure move forward from his notes. I have to point out here that Keith was also extremely good with tradecraft having the vast resources of the ICC and he possessed an uncanny ability to connect the dots as we are doing now. But he couldn't follow up on Martin's file because it may lead him to the same demise as happened to Martin and since we were working in secret we were the ones to proceed.

We dusted the entire file and contents to see who had touched it and now we were ready to use Noz Robert's contact for a leakproof AFIS search. I sent Noz a message, "Isabelle?" and that was all my message said. I knew he was on the ball and would send me the number for Isabelle Rodriguez. We were busy with the file and had photographed several fingerprints on the documents.

Nothing more to do with the fingerprints yet so we moved back to the mobile phone I retrieved from the Embankment. I was busy looking at the map showing where each call was made and was looking at the Basel location. The location was where the world banking empire was centred at the BIS Tower in Basel. What had that to do with Richard Whitehead I wondered. There was not much else in Martin's file and I thought perhaps he had another location where he was keeping his more detailed information.

I had to go back to The Hague to check Martin's apartment to see what I may find there. Since it had only been a couple of weeks since his death I hoped his apartment was still untouched. I messaged Keith with a SYS (see you soon) encrypted message. This time I would take the Eurostar to Paris and fly to Amsterdam then go by rail from there.

I would use my "Nom de plume" for my travels this time and my other travelling name was Anthony Smock, for which I had a passport and all travel docs I would need to travel incognito through to The Hague. I used these whenever I needed to travel incognito and this name was, for me, a clean skin.

My intent was to go to Martin's apartment to search if he had more information than was in his sparse file, which didn't seem to contain enough to get topped for, so I assumed there must have been more unless this file had been sanitised.

We now had a couple pieces of the puzzle, a map reference in Basel, Switzerland and a phone call made to Basel by the assassin Neil just before they flew to Geneva on their way to Val d'Isere. So Neil was getting his orders from someone in Basel and the map coordinates in Martin's sparse file were an exact location for the BIS Tower in Basel. We were still missing a piece of the puzzle, what happened in Burma between Richard Whitehead and his close friend, Wild Bill that may have started all this.

The woman who could probably help was the contact Keith told me about but he had not given me the name or contact details yet. Well, we still had the army records to follow up on.

I headed back to the office to see what Jeannie may have found and to tell her I was heading back to The Hague to go through Martin's apartment before it closed down if it hadn't been already, as he was no longer living there. But I had to go soon, possibly the next day.

Jeannie was, as usual, in before me and had updated our war board and a map showing Basel with a red threaded line from London where Neil had made the call. Jeannie was still pouring over the phone records for the number in Basel and had found some interesting data.

"Seems whoever was at the other end of that number was busy making calls to another location in The Hague and a location in England all within 2 days of Neil's call," she told me as I entered the office.

"Ok you see what you can find but I'm heading back to see what I can find in Martin's apartment if it is still not touched. I don't want to say anything yet to anyone there until we know who the leaker is."

I made my travel arrangements for the following day, then my phone rang and it was Noz Roberts telling me all was clear to let Isabelle know when we were about to search the AFIS database for the fingerprints and the DNA file that Olivia could check for any DNA found on Bridgett's phone. Jeannie could handle the AFIS search while I took Brigitt's phone to Olivia to swab for any DNA. It was a long shot but worth the walk to the morgue.

I called Olivia on the way to tell her I was headed over to see her if she had time for a quick visit. She told me she was about to call me to let me know she had some information for me. She said nothing more but would tell me in person when I got there.

I tapped on her door and showed my face in the glass panel on the door. She opened it and then locked it after I entered. It made me a little sad because I realised she was now very nervous after my warning to be careful. I liked Olivia a lot and didn't want her involved more than necessary.

She told me she had done a search on the two poisons she found from her contact at the lab in Leatherhead, Surrey. Immediately all alarms started ringing for me thinking someone may have been looking for that red flag with the poisons. She could see the alarm on my face and said, "Max, don't worry I went there myself to meet my old friend, the lab tech, who I've been working with for years."

He has a trade publication he offered to show me there, which is a regularly updated document and is only sent to crime labs as an insider monthly. It shows information on what the latest technology in the field of pharmaceutical research is being done as it relates to crime labs.

"After you and I met, I went to see my friend at the Leatherhead lab as it was fairly quiet in my office and we found a mention of a research facility in Hastings that worked regularly with both NOAA (National Oceanic and Atmospheric Administration) and also with Woods Hole Laboratory part of NOAA Fisheries in the States. We found some research data on Pufferfish poison that had been done by a research lab in Hawaii of all places. It's a small lab on the coast and I can give you the contact there if you want to follow up."

"Or I can go to Hawaii for you," she said smiling. "We left it at that and yes, before you ask I told him not to follow up on this in any way," she told me. "There is also a small lab in Hastings that is known for marine research maybe we can start there to see what they might have." "Thanks and yes I'll certainly take that info" I said, "But I've got something else for you to check, but I have to give you a contact to call before you go onto the DNA or AFIS databases. Her name is Isabelle Rodriguez and she will clear it for your search to be incognito and it won't show up in case anyone is looking and we have to assume someone is looking," I told her. "It came from a phone I retrieved and is key to the death of your John Doe, Richard Whitehead."

"Is he still on your slab?" I asked. "Yes because we have no official name associated with him and I've done nothing as you told me to hold the body until we had a further update. But time is running out and I have to know soon ok?" She said. "Yes, I know and we are getting close, we have a lead from him which we are following up on as we speak," I told her.

"Ok but only one week more and then I have to release the body for burial, you understand we have laws we have to follow," she said. "Yeah I know and ok if we haven't got more I'll call you or you call me before you have to release the body," I said. "I don't suppose our whizz kid Angel Borowa has called you has she?" I asked. "As a matter of fact she did call me two days ago to ask what the cause of death was," she answered.

"Unbelievable, she left it for a week before following up, so what did you tell her?" I asked. I told her the truth, there were no identifying causes of death and I thought it may be a case of SDS, Sudden Death

Syndrome, which was the truth and I asked her if she wanted a tox screen done. She said she would get back to me on that, "But I'm not holding my breath on that," she said.

Ok, that's telling her the truth and we have a way out if eventually the tox screen data is revealed. "You can say you did it anyway as you don't need police authority to do your job," I said. "By the way, how is that Pufferfish poison delivered," I asked her. "That was the second thing I had to show you," she said as she opened the drawer and slid Richard's body out. Then, turning his arm over, right here on the forearm," I saw a tiny mark almost undetectable.

This was how it was delivered. I missed it the first time around because there was nothing to search for until we got the tox screen back. This must have been administered, while he was on the station platform because its activation is so fast that he would have collapsed in seconds and died within a minute. "I got that from my lab visit to Leatherhead," she said.

"Ok so now that proves his murder, we know the weapon, a syringe and method of use, a jab in the arm," I said "Great work. How much poison was needed," "Glad you asked that, normally if it was the Pufferfish poison only quite a lot but mixed with Curare two things happen. The amount of poison required is reduced significantly and the time to death is less than 2 minutes maybe even less than one minute. He would have felt a numbness starting from the injection site and then rapidly spreading as it went through his body. The poor man had no chance at all, he was dead as soon as the poison hit," she said. We were both silent thinking about the killers that arranged this to happen.

I thought back to the young nurse who was standing next to him when he collapsed, wondering if she might remember seeing someone next to our man, after all, if the poison worked so fast it must have occurred on the station platform and not before. We were getting somewhere I had to go and see the young nurse as soon as possible.

I took Olivia out for lunch and thanked her for her help, reiterating that she must remain careful and not place anything online or in phone calls. After lunch, I headed back to the office. "How would you like a paid trip to hastings?" I asked Jeannie.

"And what do I do when I get there, want me to lounge around on that bunch of stones they call a beach?" she asked, "Tell you what, send me to Hawaii instead, as I told her of Olivia's search at the Leatherhead lab. I've always wanted to go there it's on my bucket list," she said smiling, fluttering her eyelashes at me. I was thinking, honestly if I could have paid for that trip, as a reward for all the help she had given me, but it was not possible right now.

"What do I do there?" she asked. "It's a long shot but if you can go to the research lab there and tell them you are a research scientist, which is half right, you are a scientist. But I want to find out about their research into that poison to find out if anyone outside the technical scientific profession had shown interest in Pufferfish venom. We can't do it over the phone or online and you never know they might have something, anything that can help." I told her

"The thing is, this assassin or assassins can do what they did in a crowded public place, with apparent ease, they can do this to anyone anywhere," I said. She got it and realised we were involved in something potentially far more dangerous to the general public than just one death. "Ok, but we have to let them know beforehand so what's our story?" she asked. "Tell them you're an independent researcher doing a piece on antidotes for deadly poisons and were particularly interested in marine poisons."

"What you are after is anyone else who may have expressed an interest in their Pufferfish poison research, but get on board with them first, blind them with your scientific knowledge and you'll do just fine," I told her. "Ok I'll work something out, no sweat and I need a break, when do you want me to go?" I told her I was going to The Hague tomorrow for a few days to search Martin's apartment before it was too late, "Best if you go while I'm away. Can you leave tomorrow?" I asked. We always forwarded our phones so we didn't need to worry about incoming calls if the office was unmanned. She agreed and said she would enjoy a drive down to Hastings.

Chapter 18

A Key and A Book

I went incognito travelling back to The Hague, using my other name, Anthony Smock. I soon found Martin's apartment but I didn't update Keith as I wanted to remain anonymous. I waited over the road from his apartment complex for a while to see if anyone was watching it. I couldn't see anyone so I took my bag of tricks with me to get to the apartment and swept it for wires and cameras. His entrance was secluded and it looked like the apartment had been left as it was perhaps when he left for Val d'Isere.

I should have done this last week but as things were so slow to reveal themselves yesterday was the first time I thought of it after the file he was working on really didn't show much. I parked a little down the road where other cars were parked and left mine in a line of other cars so as not to stand out.

I went over to the entrance checking for cameras above the door and if there were any hidden along the path as well as the opposite. Jeannie had packed a motion sensor, sensor, I smiled, "Checking the checkers," I thought and I chuckled at her amazing talent. I got in with ease using my kit of lock picks. I opened the door very slowly listening for any sound inside. As soon as the door opened the sentry alarm system started pinging.

No sweat for a master thief like me with training courtesy of Her Majesty's Metropolitan police. I had a number scanner just perfect for this system which only took 10 seconds to scan the myriad of possible combinations which after all was only four numbers. Bloody dark ages I thought as my little gismo showed one of the four green lights. I could have bought one through the dark web but mine was a custom creation courtesy of Jeannie. I remained completely motionless for a few seconds listening for any sounds and got my motion and microphone sensor out again, another creation courtesy of the one and only Jeannie.

I swept each room and found three mics hidden in a light in the living room, under the worktop in the kitchen and another in his table lamp in the bedroom. I knew Martin was better than that and must have left them in place to either send them false leads or make them think he wasn't all that careful. Whatever, they were here and I jammed them while leaving them in place. Boy was I damn good at this stuff and I mentally gave myself a pat on the back.

Ok now the secret squirrel stuff was done I started a grid search looking for anything and everything. I worked my way through the drawers, under the furniture, under the bed and bedding and after an exhaustive search I found a few papers and little else. Ok, what was I missing? I sat in his living room and started a visual sweep noticing there was a vent high on one wall so I carefully placed a chair under it and got up on a chair to take a gander (a look).

I unscrewed the faceplate using my tiny power screwdriver removed the faceplate and lowered it soundlessly onto the chair I was standing on. I then attached the small snake lens with an LED light onto my phone's camera carefully sweeping it around inside the vent. There was nothing inside that I could see. But then, as I was pulling the light out of the shaft, I noticed what looked like a very thin silver thread tucked right into one of the galvanised air shaft's corners on the corner next to where I was looking. It would never have been visible looking in. But my snake camera attachment had revealed it.

I moved my camera snake downwards to see what was on the other end but the thread disappeared downwards, deep in the duct, out of sight. I then pointed it upwards to check if anything was above, but there was nothing. Before I began to ease the thread up and out I the thread up I noticed it was quite light so whatever was on the other end wasn't very big and was not heavy. I continued to carefully lift whatever it was on the end of the thread, out of the shaft. Finally, after around fifteen feet of thread, I pulled out a key. Hmm, a key I thought, so I took a good look at it, turning it over in my hand, I took a photograph of it and climbed down to examine it further. A number of possibilities were going through my mind as to what the key might open. There was a number engraved on it, B1051.

I continued my search opening all the drawers in the kitchen living room and bedroom pulling each one out completely and looking underneath each drawer as well as the cupboard's backboard behind each drawer. I only had this one chance and had to make damn sure I did not leave before I had exhausted every nook and cranny leaving nothing unsearched.

I next looked at the other vents and looked inside. In the last vent I checked by the front door I found another thread. This one was heavier to lift out but I went through the same routine being very careful to listen as I gently pulled the thread out. On the other end was a small notebook. "Bingo!" I thought now we're getting somewhere.

I got down off the chair and sat down to take a Look at the book. I flicked through and saw It contained a series of numbers set out in long strings and several names were also there. Some kind of code, I thought, we'll look at it back at the office as I didn't want to be caught inside Martin's apartment.

I checked once again looking at the walls to see if there was anything that looked like a blemish, maybe new paint or a slight rise on the surface. The apartment was in a typical old apartment building so the walls were as old as dirt! Seeing nothing more I quietly left locking the door after me carrying a key and a small notebook. Maybe this trip wasn't a waste of time after all.

I met Keith for early doors, what we used to call having an early drink around 5.30 straight after work or as it was back then at the end of our shift. It's what we used to do as young rookie cops in Acton and Ealing and believe me there were so many pubs there as well as in Ealing. I preferred the Ealing pubs, the North Star, The Royal Oak, the Queen Vic

(Victoria), The Village Wine Bar on Queens Parade and a small pub, off the main road called, the Haven Arms, on Haven Lane. But Keith preferred the Acton pubs. Was I a snob?

At The Hague, we met at an old bar called Rootz on Grote Marktstraat. It was a café-restaurant and bar, Grote Marktstraat was just a few blocks from the sea. It was Nicknamed "The Belgian in The Hague" probably due to the strong Belgian beers they sold.

They had over 300 beers there and it was in a beautiful old, what was originally, a 17th century coach house with old exposed oak beams along the ceiling and had a great atmosphere. At the time we met, it was quiet inside so we could talk. We sat in the far corner so we could see who entered the bar.

We ordered beers and I showed him the key and the notebook which we started to look through. "I don't know these names," he said but then looking towards the back he stopped. "Fuck!" He said under his breath, "I know this name here," he said and showed me the name. It was a female called Sheri Dannetag. "Who is she," I asked. "She works in comms (communications), the hub of all we do here. She is the coordinator responsible for keeping the lines operational on missions and has a finger in every operation we do. But Martin didn't say if she was friend or foe."

"It may not be bad though maybe she was helping Martin," I offered. "Yeah, I think you're right. He was deep in thought now. She's right in the middle of all we do," he said thinking out loud. "I'm sure you'll find a way, you always have. But now we have a starting point. Did you get anywhere with your in-house search?" I asked him. Yes, he said it was someone else also a female. I knew he had the skills to get to the bottom of who was the leak.

I was cautious about how much I could tell him not that I didn't trust him, but right now, if there was a leak it would be better to keep our knowledge base very tight. I told him I would take the book back to let Jeannie take a look. I knew he had vast resources including code breakers but with a possible leak, the was no way, Jose! Keith was distracted after that name was found and I could see he was worried. "If it is her we are in deep shit," I said. Once again I told him it may not be her, maybe she was helping Martin.

Speculation at this point is a waste of time. We had to follow whatever protocols he had to find the leak. Sometimes it was with disinformation given to a few people to see where that information came out. But this was his deal to resolve.

"What do you think the key is for?" I asked him "It looks like a safety deposit box," he said which was what I thought too. "Any ideas which one?" "No, but it's easy to find and best that you find it, not me," he said which was what I was thinking too.

I would have Jeannie check this before I headed back in case it was right here in The Hague. We made small talk after that and I told him I saw Noz in Ealing and we had a drink at our old haunt The Village Wine Bar. "I haven't been there in ages," he said. "Problem was, he got some of the old team to meet me there and it fucked up the next day for me," I told him.

"Who was there?" he asked still distracted, he seemed to be making small talk now. "Our usual, Bob Lewis, John Done, Robin Perry and Pete Miles," I said, "They all came in around 9 pm." "With that bunch of reprobates, I'm not surprised it turned out the way it did, what time did you leave?" he asked. "Around 1 am," I said. "And I was fucked up till noon the next day," I said.

Talking became a little stilted after Sheri Dannetag's name had been revealed. "Are you OK I asked him?" "Yeah fine just processing this," he answered, "Let me know if there's anything else interesting in the book." He said. We left the bar and I made my way back to my hotel. He seemed off and I thought maybe the name has really set him off. But me? I would get to the bottom of this one way or another.

It was now after 7 pm, 6 pm in London, but I called Jeannie and sent a photo of the key with a question mark and a comment, "Tempus Fugit," (time flies) meaning as soon as possible knowing she would search it out post-haste. It was an hour later when she sent me the name of the bank where that key was used. It was the ABN Amro Bank at Koningskade 30 in The Hague. Now was the problem, how do I get the bank to open it when I am not Martin Ade? I sent Jeannie another message, "Name please," asking her what name was associated. Was it Martin's or someone else's name?

It took her another hour when she came back with," Keith Davies." So now I had to involve Keith in opening the safety deposit box. I admired Martin's forethought knowing that if he didn't make it Keith, who he could trust, would know what to do. I sent a message to Keith asking him to meet me at the ABN Amro bank on Koningskade the following morning at 9.30 am. I was tired when I got back to the hotel but took a look through Martin's notebook. Other names were there and we would make their connection to Martin's operation when I got back.

The following morning we met outside the bank and I gave Keith the key, telling him the lock box was in his name. "Bloody smart Martin was," he said, imitating the voice of Yoda from Star Wars, as we went into the bank. I smiled as he put on his, "Official" face and strode into the bank. They showed us into the locker room and he presented his key. A long box was withdrawn then the bank official left us to open the box. Inside was what seemed to be a fast exit kit.

There were passports, around twenty thousand in readies, banknotes of different counties, and another book, a journal, again with a string of numbers, three names and a few photos, old, faded photos that looked like World War two, taken somewhere in a jungle, not seemingly important at the moment. There was also a small thumb drive. Keith was studying the notebook as I took the thumb drive out and without thinking I pocketed it while we were both looking at the photos.

Keith went to take the notebook but I stopped him. "The fewer people who know what's in here the better and if this Sheri Dannetag is, as you say, it won't be long before she knows what we are doing. It's better if I let Jeannie take a look, outside of your group so I took the book and left."

Chapter 19

Lords and Lady's

Once I was on the train heading back I took a photo of a couple of pages with numbers on them and another of a page with names I had no idea whose names they were and sent them to Jeannie.

I was thinking about how smart Martin had been to not only keep this, whatever it was, under wraps, but to plan in case of his own demise leaving clues in different places and the route to them so well hidden.

Jeannie called me, "Can you talk?" she asked, "Yeah, sort of, I'm heading back I'm on the train to Schiphol, I can't talk but I can listen," I answered. "Well, that's a first she said, the great Maximillion Moore can't talk but he can listen ladies and gentlemen!" She said amused at her own joke. "OK then, I'll just fill you in on what I found. Are you in a bad mood, she said?" "Not at all but I want to get going with this information we retrieved as soon as possible."

"Ok then, these numbers are a mixture of grid references and some sort of code which is something I haven't come across before but they are placed in a long string so the data is mixed up. I may need help to decipher these codes," she said. "What kind of help?" I texted her with my answers rather than talking, "If I'm right the language is a code I'm not familiar with and maybe in a foreign language, but I'm not sure. When are you back here?" she asked. I texted, "Tomorrow am." "Ok, see you then and can I ask you to keep, not talking, and only listening?" I texted back, "Har bloody har har," and I finished the call.

I thought back to my meeting with Keith and the name Sheri Dannetag his change of mood was to be expected if she was so important at MI6. But in his business, a leak can and has led to many deaths. I was thinking back to our training when we were told about Harold Adrian Russell known as "Kim" Philby who was a British intelligence officer, but he was also a spy for the Soviet Union. He was revealed to be a member of the Cambridge Five, a spy ring which had passed on British secrets to the Soviets during World War II, in the early stages of the Cold War. He cost the agency many deaths and a disrupted intelligence team that took years to replace. In the meantime, they were not able to do their clandestine work which was always urgent.

I thought a little more about this as I had other leads to follow up on and anyway, Keith knew what he was doing. I went through the notebook looking for anything that might trigger something but nothing did, yet. I arrived back at Heathrow and caught the tube from terminal 2 back to Boston Manor.

I needed a drink so I stopped in at the Royal Hotel which was on my way home from the station. The pub was a very large Tudor-style building that was once a hotel but was now just a large bar and restaurant.

I went in and ordered my usual Guinness, which they had on draft. I ordered a club sarni (sandwich) as well. Man, this Guinness tasted good and after the time I had over the past week, I needed it. Everything could damn well wait until tomorrow. A few friends I knew from way back came in and came over to join me for a drink which was welcome company. We remained there and after several rounds, it was time to head home.

I slept like a log and the following morning I did my usual commute to the office to find Jeannie there already with a pot of coffee going. She knew me well! "Ok pow wow," I said as I went in. We sat at our big worktable and I gave Jeannie the book retrieved from Martin's apartment and the second one from his lockbox.

We looked at the names, "Nothing springs to mind yet but I'll check these," she said. "What about the numbers," I asked. "I'll put those through an algorithm I made some time ago for doing this. It worked last time on that Pharma case with the theft of their confidential data we worked on, let's hope it works here," she said.

I told her about the name Sheri Dannetag and how she was right in the heart of the ICC managing all the comms. "We don't know the connection yet, but when Keith saw that name he was very concerned, in fact, our meeting really went south after her name showed up," I told her. I then showed her where the name Richard Whitehead, was in the book, between a series of numbers and letters.

"But until we can break down this code the name doesn't mean diddly squat yet," I said. We both had work to do, me looking into the army records for "Wild Bill," who as I saw it may hold a clue to the starting point of this entire case.

But he would be in his 90s now if he was even still alive, so time was of the essence in finding him or his family now. I always found that handling a case with information coming from many sources confused the case. I needed to get back to who this Richard Whitehead was and Wild Bill was the only clue I had.

I went back to the Imperial War Museum to seek out the name William Standford Smith or Wild Bill as he was known, leaving Jeannie to run a check on the names and the codes in the books I retrieved hoping she could decipher the information.

When I got there the elderly man who helped me before, whose name was John Bleby, greeted me. It turned out that John Bleby was a military veterinary surgeon working with their bomb-sniffing dogs and horses back in the day. I told him who I wanted to look up and he helped me do a search through one of their databases. We found Wild Bill along with several more pieces of information which I took down in my notes.

John had a little black book of jokes, that he opened up to tell me a joke from each time we met. I suppose it was to relieve the boredom of working in the museum. I just thought John was a little quirky but nevertheless, he was very helpful and went out of his way to assist my research which I was grateful for.

Wild Bill had a long career rising to Colonel Standford Smith, showing an honourable discharge and an address at the time. He retired from service in 1972 at age 50 but stayed on as a resource for the military.

His expertise was jungle warfare. I now had an address for where he was when he retired, which was in Kings Lynn, Norfolk a couple of hours by train.

There was an old phone number which I passed to Jeannie and she gave me an alternative number for the Standford Smith residence. I called and a well-spoken lady answered. I told her I was a historian looking to write a book about the little-known operations in Burma during World War Two and the name William Standford Smith had come up in several documents. "Oh my," she said, "He was my grandfather and sadly he has passed now but if I can help I'd be happy to. He left us with several journals and there are photos and the like, so if anything is of interest you're welcome to take a look" she told me after all, it's all in the past now and nobody is interested in this old stuff any longer. Sad really what seemed so important at the time is now just gathering dust," she said. I agreed it was part of history and important at one time but few were interested now.

I decided to drive to Kings Lynn as would need a car once I got there and set off early the next day. It was a long shot I know with a fifty per cent chance of success but I had a feeling the trip would come up with something after I spoke to Wild Bill's granddaughter.

When I found the address it turned out to be a huge, gated mansion in the middle of its own grounds, which included a lake and deer running freely around, it was impressive! I arrived at the front gate and gave my name after which the gate slid open. The family obviously had money, probably old money and it was good that I called in advance as one thing for damn sure, I would not have gotten past their large front gate otherwise.

I was greeted by a middle-aged lady who was the granddaughter of Wild Bill. As I found out her name was Lady Priscilla Standford Smith. We went into what she called, "The parlor" to talk. I had taken a couple of photos from the War Museum with me and opened up my folder. "What is your interest in Burma," she asked. I had prepared my story which was in fact partly true, that I was researching some of the warfighters in Burma to see what happened after the war.

"Well I can't speak for most who were there but I can speak about my grandfather," she said. We looked at old photos and there was Richard Whitehead in several photos. "It seems your grandfather and this Richard Whitehead were close friends," I said. "They were like brothers, always together even before the war," she said. "So what happened? I could find very little about them at the war museum," I said.

"Interesting that you ask about Richard, as far as I remember from stories my grandfather told me, Richard disappeared one day, on patrol in Burma and was never seen or found again. They assumed he was killed in action but without a body, it was just assumed and not confirmed. But years later in the 60's, he turned up here at our home. My parents and Wild Bill were stunned that he just turned up one day." "So what happened back in the war," I asked her.

"Well, apparently he was captured and held in one of their jungle prison camps for years until after the war had finished. But they had no idea it was over and anyway, he finally escaped. Under the Geneva Convention, the Burmese were compelled to say they had him but they never did." "But after that, he refused to have anything further to do with the army, which he said deserted him and never bothered to even look for him. His family lived not too far from here which was why William and Richard were close friends as boys. They were like brothers they both went to Eaton together and were inseparable. They grew up together and you can visit Richard's family if you would like. I'll call them to meet with you," she told me.

"Did William search for him back then?" "Oh yes for weeks in fact he was nearly discharged from the army because of it. He always said they were so close he knew Richard was not killed in action and refused to accept that part of Richard's army record." He always said, "MIA yes, KIA no, never" and he was right! "When Richard suddenly turned up they had a very emotional meeting. But Richard was adamant that nothing be said to change his military records and we, of course, agreed," she told me.

I was looking through old photos, "Who are these people," I asked her, she told me several names and I made a note but really this was about the name more than the man, Richard Whitehead, not the others.

I wanted to tell her about our latest Richard who was murdered but decided against it, as that was more for Richard's family than his close friend and there were many holes in this story so it was probably better left as it is than unearthed at this point in time. I thanked her for her help and she gave me her private mobile number in case I needed more information.

She called over to the Whitehead who agreed to meet me. I thanked her for her help and I could see that I had brought up old memories. I had one more question, "Was their meeting a good one?" "I asked because you used the word emotional describing their meeting after all those years, but that can be both good and bad," I said.

At this, she smiled, "You are a very perceptive private investigator," she said smiling, sipping her tea. "You knew?" I said, "Well, you can't expect me to let someone into my home without first checking on who they are," she said, I smiled at that. "Was anything you told me the truth?" "Yes, I am in fact attempting to find the truth about their mission in Burma. I am looking into a case, to get to the truth," I said.

"Why didn't you tell me that before?" she asked. "I told you the truth, I am looking into what happened and I apologise for not being able to tell you more, but I didn't know you and I have to be careful," touché I thought and my words were not lost on her.

"And what will you do with the truth when you find it," she asked. "Honestly, this began as a very simple but unfortunate incident in London and I can't tell you more than that at this point, except to say I am one of the good guys and for me, the truth is all-important. So finding it is what I do." I told her. "Oh I know that your past is impressive otherwise we wouldn't be here in my parlour discussing my grandfather's war records." She said smiling. I knew she meant it.

"Look if you are interested and as a thank you for helping me, I would very much like to return to tell you what this is all about. One thing I can tell you is that with every stone we look under, we see there is more and more we don't know. It seems we are at the centre of a deep pond making ripples that are spreading far and wide. What I can say is that we are in dangerous waters," I told her. "Well, if you believe the outcome is something I would or should know then yes, by all means, call me and please if there is anything else you may need my help with I would be happy to help you," she said.

I left it at that, being caught out with a half-truth was embarrassing but, honestly, right at that moment, I didn't care as there were important things to keep secret. I would get to the bottom of this and as I knew that, to make an omelet you have to break some eggs!

She offered me her hand, though what the fuck I was supposed to do with it, kiss it or shake it, I had no idea, but being the eternal gentleman, I took it and shook it vigorously. The French have a word for people like me, "Plouk!" a plouk is somewhat of a peasant, yep that's me I suppose.

I drove over to the home of the home of Whitehead and if I thought the Standford Smith home was big, this one was huge. It was like a castle but without a large iron gate. I drove up what was at least a half-mile driveway which twisted and turned through dense woods, before opening out into a long sweeping circular driveway, with a view of their beautiful home.

I was thinking, why would someone with a home like this, want to join an elite group of warfighters, maybe my question would be answered I hoped. I parked my car next to a beautiful silver and black Rolls Royce Silver Cloud, parked on the sweeping driveway.

Money breeds money, I thought as I exited my car, which by the way was an E-type Jag (V12). Just as I did so the large bolt-studded oak front door swung open. A servant was standing in the doorway announcing that Lord and Lady Whitehead were expecting me.

What the hell? A Lord and Lady? How did this not show up on any of our searches I wondered. I would take that up with Jeannie to find out why our extensive search engine was incomplete.

Anyway, I was shown in, a large well-furnished living room that looked more like an old Antiques Roadshow episode, to see two middle-aged people waiting for me by what was the biggest fireplace ever!

They both gave me a warm welcome so whatever Lady Standford Smith knew about me she apparently withheld from her friends. Hmm, were they close friends or acquaintances now? I wondered knowing I would probably soon find out.

Standing by a huge fireplace were Lord and Lady Whitehead. He was a tall, elegant man in his mid-sixties in good shape with dark but greying hair and a moustache. Lady Whitehead was an elegantly dressed woman in her mid-fifties, dressed in black dress with some bling in the form of a four-strand pearl necklace and several gold bangles on her wrist.

"Lovely car," said Lord William Whitehead as he greeted me, "And this is my lovely wife Lady Winnifred Whitehead." I didn't know whether to bow or courtesy as I had never met nobility before. "I've always wanted one of those," he said, looking out of the leaded window to where my Jag was parked on the driveway. "Thank you I said and yes she's fun to drive but a real gas guzzler as they say in the colonies," I said smiling. "Hmm I'm used to that," he said thumbing at his Roller (Rolls Royce) parked next to my Jag.

"Please call me Bill, I insist," he said. To which his wife added, "Of course and you may call me lady Winnifred Whitehead," she said and started laughing. "No really call me Winnie, most people do," she and her husband were both enjoying their little inside joke. I immediately liked these two and the first impressions were, with me, usually the right impressions. So what can we help you with? He asked sitting in one of the two large sofa seats between which was an antique table.

On it were two crystal glasses of what I was to find out was dry sherry. Something told me I should tell them all I could, that inner voice talking and I agreed with it as I usually did. But where to begin? I thought so as not to get this wrong, "Where to start I said out loud," "Maybe try the beginning?" my new friend Winny said.

"Just two weeks ago I was at Leicester Square station waiting for my train when a man collapsed on the platform, I didn't know him but I went over to see what I could do to help," I said. "There was a young nurse kneeling next to me, tending the man, but unfortunately he was not alive, apparently he just dropped dead right there on the platform.

I checked to see who he was but he had nothing in the form of identification on him, no credit cards, no driver's license nothing at all to identify himself, which these days is unusual. But here's what piqued my interest, he had around ten thousand in cash and his clothes seemed very expensive." I told them both.

"Added to that, I found out the next day all the TV cameras all over the station went off for half an hour when this happened." They were both listening but saying nothing.

"So, I began looking into the case to find out who he was," I told them most but not all of the story, leaving out my connection with MI6. "May I show you a photo I took on that platform?" I asked. "Please do," she said and I got the photo out to show them. Jeannie enlarged it. I handed it over to them and they both sat there in silence. I said nothing letting them break the silence which by the way was deafening.

Lady W, or Winnie as she preferred to be called, looked at the photo and then put the photo face down on the coffee table and honestly, you could cut the silence with a knife. Lord William reached over and held her hand. They both shared a look. This is our son, Richard, (Lord) Bill told me and I felt terrible for them both.

"Oh no! I am so sorry I had no idea," I said because a lot of what we have found turned out to be a series of never-ending puzzles and several leads led nowhere but Bill waived me off. I felt terrible for them both and told them so, boy how to really blow it, but I kept my cool. "It's nothing you can know about beforehand," she said.

"Our son, he left us many years ago and we never knew what became of him until you showed up today. Please excuse us both this is quite a shock," Lady W said. "Again please accept my apologies I had no idea."

"But Bill waived me off again, I think there is more to this, to bring you all the way up here from London," Bill said. "Yes there's a lot more I can tell you but not all as some of this may fall under official secrets," I said.

To this, they both smiled and I wondered why. I told them about the Italian suit and our trip to Rome to find out who he was. I also told them it was there, in Rome at the Zegner boutique, that we came across the name Richard Whitehead but that we could find nothing more on any database about Richard Whitehead. I showed them the photos I was given by the staff at The Imperial War Museum which was the only link to any Richard Whitehead we found.

He was my grandfather, Bill told me, studying the old photo, and yes he was in Burma, that's where he picked up the name, "Wild Bill," though I have no idea why and he was at a lot more places too with the military. He rose through the ranks and became Colonel William Whitehead," he said and this much I knew. I paused to let it all sink in as this was a shock to them and me.

"He looks well in this photo, so how did he die," Bill asked. "He was poisoned, with a very rare poison that worked extremely fast as soon as it had been administered and my assistant Jeannie is looking through the street CCTV cameras as we speak to see who entered and left the station at the time this happened," I told them both.

Lady W started to tear up and I felt so bad for her. "Please go on," Bill said as he squeezed her hand, so I continued after reaching to hand Lady W my handkerchief, but she had one in her sleeve. I continued to tell them in more detail about the label on his suit and of our visit to the Zegner boutique in Rome where we found Richard's name. They were listening intently as I continued to bring them up to date.

I told them that there was more and how the file turned up with the name Richard Whitehead in it. Once again they looked at each other. "What is your interest now you found our son?" Lady W asked me. I paused thinking hard before telling them about Martin Ade's involvement and his death on the slopes. "Martin Ade? The Olympic medalist," Bill asked.

"Yes I answered and he was working with the International Criminal Court in The Hague, I didn't mention he worked for MI6 there, he died on the slopes while on vacation, he went into a tree at full speed and died immediately from his injuries," I told them.

"But Martin Ade was an Olympic silver medalist and had been down that slope many, many, times. I obtained the file Martin was working on at the time, from a close friend at the ICC and it was there in that file that Richard Whitehead's name appeared." I told them looking for a response, but they were both impassive.

I continued telling them of Jeannie's work looking at the video taken by Martin's friend Hillary when she was watching him from further up the slope and when we looked very closely we saw his death was no accident.

"So, now we have two deaths both associated with Richard's name and this is where we are looking now," I told them what I found when I returned to Martin's apartment in The Hague, the book and the key. "We now have two notebooks both with a series of codes and a few names which we are looking to try and solve," I told them.

"I've been in law enforcement for twenty-five years before I became a private investigator," I said, "And I know there is a lot more to be uncovered and I intend to find out who is behind these two murders. Obviously, whoever it is, has vast resources and can infiltrate the most sensitive areas of the ICC" I told them. "So, I believe this is part of a much bigger crime, these people don't want uncovered, but I don't know where, why or who is behind this yet,"

They were both deep in thought, then Bill asked me, "Why haven't you involved the police, after all a death in London is part of their jurisdiction," Bill asked me. "I did, the following day after Richard was killed, I went to the police to tell them I was there on the platform, but they were only looking at his death as natural causes. It was because I asked my friend in the morgue to do blood work that we found the rare poison used." "So, you uncovered all this, working outside of law enforcement?" Bill asked me, Yes," I replied, "I didn't trust the law to do the sort of job we could do. Anyway, until I could find out more I knew it was best to keep this under tight wraps and I did tell the local police just to complete my duty.”

“There is only me, Jeannie, Kieth Davies at the ICC, Norwell Roberts of Acton Police and Olivia at the morgue who know about this,” I told him. “Since this led us to the ICC where their operatives are supposed to be well protected but it seems they are not.”

“Who is this Norwell Roberts,” He asked, so I told him Noz and I went way back and he was someone who would not tell others and, in my judgement, he was one savvy cop who could be trusted. “Hmm, and this girl Olivia at the morgue, please tell me about her?” He asked.

“I told him she and I had worked together on many, many, previous cases and I asked her to do the tox screen despite there being no evidence to suggest at that time that Richard Whitehead’s death was anything more than a death by natural causes. Olivia did as I asked her and ran a tox screen which was how we found the poisonous cocktail.”

I added, “I could trust her with my life, she was the one who found the rare poison used on your son. Under normal circumstances, if any death of a relatively young man, in seemingly good health, ended up at the morgue they would look for the cause of death.” I paused to allow my words to sink in.

“What intrigued us was the way in which these operators, who may have been instrumental in both cases, worked. It was so simple to them to bring down two apparently innocent people with no care for the loss of human life.” I told them what I could and my job was done here and I now had another missing piece of this puzzle.

Bill, as he insisted I call him, gave me his card and asked that I keep them both informed, which of course I agreed. As I was leaving, Lady W said, “Who is funding all your work,” I wasn’t expecting the question and answered her, “I am funding this, you asked me about the local police but their officer in charge, Angel Borowa, is not someone who I consider to be careful or thorough and to date, she has shown no interest in this case, despite being told your son was poisoned."

"There are some details I'm afraid I cannot share with you right now for national security reasons and this is part of why Jeannie and I are working this case in isolation. I wish I could share more with you but I hope you understand," I said getting ready to leave. They both agreed then Bill asked me, "This code you're talking about what does it look like?" "It's a long string of letters and numbers with a few names interspersed," I replied. He nodded and left it at that.

Bill looked at my card and placed it on the table. They both got up to see me out. "We want to thank you for all your work and please keep us updated. If not for you and your clever assistant we would never have known how our son died and we want to thank you for bothering when others seemed not to," she said.

Bill saw me out to my car and outside he told me he would be back in touch with me. We shook hands and I left to drive back to London. I called Jeannie on my way and updated her. After I had finished updating her she responded, "So this Wild Bill remained in the military and his lifelong friend went incognito even from his parents. I wonder why he did that" she said. "I'm more interested in how a Lord and Lady, British nobility, never showed up anywhere on our databases?" I said.

"Well for that matter you can't find Her Majesty either," Jeannie added. I agreed but reminded her, "We are not looking in the Yellow Pages or the White Pages," I said. We're using the highest-level secure databases, the same that MI5, MI6 and the ICC use. So how can their names not show up on these databases? Remember neither Richard Whitehead's DNA nor his fingerprints were anywhere to be found, so how on earth is this possible?" I asked. Well, that was for another day and we had more important things to deal with. I drove back to London and arrived home late.

I was thinking back to the two families who had been affected by all we had uncovered. Evil spreads like a fucking cancer, affecting all who it touches! I thought this was an evil not seen since World War Two, I thought.

Well, we would get to the bottom of this case and no matter where it led us, we would deal with it as required. My intuition told me I probably, at this point, had no idea how far and wide this conspiracy to commit

murder really went. As I said this was like ripples in a pond, spreading far and wide. Regardless, my method was to build each case I worked on, lead by lead and clue by clue. It had always worked for me in the past and I was damn sure it would work here now.

I was driving and thinking the whole way back, about how a seemingly random death on that Leicester Square platform, had led us to meeting British nobility, the rare poison used and a death on the ski slopes at Val d'Isere.

The more I thought about this the more I knew we were barely scratching the surface of what was turning out to be the most fascinating case we had ever worked on.

Chapter 20

Noble Bedfellows

The following day I went to my office to see Jeannie pouring over the notebooks attempting to decipher the codes contained in them. She was using an algorithm she had developed sometime before, but despite this, these codes seemed unbreakable.

We had a Pow wow to lay out what we had and for me to redirect my limited resources. "Did you get anywhere looking for that poison?" I asked. She told me a close friend, her mentor who helped her obtain her PhD. Was looking into it. "Can you trust that he won't blow his search?" I asked her. "Yes, he was the one who showed me how to remain anonymous and he has all the same tools we use," she said. "But he knows what to look for and we don't as regards finding where this deadly cocktail was formulated." She answered.

I trusted Jeannie and knew she was one of the smartest women on the planet. So I could leave this until she had more information. "How's the code-breaking working?" I asked her. "Nothing yet, but I will break this code one way or another!" she answered and I knew she probably would. I decided I would follow up on the couple who were filming Martin's descent from the other side of the slope.

This was the part I loved, when we both had things we were working on to solve a case it made things so much faster. Since Jeannie had hacked the cameras in the hotel lobbies at Val d'Isere I could review the timeline to do my search.

We were both busy now and I was searching through the few cameras, in the lobbies and any that were focused on the surrounding areas. It was slow going trying to find the brightly dressed couple.

I finally found them checking into the Tsanteleina Hotel near the station. I made a note of the time, and since the video was in the cloud, Jeannie enabled me to access the feed and sent me the link. I went back to the time and date of their arrival and then began the slow process of bringing it forward. There was a camera in the front lobby but it was not focused on the desk, still I would see if I could find their names.

I freeze-framed the feed at the time of their arrival at the hotel and zoomed in on their luggage. It was a little blurred but I could make out letters on a label on one of their wheeled cases. It was what looked like the airport code TLS, which after checking turned out to be Toulouse in the south of France. There was another label with what looked like LYS which if it was correct was Lyon–Saint-Exupéry Airport, in France which was fairly close to Val d'Isere. I looked up the flight time which was a short hop less than 45 minutes. There were around 20 flights each week, so it was a busy route.

I next checked to find out how to get from Lyon Airport to Val d'Isere. There were several ways to make that trip, by train, by bus and train and a shuttle, these were the public transport options. But by public transport, it would take around 6 hours which if they were going for a short skiing trip would have been too long. Since they arrived on the Friday of that weekend, looking on Google Maps, the fastest would have been by car which was a two-and-a-half-hour drive. So they would probably have rented a car at Lyon airport.

They checked in to the hotel on Friday at 4.30 pm. The distance from the airport to the hotel by car would have been around two and a half hours. So allowing 45 minutes to get to a rental car at Lyon Airport, meant I should take a look at the CCTV cameras to learn more.

They would have arrived at the airport from Toulouse around 1 pm, give or take half an hour, so I was looking for passengers arriving for flights between 11 am and 12.30 pm on that Friday at Toulouse airport.

It's just math, I thought planning back from their arrival time at the hotel to when these two skiers may have caught the flight from Toulouse.

But if I could find them they may still have the footage showing the person who used a ski pole to bring Martin Ade to his death. Which made it not only a deliberate hit but would lead me to who did this.

"Bloody hell! I yelled out, gotcha, at Toulouse airport!" I shouted out to Jeannie. She came over to see the CCTV footage I was reviewing. "Good job boss," she said. "How's your code breaking going?" I asked her. "I've never come across a code like this," she said. "I'm thinking how on earth did Martin learn to use this code and why, what did he not want others to see?" I was looking at my screen now in slow motion feed so we could see their faces more clearly.

"Here she said allow me," as she sat at my desk and began manipulating the image of our two skier's faces. She opened our facial recognition program and ran it, It was a waiting game now but a long shot, if they had never been in any trouble they wouldn't show on the facial recognition program but it was a start.

I went over to get some coffee while we waited for it to run through the millions of faces. "Any chance you can get into the French driver's license bureau's database?" I asked. "Always a first time," she said. I smiled knowing she would probably manage it.

I was still reviewing the CCTV video looking for what gate they boarded at. We needed a name and an address. The program had finished with no recognition. So the next step was a name, I went back to the CCTV footage looking for them to show up again. I had been going through the CCTV cameras and I found them on my third camera video, sitting at one of the gates, waiting for the flight to be called, but I couldn't use that unless I could get to the passenger manifest.

"Unless you have a better idea, let's try the European driver's license bureau, using their facial recognition. Maybe time to stop your code-breaking work for a minute or two." I said to Jeanie and went over to look at her work. Not that I could help with it. I looked and the computer sorting through a maze of letters and numbers incredibly fast but nothing was showing. I was looking at the code in Martin's book, "What kind of code is this?" I asked her, thinking out loud. "Buggered if I know," she said.

So I'm doing a random number and letter search, to see what comes up but nothing yet. Did you know every language has its own telltale words that identify that language? She said. "Interesting, but can you leave it running while we try to find this French couple who were videoing Martin's run at Val d'Isere?" I asked. She came over and looked at the CCTV footage I had saved on my hard drive in case it disappeared.

I told her, we have a good facial shot here and if we can break into the license bureau or maybe the ticketing system we can get their names and addresses. She did a search for the French driver's license bureau. Apparently after Brexit, there was a Brexit Withdrawal agreement but it made no provision for driving licenses.

Eventually, the British and French governments negotiated an agreement so Brits like us could, if we needed to, obtain a French License, nevertheless. The British and French governments eventually settled the matter making it easier to get a French or EU driver's license.

She went onto the ANTS' (Agence Nationale des Titres Sécurisés) website. The normal route for a license would be You need to go online at Permis de conduire, (permit to drive) which is part of the ANTS system.

The application is processed by CERT (Centre Expertise et de Resources des Titres) based in Nantes. But we didn't have the required docs which were, a copy of an existing driver's license, printed in colour, front and back plus a copy of your main passport page and a recent utility bill as proof of address, none of which we had obviously.

While she was busy with that, I took another look at the notebooks lying on the table. There were three names inside. I wrote the names down and started a search on our system. The first name was Roger Brightly, so I started with that name.

The name came up as a government official but did not tell us which department he worked for. The second name was Charlene Willoughby, and my search showed an address in Gloucester. At last, I was getting somewhere, I hoped. The third name was Olivier Nicholas showing an address in Paris.

Chapter 21

An Unexpected Ally

Following the information we now have, I wanted to take a closer look at Charlene Willoughby, who, as it turned out, was seventy years old and living in Gloucestershire. I did a Google Maps search to find her address then took a look at her residence on the Google Street View program. She lived in a mansion located in Bourton-on-the-water in Gloucester. I don't know what it is with these people but she was the third person whose name came up who was living in a mansion.

I was thinking, I don't know anything about her and what if she is part of some problem, some intrigue Martin had uncovered and I was about to blow the whistle to her on Martin's work.

No that would never do, I needed to find out more about her before I went to see her. I next looked up Roger Brightly and his name came up as forty-five years old, also working for a government office, but it didn't show in what capacity.

We were seemingly in a stalemate with names we could not follow up on and a little black book, not filled with the names of adulterers, like many of my previous cases, but filled with numbers and letters in a seemingly unbreakable code. We were spinning our wheels getting nowhere and needed to regroup our actions. It was now 6.30 pm time to leave and think overnight about what we could do next.

The following morning we were both in a Pow wow considering the next step when there was a knock at our office door. I went over to open it to see none other than Lord William Whitehead standing there.

To say I was surprised would be an understatement! I ushered him into our office and he walked straight over to Jeannie to kiss her hand!

Only the British I thought! Well with that and before I could introduce him he announced himself as Lord Whitehead adding, as he smiled at Jeannie, "But please call me Bill," "It's nice to see you again Bill, what can we do for you?" I asked, showing him to a chair at our larger ops desk.

"Would you like some coffee," Jeannie asked him being overly polite, but it made me smile as she had never been like that with anyone. "Do you have tea?" He asked. "Yes of course I'll be happy to make you a pot," she said and went over to our counter to reach up for the tea and a teapot, on the top shelf, which we rarely used.

I was wondering what brought his Lordship to our humble operation. I had already told Jeannie about our meeting and my view of Bill and his wife Winnie. He sat at our large table but did not look at the papers strewn all over it. "I expect you are wondering what I am doing here," he said. I didn't react but waited for him to continue as Jeannie was attending to the tea.

"You made an indelible impression on my wife and me," he began, "We discussed what you both are doing and we were impressed, not only with how you two are working, independently of any authority, but your decisions to keep your work under a very tight lid," he said.

"And in this case, you are absolutely correct, complete secrecy is paramount. We think you have an inkling as to what this may be about and it is to this that my wife and I owe you both a debt of gratitude. "Please!" I said, "We were doing what we do, investigating," I intervened.

"Yes you were but you bothered to find out who it was, who succumbed on that underground platform and it turned out to be our only son Richard. Yes, we were devastated to learn of his death, but what you should both know is that he chose for himself a clandestine life in defence of the realm, following his father's former life. Yes, you were

getting closer, closer than anyone else on our side. It cost him his life but I can assure you he would have had it no other way. That was how we raised our son. What you don't know is that I was head of MI6 for 25 years but like our son, my name never appeared in any government forum. Who you know as head of 6 is the figurehead, a more public name and face that suited our purpose. But the power behind MI6 was me, I ran the show until a few years back," he said.

"I had been grooming our son to join MI6 but he preferred to work under my direction outside of 6. He was very effective and was totally loyal to this country." He paused, remembering his only son.

"We had people who checked out who you were and what we got back was impressive," he said as the tea arrived. I had to smile, Jeannie had the whole thing, the teapot, complete with a tea cosy. I didn't know we even had one! She brought out two cups with saucers which I didn't know we had either, with a small milk jug and a sugar bowl. "I take my tea with a little milk and no sugar," he said.

Jeannie sat down to join us, "And you Miss Jeannie, you have impressive credentials and I can see how you are both so effective. The thing is you do not have unlimited funds and for you both to have come so far with your investigation, keeping it away from the more traditional enforcement unfunded will never do. I am still involved with 6 but no one has a clue that I am," he told us.

"And, to this, I want to help you both get to the bottom of this as much for our son as for the country. I have a small very tight organisation of professionals with various skills handpicked for what they can do. We work in putting our skills to good use and although we work outside of both 5 and 6, we are all on the same side," he paused to sip his tea and gave Jeannie an appreciative nod. I smiled as she was clearly loving this.

"So, with having said this I can point you in the right direction and help you from behind. I have contacts that never appear on any search or database and as you learned from our son Richard, we are very difficult to find. But, to this point, you found us, just the two of you, something no agency has ever uncovered. Although you had no idea what you had found, Winnie and I know you would eventually have connected the dots.

You decided to find out who Richard was when local police, as you discovered, were uninterested and ill-equipped to do so anyway. We are happy you kept this away from them and must continue to do so. Sometimes they mean well but are a little like a bull in a China shop!"

He continued, "My organisation intends to pay you for your time and in fact, my wife insisted that we cover your costs to date. We are, as you probably gathered not without means and we would like you to come on board working with us to get to the bottom of what our son Richard was involved with and who it was that killed him," he said.

I was stunned and I knew Jeannie was too. "Look," he said, I fully realise your strength is working alone, outside of the more traditional means of crime solving and to this we will not interfere, but should you decide to allow us to work with you, you will see how much more effective your results will be with our vast resources that will keep you both under the radar," he said.

Wow! I'm not often stuck for words but I was now, "I had the feeling you knew more than you could say," I told him. "And I could say the same applied to you," he said smiling. "There were things I could not tell you as I really didn't know you," I told him.

"Yes, we realised that after we had you checked out and I hope you don't mind that we did. We discovered you have a friend, Keith Davies working with the ICC and he is helping you. He is known to us. So, what do you think?" he asked, "Can we become an effective team?" I looked over at Jeannie, after all, she was as engaged in my company as I was and I valued her opinion.

Imperceptibly she raised one eyebrow which was her way of saying yes. "Well, the offer of pay is good news, but the more important thing is that we would welcome an alliance in this case since we have hit a wall. You mentioned us working alone and yes this is how we've been so effective, but working with you I am certain will have benefits for both of us. it will be a new "Mode operand" for us to be part of a team but yes, we would like to work with you and your team," I said.

"Thank you this is good news, we hoped you would and of course, you two will take the lead. You must tell us what you need and we will help.

Jeannie, would you please show me the code you are working on," he asked her. "How did you know that we were working on a code?" she asked as she retrieved the notebook from her desk.

"We have fingers in many pies and we have vast resources," he said smiling. She gave him the notebook "Ah yes I thought so, this is a very old code based on a dead Aramaic language." "Aramaic?" she said.

"Based on but not purely so," he answered. "Are you interested to know about it?" he said. "Of course, since I've been trying to break it for days," she answered.

"The Aramaic language is a Semitic language from the Northern Central, or Northwestern, area of the Middle East that was originally spoken by the ancient Middle Eastern people known as Aramaeans. It was most closely related to Hebrew, Syriac, and Phoenician languages and was written in a script originally derived from the Phoenician alphabet. We have no idea where it originally came from but we do have a code book you can use to decipher it," he told us.

"Bloody hell, that's brilliant news! I was getting nowhere," Jeannie said adding, "Where did the code book come from?"

Bill smiled probably at her enthusiasm. "The code book, we believe also came from the Middle East but more than that I cannot say. We use the code as it cannot be deciphered without the code book, no doubt as you found out for yourself. It is a random base code which is why computers cannot help as they work on repetitive words and phrases. I'm sure you passed it through a language check looking for those common repeated words. In other words, a computer can be programmed to not only recognise the language but also fill in any missing phrases and words.

For example, in the English language, or to be more precise, Oxford English, the most common words used are the, be, to, of, and, and in. But there are more complicated uses of words like, "I" which may be a pronoun or a Roman numeral. "To" for example may be a preposition or an infinitive marker; "Time" may be a noun or a verb. These are just a few examples of the Oxford English language that any computer can be programmed to find.

However, this is not so in Aramaic. The letters in the Aramaic alphabet all represent consonants, some of which are also used as "Matres" (lectionis) to indicate long vowels. Writing systems, like the Aramaic writing system, indicate consonants but do not indicate most vowels other than by means of matres lectionis or added diacritical signs.

These have been called "Abjads" to distinguish them from alphabets such as the Greek alphabet, which represent vowels more systematically used in English, which is also a Latin-based language.

Abjad, is a writing system in which only consonants are represented, leaving vowel sounds to be inferred by the reader. This contrasts with the alphabets that we are used to, providing graphemes for both consonants and vowels. I know it sounds complicated and it really is, but suffice it to say all European, Latin, Greek or Germanic-based languages are systematically written and spoken, with common words used in any number of sentences on a repetitive basis.

However, this is not the case with Aramaic, so you see computers would find it impossible to understand. But the code you are attempting to crack is what is known as a random language code, which is based on Aramaic, but modified into an unbreakable code," he explained.

Jeannie and I were dumbfounded at what we were being told. "So how did Martin Ade obtain this code?" I asked him. "Haven't you guessed? He was one of us, one of our operatives working within the ICC, but in reality, he was deep cover working as part of a very small group within MI6. A spy, like James Bond, or if you prefer, he was a spy within a spying organisation, spying on other spies!." Bill said chuckling at his joke.

"In that case, was his cover blown? Why was he a target and by whom?" I asked. "Well, that is where you two come in. We are impressed with your skills and we need t to break this open. We think you are the ones to help us crack this case. If, as it seems, his cover was blown then as you can imagine, this is very serious for the organisation and this has never happened before. We hope that together we can get to the bottom of this case, but post haste. Time is of the essence."

"What do you know of a Sheri Dannetag? I asked him. He looked puzzled. "What we do know is her position within 6, she is the very hub of all communications into and out of 6, operating in The Hague," he said. "Why do you ask?" "Her name came up in one of the two notebooks of Martin's, but we don't know in what capacity yet until we break this code, and with your help we will soon find out," I told him.

I got the feeling Bill was a very canny person who never fully revealed all his cards. But while we were now on the same team, I showed him a photo I took of the tail we picked up in the bar at The Hague.

He smiled, "Yes we're aware of him, he is as you may have suspected working for someone else but we don't know who yet." "We have a problem in that case, how the hell did he know Keith and I were meeting at a bar The Hague?" "So how? Was his phone and mine both tapped?" I told him.

 "Well that's not difficult, he could have been waiting for you or Keith to make a move," Bill said. "No that's not possible because only Keith and I knew we were to meet that evening, no one else knew," I replied.

"Well, that is for you two with some help from my team to unravel. But unfortunately, I have to go now as I have an appointment, you have my number on this card, do not save it with my name, just the number. I already have your numbers and as part of what my organisation does, we will be monitoring if you are being tracked.

I'll let you know where to pick up the code book, it'll be a dead drop. It has been a pleasure to meet you both and we'll be in touch," he said. When he reached the door, he turned and said, "By the way, Winnie asked me to thank you both, on her behalf, for bothering to find out about our son when no one else would have bothered.

We'll be in touch soon and let me know if there's anything you need in the meantime," at that Jeannie said there was one thing he could help us with. She told him about the two witnesses on the ski slope and filled him in on the connection with Toulouse airport.

"We can find them easily and what do you intend to do when we find them?" he asked "They were filming Martin's run and we need their video, if they still have it, so we can prove who Martin's killer was. We owe it to him. We believe it is the Neil character who befriended them on their departure at Heathrow, but all we have is a blurred image of a ski pole tripping him up," I said.

"Consider it done and I have a private jet and a helicopter which I will place at your disposal. One last thing, can you give me a bank reference, maybe a separate one where we can begin to fund you both?" he asked. Jeannie already had a separate bank account for payments and gave him the sorting code and number. Bill, left us both still stunned at the sudden turn of events.

We sat in silence for a few minutes both going over all we had just learned from our new friend, Lord William Whitehead, aka "Lord Bill," or as he preferred, just Bill.

Jeannie broke the deafening silence. "What the fuck just happened?" she said. I told her we now had help and we needed it. I also told her this was now officially our next case and not, by the way, pro bono any longer. We would have struggled on regardless but now with Lord Bill's help, we would find out what these two murders were about. Another case to solve!

Chapter 22

Toulouse-The Rose City

After Bill had left, we discussed whether or not we could have got to the end and if so what would that mean. At the back of my mind I had become increasingly concerned about the point at which we would, if we solved this case, hand it over to the police and whether they would accuse us of interfering with their work, which they undoubtedly would do.

It didn't matter if we were right, they would spin it to have our license to operate removed. I couldn't risk that, but looking at the way Angel had responded I knew we were on a sticky wicket. So with Bill's resources and assistance, we could avoid that risk, Jeannie had thought about this too.

The part Jeannie liked best was the availability of funds as she was always counting our pennies. "Look after the pennies and the pounds will take care of themselves," she always said in her sing-song Welsh accent

It was just a day later when someone from Bill's organisation sent us the names, addresses and phone numbers of the two brightly dressed holidaymakers from the ski slope. Wow, I thought, that was bloody fast and now I had to go to Toulouse to find them. Their names were Jacotte and Jean Louis Piquet. Their address was in a town called Bruguières, outside Toulouse, which looked like a short forty-minute drive from the airport.

I decided to call Jacotte's number with a story that I was a reporter doing a story on Olympic silver medalist Martin Ade who was at the resort of Val d'Isere when they were there also. It was flimsy I know but I hoped it would work, so I called her number and in my limited French

I asked her if she was Jacotte Piquet and if she spoke English, luckily she did speak somewhat broken English but it would do for now. So we continued in English and I told her my little white lie. Honestly, I claim to always be looking for the truth, but in fact, telling little lies is a huge part of my job and is what I do on a regular basis. I know I'm going straight to hell!

Anyway, I asked her if she was at Val d'Isere a few weeks back when the famous skier Martin Ade a former Olympic skier was there. I told her I was in Paris and asked her if she remembered seeing him run, Off-Piste when he had a terrible accident that killed him. She became animated, she said she was videoing the skiers at the time and it was, "Un terrible accident," I agreed.

I asked her if I could come to see her and take a look at the video. "You want to come all the way here, to Bruguières?" she said. So my little white lie just got a tad bigger.

"Well I'm a freelance columnist, I have followed Martin's career and I want to let people know how he died, so for me it's no problem to come to see you if that's ok with you," I said. She said it was fine so I told her I could be there around 11 am. She agreed.

I caught an early flight from Heathrow to Paris and from there a shuttle to Toulouse. At Toulouse airport were photos and comments about the fabulous Concord which was created in a joint enterprise with BAC and Air France, in England and in Toulouse.

I had to chuckle at that, really. I thought, the British and the French actually getting along well enough to create something so spectacular! I would love to have been in the same room when they were discussing a joint venture between the British and the French!

I had been on Concord once from London to New York's JFK airport. The flight took just three hours and ten minutes flying at 1,425 miles per hour, Mach 2. The experience was incredible! I digress!

I rented a car and drove to the town of Bruguières a short 40-minute run. Jacotte lived on Rue des Sports just off the centre of town.

She met me at her door and was with another woman, "This is my friend Eve and she can interpret for us. My English is not good for a conversation like this," she said.

We sat at a table outside at the rear of her home by their swimming pool. The weather was warm and there was a good ambience sitting there a million miles away from London. I was thinking, I could live here and really enjoy life. But then reality crashed in, invading my lovely daydream. Max, it said, you don't speak French and for the most part, French people don't speak English! Well, I thought, there is that!

Anyway, the three of us sat at the table in the glorious late morning sun. I was offered wine or coffee. I preferred coffee which was fresh roast, strong and delicious. I could do this I thought, drinking nice strong French roast espresso coffee or sitting by my pool with a good wine, or even better a glass of Pastis 51 in the evenings. It is said that if you drink too much Pastis you get a facial twitch!

Well, then Pastis 51 is no worse than drinking "Scrumpy" at almost any bar in the West Country, in England. The West Country is Cider country and believe me it's strong. Scrumpy is raw cider, straight from the cider mill and in many cases it is not even fully fermented and is highly alcoholic. I remember drinking with friends in Somerset watching a young man hallucinating while lying on the front lawn of a local pub. Too much too strong and too many!

Anyway, back to the business at hand. Eve, pronounced Ev, spoke perfect English which made my meeting with Jacotte much more productive. I started by telling them both I was writing a story about the Olympic skier Martin Ade and I managed to find other skiers who were there at Val d'Isere at the time of his accident.

I asked Jacotte, through Eve, "Did you see his accident?" Eve interpreted and the answer was yes she was there. "Several people saw it, I lied and I am following up to find out more, after all, it's not every day an Olympic skier gets killed on the slopes," Eve spoke to her friend and they began a heated discussion with each other. Eve then told me Jacotte did video the accident but did not want to get involved.

I was afraid this might happen and told her Martin Ade had a family and they deserved to know the truth. Eve nodded and spoke to Jacotte.

It worked and Jacotte got her phone out to show me the video. She spoke in rapid French to Eve which started another heated discussion. I intervened, "Please tell Jacotte that I'll keep my source secret and since she is my source her name is protected by law." Eve explained this to Jacotte.

Just then another woman arrived, her name was Janet and apparently she was a successful local businesswoman. She introduced herself speaking perfect English and sat down to join us.

The three of them started talking together in rapid French and I was thinking, "What am I chopped liver?" Why is it that when two or more French women get together they speak twice as fast as is humanly possible to understand and anyway how the hell can they all listen when all three are talking at the same time?

Finally, they paused for a breath at which time I said to them," Umm hello, can we proceed in English please?" They stopped talking then Janet spoke to me. "Sorry, but we agreed that we would never ever talk about Jacotte's video and now you are here and we are supposed to just ignore our agreement together, because you, a total stranger show up."

It was time to level with them if I was to get the damn video. "Look, I am writing about Martin Ade and I know it was no accident. Martin had a friend with him who had also videoed what happened." They interpreted for Jacotte. I carried on, "The video his companion took was from the upper part of the slope and showed a ski pole being pushed out from within the tree line. It was this that caused his fatal crash and it was no accident."

I waited for the interpretation, Jacotte spoke and I waited for an interpretation. "She says that if you already have a video why do you need to see hers?" I was prepared for this question and said, "I'm working with Martin's family who only want to get to the truth as to

what really happened. As far as the authorities are concerned it was an accident, death by misadventure and until I can get to the truth, his family will forever be stuck with a lie about his death.

Do any of you three have families" I asked them and waited to see them nod their heads to say yes. "So, if this was your family member who was killed, your son or your husband wouldn't you demand to know the truth?" Once again they started to talk together in rapid French.

I waited for them to take a breath, thinking how is it possible for any human to be able to continue to speak so fast, for so long, without even taking a breath? Are they making it up as they go along?

I honestly believe women are given twenty-five thousand words to speak every day. But men are only given twelve thousand words so that's why I'm here waiting for their quota to be used up and at this rate, it should be around a half hour!

"Ok," Janet said, "How can you give Jacotte assurance that you will never tell where the video came from." The three of them were in agreement. I was prepared for this and told them, "If I am compelled to reveal your video, I will ensure your personal safety by getting a court order to have an agreement between you and the court ensuring your privacy, between you and a judge who will seal your affidavit so only the video and not your name will be used."

"How can you promise this," Eve said. I told them in my line of work I have a good reputation and it is based on my integrity without which I could never do my job as a reporter. Anyway, all journalists are protected by international law, and not to be forced to reveal their source. Even in a court of law and you Jacotte are my source. So your name as such is protected unless you wish to reveal your name, which I would advise you not to.

I continued, "But anyway, it's the video, not the person holding the camera that is important. So once I have the video you are really, to all intents and purposes, unimportant and since the video can be technically proven, to be an original video, that's the important thing. In all honesty,

I said, you are in more danger of keeping the video than you are by passing it to me. Once I have it, I am the target, not you," I explained. More rapid discussion between all three using up their quota of words.

"Did any of you see the Kennedy assassination?" I asked them. They all nodded their heads. "There was a video taken by a man named Abraham Zapruder, who filmed the assassination and his film became a vital source disproving what the government told as being the truth. He showed his video all over the world. Well, he lived a long and healthy life despite going public with his video and his was a video of a sitting president, being assassinated in broad daylight, which by the way was far more dangerous than the death of a skier." I added.

"Anyway, my point is, that once the video was released for all to see, Mr. Zapruder became relatively unimportant, certainly less so than the actual video once it had been released."

I waited for Janet and Eve to interpret for me. Once again, my brilliance worked and I finally had the damn video in my hands. Before I watched it with them I asked Jacotte, "Who else have you told about what you saw and were you with anyone else at the time?"

She told them and me, that she was with her husband Jean Louis, I was relieved to hear it was her husband and not the usual French way being on vacation with an affair. If that were the case then most definitely their lives could be in danger. "Please explain to Jacotte that both she and her husband do not need to discuss this with anyone else. Do you think Jean Louis told anyone?" She answered through Eve, "No he wanted the video destroyed and I told him I had destroyed it but I did not," she said.

We started watching her video of Martin's final run. He was going very fast indeed, then there it was, the man in the tree line. It was clear from the clothes that he wore, which were the same exact clothes he was wearing in the video that Hillary had taken at the open-air restaurant before the incident, that it was Neil. This meant the friendship at Heathrow was all to get to Martin who had no idea.

I thought how bloody callous to become someone's friend in order to kill them a few days later, I will get you and your accomplice and when I do you will either be dead or residing behind bars at Her Majesty's pleasure! We had him now, it didn't matter that his eyes were hidden by his goggles, I would leave that to Jeannie to figure out. I made two copies of the video and told Jacotte to take it off her phone now which she did while I was there.

I reminded the three of them once again to make sure they kept this between themselves and to ensure Jacotte's husband Jean Louis continued not to tell anyone at all. "Will you tell him I came?" I asked her through Eve. "No," she said, "We never have secrets," smiling at her little white lie, "It's the French way you know!"

"Ya gotta love French women," I thought, as I left Bruguières and headed back to the airport. At least this mission was a success, thanks to our new friend Lord William. I called Jeannie on the way telling her I now had the video and it was all we hoped Neil was the one who tripped Martin deliberately causing his death, of this fact there was now no doubt.

The following morning Jeannie and I reviewed the video in our office. Jacotte had done well, her hand was steady and the image was clear. What we saw was the speed at which Martin hit the tree, he must have been going at least 70 mph, I also saw the man in the trees crouch low and push his ski pole out at Martin's legs.

The crash was horrendous killing Martin instantly. It was very hard to watch but then we saw Neil going over to Martin's smashed-up body to check that he was dead, poking him with his foot.

There was bright red blood in the pure white snow. Then he edged out of the tree line and looked up the slope giving a very slight nod, raising his ski pole to make it seem he had just seen a terrible accident if anyone was watching. Well, luckily for us, someone was watching but unseen by Neil. This was deception at the lowest level!

What we now proved was that Neil, whatever his real name was, was a hired killer and so was his accomplice. In the video, Bridgett was

standing in Hillary's line of sight so she missed this small detail. My resolve to catch them both was what now drove me to find them and what this case was really about. If nothing else to avenge Martin's death and to give it meaning and closure.

We now had all the evidence of what we suspected now proved to be true and I would call Bill to fill him in on where we now were with the death of his son. Seeing the callous way they planned and executed their plan made me angry, in fact, I was seething at seeing what had occurred.

I believe in Karma, but for these two and whoever was behind this I would be their Karma, they just didn't know it yet!

Chapter 23

The Man in The Trees!

I messaged Bill, thanking him for the lead and told him we now had undeniable proof that Neil was a hired assassin. But now we had to go through the two notebooks using the code-breaking Bill provided to see what else we would uncover.

Someone in the past had converted the code from its original Aramaic into Latin-based letters and numbers, obviously to enable the code to be used during WWII, as Bill had told us.

Jeannie was laboriously typing the code-breaking system onto her computer; it took time but would speed things up when we entered the notebook data. She placed the info onto a separate laptop that had no internet connection just in case there were trip words that might show up if someone was looking for certain words or phrases from these codes. Nothing was too low for these killers and their organisations.

There was little more I could do to help her with her work, so I began tracking down our two killers. I went to a map to see how they would have left Val d'Isere and found them at the train station. But only Bridgett caught the train, I found that Neil if that was even his name, went to the airport travelling separately, they were professionals.

The facial recognition algorithm I was using made it possible to track their image but it was slow. I needed help and sent the new photos of Bridgett and Neil to Bill. I didn't need to add words as he would know what to do with them. They had changed from their ski gear and were now wearing common clothes for travelling in since they no longer needed to be seen as skiers. It was only through facial recognition that I was able to retrace their steps. Had this not worked I would have gone back to before they met Martin and Hillary at Heathrow and backtracked from there instead.

I sent the images of them both with their ski gear and with normal streetwear to Bill. I went back to our war board removing some of the question marks and looking how far we had come in just a few weeks. It was a waiting game now for both Bill and Jeannie.

I messaged my friend Noz for a meeting but this time we met at a small pub called The Haven Arms, on Haven Lane in Ealing. The pub was small, off the main road and also had a small beer garden at the side so we met there. I was waiting for Noz and ordered us two drinks, my Guinness and his single malt whiskey.

I didn't have to wait more than a few minutes for Noz to arrive. Once again he arrived and greeted me with his usual, "Wassup mate, things moving along?" I held up my beer for him and I said Cheers before I answered him. "Yes," I said, "Things are moving very fast I wanted to ask where you were with asking your friend, Ms Rodriguez if she can help us." It's Mrs Rodriguez and yes I did call her and she's happy to help.

She was away for a few days, but she is expecting your call, he gave me her contact details. We had agreed it was better to hand carry things like this rather than leave a trail through electronic media texts or phone calls.

I told him I had found Martin's killer I didn't tell him how or where. This was to protect my friend and I mentioned that we were working on this now. "Why not let us deal with it?" he said. I explained this was a non-starter as we were aware there was a leak somewhere and with two people dead already we didn't know what we were up against.

"Do you know a detective "Angel Borowa," over at Agar Street Nick, in Covent Garden?" I asked him. "No why what's up with her? Don't tell me you're bonking her!" He said. I told him about our meeting and her disinterest in the John Doe case and how she got really pissed about me not telling her that I was ex job. I also told Noz that to date she still hadn't followed up with the coroner or even read the report about the poison used.

"But the thing is I really don't want her messing around with this and stirring up the pot as you know once your mob gets involved we lose control and it becomes a pissing contest as it always does," I told him. "Yeah, I get that but when this blows up you better have yer arse covered mate!"

I knew he was right but we would deal with that one when we got to it. We stayed for a while and he told me he was working on a murder in Acton, but my mind was elsewhere. "What will you do with the news of the killer," he asked me. I replied that this was part of something much bigger involving other agencies but as soon as we find these killers we would think about handing the case over to the case officer.

"Be damn careful Max," he said. "I can see this whole thing going south on you if you are not careful." "Yep, I knew interfering with a case was an offence, but it's not yet, is it?" "The case officer Angel whatever hasn't even picked up the file yet or so it seems," I told him.

"Anyway we have connections that may help out with this," I said. "Friends in low places ? he responded. "You bet, very low places," I said with a wink. We stayed for a while before leaving the pub around 10 pm. I headed back to Boston Manor. On my way, I received a text from Bill, "Thanks for the update," was all it said.

The following day Jeannie was still uploading the data from the codex onto her laptop when I received a call from Noz's contact, Isabelle Rodriguez. She asked me what I wanted her to do. I told her about our need to remain undercover while using her recognition databases. "No problem," she said, "We've done this before all I need is your email and contact numbers and I'll take care of it here," she said.

"Your names and any people you come up with will not show anywhere," she told me, adding," I owe Noz big time for the help he gave me one time and anything you need I can help you" I thanked her and

asked when we could start with this. She said, "Give me one hour after I get your contacts and you're good to go," she replied.

"What about Olivia, will she be ok as well?" she asked I told her Olivia's role, checking for the poison online was finished now so she wouldn't be doing any more research into this. She would be taking a trip to Hastings for a face-to-face talk with her mentor to find out more but not over the internet.

Funny how one thing leads to another and as they say, to eat the elephant do it one bite at a time and that was how we solved our cases.

Chapter 24

Pieces of The Puzzle

Things were moving at last and I checked with Jeannie on her progress with the code, she thought she was about halfway through. After around an hour, I sent Isabelle the data noting the time it was sent. I was anxious to start searching for the real identity of our killers.

In the meantime, I updated our war board which was filling up with names and details. I had to smile at how far we had progressed with this case and how Bill had helped move it along when we had hit a brick wall. Our strength was in remaining a small company of just two people unhindered by office politics and all the unnecessary wasted time filling out reports, which, if my memory is correct used to waste around 20% of my time.

The real work would start when the code in Martin's book had been cracked, which I hoped would not be too long now and I knew Jeannie would add her own shortcuts, as she always did!

It had been a week since we obtained the code-breaking book when Jeannie announced she had completed writing the code on her stand-alone laptop. She began entering the string of numbers and letters, from Martin's book, into the program and after a while, we started seeing the results. It was like watching a puzzle slowly dissolve into a picture, pixel by pixel revealing letter-by-letter words that were forming.

Words began forming into sentences, on the screen, and we were both mesmerised as the sentences began to emerge. The opening sentence said, "If you are reading this, I failed." We looked at each other in silence and knew what this meant. Martin knew he may be killed and this sentence brought it home and we knew we had to solve this case.

The sentences were formed incomplete and each line started from the right not the left so we were reading the end of each line before the beginning. Each sentence was building up in random letters, slowly appearing pixel by pixel before we could read each sentence. We waited for more of the code to be deciphered, as I sat at my desk watching, with a coffee. After some time which seemed to take forever, we could read what had cost Martin his life.

At the beginning of the notebook, he wrote, "I am an MI6 operative working under deep cover at the ICC in the Hague. I was sent there to uncover a cell of operatives using the data in the ICC for their own purpose."

We were reading that he had found a cell working within MI6 based at the ICC. "There is a connection to the BIS Tower in Switzerland and I believe it is there that the head of operations is based. Roger Brightly is part of their operation and is an MI5 operative, based in London. Olivier Nicholas is not part of this organisation, he's based in Paris and is helping me," We read

The code went on, "I have proof of these facts. I believe this cell is part of a global banking fraud aimed at disrupting international banks to set up a global crash. This faction exists within MI6, the ICC and maybe within MI5. In case I am caught I have a video detailing my work to date. It is located with my mother. It will be in a sealed box.

I sealed it with a red wax seal. Old school I know, but the seal was made using my father's University ring. If you find this video the seal should be unbroken. Richard Whitehead was helping me with the Swiss link, he is to be trusted and is one of only three involved with my case.

I trust you will know what to do with this, help comes from high places. Contact Olivier Nicholas in Paris, he can help you. Password Falcon. Place no trust in MI5 or MI6 communique, only trust old school as I have done. I wish you good luck and I'm sorry I won't be there to see this through Goodbye." His message ended.

We both sat in silence, this was the work of a dedicated hero, one of many who are unsung heroes working behind the scenes keeping us all safe.

I remember going to meet a friend in the CIA who showed me the Memorial Wall located in the original headquarters building lobby on the north wall. There are now 140 stars on it. Each star represents an employee who died in the line of service.

There is also a black Moroccan goatskin-bound book, called the "Book of Honour." It sits in a steel frame beneath the stars and is framed in stainless steel, topped by an inch-thick plate of glass. Inside it shows the stars, arranged by the year of death and, when possible, lists the names of employees who died in CIA service alongside them.

The identities of the unnamed stars still remain a secret, though they are all now dead. Many names from the Cold War era have been released or uncovered in recent years.

I thought it was a pity we didn't have the same, but the British stiff upper lip and all that MI5 is the equivalent of the FBI while MI6 is the same as the CIA. But, regardless, to me a hero is after all a hero.

Richard Whitehead and Martin Ade were both heroes in every sense of the word and I was damn certain their deaths would not be in vain. They both knew the risks but continued regardless and sadly their work cost them both their lives.

But now at last we were getting somewhere and we now had a new lead to follow with Olivier Nicholas so I would be heading over to Paris. For this trip, I had to use my fake ID under the name Anthony Smock, since I was going to see a contact with links to the BIS Tower and Switzerland.

I had no idea who Olivier Nicholas was, but if Martin said he could be trusted then, I would trust him at least for the time being. Jeannie found him on one of her search engines and provided me with a photograph.

Before I headed over to Paris, we had to retrieve the video from Martin's mother, Marilyn. I found her address in Lowestoft in Suffolk which was just over one hundred miles northwest of London on the East Anglian coast.

Did Martin's mother know of her son's death? I would have to tread carefully until I found out. I thought probably not as his death had been kept under a tight security screen by Jeannie and me. Anyway, I had to make the trip while Jeannie was still unravelling Martin's notebook.

I left the following morning for Lowestoft; it was a brisk 118-mile drive up the A12 which ran from M25 all the way to Lowestoft. I got there late in the morning and headed to her address on Kirkley Park Road. The houses there were very large and she lived halfway down the road. She had no idea I was meeting her and I preferred to keep it that way until I could meet her face-to-face to deliver the news about her son.

I rang the doorbell and she opened the door. I prepared for this and said, I'm here about Martin and I have been told to tell you, "Falcon." She stood there in silence, knowing what this was about. She invited me inside to her back garden and we sat at a table there.

"I have been expecting your visit or a visit from someone like you," she said. "Please tell me what has happened to my son," I told her I was deeply sorry to tell her Martin had been killed on a ski slope in France. "Val d'Isere?" she asked. "Yes I said, did you already know he had gone there?" I asked her. She was dignified and careful with her words.

"Not directly, he never told me details, we were never that close, his aunt my sister was his surrogate mother, but Val d'Isere was his favourite place to ski and he had been there many, many, times since he was 8 years old. He knew those runs like the back of his hand so I have to ask what happened?" "Before I answer that can I ask how you believed something had happened to him? Did someone tell you?" I asked her. This was a test question to see if someone had loose lips.

"Though we were not that close, Martin and I had a code, he would text me just a single number in consecutive order every second day, deleting the prior number when he texted the current day's number and I would do the same, with the understanding that should he miss a single day, I was not to follow up but wait to be told what had happened. So, you see, I knew something bad had occurred when the numbers stopped being sent. But please tell me what you can."

I told her of the incident that cost him his life. She responded. "You and I both know he was the best skier in the world and that was something most of his fellow Olympians thought as well. I also know he didn't make such mistakes or take unnecessary risks doing what he loved and what he was excellent at. So please tell me what you can, by the way, I too had top-level security clearance and was part of MI5 some years back.?" She smiled, "Who do you think taught him his tradecraft?" She said.

I told her his death was no accident, it happened on the fastest part of the run and caused him to hit a tree. "How did you know this, were you there?" she asked. Once again I told her what I could without compromising our agreed secrecy. I told her his death was linked to a case I was working on with a name in his notebook.

She didn't ask what the name was and I thought back to what my mentor told me, when you drain the lake you uncover rocks at the bottom. I was relieved to know I was talking to a fellow professional. I cut to the chase and told her he left us a coded message saying he had a video which he left with you. "Please, one thing at a time," she said smiling. "What was the codex he used?" she asked.

I told her it was an ancient code and we couldn't break it, using several different algorithms, until we obtained a code book, I answered truthfully. "And who do you think taught him that code?" she asked. "I guess that was you, was it?" I said. "Yes, it was a code my former team developed in World War two. I was station chief based in the Middle East, you can check and I assume you probably will and my name is spelt with a "Y" Marilyn. After the war ended my team found the code very useful. I taught Martin how to use it, happy to find he took my advice," she said, "He didn't always, unfortunately."

She went to retrieve the video CD and gave it to me. I looked at the red wax seal which was complete and unbroken sealed onto four red threads going around each side of the CD. "Do you have your husband's ring?" I asked her so I could check the ring to the seal. No Martin had that but my late husband went to Cambridge and his ring was the coat of arms of Cambridge University.

I checked the engraving on the seal. It was a "Shield" shaped coat of arms. I took a photo of the unbroken seal before I opened it. It showed four lions in the four quarters separated by a cross with a bible lying sideways in the intersection in the middle of the cross. All along the beams of the cross uprights and cross beams were 21 smaller crosses. The detail in the wax seal was very good.

I also went to Cambridge University; after boarding school and I knew the seal was a correct representation of that university's coat of arms. I thought back to Martin's apartment in The Hague, there was no ring there and according to the coroner's report listing his clothing, there was no ring on his fingers. Where it may be was unimportant now, my guess? He probably hid the ring after using it to protect a single use of the ring with the wax seal.

"A month ago," she said, "Which would have been just before he went to Val d'Isere was the last time I saw Martin," she said. I thought maybe he knew he was being followed, well whatever I hoped I would soon find out. I broke the seal and inside the package was a compact disc, with no writing on it, or on the box it was in.

Marylin showed me back into her home where a CD player was located under a wall-mounted TV. "I'll leave you to watch the video, please let me know when you're finished and tell me what you can," she said.

I didn't wish to insult Marilyn but I would not watch the video at her home in case it contained classified information. I told her so but promised to tell her what I could after we had analysed it at my office.

"I knew that but I wanted to check on your tradecraft," she said smiling, adding, "Old habits and all that, I'm sure you understand!" I wanted to get back to London in case the information may be time sensitive. I told her again how sorry I was for her son's death.

Chapter 25

SWIFT

Before I left her, she asked, "Please do all you can to find the people behind my son's death and, as we say in the trade, treat them with, "Maximum Prejudice."

I left her to deal with her loss however she could and drove back to London. I called Jeannie to fill her in telling her we would review the disc in the morning. She was still working on the codex but I knew if there was anything new she would call me.

I took the CD into the office where Jeannie was waiting to see it. Neither of us had any clue as to what was on it. Jeannie placed in our player and we sat at the table as it started to play.

Martin's face appeared looking at the camera as he began, "If you are watching this it is clear I am no longer around," said Martin Ade looking at the camera. "I made this video on the off chance that you may not have been able to decode my notebook. I want to start by saying please pass on a message saying how sorry I am to my mother for not being able to see this through, but here we are.

I was placed in the ICC staff as part of an MI6 operation to uncover a leak inside the ICC which MI6 became aware of six months ago. We had information that led us to believe there was a cell operating inside the ICC connected to the global banking system, the Bank of International Settlements, or BIS, based in Basel, Switzerland.

Communications were picked up through a connection we had in Paris, with an operative there, Olivier Nicholas, working with the French Intelligence Service. He was tailing this man in France. Another image came up with our spook who entered the bar where Keith and I were meeting at The Hague. He was traced back to the BIS Tower in Basel, Switzerland and had been making regular trips between The ICC at The Hague and Basel.

We thought at first it was simply liaising money transfers that the ICC were involved with. But with the SWIFT banking system, no personal involvement is required, so we looked into this. We then tracked this man in Brussels at the same time the Belgian finance minister was found dead in the street with no visible signs of murder."

An image of Neil came onto the screen, as Martin continued with his monologue. He apparently dropped dead on his way home from work. His death was ruled death by natural causes, yet he had an annual medical checkup, required as part of his job as Finance Minister, just one week prior and according to his doctor he was given a clean bill of health. There were no signs of interference, no marks on his body and we had nothing further to investigate regarding his death.

We looked into his business dealings and we found a connection once again with the BIS Tower, in Basel, Switzerland according to his bank records large sums of money were regularly being transferred into a numbered Swiss bank account. We believe he was being blackmailed because once his personal account had been drained, that was when he dropped dead. The total amount he paid was twenty million Euros which in fact bankrupted him.

The end game of this active cell, we believe is to undermine the global banking system by simultaneously altering or blocking all the access codes in the SWIFT banking system. As you probably know, SWIFT is The *Society for Worldwide Interbank Financial Telecommunications* or SWIFT for short.

This system powers most or almost all of international money and security transfers. SWIFT is a vast messaging network used by financial institutions, to send and receive information, such as money transfer instructions. SWIFT powers most international money and security transfers.

We are aware that 95% of all financial institutions use SWIFT to securely transmit money and instructions through a standardised code system. Although SWIFT is crucial to the global financial infrastructure, it is not a financial institution. It doesn't hold or transfer assets but simply facilitates secure and efficient communication between member institutions.

When we looked into SWIFT, we found there are more than 11,000 global SWIFT member institutions, banks, building societies, lenders, investment banks, high street banks and the like. These SWIFT users are represented in almost every country in the world and they collectively send more than 44 million messages each day through the SWIFT network.

So, if our information is accurate and we believe it is, any disruption of this banking system would be of global proportions and would bring the entire global inter-banking system down.

SWIFT powers most international money and security transfers and its network is used by financial institutions to quickly and securely transfer money around between various institutions. It powers most international money and security transfers almost invisibly.

A disruption on such a scale would be of global proportions. We cannot evaluate the total effect but with every one of the 11,000 banking systems, of which there would be hundreds of thousands of banks affected and the entire world would be locked out of their finances.

This could lead to a run on all the banks, for cash, probably leading to the discontent of the people at all levels, insurrection and eventually war with each country affected blaming all others for their demise in not receiving agreed money transfers. When Russia and Iran are placed on a financial embargo it's through the SWIFT system, where they are blocked from using it and it works. Ordinary people would face starvation after grocery chains ran out and truckers could not use their credit cards to buy the hundreds of Euros to fill their tanks, to make deliveries. Street fighting of massive proportions would ensue starting at banks, garages and grocery stores. To put it simply, the world would be plunged back into prehistoric conditions but with gangs armed with present-day weapons out in the streets.

They would also have access to every user of the SWIFT inter-banking system's bank accounts and routing codes. This meant they had control over every company or person using SWIFT and could access or transfer all the money into their own accounts.

It would get worse, armies and governments could not be paid; police, fire, hospitals and all branches of government would be shut down, unpaid. Power and water systems would also be affected. No one could drive because garages could not take credit cards and what cash banks had before the system was shut down would soon run out. Ordinary people would demand their money in cash after which no pay could be made back into their bank accounts for work done.

We found a connection between members of the ICC and this man. A photo came up and was freeze-framed so we could see his face clearly, it was the same man we saw at The Hague in the bar where Keith and I were meeting.

We believe he is the assassin hired by someone or a group operating out of the BIS Tower. This is the second person we are aware of as another freeze frame showed the man whose name we came across in Martin's notebook. His name is Roger Brightly, and we now added him to our board we have no image of him yet but we will very soon.

There is a third man in communication with the other two but we don't know who he is. We do know that the third man is running the show at the ICC.

Chapter 26

Wheels within Wheels

Following our meeting, we found another link going right back to MI5 at Thames House and we believe it is Sheri Dannetag making the calls from within the ICC. This was the name we could read, that appeared in Martin's notebook.

His message went on, "She will be difficult to prove but that we are aware of her comms with this group means we are monitoring all her communications. We decided to leave these people in place until we can find who the mastermind is and if it is someone at the BIS Tower. I wish you well with this and I hope to God that you are successful, because if you are not." He left the comment for it to sink in, and it did.

We had finished watching the recording and sat in stunned silence. If what Martin had uncovered was correct and we knew it to be so, we had to get help to stop this as this was far bigger than just two deaths we had been following up on. The Belgian finance minister and Richard Whitehead both suffered the same fate, dropping dead with no visible signs, both ruled death by natural causes.

I contacted Bill to come to our office urgently. We placed the information "BIS" on our board. We now had a map connecting The ICC in The Hague to London and the BIS Tower in Basel Switzerland.

Bill arrived and we showed him Martin's message, he sat in silence watching the message from a deceased colleague. When the message had finished he told us he had become aware that there was something big and possibly of global proportions afoot. I told Bill we needed to combine forces as this was now too big for just Jeannie and me to be able to stop it from happening. He agreed and told us he would take the CD back to his team, he saw my concern and said, "Max, you need not be concerned, my team has been in place for a considerable time now and is the best there is."

"Perhaps it is time for you both to meet them since you will both be involved together now to stop this. I'll set it up and I can tell you we have seldom all been together in the same room so careful planning is paramount so as not to raise any red flags. I'll send you time and place and I leave it to you both to find the best way to get there without being followed," he said.

I told Bill, we had to find the third man in the ICC, monitor what Sheri Dannetag was doing and find the group in the BIS Tower. As for the assassin, now we had him on our radar and we knew that wherever he showed up someone was about to be topped.

I told them both, "We can use their assassin as our weathervane," I said and they looked puzzled. "In other words wherever they point him and we find him, we will know they have found someone who they want removed and that can be our way of knowing what they know. So keeping an eye on him will give us a heads up" I said. Jeannie knew how I think and Bill nodded his head in agreement, "Good point and please bring this to my team," he responded.

Bill left us and we would now await the location of our meeting with him and his team. After he left I talked with Jeannie about working now as part of a team which is not what we usually do. But we both agreed this was a case that had exploded right in front of us.

"We have to be one step ahead of these financial terrorists because if we are not, we know what will happen if what Martin believes is the outcome then becomes fact," I said we both knew we didn't usually play well with outsiders but this was too big so we would work with Bill's team.

Two days later I got a message from Bill telling us to meet him at a location in Norwich and we would go together to the location to meet his team. We were to meet him at the Norwich Castle Museum and Art Gallery the following day at 12 noon. The train ride was just over one hour from Liverpool Street and we would both meet on the platform under the clock at 10 am.

Jeannie was unsure to be meeting the team we would be working with; I could tell by her silence on the train journey. I was a little apprehensive too but I learned on the job never to underestimate the future, especially when the future can be something I might control the outcome of.

I left the Met because I hated the rules and regulations. For me they were stifling, all those reports and bloody meetings, to tell others who never gave a fuck about me or what I was working on only that they could make it seem, to their bosses, they were making my decisions.

The very reason I closed more cases than my colleagues did was because I liked to work alone. That way if something didn't pan out I would regroup and go in a different direction. Seemed the more success I had; the more others wanted to shoot me down.

Everything I did to solve a case was because I liked to work alone and at the end of the day I was better off doing what I loved, but outside of the Met. I snapped back to the present and turned to Jeannie, telling her not to worry because if Lord Bill had been working for so long behind the scenes as head of MI6 he must be damn good, anyway I told her, "He came to us, not the other way around!"

"Ok I said, we have time to kill let's play point-counterpoint," I said. It was a game we played going through the arguments for and against a case we were working on. One of us would think of a point and the other would give a counterpoint. It was a game but with a very real logic behind it and we used it to see what each of us was thinking.

I continued, "So why were they impressed with us finding out what happened to their son, Martin, after all, we always had success which they would know having checked us out?" Jeannie thought for a while then answered, "You went there unannounced so before that they knew nothing about us," she said. "Ok I think Bill wanted a face-to-face to check us out and to see our office because he was trained to make quick assessments of people and surroundings," I answered. Point counterpoint. "Why offer us pay for our work when he could just as easily do what we were doing, using his team, without paying us," I said. "Because we had uncovered what his team had not, around his own son's death," she countered I said. "Yes, but they didn't she said. "We blindsided him with what we found out and we offered new thinking into what Bill and his team had either missed or never found," She added.

Point counterpoint. "He came up with the name we were missing and very fast too," she said. "Yes sprats for mackerels," I answered. "Huh?" she replied. "Offering a sprat, a small fish, to catch a mackerel a much bigger fish," I explained. "So which are we, the sprat or the mackerel?" She asked. "We are the sprat," I answered, to catch the bigger fish.

Point counterpoint did the trick and pretty soon I regretted it, Jeannie was back to her old self going over the names, places and missing details we needed. She brought with her the file she had on the case and we went through it. We were missing key data, the names within the BIS Tower and the timeline they were working on.

"Could you get into the SWIFT system and rummage around to see if anything seems unusual?" I asked her. "Yes I can but what am I looking for?" "Well, I think it would be any link between BIS and The Hague, Brussels and their man Neil. There must be some common calls or messages linking those together," I said. "But let's see what Bill's team have got before we show our hand," I said.

"Do you trust Bill and his team," she said. "I don't know them yet, and until I do let's just be cautious, I think they're legit but you never know, so we go into this both eyes wide open!"

We arrived right on time at Norwich, "Good old British rail over the points and right on time," like the old song, "The 6.5 Special, my father liked" I thought. "Let the train take the strain" as their persistent ads used to say, every day and night ad nauseam! Still, they were right we arrived on time and were ready for whatever the day would bring!

We caught a cab at the station and it was a short 5-minute hop to Norwich Castle Museum. The building was a large square building set on a hill, probably to make the marauding peasants work a little harder to get into the castle, both Norwich peasants and any other marauders of the time. There were greenhouses and their famous "Bittern Line," miniature train running around the grounds.

I read the history of Norwich Castle as we were a little early. It was built by William the Conqueror around 1075, nine years after the Battle of Hastings where our not-so-good King Harold was killed with an arrow while probably looking up to see if they were shooting arrows. Well apparently they were and one arrow found his eye.

William embarked on a Campaign to subjugate East Anglia and was probably around this time that the castle was built. William I (William the Conqueror) ordered over 98 Saxon homes to be demolished to make way for his castle's earthworks and deep defensive ditches that he built in their place. The earliest recorded incident at the castle is in 1075 when it was besieged by troops loyal to William to put down a rebellion "The Revolt of the Earls," led by Ralph de Gael, Earl of Norfolk.

Old Ralphy went abroad to try and rally support from the Danes leaving his wife Emma in charge of the garrison. I would have rather gone to the pub I thought as I was reading the castle's history!

Anyway, his support failed, I could have told him not to trust those bloody Danes, so the rebellion was put down. It lasted three months and ended when Emma secured promises that she and her garrison would be unharmed and given safe passage out of the country.

The castle itself was a rather boring building on the outside, I supposed the architect, was having a bad day. In fact, compared to any of the other castles around at the time, this one was the most boring of all! It was just a huge oblong block of stone with four rows of recesses where maybe windows were once to be placed but never were. Maybe they thought it was not worth the money. But, whatever the reason, they were not there now. So they were now just stone recesses and with the exception of a few sporadic windows that was it.

The limestone used for the castle was shipped from Caen in France at a cost of over three times the original value of the stone! He was ripped off by the French! I had to smile, can't trust the bloody French either!

It didn't compare to the other British castles but then again maybe the French at the time had more basic ideas of what a castle in England should look like. Personally, I thought they built it deliberately boring to make their own castles look great, but that's just me.

Once inside, we were in a great hall with stone walls and a high wooden joisted roof. There was a balcony running around the main hall which had four large arches going right up to support the roof. The floor was polished wood and it had been converted into a museum with various artifacts dotted around. My history lesson ended and we didn't have to wait long before Bill arrived.

When we met him I asked, "Is this your extra pad Bill?" "Not mine," he replied giving the museum a look that said it all. We went outside to his Rolls. His driver was waiting, holding the rear door open for us. He looked like a cross between Jason Statham and Daniel Craig, a wiry straight-faced bodyguard come driver.

I was well able to handle myself as I had done many times, as a former university wrestling champion, but I hoped I would not have to match up to him. He was average height, with cropped short hair and a couple of days' growth, though these days it was "The look" he nodded at Bill and closed the door after we got in.

Bill joined us in the roomy back seat I had never been in a Roller (Rolls Royce) and it was everything people said it was, smooth as silk, utterly quiet as it whispered its way to where our meeting was to be. Bill turned to me and said, "After I've made the introductions I would like you to brief the team on all you have found so far."

Chapter 27

Nine at The Lodge

We drove through a winding road with dense trees on either side then after around forty minutes we turned off the road onto an unpaved track that went up a slight gradient and ended at a large, what I supposed was once a hunting lodge. Probably not used for hunting these days unless for the occasional squirrel or if you're lucky enough an unfortunate deer but bears and wolves went along with all the other species hundreds of years before.

The lodge was made of stone with a balcony around it, which gave a view of the surrounding densely wooded area. Bill showed the way and we entered into a large sitting room with 5 men and one woman waiting for us. There was a smell of coffee just brewed. The chauffeur, if we can call him that, joined us at the table as well.

Each of Bill's team there shook hands with us and told us their names, first names only as we sat down around a large oak table set in the middle of the room. The room had several animal heads on the wall and I was thinking, with their credentials, they could probably have added a couple of human heads on the wall as well.

He introduced us both saying, "I've told you a few things about Maximillion and Jeannie and how they uncovered all we are about to see, just the two of them. As you will see from the video my son died to get this information to someone who could stop, what you are about to see, from happening.

I handed Bill the CD I brought with me and he placed it into the player. Bill told them it was his dead son who gave us this information at the cost of his life. Everyone sat in silence as we all watched the recording.

After it had played out Bill started the conversation. "As you all already know, Max here and Jeannie uncovered this activity after following up on the single death of the person in the video, Richard Whitehead, who was my son."

After the video Bill nodded to me. "Here's what we don't know," I said and outlined the names we were missing which was one person at the International Criminal Court in The Hague, who we believed to be the head of these operations inside the ICC. But we would need to find who that person was or if there may be more than one.

We are also missing who was at the BIS Tower in Basel who was running the assassin and probably the entire show. I told them also that the deaths of Richard Whitehead and the Belgian Finance Minister both, we believed, had the same MO. Both just dropped dead for no apparent reason.

"We knew the rare poison used for Bill's son," I turned to Bill as if to say sorry for this, "Was a deadly cocktail guaranteed to cause death but there was no ID on him whatsoever so it took some time to get to his name which was, as we now all know, Richard Whitehead.

We also believe that what killed the Belgian finance minister, as his death was also widely publicised as from natural causes, may well have been the same poison used on Richard." Several of the group nodded their heads. I added, "In our line of work we know there are seldom coincidences." They certainly knew this to be true.

"One death was on Leicester Square station, the other on his way home in Brussels," I told them the station CCTV cameras were all off at the time but in the urban area outside Brussels, the area where the minister was killed had no cameras. This was probably deliberate as he worked in the city where many cameras are located.

Jeannie passed around the face of the assassin, which she had cleaned up and enhanced, telling them she had hacked into the CCTV images on the streets leading to Leicester Square and the same man had been seen at The Hague which was how we knew his connection to this.

She then showed the photo of Michelle Nicholas adding that he worked for French Intelligence and was probably an ally since he was seen coming out of Thames House. But why he was at MI5 since he was French we didn't know yet. "So maybe there's a link there," I paused to let this sink in.

"We know little to nothing yet about the three names in Martin's notebook, Charlene Willoughby, an elderly lady who lives in Gloucester, Olivier Nicholas, in Paris, who we are told is also an ally. Then there is Sheri Dannetag who works at the ICC managing their central communications along with Roger Brightly, who according to Richard is a government official but we don't yet know if he is a friend or foe.

Bill entered into the conversation, "We need to find who it is in Basel in Switzerland working inside the BIS Tower, there running the show and we need to know what the timeline is." To this, the other woman in the meeting, whose name was Mariah, (no last name given) told the group she did have a contact inside the BIS Tower and would be able to work with her.

Mariah was a tall slim attractive redhead, the only female, apart from Jeannie, in the group. She had a "Don't fuck with me," demeanour and was ex-spec ops with a track record of success with many kills down range. She had apparently seen action in Afghanistan, Iraq and on the Horn of Africa and according to Bill was a sniper who could hit a quarter at 2000 meters.

Bill wasted no time and asked her. "OK, would you take the lead on that and see if you can find their timeline." She agreed and said she would do it immediately. Another member of the group, Dave, the bodyguard had connections in Paris and agreed to go with me to see Olivier there.

Bill then produced burner phones that one of his team had, "Cleaned" and were loaded with each of the team's numbers under the numbers 1 to 9, including Bill and Jeannie's numbers, with no names given on each phone. "Use these from here on, to communicate with each member of the team," he said but, he said looking at me, for your internal communication between yourself and Jeannie please do as you usually do. He asked me to recap the missing details which I did.

After the video and after my recap had ended Bill left the lodge saying as he left us, "I'll leave you all to work out the details but please keep me appraised of your progress." After he left they each came over and thanked us for the work we had done and welcomed us to their small highly talented, specialist group.

One of them told us that we had really impressed Bill and he never had invited anyone into the group. They told us they looked forward to working with us both. Please use our skills and add them to what you already have. Jeannie said, adding "We don't know what your skills are," to which they each introduced their background.

As we were to learn we now had a team of ex-CIA intelligence gathering, an MI6 operative, an ex-spec ops, (Mariah) and two SAS operatives. All had seen action having been deployed downrange in various parts of the world, Afghanistan, Iraq, and Africa and we knew each could handle themselves if the need arose.

They told us they were amazed at what we had uncovered and were there at our disposal to help stop this act of terrorism. Jake, the ex-CIA operative offered to come to London and work with Jeannie on accessing the SWIFT database system.

He told her he had an amazing bag of CIA tricks, tapping his head to say, it's all up here. She readily agreed adding it was an area she was having difficulties with.

Dave, the chauffeur, arrived back to join us and introduced himself as ex SAS which did not surprise me. His name was David, "Call me Dave," he added. "I've been asked to work alongside you both and to watch your backs. We told him to meet us the next day at our office and we could go through what we were doing."

Chapter 28

Strange bedfellows

We left the meeting and headed back to the station. Dave took us in his black BMW which I noted was an M series and very fast. We left him and caught the next intercity back to London.

On the way we went through the meeting and I asked Jeannie, "Well what are your thoughts now?" She thought for a moment and answered, "Up to when Bill left I thought they were all very straight-laced, but after he left they were great and I thought, what a team!" I agreed and asked, "But did you notice anything else?" "Like what?" she asked.

"Well, to me, his team seemed heavy on the physical ability side with excellent skills at combat but seemingly light on the thinking and planning side with the exception of Jake who you will work with to hack the into SWIFT system." That is where we come in, we are the planners and thinkers adding the skills they need to accomplish this mission.

We agreed that we would use our own comms for talking and messaging between Jeannie and myself but the burner phones for the group.

The following day Jake and Dave arrived and Jake immediately started working with Jeannie. They seemed to be getting along well and were both talking about the dark web and encryption codes, bytes and terabytes.

Dave came over to take a look at what we had found so far and I brought him up to speed going through our war board. "So let's go to Paris to meet this Olivier character," he said, "We can use Bill's plane.

Keep me posted Jeannie," I said as we left. Dave drove us to Stansted airport and we talked along the way. "We have no idea what their timeline will be but I think it will coincide with something big," I said.

"Why do you think that?" Dave asked. "Well, think about what they are planning, it's huge and will give them control of the world's banking, well at least for all the banks on the SWIFT system, which is all of the principal banks. So what would be better than an international meeting or something similar, a high-profile meeting where they could have maximum impact and visibility," I told him.

"I'm thinking that they could launch their program during something like an upcoming UN, NATO, World Monetary Fund, or the next World Economic Forum or something like this," I said.

"Yeah," Dave answered, I agree it's a possibility, let's get a timetable of upcoming international meetings and work from there. He filed a flight plan to Paris Beauvais–Tillé Airport which was a small regional airport and preferable to either Charles de Gaul or Orly both of which may be monitored. From there It would be a 60-minute drive into Paris.

I left a message for Olivier saying I was a close friend of Richard Whitehead and I had some business in Paris. I told him my name was Anthony Smock which was the name I would be travelling under for this trip. He suggested we meet up so I told him I would be in Paris tomorrow night staying at a hotel in Montparnasse and I would very much like to meet up with him.

I thought I would try using the name Richard gave us and said, "Richard wanted me to let you know his pet Falcon is doing very well. I'll be meeting a business associate in a bar called The Hideout, on Rue de la Gaité. I look forward to meeting you, I hope you can make it."

"What was that all about?" Dave asked, "I answered that it was a test, if he were a friend he would know, the code word Falcon, but if he was an enemy he would ask what that was all about, just like you did." Dave gave a wry smile.

I told Dave that I chose this hotel because it was a relatively small, boutique hotel and had an easy escape through the back of the bar if we needed it, that is if he came to meet me. The bar is right across from the hotel, on the other side of the Montparnasse cemetery. So we can walk to the bar through the cemetery and should there be a shit show we can take it up there.

It was game on, we either met Olivier or we didn't. I told David he should watch the bar from across the street and when Olivier arrives give it 2 minutes then walk in. "Don't forget my name is Anthony Smock!"

I entered the bar and sat in the corner, it was quite busy with people, locals, probably there on the way home from work. I preferred it to be busy, with less attention to my meeting, that is if Olivier showed up.

I ordered a glass of wine and waited, then around thirty minutes later Olivier walked in. He didn't know me so I watched him for a while to see if he was with anyone, it didn't seem that he was followed at least no one came in with him close behind, but Dave would be in later to confirm. Olivier was a tall slim, fit-looking man with a dark beard. Seems every young person these days has a beard, but I don't. I guess I'm now officially old school!

I waited until he ordered a drink and it arrived before I went over to speak to him at the bar but faced the bar so as to look like I was ordering another drink. Olivier was standing next to me also looking straight ahead. "Olivier?" I asked him without turning. He replied facing straight ahead also, "Yes and you are,? I told him my name. He spoke English with a heavy French accent, "We cannot be seen here in public it is too dangerous," he said. "There is a cemetery behind this place with a large statue in the middle meet me there," he said.

I paid my tab at the bar to make it look as if that was why I was standing there. Olivier did the same remaining at the bar until I left I returned to my table after paying my tab, finished my drink and left the bar.

I texted Dave telling him simply, "Meeting him in the cemetery," and went into the cemetery heading for the large statue in the middle.

Naturally, the cemetery was empty at that time of the evening. Olivier arrived soon after me, and we stood by the statue. "So what is this about and where is Martin?" he asked. "Our agreement was never to meet in person, yet here you are," he said. "What is the code word," I asked him. "Falcon" he replied.

"You know this that is why I came. This had better be important to risk this meeting in such a way, and here of all places a public place," he was pissed at this. I told him I chose the bar because of this cemetery which was how we arrived I told him.

"Look we have to cut to the chase there is no time to lose," I told him. "Martin Ade is dead, he was killed skiing at Val d'Isere a few weeks ago," "And you know this how, were you there?" he asked. I told him no but his name was associated with another death in London and that was a man called Richard Whitehead." He looked shocked and asked me how it happened so I told him it was deliberate and explained how Martin was killed.

He thought for a long moment and turned to me, "Well then you know Martin and I were working on something, please tell me what you know." I told him of a code in his hidden notebook found at his apartment in The Hague. and how hard it was to break, but I didn't tell him what the nature of the code was.

"He was working on a case involving the BIS Tower in Basel Switzerland, using the global SWIFT system and he believed it to be extremely dangerous for the financial world." "Yes it is, then you are aware of how dangerous this is too and why we cannot allow this terrorism to be carried out," he said.

"That is why I came here," I told him adding, "I am well aware of the risk but as I hope you will agree we had to talk very quickly since we don't know when this will happen. We have some of the missing pieces but we need to know who was running the show in Basel." "Were you working that angle, to find the names in Basel?" I asked him. "Yes I am still and I have one name but there are more."

"There is another person working for them based inside the ICC," I told him. "But we don't know who that person is. We believe that person is coordinating with a messenger from the BIS and that is the person who killed Martin. He had a female accomplice with him and they were in Val d'Isere for the sole purpose of taking Martin out of the game. But someone who worked at the ICC knew where Martin was headed, and tipped this assassin off," I told him.

He told me this but I had to focus only on the BIS part, I am the only person working alone, not even my security bosses, at the DGSE, know what I am doing. "I was working alone too," I said but now I have a small team helping me. I know I can trust them and they have the skills we need if we are to break this before they put their plan into action. Martin was killed because he got too close and this tells us the timeline is soon, maybe too soon. But we can only do what we can and we are working against the clock," I said.

Do you know Michele Debusse? I asked, "Yes of course he works with my team but he is based in London, why do you ask?" he said. We saw him leaving Thames House in London and found it strange that the DGSE was working with MI5 who as you know are domestic only.

"This tells me he found a link probably within the Bank of England which can be the only reason he would be talking with MI5. This is worrying to me because it now means the net is wider than I was aware of and with more people involved we are at a more serious risk."

"The name I have at Basel is Claude Monserrat, He is a manager there responsible for maintaining the SWIFT system. But I don't know if he is friend or foe," he said. "For the moment I am assuming he is foe, because they, whoever they are, need his information in order to break the SWIFT codes," I said.

Olivier was definitely working with Martin and not against him, so I offered him help. "Someone will call you within the next few days who can help you, what is the best way to communicate?" I asked him. "I have a Satellite phone, not known to the DGSE, your friend can use this number to call me." He gave me the number, "It is secure," he said.

My assistant Jeannie will call you and you can trust her. She is excellent at breaking into surveillance systems. "Why did you not share this information with the DGSE," I asked. Because I, like you, do not trust anyone at this point and knowing that someone at the ICC is involved, I am taking no chances. My organisation is supposed to be secure and it is 99% but with this conspiracy of financial terrorism which will have such a far-reaching and devastating effect on the world economy, I have kept communications about my findings largely to myself.

Are you in communication with Michele in London? I asked him. "No but I believe it is best this way as it may, as you say, "Blow my cover," he said. And I agreed. "Ok, they will use the code, "Falcon," in the first sentence so you will know they are working with us. We shook hands and parted we both went in different directions.

I sent a message to Keith at the Hague saying "Met with O.N. in Paris meeting M. D. in London next. Talk soon. It was cryptic I know but sometimes as we say, "Less is more."

I had a lot to add now to our war board and I needed to update Jeannie on my meeting with Olivier. We were moving two steps forward and one step back, but at least we were finally getting somewhere. We had a new name at the BIS Tower, Claude Monserrat, to follow up on but whether he was a friend or foe was yet to be seen.

We could now place Olivier in the "Ally" column which was also good to know. The next stop for me now was to set up a meeting with Michele Debusse in London who, right now could be either friend or foe, but we'll know this very soon when Michele and I meet.

Our meeting would be in London as I needed to see him face to face to assess who he was and what he knew. But more than this was he with us or against us? Well, we would know very soon and I would have Dave with me in the background.

Chapter 29

Friend or Foe?

As I began to walk back across the cemetery, following my meeting with Olivier, Dave joined me." Did you get what you came for?" he asked. "Mostly," I said and we now know Olivier is working with us, not against us and we also have a name inside the BIS Tower.

"Well I had some fun too," he said, "Someone was following you both, she was waiting across from the bar and followed you here to the cemetery. She was aiming a gun at Olivier, so I took care of her," he said casually. We kept walking as I didn't want to be there any longer than necessary.

"What did she look like," I asked. "She was a blonde, slim and professional. She was using, or trying to, a suppressor on her weapon." He answered. "She would have taken you both out had I not stopped her. I took her down and I took her weapon and her phone and this," he showed me a photograph of Olivier. "It will look like an accidental death and will take some time to even find her body," he said but I didn't need the details. I thanked Dave as we were walking back to the hotel.

I called Olivier once we were back at the hotel and told him he had been made. You must move away as soon as possible my man took care of it while you and I were talking. "Thanks for this, I was always aware I risked being found and I have a place to go to." He said. We left it at that as he needed to get the hell out of dodge and fast.

Olivier was now made by this group and was, as a result, done with this. I asked, "Dave, did she make me?" "No," he said, "Only saw your back and you both left the bar separately so no, and anyway, she's out of the game now," he said.

He had taken a photo of her and showed it to me. She was in fact the same woman, Bridgett, who was with Neil at Val d'Isere. "Did she make any calls?" I asked him, "Well as a matter of fact I have her phone so we can check." He gave me her phone and I looked through it, there was a photo of Olivier but nothing of me. I breathed a sigh of relief knowing I had not been made, yet!

We left Paris and arrived back at Stansted in the early hours, Dave drove me back to Boston Manor. I thanked him for saving us both, he said simply, "Doin' my job mate that's all!" and drove off.

The following afternoon I arrived at my office to see Jeannie and Jake busy working with the SWIFT System. "Bonjour," Jeannie said as I went to join them, "Ow was gay Paree," she said in an overdone strong French accent. "Tres bon merci," I answered in my limited French smiling, I loved my Jeannie! I grabbed a coffee and sat at our big table.

"Pow wow," I said and they both came over to join me, I filled them in on Olivier and gave them the name of the only contact we had inside the BIS, but it was a start. I told Jake, that Dave earned his pay last night by taking out a female assassin who was by the way the second part of the team that killed Martin. "Good, Jeannie said holding her coffee cup up in a cheers gesture," one less to be bothered with!"

"I'm glad you had Dave with you," she said turning serious for a moment. "Me too," I said. "So back to business, when you break the SWIFT code you now have a name to follow up with Claude Monserrat, but we don't know any more about him yet,"

"We soon will, this stuff the CIA uses is amazing," she said. "OK, I'll leave you with this as I need to meet Michele Debusse who is also with the DGSE now seemingly working with MI5." He and Olivier were both working on this but separately, not sure how that worked but as we know the fewer people in contact the better.

Jeannie had a contact number and an address for Michele, in Bayswater just off Hyde Park. I texted the number using my burner phone. All I said was "Falcon" and Black Swan at 7 pm. The Black Swan was a pub I knew on Bayswater Road and would work for this meeting.

I arrived early so I could observe Michele entering the bar. I had a newspaper and sat outside with a coffee watching and waiting. He arrived on the dot at 7 pm.

As he passed me I saw a lump at the back of his jeans meaning he was carrying, but then so was I. He went to the bar and ordered a glass of wine. He looked around as I came in and I nodded to him. I did the same as with Olivier, I stood at the bar, next to him but not facing him and said quietly, "I am Falcon, meet me in Hyde Park opposite," and left the bar.

I went into the park and sat on a bench next to the horse path which went around the entire park. It was evening so no horses were trotting along the path. The bench I sat on was partially secluded with trees behind and with no clear vision of either side. Michele arrived a little later and joined me.

I didn't know where Dave was but I knew he was close by. "Oo are you and why are you here?" He opened with a strong French accent. I thought here we go again another arrogant DGSE operative. "Why don't you sit down and we can talk about why I am here," I answered. "I prefer to stand," he said as he stood next to me looking up and down the horse path to see if someone was watching us.

"OK, stand if you prefer," I said. "I'll ask you again, who are you and why are we here?" he repeated. I was wearing a wire linked to Dave who was waiting nearby. "I used the code word so you already know why I am here and if you didn't you would not have come here to meet me, a few minutes ago and second you have come packing heat" I replied. "So shall we get on with this and stop wasting each other's time?" I said. "You have two minutes to answer my question," he said.

I was too far into this to be bothered with this stupid game, so I stood up and went to leave. He pulled his gun and pointed it at me which was a stupid thing to do and said, "I wouldn't if I were you." I moved in closer looking past him as if someone was coming. I put my finger to my lips as if to tell him not to say anything and I looked as if I was going to say something.

He moved his gun menacingly and I saw his finger was on the trigger.

Then I slapped his hand hard, as I quickly twisted the gun out of his grip, more of a punch to his wrist, pointing the gun away from me. He wasn't expecting my quick movement and looked shocked as he rubbed his wrist and I now had his gun. I was deliberately hard because I was fed up with this DGSE operative's attitude.

He moved in to hit me, I sidestepped and pushed him past me. As I did I told him to look at his chest pointing my finger. He saw the tiny red dot trained on his left side and realised he was being targeted by a laser sight by someone out of view. "What is this and who are you?" he yelled becoming angry.

I sat down and told him to sit down on the bench so we could talk. He was fuming and for no reason. He reluctantly sat next to me and started to talk in French, because he was so angry. I realised he was not as professional as Olivier had been otherwise he would never have drawn his weapon, but here we were.

He sat next to me still rubbing his wrist, time to take the lead, "Look I am not here to waste yours and my time and if I intended to hurt you I would done so already," I told him. "I am here because you were seen coming out of Thames House and I decided to meet you to ask you what a French DGSE operative was doing meeting our MI5."

"That has nothing to do with you!" he said, "Well, as a matter of fact, it very much does and here's why. We are investigating a situation with others of your DGSE in France (I didn't say Paris in case it gave Olivier away) who are helping us to stop a catastrophe of global proportions. Now you either work with us or we cut you out of this operation and when it's over you can discuss your future with your Director General," I told him.

"And, since we are having this "Friendly" talk, let me remind you of your sworn oath to your country," I told him. You swore an oath to bring reliable intelligence to your government in order to shed light on its actions. You also swore to detect and block, threats coming from outside the national territory, the threats targeting France and French nationals. You also swore to promote and protect national interests and security levels.

"Now, having said this, which part of your oath do you not agree with?" I asked him, because from where I'm sitting each part of your oath relates to why we here at great risk to both myself and yourself, by the way, representing a secret organisation formed for the sole purpose of breaking an imminent act of global terrorism. "Now are your job and my job both aimed at ultimately keeping the world safe?" I asked him and I let my words sink in.

He thought for a while, weighing the pros and cons of my short speech, before answering me. "Of course they are but the reason I am still alive is because I'm extremely careful," he said. "Aren't we all, but I want to know what you were doing at Thames House," I asked again.

"Then why don't you ask them that, after all, you're British and it is your organisation, not mine!" He said. "The reason I will not do that is because there is a leak and two excellent people have already been killed and until we can find this leak, the fewer people who know about what we are dealing with the better. But you know what I'm fucking done with you. I've asked you three times why you were there and three times you have avoided answering me," I said angrily.

"So, with that said, you are on your own and we will not be needing your help or using you as part of our team, I wish you good luck," I said and got up to leave. "Wait a minute," he said, but just then I heard a pfft and Michele dropped to the ground. I immediately ducked down to see he had been shot in the middle of his forehead and was dead instantly. I was covered in blood splatter as he was hit.

He was facing me when it happened so I knew the shot was from behind me. I drew my weapon and ducked behind the bench. I quickly went through his pockets and retrieved his phone and wallet so we could look at it later. I felt bad for Michele but why was he being so difficult?

Dave was somewhere but I didn't know where. Then he came out from behind the trees and came straight over to me. "I got him but not before he got a shot off. I got his phone and his wallet the gun I left so he is linked to Michele's death. My shot went right through his killer and into a tree. I dug the bullet out he said showing me his 45 magnum.

His gun was a people stopper and the killer was shot through the heart, compliments of my new bodyguard, Dave!" "The leak came from his side, not ours," I told Dave, "There's always a chance of that and no matter how many precautions we take we can never know who the enemy is talking to," Dave replied. "I don't know why he was so pissed off, right from the get-go and pulled a fucking gun on me with no reason!" I answered.

It could be that he suspected he was being followed and wanted to show whoever it was that he was with their organisation not against them. That's the only explanation I can come up with as to why, for no reason, he would pull a gun on me. "Well, it doesn't matter now he's brown bread (dead)," I said. "I had him covered and was ready but his killer caught me off guard," Dave said. It's possible he already blew your meeting and we'll soon know when we go through his phone.

We left Hyde Park quickly, leaving two bodies there and Dave gave me the killer's credentials. I would take them into the office where we could study them and match up the precise times and locations of his calls and any texts.

I felt bad for Michele as I believed he was deliberately being difficult to offset his double agent status. But we had to meet and that is always a risk that goes with the job. I believed now that Michele was indeed a double agent working with us and had probably infiltrated this terrorist organisation. He was deserving of a star, if one exists, for the French DGSE who he worked for.

This killer was not the same one that took Martin out so they had more than one, which didn't surprise me. But we were both aware that our enemy was more devious and far more deadly than we knew. Well, they were up against me, Maximillion Moore and my small but highly effective team and we would beat them no matter what!

Chapter 30

Phones and Photos

The following day I went to the office, I had called Jeannie on my way home the previous night and gave her a quick update. When I arrived they had some good news about the SWIFT codes. Jeannie was bursting to tell me. "We're getting closer now to breaking in and we've found some source codes that will help us," she said.

"How long do you think?" I asked her, she told me it was, at this stage, difficult to say. Jake then entered the conversation and said, "Finding their source codes has been extremely difficult but now we can assess the code writing style, of whoever wrote their OS (operating system) we can move faster but this will still be one step at a time so as not to allow them to know their system is being hacked," he told me.

"Can you be certain you won't be caught?" I asked them. "There is always a chance of that and if it happens we will have to work very fast, but until that time which we hope will never happen, we can keep moving forward," Jake said. "The SWIFT system has many dead ends and lock codes which are what is slowing us down, but it is to be expected since the world banks rely on its security measures which they would have had to sell to these world banks if they wanted them all to hook onto it." He told me.

Jeannie added, "Every day their codes are changed and this is an automatic event. Once we can see how that system works our algorithms can predict the next day's codes. That is our next step after we have successfully hacked into their system," she said.

"Sounds like a plan I said keep going. As for my meeting with Michele Debusse, he is now no longer a factor," I told them both.

"What happened," Jeannie asked. "He was shot, right next to me," and I tapped my forehead showing where he was hit. "What the fuck!" Jeannie said. I told them how and where it happened and added, "Michele was being very difficult and refused to answer a simple question I asked three times as to why he was at Thames House. He refused to answer and drew his weapon on me. It was then that he was shot dead. Dave took the assassin out within seconds but not soon enough to save Michele," I said.

"So with that said, I believe the sole reason he drew on me was to show whoever it was that had him in his sights, that he was one of them and not working with us. He also had a wire so obviously they were listening in. They killed him to stop him talking which tells us whoever it was who met him at Thames House, is probably not a friend," I said.

I placed their cards and phones on the table. "We need to go through these two phones and get whatever is on them as soon as possible without them being traced. They are off now and I removed the batteries while we were still in Hyde Park so their lead stopped there."

Jeannie and Jake both took the phones and plugged them into Jeannie's software which would stop these phones from being tracked. We started to look through the images on Michele's phone to see his contacts and any photos he had.

It was no surprise he had a photo of Richard Whitehead and looking at the date it was taken a year ago. He also had photos that we didn't recognise but Jeannie started the facial recognition program that Isabelle Rodriguez had set up so their account name, for using the program was hidden from anyone in the police or other agencies from tracking us.

Jeannie sent Isabelle a text to let her know she was using the facial recognition system just in case something had changed. That was the system they both set up as a safety precaution before Jeannie or Jake went onto the system.

I was looking at their credit cards and the names they used. The killer's name on his card was Chad Denton. Regardless of the real name, we could now check where he had been who he planned to meet and hopefully any air tickets and hotel reservations he had made. From that, I could see who he was meeting at Thames House.

Jeannie and Jake were running through the photos on Michele's phone uploading them onto the facial recognition system while I was looking through the killer's phone after Jeannie had broken the code. She had written a code-breaking program which ran through a sequence of numbers and letters mixed with predictive wording that could guess names and dates very quickly.

She added a piece to her program which could accommodate most languages which helped to speed things up. We would be checking his encryption code too as many people including agents use familiar names and dates.

I knew we would have a lot of data to go through now with contacts, photos meetings and all the stuff one usually puts on their phone. Michele's phone did have an encryption system on it but keeping it offline meant we could take a good look through everything on it.

I put the news on to see what, if anything, had been said about the two bodies that may have been found in Hyde Park. But so far there was nothing at all. I let it run all day switching from BBC to Sky News to ITV News but nothing was showing yet. If after a day still nothing we would know that both bodies had either been taken by our own Met or perhaps MI5, or whoever it was it was kept a secret.

I was interested to know who had removed the bodies so I called Noz and arranged to meet him at The Village Wine Bar at 6.30 pm later that day. To see if it was a MET operation. That would eliminate one of three possibilities. The other two were either enemies of ours or maybe MI5. I asked Jeannie to go to any local street CCTV cameras and look from an hour before the time Michele met me, through all night looking for a van or car parked, on Bayswater Road, near where we met.

I had taken several photos of Michele before he was killed, which would allow Jeannie to re-trace his movements before he met me at the Black Swan pub, I also took a photo of his assassin.

We were expecting names places and other contact details we didn't yet know the group of terrorists may have connections with. So killing both Michele and his killer gave us a goldmine of info we could follow up on. At least, that was what we hoped to find.

We had faces we had no idea who they were and names in both Michele's and his killer's phones to follow up with. Among the phone numbers was the number for the ICC but it was a switchboard number, not a direct line. But this alone proved this terrorist group were in contact with the ICC. There were also calls made to Thames house from Michele's phone and the number called several times proved to be the direct line to Roger Brightly so the loop was closed now with his name linked to Michele's.

Maybe this Roger Brightly didn't know Michele had been killed yet and I was thinking of contacting him but, at this stage of our game, we needed to know more about him before I broke cover on this. But what we could do was monitor his phone, now we had the number, to see what other phones made contact with him from our list of numbers on Michele's phone.

Jeannie entered the numbers into our database which meant when one of them made a call we would be notified and the connection monitored. We couldn't listen in, without a warrant, but we could establish what number called another number in our database and for what we were up against that was enough for now.

Jake called me over to see what was on our killer's phone. There were not a lot of calls made but several photos which we could check up on the dates they were sent. We would enter these photos into the facial recognition system to see who they were and to learn if they were alive or dead. There were 11 photos in all and I was hoping against hope this was not a gallery of people this assassin had killed.

We started a separate board for the names and photos on both Michele's and his killer's phones. We could now build up a contact list for both of them. Later that day Dave came in and told us he had looked into the CCTV cameras from their operations room and saw him following Michele.

He told us that the killer must have tracked, or listened in to Michele's phone because he was in the park ahead of Michele entering. What was interesting was a call Michele made to Thames House just before he joined me in Hyde Park. We would find out whose phone that was very soon. I realised we needed more help from Bill's group as there was too much information for the three of us to handle.

I called Bill to bring him up to date and to let him know what happened in Hyde Park. I asked him if he could assist us with some help to establish who Michele's and his Killer's phones were connected with. "I'm concerned with not knowing any timeline and time may be running out." I also told him about my thoughts of this going down timed to occur with an international meeting, perhaps an IMF meeting or World Economic Forum, something the world would be watching when they would announce their intent.

"Dave is making a list of international meetings including the UN and NATO, WEF and IMF with dates for each as I think it will be one of those meetings when this goes down," I told Bill. "We will need to upload the names and faces retrieved from the two phones and split them up between us all in order to speed the recognition along," I said.

"Maybe I didn't make myself clear and I apologise if I did not, but my team is now your team. They now report to you so please use them as you see fit. They are each paid to safeguard our values and to prevent acts of terrorism. But please keep me informed of your progress and if need be I can and will help you with this. I had to let my "Team" know what help I needed which was to look at the names and faces we now had to see if any of them recognised any of these people Jeannie and Jake were uncovering from the two phones."

I sent a text with a photo taken from our assassin's phone to each of the team and asked them to follow up and check on each of these people who were shown and probably killed. We needed to know what the link was with each image.

I hadn't worked with a team since I was a cop in the MET and this was new to me but because of the magnitude of what this case was all about I needed all the help I could get. At some point I would have to bring in the police but to what? Right now, all we had were photos, names and a future act of terrorism but we really didn't have enough details yet.

But the real issue was that so far this group had been eliminating anyone who got in their way or who was a risk, as in the case with Michele Debusse. So, I was not about to go outside of this group that Bill had put together and risk all our lives.

I knew our Met cops were good otherwise I wouldn't have given them so much of my life, but I also knew they would have to go to Interpol and once that happened this left our control and we would be at risk. My decision, my choice, was to keep this under wraps until the time was right and even then, this was a group of world bankers having vast sums at their disposal so things they could do were boundless.

Nope, my decision was about keeping these men and women in my team safe so they could work undercover for the time it took in order to break this conspiracy. As for letting others in, I would cross that bridge when I got to it.

Chapter 31

The Hardest Job

I called each member of my new team one by one to explain what we now had and to tell them where the photos came from. I could have done a video call to all but I wanted to gauge each of their reactions and to give them a chance to ask questions.

I told them we didn't have time to plod through each photo and to ask each of them to be very careful not to be discovered while checking each name. I needed their help in order to piece this puzzle together faster than just Jeannie and me working on them.

One name I wanted to know more about was Roger Brightly, whose name was in Martin's book as a government official but other than that we knew nothing more. Was he friend or foe, how could I find out?

I asked Jeannie to find Roger Brightly's name in Martin's book and see what was said about that name while Jake continued the codebreaking of the Aramaic code. But, after several hours of research, she found nothing. He did not appear in any employee list for any government office, yet we believed Martin's research and if he said Roger Brightly was a government official we needed to find out who he was.

In addition, I needed to know who Charlene Willoughby was. All Martin said about her was her name and nothing more. My intuition told me she was a friend so based on that plus the fact that we knew we may be running out of time, I decided to go to Gloucester to meet with her.

I had seen her mansion, in Bourton-on-the-water, looking through Google Maps and since it was under a two-hour drive I would go there tomorrow morning to see what I could find out. Her name did not appear with any explanation, only as a woman of seventy years old, retired, but no work listed.

I left Boston Manor at 8 am and headed for the A40 which would take me all the way to Gloucester and since I was going against the usual rush hour traffic I had an easy journey. I went around Oxford through Witney then took a right at Northleach and on into Bourton-on-the-Water.

My journey reminded me of the Black and White coach ride to my boarding school in Cheltenham. That always took four hours, with a stop-off at an old coaching inn at Northleach. But with the roads now it was under 2 hours.

I found her mansion set back from the A429 before I got to Upper Slaughter. How on earth did "Olde England" come up with these names of towns? She too had a large iron gate with a talk box and camera above.

"Can I help you?" an upper-class voice asked me. "Yes I'm here on behalf of my friend Martin Ade," I announced. "Martin?" She said, "Yes," I answered, "May we talk?" "Of course, she said please come up to the house." House? I thought, who calls a fucking castle a house, I asked myself as I drove around a very large lake. I suppose that lake is a paddling pool to her, I mumbled, as I drove up her graveled driveway.

She greeted me at the door, a huge solid oak job that no police battering ram could ever make a dent in. "Please come in?" She was probably a slim, attractive woman in her younger days, I thought as we went into her kitchen, which had oak beams on the ceiling and a large solid pine table in the middle.

There was an Aga cooking range off to one side and on another side of her large kitchen was a shiny espresso machine which was not your home version but a full professional café version with gauges and levers which had already made a coffee which smelled irresistible.

"Are you a morning coffee or a tea person?" she asked me. I would love a coffee, thank you" I answered. She went over and made me a cappuccino which was perfect. We both sat at her large table and she asked, "What brings you here about Martin?" she asked.

"I'm afraid I have some bad news to tell you and I wanted to come here to tell you personally, Martin was killed a few weeks ago while skiing on the slopes at Val d'Isere," I told her. She remained still and said, "Skiing? You know he was the best in the world?"

"Yes I know this and now I am so sorry to have to tell you he did not have an accident, he was killed deliberately," There was no easy way to pass on bad news like this.

"I wondered why he hadn't called me in a few weeks, he was usually very good at keeping in touch," she said, as she brought a handkerchief up to her face holding back tears. I reached out and placed my hand on hers to offer support at this difficult news. I had done this many times but every time I was talking about someone's loved one or a friend, it was always the most difficult news to break.

I'm so sorry to be a stranger and to have to give you this news, but there are things that I cannot tell you yet. But what I can tell you is that Martin was a hero and he died in the course of his work which I have to tell you was of national, if not global, importance and I am not a person to exaggerate something like this. "I understand that you and he were close," I said.

"Yes he was my sister's son, my nephew and she sadly passed away of cancer when Martin was just five years old. His father re married to Marilyn but at that time Marilyn was working in her job that took her away for long periods of time. So I took it upon myself to bring Martin up as my own though I was never married. He was a lovely boy always inquisitive and from the first time I took him skiing, to Val d'Isere he loved it, we both did," she said.

"I expect you are in the same line of work that Martin was working with, he was always travelling to far-off places," she said. He worked with the police for several years and loved it, "Me and my mates are keeping

you safe Aunty," he used to say proudly. "Then one day he came to see me telling me he was attached to the International Criminal Court and would be moving to The Hague. I was so proud of him. He was in love with a beautiful girl, Hillary, she used to come here to see me when he was away. I did hope they would one day be married, but now that can never be," she said. I let her speak knowing how difficult this was. Then she asked me about what happened.

"What I can tell you is that his death was instant and it was made to look like an accident while he was coming down one of their black slopes, "Off-Piste," I told her. He was at full speed when the incident happened. My assistant and I realised it was no accident, for various reasons which I cannot tell you at this moment, so we began looking into it.

I am a private investigator and I was also formerly with the Metropolitan Police. So what we realised was that his death did not make any sense. Did he ever mention the name Richard Whitehead?" I asked. "Not that I can recall," she said.

"Did he leave any notebooks or ever talk about his work?" I asked. "No, but he did say that one day he would save the world," and she began to cry. "Well as to that I can tell you what he uncovered, is exactly that but I can't tell you more right now."

"I would like his remains brought back here so I can give my darling nephew a proper burial," she said. "I will see what I can do," I said thinking I had not even thought of his burial.

"I have to ask you to please do not mention what I have told you to anyone and If Hillary gets in contact tell her I came to see you but I couldn't say more. This is for yours and Hillary's safety and I promise when this is finished I will come to see you both to tell you what happened and what he was working on, but I can say is he was onto something very big."

There was little more I could say to her so I said I would keep her informed with more details as soon as I could. I left and headed back to London. I arrived around 4 pm and called Jannie and Jake to see how they were doing. "We'll have something to show you when you get in. I told her about having to deliver the bad news to his aunt and I also told her what Martin had said about one day he would save the world." "Well, at least that part is true and we will pick up where Martin left off," she said. I finished the call thinking about the impending terrorism.

I arranged to meet with Noz later and asked him how we got a fallen hero back to his aunt to effect his burial. He agreed to send me the details and help set it up for as he said, "An old mate." I needed a drink after having to deliver the bad news to his aunt and we discussed how many times we had to do this. Noz won, as he had done it many, many, times whereas I had only had to do this maybe ten or eleven times. I thanked him for putting Jeannie in touch with Isabelle Rodriguez and how she had helped keep our search off the radar.

Any thanks with Noz usually involved a double (gentleman's measure) of a single malt whiskey, preferably Glenmorangie. Although as I pointed out the old distillery was now owned by Louis Vuitton of all people and Moët Hennessy so maybe the location was Scottish but the owners were French. That always pissed him off but still the Scotch was still as good!

We were sitting in the garden at The Fox Inn, a busy little pub in the old part of Hanwell. It was located at the bottom of a cull de sac, in Hanwell close to the canal which was just on the other side of the cull de sac.

A couple of Gunnesses for me did the trick and I left three hours later in a far better mood than when I arrived. Time to move on and get to the bottom of this puzzle I thought.

I was thankful that Noz didn't feel the need to quiz me on the case and was ok with the parts I told him. But also when we met I wanted to know what he was up to, so I asked him how things were for him.

"Well as a matter of fact I'm a pop star!" he said. "What does that mean," I asked him. "Well, the Met need a poster boy to bring in more recruits, but not white ones. They asked me to be their poster boy to help them reach black and brown recruits. They told me they need to reflect the general population of London which now has all nationalities

not just white," he told me. "So what do you have to do," I asked. "I'm being photographed all over London wearing my old uniform, even though I'm a detective now. By the way, I was a skinny dude back then so they had to let out my trousers to fit me. But they are pushing the "First black policeman in London's Metropolitan Police" story and honestly, after all the crap I went through in my early days things are different now," he told me.

"I've appeared on the underground stations, on posters, on those advertising posters inside the tube trains and all over the place," he added. I was impressed since Noz was never a limelight kind of bloke. He preferred to do his job and be left alone doing what he loved, nicking villains!

"So how can you do your job now your face is plastered all over London?" I asked him. "Well that's the thing, people love it and I get stopped in the street by people who love the photos. But it also makes it a little difficult when I have to do my job and actually nick someone," he said.

So my old mate was now a model! A pop star! I had to chuckle at this news. I raised my glass, "Here's to you mate, you never cease to amaze me!" We left later and I headed home, still smiling at how Nozzer, the cozzer, the high-flying rozzer had now made the big time!

Chapter 32

Casting a Wider Net!

The following day I sat with Jeannie and Jake, they had finally broken the code and were going through Martin's detailed account of what he had been working on. It was far bigger than we understood from his video.

He found links to government officials in China, Switzerland and Russia who were all to some extent part of this massive conspiracy and he alluded to the fact there may be more. His knowledge was extensive, no wonder he made it so difficult to break the code.

But what was even more interesting was the fact that the names he had were not the leaders of these countries, but the finance ministers only. Were these ministers in fact staging a Coup or were they passing on the information up to the top? We would I was sure find out later.

The work that Jeannie and Jake had done was excellent and now we were finally getting closer to uncovering the extent of this cyber terrorism. There were still no details of when or where but that was now our job to find out when it would begin.

"Have you deciphered all that was in Martin's notes?" I asked them both. "All but one small part which is giving us problems," Jake answered. "Show me," I said, not that I could help but sometimes a new pair of eyes helps. It was one paragraph. This part of the code looked different from the rest. I told them he must have done that on purpose so we must find out what it was.

I asked them both if we had any names in the BIS, anything at all because we need a starting point there that we can follow up on. "We went through their list of names without knowing what kind of name we were looking at," Jeannie said. "OK," I said, "Time to change focus and start looking into these names and stop working with the code for now. One or more of these names is part of this and we don't know who or, what role, or anything else yet."

"These are our priorities right now. Is this Sheri Dannetag part of the conspiracy or not? Jeannie and you Jake is there a way we can set a trap to find out if she is a leaker of someone to trust? Here are the facts, she must have known Martin was going on a skiing trip as he would have cleared it with admin. So, look for his number in association with hers.

Also, find out if she has another means of communicating or if she was talking with any of the names we now have. Look for locations of calls as well as the numbers. A long shot I know but if we can triangulate on any cell phone towers we may find out whose side she's on." We were clutching at straws and we didn't know how much time we had before this thing was to be triggered.

Dave came into the office with a list of major upcoming events with the UN, the IMF (International Monetary Fund), the WEF (World Economic Forum) and the next NATO summit. He put the dates on our board. Which one of these do we think will be the trigger? At this moment it could be any of these events, but my money is on either the WEF or the IMF meeting, but we couldn't be sure. So how long do we have before the first of these occurs?

We stood back and looked at these events, the first of these which was in just two months' time, was the U.N. General Assembly conference taking place in September in New York. How many members are in the WEF? I asked. Dave answered, "There are twenty-four members of the executive board." "OK let's see if any of those names are linked to our list," I said. "We need help from the team, we have to split these names up and get the team to help. Jeannie, how many names do we have?" "Twenty in all," she answered.

"OK, can you and Jake split these names up and send them to the others? I'm setting a conference call with them all in one hour to fill them in on what to look for.

We need to give them the names we now have but tell each to focus on three names only. You and Jake set those names in motion but you two take the remainder." I told Jake and Jeannie. Dave, can you work with these two to speed things up?

We set the conference call up on Jeannie's VPN and each of the team had untraceable numbers as well. When all of the team were online I explained we were up against a fast-approaching deadline and told them each would be given three names to focus on to see if they were in contact with any of the others or in particular with any numbers located in the BIS Tower, or with any number in Basel, Switzerland. We'll give you the area codes.

Each of the team was now involved and each was, according to Bill, who handpicked them all, excellent at this type of work. Well, we'll see just how good my team really was and now was the time for them to demonstrate their abilities.

I looked at the dates on the board in September for the next IMF meeting in New York and the World Economic Forum which will take place in Davos, Switzerland, from the 15th to the 19th of January. My guess would be the WEF because it's in Davos Switzerland the same country that the BIS Tower is located and is only a two-and-a-half-hour drive between the two locations. Also, because it was a financial summit which would make their plan an ironic event which would not be lost on the financial world stage they wanted to control.

With the entire team now involved I could do nothing but wait to see who came up with what. In the meantime, Jeannie was looking into Ms. Dannetag in central comms at the ICC.

It was later that day when Jeannie called me over to show me what she found. It was a call made from an unknown number from The Hague to a number in Basel, Switzerland. "Bingo we've got a link," I said. "Can you monitor both phones to see if they change locations where we can perhaps put a face to whoever made and returned that call," I asked.

"We don't have time to watch both but they are both mobile numbers so what I can do is set them so when either phone changes location makes another contact or is using a different cell phone tower we will be notified," she said. "Ok good enough" I replied.

Just that piece of news confirmed that we were on the right track, I wasn't certain of this before but now it was confirmed. I went over to speak to Dave about the next WEF meeting in Davos. "Do you think this will go down at Davos or somewhere else, maybe close by?" I asked him. "Dunno what to tell you mate, how will we know?" he asked.

"I was thinking about that and if they are using a different location other than wherever the meeting is in Davos they will need some pretty advanced communication equipment to hack into the SWIFT system while it is online and until we know how many people are involved we can't guess the location. But in the meantime can you give this some thought and let me know what you come up with?" I asked him.

Later that day we had another ping from the phone located within the ICC, "Whoever it is, is now on the move!" Jeannie told me. So I went over to see the movement on a map. Normally we wouldn't bother monitoring a connection like this but the fact it originated from within the ICC to one of the contacts Martin had flagged meant we had to.

The phone was moving along a main road, but no calls were made at that moment. Then the phone stopped moving and on checking the location it turned out to be a garage, "Perfect," I thought. Jeannie was already on it, checking the location and moving to street-view so we now had the possibility to see the car and the driver on that garage's CCTV cameras. But we couldn't do that from our office, far too risky.

Chapter 33

A Name and a Face

I told the team we needed eyes on the garage CCTV asap, I said, as Dave was already heading out of the office to use Bill's plane to get to The Netherlands as soon as possible and to see if he could get to the CCTV footage in the garage. This was the second big break we now had and I hoped we may be able to see who it was from within the ICC that was in contact with the BIS Tower.

While Dave was on the way to Stansted airport to pick up Bill's plane I called him to tell him Jeannie would be keeping tabs on the mobile number he was looking for and when he touched down in the Netherlands we would pick up the contact and pass the live feed over to him to keep him posted. "What do you want me to do when I find him or her," he asked. "For the moment, just watch, take photos and send them back to us here. Then we can establish who it is. We need you there, Dave, for eyes on the ICC and to run local ops there anyway," I told him. "Understood boss, I'll see what I can find here," he said and I knew he could work well alone.

If Bill had placed his trust in Dave as his own bodyguard and being ex SAS he would have been well trained to operate alone and that was good enough for me. Dave would be back in contact in just a couple of hours when he landed and would provide more intel on the ICC.

At this stage, I preferred not to involve Keith in our local ops at The Hague just in case he was compromised and anyway, we didn't know yet if Sheri Dannetag was friend or foe and until we do, communications with Keith need to be strictly limited to secure burst texts only. We had a lot of irons in the fire right now and I was happy I had a team to help us.

It wouldn't be long before the other members would, I hoped, get some hits on the names we sent them. In all other cases I worked on I worked only with Jeannie but as we uncovered more about this case I realised we needed more help especially if there was a showdown with whoever was behind this.

Later that afternoon I began to get calls from the team, the first was from Mariah, our bad-ass ex-special forces girl who had a hit on one of the faces. "This number, in Paris she said has a link with a here in Basel," she said. She was the one who told me she had a contact in Basel so I asked her if she spoke any languages other than English. "I speak French and Spanish," she said, "Oh and some Farsi, from my prior deployments, in Iraq, Afghanistan and a few other places" she said. Mariah was a sniper she held military medals for her accuracy up to 2,000 meters.

"OK, Mariah, we need you in Switzerland to follow up with events there and to see what you can find out when Dave sends you the details of the phone and user he is following up on at The Hague." "Ok boss I'm on my way," she said. I thought, "Boss?" really? I'm not used to being called that, and I have to say, it had a certain ring to it that I could get used to!

We had three of the bases covered; London, The Hague and now Basel, so we had people in place to give feedback intel to us as we learned more. I should include Paris with Olivier but his section was not critical at the moment. We had covered a lot of ground but until we knew who was running the show and when this was going down, to me, it was all just background information.

It was now 6 pm in London, and 7 pm in The Hague when Dave called in. He touched down at 5 pm and went straight to the garage to get into the CCTV footage.

He took the name of the security system, shown on one of the cameras and told the garage manager he was from the corporate security system headquarters. and needed to ensure the CCTV system was working properly. Because one of the systems they had installed in another location had failed through bad maintenance.

They showed him the unit which was cloud-based so he was able to send back the CCTV protocols to allow Jeannie and Jake to go through the footage at the time the car and cell phone were there.

He went on to the next location following the movement of the mobile phone and was within sight of the phone's current location. "Looks like whoever the user is, is now at home. I'm sending you the address, it's in a town called Leiden a few clicks north of the Hague and the N44 route was the fastest route here." He messaged me letting me know he had eyes on the car and was waiting out of sight for the driver to emerge from the house.

Like everything we were up to it was a lot of waiting and not much action at the moment but things were falling into place. The number plate was a diplomatic plate belonging to the Swiss Embassy, so no luck finding the owner yet. This complicated things if she was a legitimate embassy employee assigned to the ICC.

A few moments later the driver came out of the house so Dave sent a photo of the woman, it was not Sheri Dannetag but we needed her name so we loaded her image onto the recognition software linked to Interpol's database and waited. "Fuck! back to square one." But we now had eyes on location at the ICC and no one knew we had an asset there. Dave didn't need instructions he knew what to do.

Back at the office names and links began coming through from the team. Jeannie was busy linking names to locations. "Bloody hell," I thought. "Martin had done an amazing job working this case and with no help!"

Two of the names had not shown up yet but we had quite a lot to work with now. Jeannie used red lines where the names linked to either military intelligence or Basel and there were three of these red lines. She used blue where the name was linked elsewhere. We would focus our time and energy on those three red lines, monitoring call traffic for the time being, the others would have to wait for now.

I decided to pay Roger Brightly a visit, we now had a photo so I knew what he looked like and maybe he didn't know Michele was dead, after all, when Dave took him out, no one else knew. The body had been removed and we didn't know by whom yet, but one thing for sure whoever removed his body did it in secret. There was nothing in the news about two dead bodies found in Hyde Park.

We now had Brightly's phone number from Martin's notebook. What would I say? I had no idea but since we had his phone we could track his movements. We had him pinged and were watching where he was going. He was at Thames House so we knew he was with 5 so what was the link with Michele?

It was around 12.30 pm when I saw, from watching his phone, he was heading and judging from the slow speed of his movements he made his way to the Embankment and was walking along it. I saw his movements on my phone then left the office and caught a cab to the Embankment. It didn't take me long to see him standing by the wall, looking out at the river.

I sat on a bench with a newspaper watching him for a while then a woman joined him. She was attractive, in her late thirties slim and dressed in a blue anorak, skirt and boots. Was this just an affair or what? I took several photos of them both then I started videoing them. They were pretending not to talk to each other which was a little lame as there was no one else near them making it clear they were, at that point, obviously both together. Both were standing a few feet apart facing the river, talking.

Their conversation grew heated and I had my phone mic on while videoing them both from a distance of around 30 yards. I was faced slightly the other way but using my phone, hidden from view by my newspaper, to video them both. There were people walking by as there always is on the Embankment. I hoped maybe Jeannie or Jake could enhance the video and sound recording later.

The two of them were now animated in their conversation seemingly having an argument but both were still facing the river. After around fifteen minutes she left him and I decided to follow her. We had her phone number because she had called Brightly's phone, probably to set up the meeting. Jeannie had sent me the link to her phone so I could track her. She left with him still standing by the river, he then made a call but I would now follow the woman from a distance so as not to blow my cover. She then made a call, while she was hurrying along which we would be able to track, to see what number She called. I was thinking, "Ya gotta love technology, especially in my line of work!" It made me smile.

After her call, she started walking faster which made it difficult for me to keep her in sight without being seen. But with the phone app, I could see her movements so it didn't matter too much.

A van pulled up alongside her and she got in. I hailed a cab and asked him to follow the van, I had to smile at this since it was like almost every criminal film where someone says, "Follow that car!" Well, I just said it.

They were headed back into the city, but because of the heavy London traffic, following them was difficult. I soon lost them so I asked the driver to keep driving in case we could see the van again but after ten minutes or so, the traffic was so bad I gave up looking and asked my cabbie to drop me off at Leicester Square. He probably thought I was following my wife or girlfriend but whatever.

As soon as I arrived back at the office, I gave Jeannie my phone to download my photos and video and we started watching Brightly and the women talking. While we were watching the video, Jeannie ran the facial recognition to see if the woman's face showed up there.

We enhanced the sound but only some of the words were audible. I was writing those words down but it was difficult to hear all that was said. The woman had an accent but it was indiscernible to us. We listened to the recording several times adding several missing words to their dialogue but it was still bitty.

I wrote their conversation on another whiteboard with missing words shown as a series of dashes. Standing back, to see what was said, it was obvious they were discussing Michele as his name came up several times. My guess was that she was working for the DGSE and that would account for her accent which was probably French. Other words we pieced together were "Meeting with you," and," You blew it not us,"

So the DGSE now knew that Michele was missing following a meeting. Soon after his meeting with Brightly. The good news was she had no idea Michele was meeting me, otherwise either the name, The Black Swan or Hyde Park would have come up. So the mystery deepens, who removed the bodies?

We now added the French woman's face to our board with a red line attaching her with Brightly and Thames House. But we still didn't know if either of them was friend or foe. For all this, we only added more confusion to our case. I told Jeannie and Jake this was a red herring and we had to get back on track.

With Dave and Mariah both deployed one now located at the ICC and the other in Basel, we at least had "Eyes on" in both locations. Both of them had the phone numbers tagged so they also could follow up if any calls were made using the numbers Martin had been killed to give us.

I called both of them for an update, Dave had nothing yet but Mariah had contacted her friend, who was a banker and worked at the BIS Tower. She told me she was playing it down and told him the reason she was there was on a vacation touring Switzerland. The two of them went way back to their time as students at the LSE (London School of Economics) before she joined the military.

They were both independent operators and although I didn't need to keep tabs on them we didn't know how much time we had before this would go down.

Chapter 34

Regroup

We were missing something but I couldn't figure out what it was yet. It seemed we were spinning our wheels getting somewhere but nowhere close to where I knew we should be. Thinking back, so much had happened since Martin's death which was just one month back. I looked again at our board and called a Pow wow. The three of us sat at the big table. I worked my best with a hot and strong black coffee, preferably a double shot espresso, which I now had in front of me it helped me to think.

"We're missing something here," I said to them both, "We're all working at uncovering phone numbers and connecting names and faces but these are getting us nowhere. What we need to be focused on are just four things; who is the leaker at the ICC, who is running this financial terrorism, from where and when is this going down?" They both nodded but had nothing to add at this point.

"We're spinning our wheels until we can get a definitive lead on any one of these four things and what we have done so far is building up our knowledge base adding a distraction from our mission. We have to focus on these four things. The critical part now is to find out who is running this entire program and then to track their movements and contacts. Mariah in Switzerland is monitoring the BIS Tower traffic and is closest so how can we help her?"

"We should consider Who could possibly benefit from this," I said out loud, "It's not the people at the ICC nor is it the staff at the BIS Tower. The only people who would benefit from bringing down and taking over control of the entire world banking system could be the mega-rich banking families who own the banks that were controlled at the BIS Tower, as long as they remained as the post-SWIFT's collapse new banking oligarchs.

The banking families within this global banking cartel are Goldman Sachs, the Rockefellers, Lehman's and Kuhn Loeb's of New York. The main four are, the Rothschilds of Paris and London, the Warburg's of Hamburg; the Lazard's of Paris and the Israel Moses Seifs of Rome. These came to be known as "The Four Horsemen of Banking." They include Bank of America, JP Morgan Chase, Citigroup and Wells Fargo.

These banking families compare to the Four Horsemen of the Oil industry, Exxon Mobil, Royal Dutch/Shell, BP and Chevron Texaco, who work in tandem with Deutsche Bank, BNP, Barclays and other European "Old money" behemoths.

But, having said this, would any of these mega-banking families be interested in stopping their gravy train of interest payments for loans made, which are repaid by the taxation of working people? They already control the entire banking and money transfer system, so I very much doubt it, because they already have all the control they need, albeit with a legitimate board and with globally accepted checks and balances.

So it must be an outsider or an operation that would benefit from controlling the world's finances, someone who does not have that control presently. To set this up and to have a web of operators that includes London, The Hague, Switzerland and Hong Kong, to be able to get into the BIS system must be a hacker perhaps sponsored by a super-power or person that has been affected by sanctions.

We listed those countries that had been affected by financial sanctions these were the usual players, Iran, Iraq, North Korea, Russia and even South Africa during Apartheid. However, South Africa's sanctions were lifted after the inauguration of Nelson Mandela as president of South Africa in 1994.

"Would any of these countries risk world war, over this, which was a dead certainty? I very much doubt it, because the entire world would be affected and would be after their blood. So, I think we are looking for a faction, a small group, or even a single person, with nothing to lose but who has the resources of a global power or a mega-rich oligarch.

Jake was first to respond, "I agree with your thinking, there is far too much at stake for a country to do this and as for these financial leaders, within the IMF, WEF, the BIS or others, they already have pretty much all the control they need and are all extremely well paid.

So, we are looking for an independent person or terrorist operation who has an axe to grind with banking or finance," he said. "Could it be someone who was fired from a prominent position within these financial groups, the BIS or from within a world bank?" He said.

"Ok, let's switch our focus on the news media and look for someone high-profile who fits this description," I told them. "How far back do you think?" Jeannie asked. "Let's go back five years and start from there," I told them as they both went back to work looking through all the news media networks. "But time is running out so let's do more than just scan the media, we are looking at someone high profile, vocal about being fired and with high-powered connections," I added.

I thought we were on the right track now but something was still bothering me and I couldn't put my finger on what it was, but I knew it would keep bugging me until I figured it out. I had a method that usually worked when this happened. I sat at my desk and doodled as I was mentally backtracking to figure out what was bothering me. It was late afternoon and I could do with a cold Guinness right about now but a double espresso would have to do. I was backtracking to find what it was that was bothering me.

Was it the leak at the ICC? Was it the spider in the web at the BIS Tower? I couldn't place what was at the back of my mind as I sat thinking. No, it wasn't those things although we still hadn't solved these things yet. It was a nagging thought at the back of my mind.

I went over to see how Jake and Jeannie were doing, scrolling through old newspaper headlines online and looking through various other media. They had a tough job to do but I was certain we were on the right track now. I went over to our war board and added the words, "Financial Leader, Bank President, Financial Director, FIRED and Fraud, in big red letters." We were doing all we could but were going to run out of time at this pace. In these situations, I usually backtrack to rebuild the case from the starting point and that's what I was doing now.

I went back to the point just before we found out about the leak at the ICC, I had mentioned the leak to Keith, and I was trying to rebuild how he responded. He was shocked but seemed not too surprised. Then I recalled the conversation where he mentioned getting close to finding who the leak was, he told me it was a she. So, did he already know it was Dannetag and if so what was he doing about her?

He also told me he had a proven method of finding a leak, had he put this proven method into action? I should set a meeting with him to go through our options. One thing or damn certain he had to brief me on where he was with this situation and we couldn't let it remain in limbo.

I could think of three alternatives; if he had a proven method for finding a leak why hasn't he found it? Or maybe he had and didn't want to say which would be out of character. The third alternative was unthinkable, he knew who it was and he was part of this conspiracy.

I would message Keith for a meeting, this time in London without Dannetag knowing. Right now though I had engaged the entire team on the face search to find out who was who, so I decided Keith could wait for the time being.

Chapter 35

A Secret Game

I got it, what was bothering me was the missing code in Martin's book, the code that was different from the Aramaic code he used for the rest of his information. I went over and started looking at this section of code, though I didn't know what I was looking for, I looked anyway. I tried the reverse alphabet on the first, what I supposed would be, a sentence. But nothing made sense.

Then I tried various languages looking at the most common words. I tried English, but nothing, then French, German, Portuguese, Russian, and Spanish still nothing. Then, after several hours of trying I had an idea, I called Charlene Willoughby in Gloucester and arranged to go and see her the following day. I told her I couldn't discuss it over the phone but I needed to speak to her.

I left Jeannie and Jake to their task of scanning news media and told them I had to go to Martin's Aunt in Gloucester. "On a hunch," I told them. I left the following morning and arrived there at Bourton-on-the-water at the decent hour of 10.30 am. Charlene greeted me at the door with a smile and a hug, what a lovely lady she was.

We went through to the back garden where she had a pot of tea already made. It was sitting under a tea cozy which I guessed was hand-made. Her garden by the way was absolutely beautiful, with the most amazing array of flowers and plants all raised on beds of what looked like pure black dirt with not one single weed in view. All the edges were trimmed with razor precision and not a single blade of grass was out of place. She had beautiful fully grown huge Cedar trees and Weeping Willows, down by her lake, with a row of tall slim Poplars lined up along the path, giving her path down to the lake some shade in summer.

There were also flowering bushes dotted around on dark well-manicured flower beds along with perfectly shaped sculptured bushes. Whoever had done this was very skilled.

We sat at her garden table and I asked her if Martin and her were close. "I was Martin's "Other mother" I am his real mother's sister his aunt. Martin spent more time here with me than with his own mother," she said. You see Martin was a spitting image of his father who died overseas in the course of his work with the home Office.

For some reason, my sister never got over his death when Martin was just five years old and Martin reminded her so much of her dead husband. So she became distant from him and since he had spent all his holidays here we became very close. He loved it here at my home and especially the lower garden on the other side of our lake. I seemed to have become his surrogate mother which, since I had no children, I didn't mind at all.

I understood what she was telling me, he was like a son to her. But I was on limited time and showed her Martin's undecipherable portion of the code. "What is this you are showing me?" she asked, "It looks like gibberish," she said smiling as she poured us both a cup of tea. I explained what it was.

"So what do you want me to do with this?" she asked and I told her what it was. "The thing is we cannot decipher this part of his code. The rest was an Aramaic code but this section was something else," I explained.

Can you recall if Martin ever played a game as a child, or made up any secret codes as part of a game?" I asked. I know it's a long shot but that's why I came to see you." "Well, she said, "He was in fact often playing a secret agent, hiding and playing with his friends," she said. I told her the game had become more serious and I thought his secret game as a child had just become the missing piece of our puzzle.

"There is his tree house still hidden in the large oak tree on the other side of the lake, where he was always playing with his friends. He often spent hours down there by himself, though God knows what he found so interesting, but then again, boys will be boys. "Mind if I take a look?" I asked, "Not at all, in fact, take the golf cart, I always did whenever I took him to lunch or dinner in summer so he could keep playing. His tree house is some way down on the other side of the lake. That's why he loved it here," she told me. "You'll like riding the golf cart," she said with a chuckle. I finished my tea looking out over her beautiful garden marvelling at the perfect stripes on her, very English, lawn.

My American friends would perhaps have called what Charlene had a "Back Yard" but to me, a yard was always and only will be, "36 inches." What she had was a beautifully landscaped garden on par with Kew Gardens, not far from where I live in Ealing. Kew Gardens was a magnificent park with huge walk-through greenhouses each one set as a complete environment from jungle to desert with all the flora one would see if they were there in the real thing. They also did a lot of botanical research used worldwide by environmental and research scientists.

I went round to the stables, yeah she had horses too! The golf cart, if I can call it that, was parked by one of the stable doors. But this was no ordinary golf cart it was a done-up vehicle made to look like a Rolls Royce! It made me chuckle to see what Charlene found interesting to do. I got on and drove it down the path around the lake. The drive was around a mile and I put my foot down to see what it could do. This thing could really fly!

I was nowhere near full speed and before I realised it, I was doing 40, in a bloody golf cart, on a small, paved path driving around the edge of her lake and had to slow this souped-up set of wheels down before I killed myself!

I slowed down to look for Martin's tree house and eventually found it in the midst of several other very large, very old, oak trees. The tree he had chosen was a huge old oak, the biggest one probably several hundred years old. He had a rope ladder going up to his tree house, tied up to a branch sticking out of the huge trunk. The house itself was very well built and had not in any way been damaged by wind, rain, snow or any of the elements, Martin had made his tree house very well and it had lasted for several decades weathering all sorts of storms and the like.

I climbed up the rope ladder and reached a platform around 30 feet high. This was no ordinary kid's tree house but a well-built, well thought out, structure in this huge oak tree, the biggest one in the woods. It had a door and once inside there were seats and kid's things dotted around. There was a bow and some arrows propped up against one wall with look-out window frames on three of the four sides. It was around 15 feet square, enough to hold several kids there.

I looked around and there was a small cupboard next to one wall so I opened it to look inside. It was empty and I was thinking, what would I be doing if I was a talented kid who built this tree brilliant tree house and played secret agent and spy games? I would hide my stuff somewhere but not in an obvious location. So I moved the small cupboard away from the wall, there was nothing behind it. I knew that would be too boringly obvious, so where did he hide his stuff?

I looked around and there was nothing hidden here. Maybe I was wrong, maybe he hid whatever it was in his bedroom, or in the huge mansion but no, not this kid. A kid like Martin I am sure, would have hidden his secret stuff somewhere close by or inside his hideout. Maybe he had written his code while sitting quietly here in his tree house. But if he did, where did he hide it, I just had to look closer.

I looked outside his tree house, even on the roof and looked around at the surroundings. There were many other huge trees around, so I did a grid search, studying each one close by. Then I noticed there was a tree swing a little distance away so I studied both the swing and the tree it was hanging from.

I climbed down from his tree house and went over to have a closer look at his tree swing. I stood on the swing to see from a different viewpoint I looked around at the other trees. Well, I might as well have a swing on this thing, I thought so I started to use the swing.

Then as I was swinging higher, I noticed a hole in the bark of a tree nearby. I stood on the seat to see better and yes it was a hole in the tree, but a little too high for me to reach.

I drove the golf cart over, carefully avoiding hitting or scraping any of the trees that were all around. I parked the golf cart right next to the tree and managed to climb on its roof. It was a sturdy cart, not like the others I had seen and used, playing golf at other courses. I carefully climbed onto the roof and peered inside the hole in the tree, but it seemed there was nothing inside.

Then I remembered what Martin had done in his apartment, using string inside those air ducts to hide his notebook so I gingerly reached inside the hole and felt around, I hoped there were no spiders inside. Yes, there was something here, it was a length of string tied to a piece of overhanging wood inside the hole. I carefully reached in and grabbed the string, which by the way was not visible at all, from the outside as I slowly started to pull it up.

I could feel there was something attached to the other end as I drew it slowly, carefully, upwards. I had to be careful not to let whatever it was on the other end, come off the old piece of string as I drew it out of the hole. I noticed that parts of the thread had become frayed which made me even more cautious. Finally, I had what was on the other end, in my hand. It was something wrapped in a plastic bag tied to the end of the string.

I took it out and climbed down off the roof of the cart to undo the bag to see what looked like another notebook. I had to smile, Martin and his bloody notebooks! I opened it to see writing in faded pencil.

It said, "My secret code, if you read this you are in grave danger," I had to smile, according to his aunt Charlene he was twelve when he used to spend a lot of time here and that was when he showed her his newly finished and marvellously built tree house.

I undid the plastic bag and opened the notebook. I read on and it was an explanation of his code. Honestly, this boy was a bloody genius! The code was in Latin, no wonder we couldn't break it in the office.

Then I remembered he had gone to a private school, here in Gloucester which meant he must have learned Latin which used to be taught in grammar schools and private schools, at the time he attended school. In fact, Latin was taught to a similar degree as English and was tested in the finals, so school kids had to learn it properly.

Well, I had what I came for and drove carefully out of these woods and up the path around the lake past her beautiful garden. Charlene was still sitting at the table. So I went over to see her and parked her mini-Rolls close by. "Well, did you find whatever it was that you came for?" She asked smiling. "Yes I did Charlene and thank you so much for allowing me to look around," I said.

I felt I owed her a little explanation as to why this was so important. "Charlene, I can't tell you everything about what Martin was involved in. But I will come and tell you more when this is over. I can tell you that your nephew was a genius and was working on something of national importance, which is why he was killed. I promise I will return once this is over and explain what it is about," I told her.

She looked at me, smiled and said, "Thank you, Max, for bothering to come here, I really appreciate you driving up from London to tell me all you have and of course, I understand why you can't tell me more. I will await your return and I am so glad Martin's life was not in vain," she replied. "It certainly was not and I'll see he gets recognised for his work," I told her.

"You can Leave the Rolls here," she said smiling at her joke as she nodded to her luxury golf cart. The thing is, she had a full-sized one parked in another of her stables, not occupied by her horses that were at the time I was there in a large field on the other side of her lake. It was a beautiful Silver Shadow. Though it was an older model it had the upright grille which I always preferred.

"I think I'll take a ride down into the woods myself and spend some time there alone, I loved my nephew so much and I miss him not being here. He used to come regularly to spend his weekends and his school holidays here. I know he was busy but he always thought of me," she said and I understood completely.

She offered me another cup of tea which I accepted as I wanted to keep this lovely lady company and anyway, it would have been rude to just leave as soon as I got what I came for. So I stayed with her listening to stories about Martin. She told me a little about her life too which was extraordinary. She had been in military intelligence for some time, the same as his mother, continuing after the war and told me she showed a young Martin how to build codes which he loved to do.

I listened to stories about a boy who preferred to be alone after the death of his father. She never told me why she, as a chosen spinster who never married, a choice that was hers to make, loved having him live with her.

She explained that all this, pointing around at her huge home and grounds, was her family inheritance from a business her grandfather had started during World War 1. He was an engineer who was into munitions and ballistics. Then as an ex-military man, he developed many new highly specialised weapons for the British army. The contracts were huge and they paid him well for his work.

He bought this home from Lord and Lady Belmont who couldn't afford to keep up with the costs any longer. But he, being a gentleman, wanted them both to remain living in their home until they passed. Then he moved in and carried out many much-needed repairs to bring the home back up to standard.

"The work on these grounds, which before was just a large field for their horses, was my love to take on and I did it all creating this beautiful garden which I adore to sit in and pass my time," she said.

I told her these gardens were stunning and a pleasure to enjoy. "I love London, I told her it's where I've always lived, but now seeing all you have done here I realise what I am missing in my life. It's this, exactly this," I said pointing around her grounds. I was lost for words at what this lovely lady, Charlene, had created.

"Do you like gardening," she asked. "Honestly, I've never had the opportunity, living in London, but to create or keep a garden like this? Yes I would, it's perfect." We carried on talking and I asked her if I could visit her again and maybe just sit here and talk in her beautiful garden.

"I would love that," she said, "Yes please come as often as you like and I would be happy for your company," she said. "I know the line of work you are in, it's similar to what I used to do and though we can never talk of it, in detail, there are many stories to tell you. No one else knows these things and it will be fun to fill you in," she said smiling.

We said our goodbyes, as I headed back to London. The weather on my drive back was sunny and I had a lot to think about especially now I had the missing code. I called in and told Jeannie I found Martin's missing code book and told her it was based on Latin.

"Damn right," she said, "Of course is! It had to be some bloody upper-class language only taught in bloody grammar schools and the like, why didn't I think of that? "Well no one's perfect," I offered trying to be helpful. I had worked on a hunch based on Martin's knowledge and tradecraft and I thought what would I do if I was building a code of national importance?

I would do exactly as Martin had done hide them in separate places." "So What did Charlene think?" Jeannie asked "Well, this is the good part, she taught a twelve-year-old Martin about code science and showed him how to build and use his codes. It was Charlene who taught him the unbreakable Aramaic Code used by her and her team of spies after World War two. She and Martin used to play spy games and he loved it," she told me a lot about Martin. I know she will miss him; he was like the son she never had and I promised to keep her informed when I could about what he was doing.

I did tell her he died in the line of duty, doing what he loved and that he was a real hero. "Did you know that Charlene that lovely old lady was herself a spymaster, can you believe it?" "Well he had to learn his trade craft somewhere and he was a cut above the others we've dealt with," Jeannie said.

I told Jeannie `about the beautiful garden and her incredibly souped-up golf cart and where Martin had hidden the code book. Martin was a real hero and Charlene wanted his body returned so she could bury him in the one place he loved to be, in Charlene's beautiful garden.

Chapter 36

The Missing Piece

Although I didn't know how we would do this, we had to make it happen, to bring back Martin's remains, for both of them! I would ask Bill how to go about having Martin's remains sent to Charlene for his burial on the grounds of the home he loved.

As I was driving back to London, I couldn't help smiling at what Charlene had told me, what an incredible lady and what an incredible family Martin had been brought up with.

I would see to it that he gained recognition for all he had done and now more than ever I felt compelled to resolve this and beat these terrorists, of that I was damn sure!

I arrived at the office around 6 am, but once again Jeannie was there already and the aroma of freshly brewed coffee filled the office. "So that's why we couldn't decipher it," she said as I entered the office. I told her we would have probably found it with more time since Martin's original code was also in Aramaic which was also a dead language.

But the problem was, we didn't have the time. I gave her Martin's book and she began entering the data into her code-breaking algorithm. It didn't take long and she had to make some adjustments for the Latin-based language. The only Latin I knew was what was written on one of the cards given to me at my leaving at The North Star pub in Ealing when I left the Met. It said, *"Illegitimi non carborundum,"* meaning don't let the bastards grind you down, and yes, I also learned Latin at school.

By early afternoon she was ready to run the program so I went over to watch as her program began to decipher Martin's code.

"Unbelievable, a boy of twelve built this code and an advanced computer program has to decipher it!" I said. We both watched as the letters began to form on Jeannie's screen, once again, not in any order, but random as when the other code had also been broken. The words appeared as single letters dotted around the screen in pixels gradually forming complete words.

We began to see a message forming telling us who was the mastermind of this soon-to-be attack. We were on the right track looking for a disgruntled Finance director, but we didn't know who it was. The originator of this scheme was none other than the Belgian Minister of Finance. "Of course!" I said out loud, "He was the one murdered in Brussels and now we know why!"

The code was still piecing the letters together as more of the code was deciphered. I remained looking at it as the words were forming. It went on to tell us who was also behind this conspiracy.

It was the Belgian financier who was part of the BIS board, who had originated the plan to destroy the world's banking system. But according to Martin a man called Boris Neumacher, a Jewish-Czechoslovakian billionaire, who was a relatively unknown name unless you were into international finance. He had taken over the finance minister's work and had him killed on the streets of Overijse outside Brussels, just to close a loose end.

No wonder we couldn't make the connection. But now we had the final missing piece of the puzzle and we could begin the work of breaking down his communications, who he was talking to and we had to know who he was seeing. So it was, once again, back to Jeannie's skill with CCTV cameras but now they were in Brussels.

Our work was cut out now and thanks to Martin, we could focus on one man, not all the other names who, I am certain will be relevant at some later point, but right now we have what we need to solve this and prevent this terrorism from being implemented.

I called over to Mariah, who was still in Switzerland, to fill her in. We sent the address and contact details for Boris Neumacher for her to follow up on. Boris Neumacher was well known in the world's top financial circles and we now had photos of him attending the IMF and the WEF annual meetings.

It was obvious now we knew who was behind this and we could focus on this monster, who as we began to piece all he had been doing, it became clear as to why. He had been pushing a socialist agenda and had been using his massive wealth of billions to undermine many countries in Europe and the US. It had become his personal mission to use his billions to bring socialism to Europe and the US... He was portrayed as a hateful man, who was now a monster.

He was Jewish and was originally from Czechoslovakia but now, although he was a Jew, he had become antisemitic choosing policies that would make Europe and the US. both socialist and as a result antisemitic.

Why he was doing this when socialism had failed in every country it had been forced into I have no idea but it is what it is. Maybe that was his plan, to utterly destroy all that had been built by the EU and the US. By destroying the global financial system, Boris Neumacher had become a monster!

I remembered reading about the damage socialism had done in other countries and I read about *"The Baltic Way,"* in 1989, which was an incredible act of protest involving Lithuania, Latvia and Estonia. Some called it *"The Chain of Freedom."* It was a peaceful political demonstration that occurred in August 1989.

What occurred was that approximately two million people joined hands to form a human chain spanning 690 kilometers which was 430 miles long. It spanned across the three Baltic states of Estonia, Latvia and Lithuania, which at the time were occupied and annexed by the USSR.

They were annexed by the Ribbentrop agreement after the Second World War and had a combined population of approximately eight million people. The central government in Moscow considered the three Baltic countries republics of the Soviet Union and ruled them as such but gave them less standing than was given to Russia.

The 1989 event was organised by a Baltic pro-independence movement, to draw global attention by demonstrating together and showcasing solidarity among those three nations.

The Soviet authorities failed to do anything that could close the widening gap between the Baltic republics and the rest of the Soviet Union. Seven months after their protest Lithuania became the first Soviet republic to declare independence. It stuck in my mind as the most incredible silent revolution I had ever seen.

I remember thinking, at the time, if socialism was so bloody good, why would two million ordinary people risk their lives to go against their strong Russian leaders by forming this massive human chain? This one event stuck in my mind as one of the bravest acts of human determination I had ever seen. I bet it went down like a lead balloon with Mikhail Gorbachev, Russia's leader at that time.

As for me and my political beliefs, I never bothered about right or left as both sides had some good and some bad concepts. But these politicians' actions once elected on both sides, left and right, were based solely on keeping themselves and their party in power. To me, their personal ambitions came before any decision that was based on what their communities or their countries needed or wanted.

Neither did I believe the press or the TV news media who, like the politicians always slanted their programming to gain more readers or viewers and to use their power to sway their nations into believing what they were telling us all as being the truth.

My work both as a cop and as a private eye taught me that people at all levels lied and cheated, on their companies, on their wives and friends and in fact on anyone who, in their opinion, did not agree with them or got in their way and had to be removed. To me, a half-truth, as told in most of the media, is still a lie!

Now we knew who was behind this we were researching into Boris Neumacher. All we were reading about Boris Neumacher was negative, it seemed he was not a popular person despite the fact he gave billions to various charities and organisations probably to be seen as a charitable philanthropist which he was, on the outside, but underneath his determination to corrupt Europe and the United States into socialism was his ultimate goal. I read that he was attempting to buy up all the independent radio stations, probably to control what they were broadcasting.

We learned more about the head of this tyrannical snake and the more we learned the more damage we understood he had already done or tried to do. Among other things, he had led a group to bring Iran and North Korea into the World Economic Forum, but he failed, which probably added fuel to his fire of pure hatred against these accepted organisations of which he was part.

It was alleged that he had undermined elections in Germany, Great Britain and the US, by giving the socialist parties in these countries, millions to support advertising and events to promote socialism. We saw he had been buying up news and TV media as well, using his vast wealth to control what the people were listening to, reading and watching. His was a desire for ultimate control which made Boris Neumacher the most dangerous man alive.

What an evil monster we were now dealing with, but as this murky deep lake had been drained and now this murky dark rock was now exposed. He was our target to be dealt with thanks to the incredible work Martin Ade had done before he was killed.

Jeannie called over for me to look at her screen as words were forming. At the end of his code he said, "Do not underestimate Boris Neumacher, he has eyes and ears everywhere!" A dire warning from the grave!

One way or another we would stop Boris from his act of global terrorism. It was time to meet Bill, to fill him in and to seek his guidance about whether we should inform Interpol and the intelligence community about what we had found out about the head of this snake.

Jake and Jeannie were working together with Mariah setting up surveillance and communication connections with Boris's mobile phone, his car and his home in Grindelwald, Switzerland.

We could now gather information from the head of the snake but we had to be very careful.

I called Bill to set up a meeting, he decided to come to London, to meet with us at our office where, as he said he could see all that we were now working on. He arrived later that day and I called a pow-wow where Jeannie, Jake and I could brief him and bring him up to date.

When we had finished updating Bill, I asked him about letting our intelligence community know about what we had discovered. What he said next surprised me, "They already know," he said, "I filled both the PM (Prime Minister) and the Home Secretary about adding you to my team after you had uncovered the truth behind the deaths in London and Switzerland," he said, "And they both agreed with my decision."

I had no idea he had done this but I was happy he had because it took a load off my mind and I didn't have to worry now about being admonished, or worse, for not involving our intelligence community. Bill had notified them as a former head of our intelligence network and he had notified the Home Office as well, albeit from a position of secrecy.

He decided to keep me out of that loop so I could focus on what we had to do to stop this act of global terrorism from being implemented. Bill's reputation and his knowledge allowed him to make decisions like this and be trusted by the current PM and the Home Office.

"We still need to know who will be implementing this and when and I still believe it may be coordinated to be launched at the next IMF or WEF annual meeting for maximum coverage since both are covered in the world news and press," I told Bill.

"What do you need?" he asked. "I think we are going to need a few more operatives when this goes down because they won't be doing this quietly I think they will have a small army to prevent any interruption when they implement the takeover of SWIFT and even if they don't we must be well prepared with a small but overwhelming force," I told him.

Bill thought for a moment and agreed, "OK you've got it. When you know where and when you need them let me know and I will have operators from the SAS in Hereford join you," "How long will you need to get them deployed?" I asked.

He replied, "Twenty-four hours, I'll prep their commander personally beforehand and ask him to place them on standby, with no missions after that time. But this has to happen when you have the final plan you intend to put into motion," "OK I'll get the intel from my group and prepare you with all we have, to have maximum effect when this goes down. Whatever happens, we cannot and will not allow Boris's act of financial terrorism to be played out," I told him.

Bill left a little while later after thanking Jeannie and Jake for all their hard work. "You've all done an incredible job so far, now all we have to do is take this over the finish line. If there's anything else you need, fast transport, feet on the ground, anything, you must let me know." He paused thinking, "Then he turned to us as he was opening the door, good luck to you all and I'll inform the PM and the Home Secretary of this update," he said as he left us to carry on with our work.

After he left we were now more determined than ever to do whatever it took to stop this man from his evil intentions. We each had our work cut out now and time was running out.

I called Mariah in Switzerland on her encrypted sat phone to update her on the name we now had, "Boris Neumacher" I told her to find out who he was in contact with and anything at all about his movements. She was already set up and knew what to do.

I then called Dave to brief him on Boris's actions and told him to monitor the intel at the ICC. I also filled him in on what we had learned from Bill about the PM being informed. "I thought he might do that," he said, "After all he was head of 6 for a long time and his web of contacts goes far and deep," Dave said.

Do I inform Keith at the ICC because we still had a leak there? I decided to wait for the time being, it was always better to apologize than to ask permission and I could not risk any breach through him at this point. I would explain everything when the time came, but right now our actions were in Switzerland as well as The Hague and I had Dave there to monitor intel from the ICC.

We were moving fast now and thank God I had a team to help me, it was a good call from Bill to bring his team onto this case to help us break this conspiracy and stop them. From my prior experience in Ealing Nick, I knew there was only so much one person, or as often was the case in our line of work, a two-person team could do and this is new territory, but I liked the thought of doing something more meaningful.

We were now working on several fronts, Jeannie and Jake made a good team, they worked well together and they were getting results fast.

I decided to make a visit at the weekend to see Charlene, it would be a break for me. I called her and she was happy for the company. I headed out on Friday afternoon and arrived at Bourton-On-The-Water in the early evening.

We sat at her garden table and I told her that my prior trip had given us a wealth of new information, enough to be able to break the case. It made her happy to hear that she had been able to assist us. I guessed her clandestine past had never left her.

We went for a walk around her beautiful garden and she explained about all the flowers and shrubs, telling me how she had planned her garden before planting all she now had there. She told me she had beds of roses that each bloomed at different times of the year so she had colour in her garden all year round. I was fascinated.

That evening I took her out for dinner and since I was staying at The Mousetrap Inn, at Bourton-on-the-water, I took her there for drinks and dinner. It was a small inn with a pub and had an excellent reputation. She was so happy to be going out and told me she seldom gets out, except to go to church on Sundays.

When we sat down in the restaurant, several people including the owner of the pub came over to say hello to Charlene and I could see they had genuine respect for her. Dinner was excellent and she invited me to see her the next morning. We went around her grounds in the "Rolls" and believe me she was an excellent driver!

I had grown to love her garden and after our chats, I understood more about Martin and why he became the man he was. She had been a major influence on his education and had honed his skills which made him an asset as an operator with MI6. The fact that her sister, his mother and his father, were also in the clandestine world made it impossible for him not to join the "Family" business.

I felt sad for his mother but I knew life is sometimes like that since we are all wired differently. I liked Charlene and all she had done over many years in making Martin the man he had become and what a skilled man he turned out to be.

If not for his work we would all be completely unaware of what was about to happen with the global banking system and we were now well on the way to prevent it from being implemented. Time will tell if we were able to stop it in time.

Chapter 37

A Trap

Intelligence is often exactly the opposite of its name when it comes down to actionable intel. Often, as it is here, it is based on related and unrelated intel from seemingly random places plus HUMINT (human intelligence) and more guesswork or as we referred to it- "Informed decision making, based on the skill and thinking of the operative." I was making a guess on when this would go down, a guess which, if I was wrong would allow the most devastating act of global terrorism, locking out all 11,000 financial institutions, with hundreds of thousands of outlets, affecting millions of hard-working people from their legitimate need to transfer their funds and their pay for work hard-earned.

We learned that SWIFT is run from data centres, located in the United States, the Netherlands, Hong Kong and Switzerland. They share information near real-time twenty hours seven days each week. In case of a failure in one of the data centres, another is able to handle the traffic of the complete network via an automated switch-over. SWIFT also uses submarine communications cables to transmit its data.

The location was Zoeterwoude, in the Netherlands, which was an operating centre. Culpeper in Virginia, United States also an Operating Centre, Diessenhofen in Switzerland also an operations centre and Hong Kong was Command and control.

If I were right, the WEF annual meeting at the end of January in Davos would bring together some 3,000 paying members plus selected participants including investors, business leaders, political leaders, economists, celebrities and journalists. It usually lasted for up to five days to discuss global issues across 500 sessions with each delegate taking part.

So, with this in mind, we would need to have teams in all main operational locations including Hong Kong when we acted. We would need to breach each location simultaneously to prevent an automated switchover to any of these three centres.

It was now September and if Boris was aiming at the next WEF meeting we had until January when the next meeting would take place in Davos. I messaged Bill to tell him we may be deployed not only in Davos but also in these other locations, so he could update the SAS commander to study the best routes for infiltration.

If we had to go through normal channels, there would be all kinds of permissions required to bring this down, a myriad of paperwork, courts and countries with different laws involved and all this would take months. We didn't have the time to do this so our operation, when it happens, must be covert. I would leave the semantics of laws and legalities to Bill and others, including the PM after all Bill had been doing this for a long time.

It was complicated for damn sure and we, as yet, did not have an action plan but we would before the time came. Dave was working on finding the leak at the ICC and I told him to focus on communications to and from Sheri Dannetag to anyone within our group of names supplied by Martin and to use Jake and Jeannie if necessary to help set up a trap to see whose side she was on.

The trap was set, in the form of a phone call to Sheri Dannetag, supposedly from Boris but actually sent by Mariah in the close vicinity of Boris's home in Grindelwald, Switzerland. She travelled there and sent a text from Boris's Grindelwald home location which we knew Sheri would receive and probably trace back to where Boris lived. We made a massive guesstimation that there would be no reason for her to have any contact with Boris and if she did then she was part of Boris's team.

It was a rough trap I know but it may catch her if she knows who Boris is or recognises the location where that call came from. The message said simply, "Things moving along, keep you informed." It was timed for a Thursday afternoon hoping she wouldn't be working at the weekend.

If she responded with anything other than, "Who is this" or similar, or she informed the ICC head of station about the text on either that Thursday or Friday then we would know she is a spider in their web.

At worst, if we were wrong then an apology was far better than interviewing her about her relationship with Neumacher, either way, it was the best we could do with so little to go on.

Of course, we knew she might do nothing which would complicate things but regardless it was worth a try. Two days later the trap was set, by Mariah in Switzerland and we waited for a response. We didn't have to wait long, she answered within twenty minutes, saying, "New phone?" Mariah responded, "Sat Phone keep this number." We had her so now we removed the question mark next to her name on our board and we knew this would complicate everything as we could not now involve anyone at the ICC.

But we were also looking at Keith to see if there was any phone communication from her to him immediately after receiving the text from Boris (Mariah). But since they both worked at the same location maybe they would communicate face to face, not through any other method.

It also meant we had to arrange a takedown, timed before we took down their network, in case she could stop us, or worse, inform others on their web. We were now going to monitor her phone and Jeannie set it up with Dave at The Hague who was monitoring communications there also.

I sent a message to Bill, so he would know Sheri Dannetag had been linked directly with Boris Neumacher. I was now keeping Bill in the loop on any new findings so he could inform the PM and Home Secretary as he saw fit. We would need all the help we could when this went down.

I returned to Boston Manor later that day and went to the North Star pub, in Ealing, as I wanted to be in young, noisy company. I found it always relieves the stress of a busy day. They had a band playing so I went to the outside seating area at the side of the pub, seeing several people I knew, perfect!

I had to smile as Robin Perry, one of my former colleagues, came over to join me. He had a nickname, "The Terminator," as it was known he always got his villain!

We talked about cases he was working on when one of his informants came over to join us. He knew we would talk about what was going on in his world but he knew not to ask about mine. His informant's name was Josephine, "Josey," she was apparently a former prostitute, who he had once nicked, for soliciting, but now she was reformed and taking a nursing degree at college.

Robin, or the Terminator, always gave his suspects his time and treated them all as people not just villains. Many became friends of his and even appreciated his help. Robin was the most decorated cop in Ealing and Josey was a hoot. Her stories of how Robin caught her with a "John" in his Jaguar, parked in the upper-level parking at the Ealing Broadway Centre, "We were bonking like there was no tomorrow!" She said, "I don't know how he caught me," to which Robin said, "What! all the windows were steamed the fuck up and the car was rocking like a bloody rocking horse!"

I had to smile, Robin and Josey had become good friends now and often met for drinks. I was impressed that she turned her life around and wanted to become a nurse. There is hope after all! I left the pub around eleven thirty leaving Robin and Josey still there, feeling no pain as they say, well on their way to becoming legless!

The following morning, I craved a huge breakfast, so I went to a small café I knew on Northfield Avenue, Café Nell, a small café with seating for maybe 20 or 25 people. They had the best value "Full breakfast" around. I had their full (English) breakfast, bacon, eggs, sausages, grilled tomatoes, baked beans toast and a cuppa, but I didn't have the black pudding. All this for under seven quid, brilliant value! I was now all set to work at home all day nonstop on the case, after my "heart-stopper" breakfast.

I went home and started to review all we had done piecing together where we were and what we now needed to get done.

Chapter 38

Names in the Hornet's Nest

Thinking hard about two things, the timing and the implementation, I thought we had to have our people in each of the SWIFT locations in Zoeterwoude, in the Netherlands, maybe in Culpeper, Virginia, in Diessenhofen in Switzerland and in Hong Kong.

I thought Hong Kong might be the trigger point since that was the operations centre so it would make sense for them to go there to initiate their operation. I marked a question for Jake and Jeannie the following day, asking the question, "Could they trigger this from a remote location, over the internet from Boris's home, or would they need to be at each SWIFT location?" We still needed to know when this was going down.

I was also thinking of Bill's offer to use the SAS as required. I thought we could use them best at the Hong Kong SWIFT head office. Not so much that we needed them to implement the downloading to their computer, but we did need them to take care of the guards there, to allow Brian and Jack to do it.

If we did deploy the SAS team, we would have to maintain operational control at the location where they were working alongside my team and since several of mine were ex SAS they would know how to coordinate.

We were at the point where, as I saw it, we had everything but we still had not enough. We had an extensive list of names, locations, contacts, and a terrorist conspiracy but the "When and where" were still missing. That was going to be our immediate focus when I got to the office the following day. Mariah had an update for us and called in on her phone. "There's been several calls made from Boris's phone," she said, that could mean our message to Sheri Dannetag had been caught or it could mean he was setting things in motion which, if true, might mean his plan was being put in place sooner than later. I told Mariah, don't spend time tracking the calls just log the numbers and the time then send the numbers to us and we'll check them out.

As I said, gathering intel is exactly the opposite, it's accumulating facts from different sources and making an assessment based on limited knowledge added to a lot of guesswork. We had to find who he was calling and messaging. Jeannie and Jake entered the numbers he called into the Interpol database. Sure enough, calls were made to contacts in Hong Kong, to a Michael Kwang and to a John McGuire. He also made calls to two numbers in the Netherlands.

On checking both names in Hong Kong we found that John McGuire was ex-spec ops meaning he was heavy while Michael Kwang owned a software development company. So now we thought we knew who we were up against and we had to monitor these two, especially Kwang, since he would probably be implementing the take-over of the SWIFT system or perhaps he had created the take-over software to control the SWIFT system.

I had a friend, Peter Collins, now an inspector with the Hong Kong Police Force (HKPF) which is the primary law enforcement investigative agency there under the Security Bureau of Hong Kong. Pete moved there after marrying a girl who was from Hong Kong.

He was now Inspector Collins there. He used to work with me at the MET in Acton Nick. Maybe he could arrange a takedown of these two when the time was right, or at least help my team to implement it.

In our last conversation, he told me many things had changed in Hong Kong since the handover to China, in 1997. Most were not good changes, in his opinion, including banning English from being taught in their schools. But regardless of the many changes, there was still an ex-Met, old boy's network still in operation there. I sent him an encrypted message giving him the two names, Michael, Kwang and John McGuire and the words "More to follow." sending a download please use it.

He would know what to do, I set a time to call him the following day with the words "Encrypted only." We hadn't been back in contact since my last big pharma case when I brought down a back street operation in Kowloon, near the old town. They were making Fentanyl, pressing it into small tabs and shipping millions of tabs over to Europe and the US. These tabs were ten times stronger than opioids and easier to ship.

We were getting heads up from both Dave and Mariah telling us that the communications were continuing from Boris to Hong Kong, from a location in Switzerland and to The Netherlands also. Each location was where a SWIFT operation was based.

Hong Kong was seven hours ahead of London so we set the call for 9 am GMT, 4 pm HK time, I wanted Jake and Jeannie to listen in. Peter's call came through on the dot of 9 am. "Hey wassup you old fucker," he said which made Jake and Jeannie laugh. "Where the fuck have you been my old mate!" were his first words. "A lot to tell you, Pete," then I asked him if the call was strictly private. He said, "Absolutely, what's this all about?"

I'm coming over to HK to see you as I'm going to need your help and this is going to need your complete discretion. Tell your friends there I'm an old friend coming over for a visit and nothing more. "When I come over to see you I'll fill you in on what's going down when I get there," I told him but, and this is important, our meeting must be kept secret.

"Understood, I'll meet you at the gate just send me your ETA," he said. I told him I could only stay for a few days, or long enough to set a few things in motion with him. We terminated the call and I turned to Jeannie and Jake, we need direct intel in Hong Kong and I don't want to risk discussing this over the phone even though you sent him the encryption file, in case he discusses this with a colleague or two then we lose our secrecy I explained.

I made flight arrangements and left the office that Friday so I could spend a long weekend in HK while my office was closed for the weekend. That way I was wasting no time that I would have used in the office.

The flight from Heathrow to Hong Kong is about twelve and a half hours. I slept through the entire flight which I knew would mean I was good to go when I got there.

I couldn't afford to lose that time I had to be on my game when I got there. I have several friends who travel long distances choosing to drink for the entire flight. When they arrive at their destination they arrive drunk and suffer jet lag for the first few days on longer trips. I couldn't afford to lose time like that.

I asked Jeannie to give me a thumb drive with all our data on it, to use when I got there, so I could decide what to transfer and where to transfer it to. I told her to mark the files and separate them into absolute and incidental. I knew Pete was discrete but I needed more than simple discretion. I needed utmost secrecy from him. I reviewed every file and note on the drive, removing some of the data, just in case. Depending on how my meeting went I would decide how much I could tell him.

After I leave HK I want to be certain Pete understands how important this is and the need for him to be discrete and I knew I was placing him in an almost impossible position to set this up, but at the same time, he had to keep this on the QT! I had no choice; it is what it is and we will have to deal with it.

The consequences for a failure, at this late stage, are unimaginable and if push came to shove a few of Bill's team would deal with this ourselves with no hesitation.

I hoped it wouldn't come down to this but in my line of work, I've had to kick a few doors in and break a few bones myself. This will be no different! Right now nothing was off the books and we would do what it takes! In the words of my SAS friends, "Who dares wins" and that was how I saw this. We would dare and one thing for damn sure, we would win.

There is no second place when we are dealing with billionaires who have made it their life's work to undermine elections, governments, and people's safety and well-being for their own fucked up view of the world and their desire for ultimate power. There are a few of them, that I know, running global social media, news media and other things like banks and the like, but those stories are for another day.

We discussed the fact that Pete would need additional help and we should send two from Bill's team. I asked Jake who he thought would be the best for this mission. He told me that would probably be best coming from Bill. So we called Bill and the two names he gave were Brian Phillips and Jack O'Donnell both he said were good for this. He knew his team and if Bill said they were the best then I was fine with his assessment.

I headed to Heathrow that Friday with my go bag, which was always packed in readiness and sat on the window seat at an exit so I had plenty of legroom. I hoped Pete would be up to helping us take down the Hong Kong connection. There were plenty of flights weekly to HK around 49 each week.

On the way over I was thinking about the US connection in Virginia, but we found it to be relatively unimportant. Once we had inserted the software Jeannie and Jake had developed all locations would appear to be back to normal operation.

Our target remained the mainframe at Hong Kong and that was the most important part of the operation. Having a small contingent of SAS to help would make that part much more straightforward as long as there was no connection to either my team or them.

I went through what we had to do in Hong Kong, there would be Kwang and his bodyguard to deal with and his operation wherever that was located. As I saw it that would be phase one taking them and his operation down.

Then the most important part would be the SWIFT building itself and all I had to go on at present was the Google Maps image and some search engine photos. I didn't use Google for my basic search I used DuckDuckGo since they don't track the user and for basic photos or images, I got what I wanted.

But I also mixed my search for the SWIFT building with other images of buildings and landmarks from random locations just to make it appear

I was searching generally at large office buildings, just in case. I downloaded several images of the SWIFT building along with several other locations just in case. But being in Hong Kong, especially with Pete who lived there, meant I could go there and see for myself what the building was and how much security they had.

This would be the main part of our operation and I hoped Pete would be able to help us. Words are cheap, it's actions that count in my game.

Chapter 39

Hong Kong

When I arrived, in Hong Kong, Pete was there at the gate waiting for me, "Max you old bastard, great to see you!" He greeted me with his usual London talk. We made our way through the airport to his official car parked outside in the restricted zone, he was known to the security there and we went straight through.

We made small talk while we were driving to his apartment. He told me he had learned to speak Cantonese which I thought might be useful if I wanted a Chinese wife. I asked him if he was certain his apartment was not bugged. "Tell you what mate, we'll check it out before we talk," he said and we did just that. I apologised to him but explained why we needed to be in complete secrecy with this.

After we went through his apartment and ensured it was clear of bugs we sat down to talk. "So what's this all about, you've made it clear this is top secret so I'm all ears" he said. I told him we were dealing with a global terrorist organisation and I needed his help and his complete discretion.

"Do you remember our old mate Martin Ade?" I asked. "Of course, he said, top bloke, I thought he was part of the ICC now. Oh and wasn't he a top-rated skier, he won a silver at the Olympics if I'm not wrong I remember watching his race it was bloody awesome?" he replied.

"Yes and yes, well, Martin was murdered, doing what he loved most, skiing, a little while ago which is a case I am working on now," I told him. "Fuck that! What the hell happened?" he asked. I told him what we had uncovered about Martin's murder, made to look like an accident and about how Richard Whitehead had also been murdered.

I also told him we now knew these two murders were linked. I explained how we had uncovered Boris Neumacher's intent to take over the global banking system using the SWIFT program to lock all banks and everyone out of the system.

When I had finished he was silent for a few moments letting this sink in. "Fuck this, no wonder you're being so careful, if this goes down it will affect the entire world banking system," he said.

"Worse than that Pete, it will cause massive unrest the like of which we have never seen and it will be of global proportions," I explained, adding Neumacher will have everyone's bank account data and could at any time transfer all their money into separate accounts they own and when people, companies, governments and military cannot send or receive money or have their money stolen, this will become a shit show and very fast.

"So what can I do for you and for my late friend Martin? By the way, he still owes me a score (twenty quid), when Arsenal lost against United. 'S'pose I'll have to put that towards a pint in his honour," he added.

"This is where you come in, these two names, Michael Kwang and John McGuire, will be the ones to initiate this at the SWIFT operations headquarters here in Hong Kong. We don't know who else they will have with them, but since SWIFT operations headquarters is based here, along with Kwang's software company, we have reason to believe it will start here in Hong Kong and will be initiated by them both.

Kwang has a software company, "Kwangtech" here in Hong Kong so we believe he will be the one to initiate the infiltration and the takeover of the SWIFT program. McGuire is his bodyguard and he is badass, he must be taken down, with no second-guessing as soon as we start our takedown operation.

All obstacles must be neutralised with no hesitation as fast as possible. I have the use of a small team of SAS operators, who will be deployed here to help and to ensure this is taken care of with maximum speed. Do you understand what will be required? I asked him. "Yes I do and I'll take care of business at this end you can be certain of that," he said.

When we know the times, dates and what will be actioned I'll brief you. I will also have a couple of my own team who will be over here before any action begins, to reccy the building and assess the best way to infiltrate the SWIFT building. They will be the ones to upload some software to prevent Kwang and Neumacher from doing what they intend to do.

You will need to grab Kwang and McGuire and fast. We believe Kwang will be opening up an internet connection to start a sequence of events that will bring their plan into action. Kwang will initiate this from the SWIFT headquarters, "Do you know where that is?" I asked. "Of course I bloody do, is the Pope Catholic?" he said. "Understood, just checking!" I answered. I'd like us both to get eyes on that building to see what we're up against there and to see what security they have as soon as possible.

Kwang is someone who must be stopped with "Deadly force," when this goes down. "McGuire," as I said, "Is a badass, ex-spec ops, in fact, he was "Eleven Xray" and is also a sniper. He will try to block the team so be prepared that he will have help. He will have to be incapacitated. Oh and just so you know, you are part of a coordinated team of operators in at least two other locations so timing is everything, ok?" I said.

"Wow, you're not joking about this, are you?" "No, this is no joke" I answered, "And I'll send you two of my team to work with you and trust me, they too are badass and I would like them to take the lead, but they'll work with you. I'll try to give you the maximum heads up I can, but it may only be 24 hours' notice, so base yours and the team's readiness on that window," I told him.

"How long do I have to prepare," he asked. "That I can't tell you yet but communications traffic has recently become busier so we can expect it to go down sooner than later, maybe a week, maybe a month we don't know but please keep whatever your plans may be only with my people who you can absolutely trust, because this cannot be leaked, ok?" I said.

"Ok I understood what do you need?" he asked. "Hard to say, at this point but I'll tell you what, my two operatives can help you assess the SWIFT building's security and from that you can assess with them what force you will need. My men are pros at this and they will not steer you wrong, you can trust them, they have both got impeccable credentials otherwise I wouldn't be sending them to help you" I told him.

"Their names are Brian Phillips and Jack O'Donnell," "Brian is formerly SAS and Jack was with MI5 but before that, he was in special operations and was a Green Beret. Both are seasoned pros able to handle both this job perfectly while working with you, oh and they will have your six you can be certain of that" I told him.

The following day we headed for the SWIFT building to observe it from a café close by. It was a tall high-rise glass-fronted building on the corner of Westlands Road and Tai Koo Shing Road, just a few blocks from the waterfront. It had a curved flight of broad steps leading up to a large modern reception area.

The building was highly visible and would need nighttime infiltration. But I would leave the details to Brian and Jack. I would brief them on what I have seen back in the office but I also had a camera in a button on my jacket with live feed going back to our office.

The location and style of the target building were, to me, cause for concern. It was in a highly visible location on a busy corner and would need their expertise to infiltrate. "Do you ever do building inspections?" I asked Pete. "Yes we do often, banks, public buildings and the like, but it's the fire department who usually do that" He replied. "What about the SWIFT building, ever done an inspection there?" I asked. "I can check but they could be due, even if they are not," he said.

"OK You'll want to have Brian and Jack pose as fire inspectors to gather intel from inside that building, we need to know exactly where the SWIFT computer is located as that is our target. They could do it with someone from the fire department, or better still together with you as a fire inspector," I said. "Ok I'll set that up how soon can they be here,?" he asked. "They'll be here in a few days. I'll brief them before they leave along with the contact details for the three of you to deal directly with each other."

Chapter 40

Setting the Pieces on the Board

We were sitting in the café monitoring the foot traffic going into and coming out of the SWIFT building. We also did a walk-by with me sending live camera feeds back to my office. There were a lot of people entering and exiting the building, so I asked Pete if this was a normal volume of traffic. He told me it was fairly normal as Hong Kong, which although it was a small country, was a very crowded place, especially for the banking world.

I called Jeannie on my way to the airport from Pete's car, to get Brian and Jack to the office for when I arrived back. I met them both when I arrived, Brian was a big man and nearly broke my hand when we shook hands. He knew Jack from prior missions and they greeted each other.

Brian was a swarthy man, with red hair and beard and looked at every part of the SAS training he had undergone before he joined Bill's team. Jack was medium build, to me typical MI5 and a former highly trained Green Beret, smart, short dark close-cropped hair, wiry build and stubble on his face. If I saw him in the street I would not think anything, he blended in. I knew both of these could handle anything. I greeted them both and called a Pow wow to brief them both and my two Jeannie and Jake.

I filled them in on the entire conspiracy and what they would be up against. I asked Jeannie to be ready to work closely with them when they went into the SWIFT building and showed them what it looked like from our walk-by and from the images I took at the cafe.

"Jeannie, we will need your guidance on what they need to do when this goes down, to secure that system and to lock it down so no programming can be placed or operated from there." One thing that bothers me is if Kwang has placed an automated start point for the nefarious program or has set booby traps in place to run or to be implemented regardless of anything happening to him. Is there a way you can tell these two what to look for while they are there?

"In short, no," she said, "But I can give them a thumb drive to put in which will rummage around the system and take a look. Once that is done then they place the re-programming thumb drive in. Jake can help me with this." "Do you two think you can get into the computer room?" She asked. "Leave that part to us," they smiled and looked at each other as part of some private joke.

"I don't mean that as an insult," Jack said, "But if we can't get that part done as fire inspectors we can get in at night to set up whatever Jeannie needs." "Yep," Brian interjected, "We've never come across a building we couldn't get into," he added. "Even banks and safety deposit rooms are a breeze. That's the fun part of what we do and unlike the movies, it's not always kicking doors in. We work better using stealth rather than brute force. But, believe me, if shit happens," they looked at each other and laughed, "We can do that too!" I had to smile at their confidence.

"I don't want to point out the obvious and I understand you both know what you are doing, but the difference here is that there is no possible room for failure, because if this conspiracy does go down the world will be a shit show, nothing we can imagine would be worse. This would be like a nuclear bomb going off all over the world, the damage would be incredible. You two must make the assessment and tell us what you need in personnel, equipment and anything else." I told them. "You will both be the spearhead of this, working in Hong Kong. Speed and stealth are critical. There will be at least two other teams set up in Switzerland and The Hague or in another location in The Netherlands.

Boris Neumacher, in Switzerland, will initiate this and Mariah is there to deal with him and whatever else is there too. Who do you think should work with Mariah? Both of you two as well as Dave and Jake are in in play so who else do we have?" I asked.

"Well, it only leaves Scott, Scotty Brown," Jake replied. "OK then let's get Mariah and Scott on the call along with Dave, right now, so we can get everyone on the same page, time is of the essence now" I said. Jeannie got hold of them both and they came on the speaker. I filled them in on what we were doing in Hong Kong, The Hague and in Bern.

"Scott we need you to team up with Mariah to stop Boris who, we have good intel, that he is the mastermind of this conspiracy. We will need him taken care of when the other teams are ready. Timing will be critical so we will coordinate all three locations from here.

"How long do we have before the shit hits the proverbial?" Scott asked. Mariah is in the driver's seat for your operation presently, because she is in situ there and when she sees calls going out to the locations I've mentioned and possibly an increase in phone and text traffic, to and from Boris, that will signal when we start.

The call sign is "Falcon," as that was the name Martin gave for this. We will act fast and with deadly force. But when that happens all locations are a go. I hope we will have 24 hours but I doubt it.

Make no mistake this megalomaniac has engineered this and cares nothing for the irreparable damage he will cause to everyone in all locations, governments, the military, and hospitals and most of all, no one will be unable to get food, energy, medical, water or anything it will all shut down and once the stores are empty panic will follow and on a global scale. So, we are it as far as their future goes.

Mariah, you and Scott will take Neumacher down and neutralise his communications and his operation, preventing all communication into and out of his base. Jeannie has located his comms which are to and from his home in Bern Switzerland. He probably has a sophisticated warning and alarm system as he has been planning this for a long time. With his almost unlimited funds, we must assume he will have thought of everything.

I know I don't need to say this but be well prepared, he arranged for his assassin to take out the Belgian Finance Minister just to close that loop as well as Richard Whitehead and Martin Ade using sophisticated methods.

You will be going in at night and all will be wearing body cams and new lightweight body armour, the latest technology thanks to Bill, night vision on your cams will be clear as day. We're doing that in case there is some blowback from another of your locations which we have not anticipated.

Jake you and Jeannie, together with me, will have our hands full coordinating everything from here in the three locations, with body cams and sat phones. You each will be clear to take down whoever gets in your way.

We plan that no one will see you or know you are there. One small wrinkle, we found a leak in The Hague and will be cutting that person out of any and all communications. Dave will get that person to a remote location for questioning later.

Mariah, you are in the lead to let us know what is happening in Bern. Jeannie, is there a way you can patch in Boris's comms to our office so we can be in the loop in real-time? "I think so, yes," she said.

Hong Kong is team Alpha; Bern is team Bravo and The Hague is team Charlie. The team were now all updated on our current intel and their hardware was being shipped to the three locations, Jake took care of that as he apparently usually did on other missions they had been involved with. I did not need to know the details, I needed to be focused on where we were with this and to ensure there were no missing pieces.

I was concerned about the Hong Kong link; they had a tough job there. They would be operating in a glass building in the middle of town on a busy corner and would need to be fast and stealthy. That was a location where we needed the SAS to help us. I will arrange that with Bill.

We were once again in a waiting game for this to begin. It was now October, would they wait three months until the WEF annual meeting, or would they start this on their own timeline before then? I messaged Brian and Jack to find a way into the SWIFT building and if successful, send us vids and photos of the computer room, especially the back and the racks if they could, meanwhile Jeannie and Jake were working on getting them the program to disconnect any traps and another to lock out the SWIFT computer so it could not be hacked.

Destroying it was not an option as we needed to upload Jeannie's program, while it remained online so as not to force a disruption of its operation. They would be sent two thumb drives to accomplish this.

I went over to sit with Jeannie, "Don't stop what you're doing," I said, "When you develop those two programs to de-bug and block the SWIFT computer can you send the programs to them?" I asked her.

 "Yes, I'll send it through a storage program and send the code and operating info separately," she said, "OK, do we need to do a dry run" I asked. "That's not possible she said, it's a one-time use program which will self-destruct once it's loaded," Jeannie replied.

I messaged Pete in Hong Kong asking how it was going there, I told him we should talk tomorrow. It had been a little over a week since I was there and the two-man team of Jack and Brian, had been there a few days.

The following morning Pete called me, "Allo mate," he greeted me. "Right back at yer," I said. Then he started to brief me on what Brian and Jack had been up to. "They went into the building late last night, security is high, they counted ten guards dotted around with four on the ground floor and cameras everywhere." "To be expected," I said. "What floor is the computer on?" I asked him. "It's on the sixth floor with four elevators going there. Two guards are at the elevators at all times and all floors are key card access only,

but that won't be a problem, as I have a master key card for every building under my responsibility and I'll get a new card from the SWIFT building in case it has been changed which wouldn't surprise me," he said. They also had a Halon gas system in case of a breach, it won't affect the computer, but it means you'll have to wear masks.

"Pete, your team in Hong Kong is Team Alpha ok? Bern team is Bravo and The Hague is Charlie. Have they told you what they need yet?" I asked. "We've only made tentative plans so far but we are meeting later. I'll have them call you when they've made their final assessment," he answered.

"Ok when you do your fire inspection you need to get the latest key card updated will open every door, tell them this is a must and if the SWIFT people give you shit, tell them you will shut down the building."

"By the way, I'm deploying a small team of SAS operatives over to help secure the building leaving Brian and Jack free to download the program Jeannie has made as planned. Tell them you will need the key card to keep it at the local fire department in case there is an emergency and all buildings in the city must comply." I told him.

"There's not usually a problem with that, but since they are planning this attack they might be difficult, so yes, I will get the master key card," he said.

"OK I'm looking at the building via their CCTV cameras live feed as we speak, would there be a problem getting a boat for your own exfil? I expect the Hereford guys will have their own exfil and will probably liaise offshore, but I'll check with their commander. Pete, you need to run this by Brian and Jack as it will mean splitting the work between yourselves and the SAS guys?" I said.

"Getting a boat is not a problem as there are many available and anyway I have access to several police launches. I will have a driver here who will be responsible for our transport and exfil. But I'll make sure there's a boat standing by on the night we need it," Pete told us.

Theirs was the most difficult task of the three locations and this concerned me, but time was running out and we would have to make this work. I was looking carefully at the images of the building they had sent us and I noticed there was an access door at the side where there was a loading dock which could be used to enter the building. I would check that with them.

Chapter 41

Details Details!

Following my call with Pete, I spoke with Jeannie and Jake needing their assurance that we could cut off the cameras in the streets around the SWIFT building and also in Boris's castle in Bern. "Can you do it from here or will they have to do it at their locations?" I asked them both.

Jake answered, "We're used to cutting camera feeds, they can do it in each location," "And in Hong Kong?" I asked. "Jeannie and I can do the street cameras but inside the building, they will have to do it," he said.

I made a note to check with Brian and Jack if the loading dock would be their location to ingress the building. If this was the case Nick would be waiting on that side street which was a one-way street leading in the direction of the waterfront. In the early hours of Sunday morning, when this went down, I didn't expect there to be much traffic, if any, unless a guard or perhaps one of the team had triggered an alarm.

I made a note to talk to Jack and Brian about that when they called in to go through their final plans and tell them they would be working with the Hereford boys. I told Pete we would be monitoring Scott, Brian and the others from here and would see everything in real-time, to monitor not only what they were seeing but also the CCTV cameras for unseen threats'

I knew I was being everything I hated from my former bosses, but this was not just a robbery or a theft of sensitive information, it would be far too risky to simply let each team manage the planning process as they were each operating remotely from the others.

Jeannie and Jake were both listening in and I looked at them both to see if they had anything to add, after all, they would be the ones doing the monitoring with me, in what would be for this mission, the command centre.

I told Jeannie and Jake to expect any change in the timing based on intel we may receive from Switzerland indicating the plan must be brought forward. I sat with Jeannie and Jake going over some details of the call. Our next call was with Team Bravo who were Mariah and Scotty in Switzerland.

I was now thinking that we should start the end game on our terms, not theirs. Surprise is key and playing catch up, if we wait for Neumacher to start his plan would place us at a disadvantage not knowing where and when he would strike and this is what had been bugging me all along.

I was thinking, what if we assessed when they were starting and we weren't ready? Or perhaps our teams hit a snag right at the onset, after all, we were acting in three locations and even with the best thought-out plans, things can and often do, go wrong.

I remembered talking with the team leader of a small force that entered Iran, in 1979, to free the American hostages in which militants seized 66 Americans at the U.S. embassy in Tehran. They held 52 of them hostage for more than a year in the UD. Embassy. It took place after Iran's Islamic revolution in 1978-79 and poisoned U.S.-Iranian relations ever since.

He told me they arranged for eight choppers loaded with trucks and weapons to land near Tehran. An expeditionary force was sent ahead to locate a landing zone for a massive C130 transporter to land. They found a dried-up riverbed and they had agreed the termination of the plan would be if four of their eight choppers, loaded onto the C130, for any reason, went down while on mission.

Two of the eight helicopters sent for the operation malfunctioned before arriving at the first staging area one of the remaining helicopters collided with a support aircraft and eight U.S. service members were killed. Well shit happened, there was a sandstorm which took out one chopper when the engine was choked up with sand just as they were beginning their daring operation. So, unforeseen circumstances forced the termination of their carefully planned operation.

That was a valuable lesson I learned from him, expect the unexpected, plan for everything you could and make damn certain you allowed for the unforeseen. I called a Pow wow with Jeannie and Jake. "I know you have your hands full and this won't take long. I want to up the ante with this, we know it's going to happen soon and we must take the lead by acting on our terms, not theirs. Therefore as soon as all the assets are in place and ready we will move in and take Boris by surprise. What do you think?" I asked them.

They thought about my change of plan, Jeannie was first, "OK I don't see a problem and I agree that we need to take the lead but we need everything ready before we move, the risk for failure is very high. I agree, we need to clear the board now and make a checklist for each location's actions to be completed. Then when all tasks are completed we will be ready to go. I'll ask Bill to speak to the Hereford Commander and let him know the plans have changed. Also, we need to pass on the intel from inside the SWIFT building and where they will be deployed. Let's get the task list done here and send it out to each team for their input ASAP. Then when the action list is completed will be the ones to implement our plan to stop Neumacher." I told them.

The more I thought about it, the more I knew this was the best plan for us to take the lead and not sit around waiting for Neumacher, or whoever, to make their move. It made sense for us to take the lead so I called Bill and told him about the new plan.

I made the call as Jake and Jeannie were updating our war board in readiness for each team's task list. I told Bill we needed to meet and that I would go and see him and Lady Winnifred at Kings Lynn immediately.

He seemed concerned, that I was asking for a face-to-face, so I made sure all was ok but told him we should meet for a final briefing and to ensure the SAS boys would be in play already at the Hong Kong location before this goes down. I would appraise him in person for our change of plans at each location. He readily agreed to a meeting at Kings Lynn and offered his helicopter to get me there. I agreed and drove to Stansted Airport to meet with his pilot.

There was no direct route to Kings Lynn or the airport but it was a lot faster than the three-hour drive to his home, so I headed northwest through Borehamwood and Potters Bar then I picked up the M11 to Stansted airport.

The guards there had been notified to look for my "E-Type" Jag and let me through to his helicopter. They pointed me in the right direction and got on board. The pilot was already waiting and the chopper was warmed up with the rotor spinning. We took off and headed north and landed on Bill's back lawn. I thanked the pilot who would wait for our meeting to finish and went over to meet Lord Bill and Lady Winnifred who were waiting for me on their back terrace.

The weather was beautiful, dry sunny and warm, so we sat at their garden table to talk. Lady W went inside and told us she would join us later. Bill asked me how the progress was coming along. "It's all going as well as can be expected, as you know we now have assets in each of the three locations but the thing is, the reason for this meeting, is that I don't think we should wait for Neumacher to make his move. If we do, we are at a disadvantage with not knowing his plan and how fast he may implement it," I said.

"So you want to make the first move?" Bill replied. "Yes, we need to take control of how and when we make our move. To allow Boris to make his move first places us under his control and timing, with us following or trying to prevent what he will have already started. I don't think we can achieve the end game by playing catch up with his plans. So, we will take the lead and if he's planning to coincide with the next WEF, NATO or IMF meeting, he again has the advantage. Bear in mind he's had years to plan this and if he still thinks no one knows about his plan we will have the advantage of surprise." I said. "What do you need from me?" Bill asked.

"A couple of things first do you agree with my assessment? Second, we need your SAS boys in Hong Kong as soon as possible, in readiness for a go within the next few days. We've decided they will take responsibility for neutralising the SWIFT building's guards, leaving Brian and Jack free to work Jeannie's software onto the SWIFT computer. Who should we communicate our plans to?" I asked him.

He gave me the number for the camp commander at Hereford who I would call immediately following this briefing. "Has he been briefed about the mission?" I asked. "Yes he was in on a call with me, the PM and the Home Secretary had to update them on your plans," Bill said.

"Ok, just one more detail, we don't want any blowback if we use deadly force when this happens," I told him. "Well to your first point, yes I agree with your thinking and if our assets are all in place, as I believe they are, or very soon will be, we should move at our discretion, not his. I also agree that we should act sooner than later when you and your team choose the best time," he replied.

I've set up the final tasks for each of the three locations, Alpha, Bravo and Charlie. The outstanding tasks we have identified will need to be completed before we are ready. The SWIFT computer is on the 6th floor with four elevators going there. There will be two guards outside the computer room, four at the elevator locations and a total of at least ten guards.

Team Alpha has the most difficult task in Hong Kong and everything must be in place with your SAS boys in full readiness to enter in front of them and neutralise all their guards as quickly and silently as possible. Brian and Jack will follow on their heels and will head directly to the 6th floor to focus on downloading Jeannie's software. "That will take 4.5 minutes to complete, probably the longest 4.5 minutes of their lives," I told Bill.

He replied, "The faces and DNA of my teams are not on any database, anywhere, so they are for all intents and purposes, ghosts. I can't speak for the Hereford boy's commander for you, but they are well used to clandestine operations so no problems there. What I am saying is this, the team you now have, your team, will make their decisions in real time, and deal with whatever they face that is how they have always operated and if they need to take lethal action they will without any hesitation.

Also, these crimes have been planned regardless of what they will do to innocent people, so the answer is no, you must take out everyone concerned and with maximum prejudice. I have taken this up with the PM who together with the Home Office will deal with any fallout, in parliament if needs be, in the unlikely event there is an issue. I have prepared all your evidence and your intel will be given to the PM and the Home Secretary, for use as they see fit, so no worries there.

The only thing I ask is to bring whoever is working with the terrorists at the Hague, back here for questioning. I know it adds a degree of difficulty but this is important, we need to have answers as to why our own people betrayed us and to this megalomaniac, Boris Neumacher" he said.

"I appreciate you seeking my permission but as I explained when we brought you into the team, you are running the show and so far you and Jeannie have done an outstanding job with this. Others and I, believe you can handle this and you have our support should you need it.

Our biggest fear is for one of the team to be caught but that is always the risk with this type of operation and each of the team being handpicked is well used to the risks they take and believe me this isn't their first Rodeo" he told me.

"OK that's good to know, but I also wanted to let you know we need the boys from Hereford to take out the guards and secure the building to allow Brian and Jack time to get the computer system secured. I know what we must do but I wanted to run this by to bring you a final update.

As I said, Hong Kong will be the toughest, the SWIFT building is right downtown in full view all around and the SWIFT computer is on the 6th floor," I said. "Well, you have sent two good men there and they will

prevail, they are experts at infiltration and takedown. You can rely on their assessment and I agree to send the SAS boys with them. How many do you need?" "Four should do the job," I told him. Maybe two would be ok but I was not cutting any corners at this late stage. "What will your role be?" He asked. "I together with Jeannie and Jake will be at the centre of operations and will have eyes and ears on each of the locations through their body cams. We will also be tapped into their security and street cameras so we can help from the office if we see something they do not."

"Excellent! I also will be aware of what is happening in real-time. The PM and Home Secretary both personally wanted me to wish you well with this on their behalf and only want to know if we have stopped him not the details. That's for you and your team and I have faith that what you have set in place will lead to success."

"Is there anything else you need from me?" He asked. "No, not at this stage, Dave has your aircraft at The Hague and will use it to bring the traitor back. Right now we are poised to go ahead. I'll message you with the words "Falcon is flying," to say we have begun. When I message you saying, -"Falcon has landed," it means we were successful."

"Lastly, I don't foresee any real issues at the Neumacher castle, according to Mariah, there are many ways in through tunnels where the moat used to be. She will prevent him from making any calls or moves to implement his plan. The only problem will be to locate him in his castle. But she's been there for over a week studying him, his movements and his castle. So I don't anticipate any overwhelming issues there."

"We found the leak at the Hague; it was a woman named Sheri Dannetag in central communications at the ICC. Dave is located there and will bring her back for questioning." Bill looked shocked but I didn't ask why. "We are uncertain if she worked alone or if maybe there is another there but at this point, we have no proof. But notwithstanding this, we remain on watch for all communications from Neumacher. We are aware of another phone he is communicating with, at The Hague, but who that is we don't know yet. But regardless Dannetag will be removed and brought back here,"

I told him. "We don't believe she has any idea what we are planning and whatever her role is her part is irrelevant right now. We will however have to ensure she is not in play," I told him.

"The most difficult location, as I said, will be Hong Kong and we are unsure at the moment whether they have some automated triggers set in place, word is they do, so if that system goes down before we have neutralised it, or taken the others offline for a few seconds, the system will switch over to one of the other locations."

Jeannie and Jake are working on a software program that will incapacitate the SWIFT computer from communicating within its network until we have incapacitated it operationally in Hong Kong.

One thing is for sure, this relies heavily on perfect timing with Hong Kong when we begin implementation of this plan and I'll be going over the HK piece with Brian and Jack, in detail over the next few days. That is where we need a small contingent of four of your Hereford boys."

As if by magic, as soon as I had briefed Bill, Lady Winnifred came out carrying a tray with tea and biscuits. I looked at my watch, it was 4 pm. I was thinking, "Ya gotta love the upper crust, tea at four which made me smile, everything in its place and a place for everything. It was the British tradition for people like Bill and Winnie, tea at four in the garden!

Our meeting was over and now I was admiring their home and the view, it really was magnificent, they had a view all the way to the sea and the heritage site of "Castle Rising." The "Great Ouse" river was off to our left in the distance and joined the sea at "The Wash." It was there, according to my old history teacher Mr. Ritchie, where in 1216, King John attempted to cross "The Wash," at its estuary in the East of England at East Anglia.

"Johnny boy" misjudged the tide, which many have done before him and since, because it sweeps around behind you if you are on the long sand flats when the tide is out. It traps a person into finding themselves out at sea, which in his case led to his crown jewels being lost in "The wash," so the story goes. King John was the son and younger brother of Henry II and Richard the Lionheart. King John was best known for being forced into signing the Magna Carta, which dissolved the Divine Right of Kings. Then losing the crown jewels merely added to his tarnished reputation. His depiction in the popular Robin Hood stories further cemented his reputation as Bad King John. Boy, did we have some quirky royalty back in the day and I think in some ways we still probably do!

Lady W told me how pleased she was that we were going after those who killed their son Richard. I understood her feelings and agreed that we would get those responsible. I looked at Bill as if to say, you need to have this conversation with Lady W, as it is not my place to, but I suspected they did talk and she probably had a good understanding of what their son had started.

I was glad I decided to brief Bill in person for many reasons, not the least of which was because he, or as I suspected maybe a government body, was paying our costs either directly or indirectly. But quite apart from that he had vast experience as the power behind MI6 and I was looking to him to find any holes in our logic. I was happy to say he found none and I left in his helicopter for Stansted and home.

On the way back I was running through the meticulous planning we had put into place and the amazing job Martin had done in piecing this together, he must have worked with Richard Whitehead to have mentioned him in his notes. What a pair they must have been to unravel all this from nothing!

Charlene had created, in a very young boy, a master spy and I was happy he had been working with us, not against us. What he had exposed was far more dangerous than military weapons no matter how many, or how big an army is. If this was to be implemented no army could stop it and like the Hydra, a snake with many heads, we cut one off and another grows in its place. That's the inherent danger with the internet it can be used for good and for evil.

These thoughts were daunting but I knew if we remained focused on the mission we would succeed. Mentally I was going through each location's tasks and operations checking off what they would be doing.

My plan to bring this entire operation forward made more sense, looking at the tasks we now had to complete. My team was excellent, each had specific skills that would, regardless of what they had each been involved with prior to this, now be used to stop a megalomaniac.

I decided we should act on our own terms in Hong Kong late on a Saturday night into the early hours of Sunday morning. That would give them the best chance for success there and unless we had been made, or the leak had blown it for us, they would not be prepared for an assault. My team would go in hard and fast and I knew they would succeed.

Chapter 42

Complications

Our board was updated with tasks remaining including a set of actions for Jeannie and Jake to complete. It was comprehensive and I knew there would be a growing number of red lines through each task as it was completed.

I called each of the three teams to ensure there were no issues before we decided to go. I also informed them we were moving the operation up as soon as all three teams were ready.

I started with a call to Mariah. "Any problems with the plan so far," I asked her. "Nope all should be fine here," she said. "Scott and I will knock his CCTV out and all power to his location we hope he will be asleep as he usually is around 9 pm. We know his movements and provided he doesn't go out to see his girlfriend we're good to go. If he does it leave to see her it just adds a small complication but we're all good here. We've completed all but the CCTV and internet actual shutdown procedure and we can't do that until we're ready to go." She said.

There will be an alarm on his security system but Scott will be right there to stop it when we shut down their power. It won't be able to communicate with the local police either as we will take out their internet.

But there is one thing, he's made several calls to a number in Paris and I can't find who it is. I've sent the numbers to Jeannie and Jake. "Can you guys follow up for me and let me know if we have a problem," she said. "OK, we'll take it from here. Anything else?" I asked. "Nope and it may be nothing but I like to block all exits to be certain," she said. "Understood we'll find out who it is," we then hung up.

My next call was to Brian and Jack in Hong Kong, "How are things there, any problems so far?" I asked them. "No problems we haven't already anticipated, but we will definitely need extra manpower," he said.

"In that regard, we will be sending you four SAS operatives directly from Hereford to assist you. They will arrive tomorrow so you can brief them face-to-face about the SWIFT building and what to expect. They will have already been briefed on the mission from here. Their role will be to neutralise the guards, so they will enter with, but in front of you. They will communicate directly with you on their ETA and you both can arrange logistics directly with them.

They will remain guarding the corridors and entrance to give you both the time to download Jeannie's program. Nothing is ever one hundred per cent and you both know this, but as long as the two of you are running the ops there, which you are, we should be ok."

I called Peter the next day to inform him we would be sending a team of four SAS operatives to help. "Have you told anyone about this?" I asked. He didn't answer immediately so I knew he had loose lips. "OK, who have you told? I have to know Peter this is too big to risk failure so who have you told?" I asked him again.

"I have one guy and I know I can trust him, and before you told me you didn't need more than just me I told him about this," "Who is he?" I asked. "His name is Nick, actually it's "Big Nick." He helped me when I first came over here and I know I can trust him. I've told him before about current investigations regarding the Triads and he said nothing to anyone." I had to tread carefully with Pete as we hadn't worked together for twenty years and I needed him on the ball with this.

Had my friend changed? Was he still the cop I knew back in the day working cases together in Ealing and Acton when we were both with the Met? I was worried about his discretion now but then again we were too far into this to second-guess ifs and maybes at this stage.

He had thrown us a curved ball, but maybe there was a way through. I was now even more concerned because if Big Nick was so big and was seen he would be easily recognisable, so no, Big Nick couldn't be part of this takedown. I knew from my work as a private eye, that blending in is crucial to the success of any investigation before whatever we are working on goes down.

We work investigations always in the shadows until it's time to go. "Pete, we can't use him and you know why. Your friend Big Nick is too easily recognisable if he's as big as you say, we can't risk him or any of the team to be recognised, especially as we may need to use deadly force with these security goons. But I'll tell you what, he could be your driver, as long as he stays in the car and you make damn sure he does. That frees your team up to be deployed inside the building as planned."

He didn't answer immediately and I knew he was unhappy with what I had told him. "Ok," he eventually said, "Understood. Sorry, I didn't think of him being so easily recognised especially as "Little Nick" is the biggest man in Hong Kong," he said. "Please ensure he understands that his discretion to keep his mouth shut is vital and make sure he knows why we can't use him more than as your driver. Get him to do a drive through the route in case there are problems when the time comes," I told him. He understood what I was saying, even if he was disappointed.

I had to leave this on a positive and told him Noz wanted to be remembered by him, he laughed and we both said in unison, "Nozzer the cozzer the high-flying rozzer," and laughed. "Yeah, Noz! Now that's a name from the past, how's he doing these days? I thought he had retired," he said. "Nope still alive and kicking, doors that is," I told him.

"He helped me with his contacts on some of the past cases I've been working on. He's a good bloke and I remember he had a lot to put up with being London's first black cop but he made it through and is highly regarded within the Met. Please pass back to Noz my regards and I hope he's doing well," I agreed I would pass back his regards to our friend Noz.

We finished the conversation on a good note and I told him I was trusting him on this and that the team needed and depended on his discretion and input. He gave us his local knowledge and told us of a way into the building from the docking bay around on the side street which the team would use for entering unseen. It was always the tiny details that could make or break any case and we all understood this. I needed Pete to be part of the team and since he had learned to speak Cantonese, it may come in handy at some point.

My next call was to Keith at the ICC. I messaged him for a meeting knowing I had to have a face to face. We had found the leak there and I could only tell him so much but not what our decisions were now to move the timetable up.

I flew to Schiphol and drove the rest of the way. We met at a different place called "Frites Atelier," on Venestraat. Their speciality was "Loaded fries" I loved "Chips" as we call them and I was starving when I arrived.

As usual, Keith was already there when I arrived sitting in the corner. "So what's happening Max, you've been quiet these past few weeks," he said. "Yeah, working this case getting closer and that's why I'm here to fill you in" I answered. I told him we were putting pieces in place but I didn't tell him all the details, less is more, I know. I had decided to tell him we found the leak with Sheri Dannetag and were keeping communications with him at the ICC to a minimum.

"Are you certain it's her? She's crucial to our operations here," he said. "Yep, we are sure 100% it's her and that's why I've kept you out of the loop," I told him. I didn't mention that she would be taken before this went down, or any details of the operation, because of her part in this conspiracy.

"I'm blown away that she would be part of this and you're absolutely certain," he said. "Yes we are and we have proof," but her part is minimal so we're not too worried at present. "What I'm saying is keep any comms to us or anyone to a minimum and whatever you do, don't mention what I'm telling you." "When is this going down," he asked. I didn't tell him we were moving it up to a point as soon as possible, just in case.

"We think Boris will plan this for the next WEF meeting which is in January," I said. This was true we did think he was planning it for that meeting, but what I didn't tell him was that we wouldn't wait for the WEF meeting, we were ready to go and would trigger our actions as soon as my teams were ready.

"So is that when you're planning to act?" he asked. "That's the plan but we have to be ready to act if things change and if they do we will have to act at that time. Nothing we have seen indicates he is doing anything yet," which was also true. "Anyway, we are not ready yet there's a lot to put in place before we're ready so January will be our target," I told him.

But Keith was savvy at hearing the unsaid and I could tell he knew I was holding back more information so I elaborated. "Look, Keith, we know there is a leak at your office so we have to be very careful with our information," I told him. "Understood but you called this meeting Max, so is there something you need from me?"

I was in a difficult place with this meeting. Keith had helped me so many times in the past but this was just too important, too big, to allow any risks at this point especially knowing we had at least one leak at his office. We didn't know if Dannetag was working alone or if she had an accomplice there so I didn't elaborate on the leak to say we were still monitoring her comms. If there was an accomplice we would find out soon enough.

He would understand as he too had worked on many cases, all of which demanded secrecy and even now many years after some of his early cases were closed, some even made international news, but even so, he would never discuss them. This case was a new learning ground for me and I was working my way through this. I was used to working alone but now I found myself leading a team of specialist operators in locations from Hong Kong to Switzerland.

"I do need your help Keith when this goes down I need someone here in your group to monitor comms and I know you guys are plugged into communications in many countries, meaning you can help by letting me or Jeannie know if you pick up traffic when this goes down," I told him.

In this part of our talk, I was referring to his role as an MI6 operator, not as an ICC officer and I knew he would understand this even though he never admitted to being part of MI6. "Yes, I can do that even if we have to keep it away from Ms. Dannetag." He said.

This meant he would involve communications through MI6 not through the ICC, which was what I wanted, not that I needed their help but we did need to know if there was a heads-up in any of the locations we were working at. If that were to occur things would get nasty very fast.

The last thing we wanted was to involve local police to muddy the waters, clumping their way through in plain sight. We would go in fast and stealthily; we would get the job done and leave hopefully with no one even knowing we were there. Of course, if the shit hit the fan there would be a few dead bodies lying around but nothing to do about that. The mission was to stop Neumacher and his team from succeeding from achieving success at all costs.

A thought crossed my mind, was Keith, my old and trusted friend in with Dannetag or not? I would ask Jake and Jeannie to monitor phone traffic from his phone. I hated doing this but I had to know if I could trust him. In my mind, I was constantly thinking of what would happen if we failed. The damage to the world's financial network would be devastating and millions who never knew about me and my team, or about the importance of the SWIFT process, or for that matter what Boris Neumacher was planning. Should we fail, they would know soon enough, but then it would be too late.

Keith and I had drinks together and I hoped the information given to him would suffice to justify this meeting. The real reason we met was for me to gauge his reaction when I informed him about Dannetag. I think it did suffice and I was not telling my friend any lies, I just didn't fill him in with the entire details.

I had to smile; I was now playing his game of half-truths stopping short of deception, I was becoming even more of a spook than he was!

Chapter 43

Three Fronts

I returned to London and had to call Olivier in Paris to follow up on the number Boris had called to see what Olivier could find out who it was since we could find nothing from my office.

When I got back to my office the following day, Olivier called me, he told me that the name on the number I sent him was associated with a French military supplier who the DGSE had been looking into for supplying terrorist organisations with military-grade weapons.

"How did you get his number?" he asked. I told him it was a number that was connected to the conspiracy case we were working on. "Can you monitor the calls in and out of that number and if they are to The Hague, Hong Kong or Switzerland let us know."

He agreed but I had to ask that he did not make a move until after our operation was concluded. He wanted to know when this would be and I couldn't tell him too much for obvious reasons but what I could tell him was that as soon as we had concluded I would call him. He was happy we had given him the number of his long-sought-after enemy but he understood that there was a much bigger game in play.

"OK what I can do is now monitor all his calls to find his network which we are doing right now, he's a very busy dealer making many calls and texts. But as long as I can monitor his actions I can hold off taking him. But you understand we have been looking for him for ten years," he said.

"Yes, I realised that but if it comes to priorities, I can promise you I'll tell you what I can after we have acted." I explained "D'accord" he said and we hung up.

Jeannie and Jake had completed the software programming to check for traps and to block the SWIFT computer from access to the other locations but she needed Jack and Brian to go back into the SWIFT building to download the program.

Their system was on a VPN with multiple firewalls. The internet firewalls were very sophisticated and used a "Random Access algorithm" with a one-off key, which was a time-activated code. It used a separate key code reader where they had to touch the master key onto the small remote keypad then an access code is time stamped to use within 20 seconds in order to access the computer room. It could not be accessed from our London office.

But they were no match for the abilities of my team! Brian and Jack had breached the building a few nights ago to gather intel and no one knew. Jeannie sent them the program to be loaded onto a thumb drive. The program was very large so the thumb drive had to be three terabytes.

After Jack and Brian received her files she sent them separate instructions for accessing the drive and downloading the files from their thumb drive. It would take four and a half minutes to load but would lock out any traps from shutting down the system. Jeannie was a bloody genius!

As she often said, "The funny thing is that it is so easy to get into any system, from inside the system itself." In this case, they made it impossible to access it from outside to download our files onto their system. But from their live feed video, taken when Jack and Brian infiltrated the SWIFT building, we saw they have USB inputs, so we could access their system from inside their system's location.

"We didn't need to break into their VPN so they will have no idea we have already penetrated their computer," she explained. "Once the download was done, we could control their computer from our office but we would have only a limited time to do this and the link to us would be untraceable," Jeannie told me. "The SWIFT system would recognize our site, here from this office, as an administrator and respond to our commands." Jeannie even made a code for entry, mimicking the codes they used, since their system would only respond after a code had been typed in. Her code was "Falcon." A countdown clock appeared on our large monitor, timed to start once she had initiated the lockout. Once it was started we could let the team know how long they had to complete their tasks. But they also had a countdown on their watches that was in sync with our clock.

After Kwang, his factory and McGuire had been dealt with we had 30 minutes to get the entire takedown completed, once we entered the SWIFT building. After the thumb drive had been loaded Neumacher was next.

We would take out Neumacher in Bern Switzerland and shut down his access to the system, in fact, they were going to bomb his computer room to ensure nothing was ever useable again. But before we start the countdown clock, Bran and Jack had to take down Kwang and McGuire in Hong Kong.

They were under instructions to blow up Kwang's operation in case he had software there that could be re-used to try this again. We would do this to send a loud and clear message to whoever may be left in their organisation.

This would happen at midnight, in Hong Kong, and 5 pm in Europe so the starting point was to get McGuire incapacitated and then take out Kwang. Because of the seriousness of their intent. Kwang knowingly wrote a code that would prevent millions of people and businesses from accessing their money, the team would use deadly force to prevent anything like this from ever being considered again.

We were now waiting for each of the three teams to give us the go-ahead when all tasks were completed and we would be monitoring each location's actions and giving real-time assistance from the office. No one would know who took this operation down and honestly, I preferred to keep it quiet. Jeannie brought in and set up additional screens which we would use for monitoring all that was going on. Our office now looked like the situation room and the Pentagon!

The genius of Jake and Jeannie was that although the camera feeds were turned off in HK and Bern, we could still access the camera feeds to monitor the streets, as well as the live feed from their body cameras, to see that no authorities were aware of what was going down. Of the three locations, Hong Kong was the riskiest by far.

Each operation would message us to say they were ready; we would start the action on a Saturday night when the offices were closed except for security staff. Hardware (weapons) including C4, smoke grenades and breathing masks in case the halon gas was initiated.

We did not see masks as part of the guard's gear so if the gas was released they would succumb unless there was a safe room somewhere. The gear had been received in each of the three locations. Mariah told us Neumacher had made several calls to a location in The Hague and sent us the number.

We checked them out and the calls were to two locations, to people or phones we were not aware of within our network of people involved. One call was to an unregistered mobile phone close to the ICC building. This could be a burner phone but regardless it was unregistered. We were now three days from the start so I called Dave to take the jet and make a visit to The Hague to follow the number and tell us who that call was made to.

I had a bad feeling about this! Why would Neumacher be calling anyone at The Hague? Anyway, Dave would be there around 4 pm to track that number. My thinking was that someone of Neumacher's money and stature, working the SWIFT angle would be calling Hong Kong, which he was doing; Paris which he did call and possibly Davos or calls to WEF members. We knew who they were and he was not calling anyone of them. This close to our plan meant I couldn't take any risk to our plan.

Dave called in at 4.30 pm London, 5.30 pm EU time, telling us he had landed at The Hague airport, with a 26-minute drive to the location of the ICC building, but he was making his way to the phone's location which was now moving away from the ICC. We would know who the owner of that phone was very soon.

Chapter 44

Friend or Foe?

It was 9 pm when Dave called me, "I'm at a restaurant near the Hague following the mobile phone watching two people talking. One is Sheri Dannetag and the other is your friend, Keith Davies," he said.

"What!" I said as my mind was going into overdrive, why was Keith using an unknown phone to have dinner with Dannetag following a call from Neumacher? This was not good, not good at all!

Dave was sitting about 20 feet away at the bar, while they were sitting at a corner table. "Can you record their conversation?" I asked. "Already on it, it may be difficult to hear but I'll do it and send it in and I have photos and a video." "What do you want me to do?" he asked.

Stay on Keith, see where he goes, but be very careful, he will know when he's being tailed, "Roger that" he said and we terminated the call. I wasn't about to throw the baby out with the bath water yet, but my mind was racing.

I called Jeannie and told her what Dave had just found out, "What the fuck is he doing speaking with Dannetag after a call from Neumacher?" She asked. "That's exactly what we need to know. Dave is there with eyes on so there's no mistake, the two of them are talking over dinner and however this pans out this is very bad news," I said.

"How much does he know," she asked. "He knows about the Dannetag leak and thinks we are moving in January. I haven't discussed the new timeline or the Hong Kong link. He also knows about Neumacher's plan as that was what started all this," I told her. I told him about Dannetag to see how he reacted, now we know where that is!

But let's not jump to conclusions yet, we don't have all the facts. I've asked Dave to remain there, at the Hague, to stay watching Keith. He knows his tradecraft as well as Keith does so let's hope he isn't made," I told her. "One thing for certain, Keith is using an unknown phone and Neumacher already has that number. So regardless of his dinner with Dannetag, Neumacher called him on his other phone!" I said.

"I was careful not to tell Keith our complete plan but he knows enough to blow the whistle with Neumacher who will move immediately if Falcon has been blown. Let's follow up in the morning," I said and I terminated the call. The following day Dave had sent the audio to Jeannie, she and Jake were loading it up when I arrived.

I hardly slept at all running through all the things that this could mean. It was at times like this that my police training made me remain objective since we did not know all the facts. I was thinking about the implications of this. When they had filtered out background noise and adjusted the audio, we listened to it, it was unclear in parts but some words were discernable.

Keith was telling Dannetag about a leak at the ICC, she was asking how he knew and if it was a certainty. He told her yes it was one hundred per cent certain. She asked him if he knew who it was. He answered it could be one of several people but didn't say it was her. "But that's as far as we know right now," he told her. He was toying with her gauging her reaction.

From her voice, she was being very cautious, seeming to be nonchalant about the information, not pushing for a name. "Can you think who it might be?" he asked her. "Why are you asking me that?" she answered a question with a question. "Well you're in the communication centre, I thought maybe you might have seen some unusual traffic," he said. "No nothing but neither have I been looking for anything," she replied. Dave told us he was writing something on the napkin but couldn't say what it was.

Now I understood why he arranged this meeting and why Keith was discussing this with her. Did he want us to think he was on our side, questioning Dannetag, who he knew was another part of this cabal?

But in reality, was he warning her of the fact we knew she was part of Neumacher's group? We were guessing I know, but he had played his game. "Do we have Dannetag's phone hacked," I asked Jeannie. "No, but if she calls Neumacher we'll know." "Let's hope she isn't calling anyone we don't know," I said.

Something else was at play and he had done this just three days before we would move on our plan but thank God he was unaware of our true timetable. Our enemy was now aware of the fact we knew there was a leak at the ICC. Whether that enemy was Keith or Dannetag, didn't now matter, they were both in on this.

Keith was unaware that we had moved our timetable up and still thought we were planning for a January takedown. But none of this mattered as a reason why he was doing what he was doing, warning Dannetag. If we were right he was giving her time to escape.

I wanted to meet Keith again and called him to set it up. He asked "Where," I told him "Brussels, 3 pm at La Chaloupe d'Or." We met at the "Grand Place," the busy centre of Brussels, where I was waiting for him at a table outside the restaurant. We would be right on Grand Place because I wanted a busy location. I told Dave to sit close, which he did, watching from a location nearby; I couldn't see him but he came through on my earpiece to let me know he had "Eyes on." It would be easier for him to blend in, as our meeting was at a busy restaurant right on the Grand Place in the centre of Brussels.

I looked around, it was typically busy with people and tourists everywhere, just as I hoped it would be. Keith arrived a little after 3 pm and sat opposite me, "What's up Max? This is a sudden meeting, I had to drop everything I had on today for this, so what's happened?" I didn't beat around the bush, there was no time for mind games.

"I understand you had a meeting with Sheri Dannetag, what was discussed," I asked coming right out with it and I waited for his reply. Depending on how he reacted, I would know if he was either in with us or out. "How on earth do you know that?" He asked, not a good response! "Does it matter, we know you met with her after I told you about Dannetag being the leak, so again Keith, what did you discuss?"

He thought for a moment, another bad sign. "I often meet with Sheri, we work together as you know, so why is this even an issue? You've never bothered about other meetings Sheri and I have had and to be honest, I'm a little miffed that you called this meeting, getting me to come here, just because I chose to have dinner with my colleague, we often meet outside the office," he answered.

It seemed he was being evasive, but we went back a long way and he was being his usual calm personality. I knew I had to be cautious with what I said at this meeting. If he was on the wrong side of this then all we had discussed before was now at risk of being passed over to our enemy. If he wasn't then he needed to explain what they discussed.

"But this time it was after I trusted my relationship with you; to tell you she was the fucking leak. Do you see the difference? Did you tell her we know she is the leak?" I asked him. "No of course I didn't, why on earth would I break cover to the person who is, according to you, the problem? Do you know for certain she is the leak?" he answered. "Yes, we know it I already told you that several times already. But I have to ask you again, did you tell her we know there is a leak?"

"Of course, not why would I let on to her what you told me?" He asked. My heart sank, but I couldn't show my feelings. We knew, with certainty, that he had discussed the leak with her, we heard him say the words. I was both angry and sad that my trusted friend had just lied to me about something I knew for certain.

"Ok, so why did you meet her then?" I asked, though now the conversation from me was irrelevant, I had just caught him out in a blatant lie. "I told you we often have dinner, it was nothing more than that, she is my backstop when things get interesting and since Sheri is at the heart of our communications, she often helps with background info," he said.

"I understand that but you're telling me, you never discussed the leak with her at that meeting," I asked again. "I've already answered you, no we didn't discuss the leak," He lied again. "Look, Max, you and I go a long way back and we've done a lot together, we're good friends, but at the end of the day, I don't report to you and you understand I have my own work to take care of. My meeting with Sheri was nothing more than a friend meeting a friend," he said. I couldn't let on that I knew he was lying, I wanted him to believe I was just probing. "Ok good enough for me, but I had to ask."

"Are you still planning for the WEF meeting in January?" He then asked. "Well that depends on what Neumacher does but yes, we still believe he will do this either at the WEF meeting at Davos or at the IMF meeting later on and anyway we are nowhere near ready," I answered, doing the same as he was, telling lies.

I changed the subject, as I found it hard to process all the things I had discussed with my trusted friend about this conspiracy. What do I do with this now and can he stop us? There were so many questions I now had. "So, how's everything else?" I asked him eager to change the subject. "I should be asking you that he said, "You're in the middle of this not me," he said.

I was watching for his, "Tell," like I would do if I was playing a game of poker with him. But we weren't playing poker this was real life and the possibility of failure was now moved up several rungs on the ladder.

Part of me still wanted to believe my longtime friend had another agenda that he hadn't, or couldn't tell me yet, but that door was closing each time he lied to me in this conversation. I wanted to get the hell out of Dodge as this was a stunning revelation and so close to our launch. But we also knew Keith had another phone that Neumacher had called so that was a second, and for me, the final nail in his coffin.

I paid the waiter for the coffee and got up to go, "Are we still good?" he asked as we stood to leave. "Of course, we are, why wouldn't we be, I had to follow up on this and you know that?" I answered. "Ok good he said," In our world things are never quite as they seem," he said as we both headed for home.

Dave messaged me that he had recorded our conversation. I walked away from our location and Keith had gone in a different direction. I called Dave, "Track any calls he makes on either phone," I told him. "Already on it boss."

We decided to go via Bill's plane which Dave had used to get to our meeting. I wanted to get home quickly to discuss what, if anything, Keith's role in this might mean. I was over his deception and that is now what would lead to the actions we would take to deal with my former friend. I was more sad than angry but, as they say, it is what it is and now we have to deal with it!

Chapter 45

The Eleventh Hour

We took off in Bill's jet, "What do you think?" Dave asked, I was miles away, "He lied twice and it looks like he's working with the enemy, but did you catch what he said as we parted company?" I answered. "Yes, things are never as they seem. What the hell does that mean?" Dave answered.

I told Dave we would keep Keith out of the loop now and as I said his phone pinged. "Your friend is calling Dannetag," he said. "Pity we can't hear what he's saying," he added. "We don't need to, the fact he's calling her now after our meeting is enough and anyway we will keep him out of the loop on this now and see where it leads us."

I was feeling like shit now, I knew my old friend who I had spent years developing our friendship with was now my enemy. Still, it was what it was and we would deal with him as we would with Dannetag.

It was Friday, with one day to go and I was back at the office looking at all the screens Jake and Jeannie had placed on the office walls. "Bloody hell, I leave the office for one day and this happens," I joked. I knew we would need these to monitor events about to happen in three locations.

Each screen had a note above it, Alpha Hong Kong, Bravo Bern and Charlie at The Hague with several split screen images now showing on each monitor. We would need to know which was which as this would take place at night and one street scene looks much like another on CCTV. The monitors currently showed street scenes, in real-time, from each location from the CCTV live feed they had hacked into, to provide, "on-scene" images to back up each of the three team's body cams.

I filled them in on my meeting with Keith, Jeannie knew how far back we went and was as surprised as I was during the meeting when he had lied. "Did you tell him we knew of the call from Neumacher's phone to his other phone?" she asked. "No I let him think it was just a probe," but one thing he said as we parted ways, "Things are never as they seem," "I don't know what the bloody hell he meant but we'll soon know," I told her.

Anyway, that aside, I had to keep my team focused and Dave had his job to remove Sheri Dannetag when things began. We had our own safe house 20 miles away from the ICC, in a remote location, where Dave would stay with her until everything was over. Scotty and Mariah would be breaching Boris's castle to take him out and block all communications while Jack and Brian went to work in Hong Kong, together with the SAS contingent which would be the most difficult part of the mission.

I called Bill to bring him up to speed and to tell him we were almost ready to go. I also told him about my meeting at the Grand Place in Brussels with Keith, he listened without saying anything. When I had finished the update, he said, "We'll soon know if he has affected your plans, does he know your timeline?" he asked I told him no and that I let him believe we were still looking at the next WEF meeting in January.

I asked Bill if he was planning to be here when it went down. He declined saying he trusted our actions and to let him know when it was done. "All you need to tell me is "The Falcon has landed," meaning all went well," he said. "We brought you on board because we trust you Max and we know from your past cases, that you will complete this mission. You can tell me the details when we meet next time and we can leave it at that."

I went into the office the following day, two hours early thinking about our plans and going through the sequence of events in my mind, looking at our screens. It was nighttime in Hong Kong and our team Alpha was already geared up wearing all-black vests, night vision cameras on their helmets, hoods and weapons and were ready to go. I was a little awestruck now seeing them ready for action and I certainly wouldn't like to be up against them. This wasn't the movies though; this was real life!

Jeannie arrived at the office then Jake shortly after me. They went over to the monitors and began adjusting the images brightening them up so we could see clearly what was at each location. When the operation began, in less than one hour, they would both be working on the images to watch what was happening and to help each team with live feed updates.

We had gone through how we would support each team in several briefings we had over these past few weeks. Jeannie confirmed the CCTV cameras would be offline locally but online to us. God knows how she does these things but she's a wizard with anything online or electronic, especially surveillance equipment.

I sometimes think she is the real-life "Tron," able to enter the software and travel around inside it dismantling it "Byte by byte!" And I smiled at my little joke. She told me once that she sees hacking into these security systems as a game which she intended to win every time. As I watched the view was being rapidly switched from each camera, so we could see from one camera to another what would be going on.

Jack, Brian, and their SAS team in Hong Kong were now there with Pete and their driver Little Nick. They would take down Gwang at his residence first, then destroy his company's operational headquarters. Following that they would go to the SWIFT building to take down the computer on the 6th floor. They would then head for the waterfront, a short distance from the SWIFT office after their mission was complete.

They had gone over several options to get to the waterfront should things become difficult. They decided to use Pan Hoi Street, which was a one-way street, to get away from the SWIFT building, avoiding the main roads, since Pan Hoi is a narrow one-way street and would have little to no traffic when they exited. The total time at the SWIFT building should be 30 minutes.

Little Nick will be waiting for them at the side of the building, on Pan Hoi Street in a car ready to take them to the waterfront, just a few blocks away, where they will pick up a speedboat courtesy of D.I. Peter at Parker Court.

The boat would take them to a second location ready to get them both back to London.

Meanwhile, in Bern, Mariah and Scott would initiate the shutting down of the cameras, timed for when the mainframe computer in Hong Kong, is switched off. This would be coordinated by Jeannie and Jake, to give them the go-ahead using the codeword "Falcon" Then they would breach the castle from the dried-up moat. There was a tunnel under the castle they would use to get into it. They had already been there to assess the breach.

They had a live feed from Jeannie telling them what room Boris was located in and she would be monitoring the camera feeds to give them a heads-up if any tangos were around. They knew what to do then and would set charges in his computer room that would destroy all his communications while they went up to his bedroom to take him down.

His crimes were too serious to ever leave him to the authorities as we anticipated he would have them in his pocket, but we had no time to find out who was good and who was bad. They would use the same cocktail, Curare and Pufferfish venom, that Neumacher had used on Richard Whitehead. That minor detail was at the insistence of Richard's father, Lord Bill. and would be used on the assassin who murdered Martin who we knew was staying at Boris's castle as his bodyguard.

At the Hague, Dave would grab Sheri Dannetag, from her home, and take her directly to the jet, parked close by ready to bring her back to London. No violence would be required, she would be given a drug to make her lethargic and easy to move.

Chapter 46

Team Alpha

We were now ready to begin the takedown of this massive conspiracy and there was no room for failure. As each of the three-pronged attacks were completed each would use the codeword, "Falcon has Flown" just three words telling us each of the three missions had been successful.

This was far more exciting than the corporate jobs I had done before and this was doing far more than saving some corporation from the theft of a drug formula or other. But That too was also important and had helped get my company going. Now I looked at what was in my office and was amazed at how far we had come in just a few months.

I was damn sure we would pull this off and no one outside our small specialist group would even know we had. We were in the office watching events unfolding it was Midnight in Hong Kong, 4 pm in London.

Team Alpha had begun and had made their way to the Kwangtech building which was on the edge of an industrial park 10 clicks from the SWIFT building. They immobilised the two guards in their guard house using sleeping darts.

We watched as they made their way through the wire fence and into the grounds like ghosts. There was a guard office by the front gate and the guards walked the grounds every half hour. The CCTV cameras had been switched over to a still image of the building, courtesy of Jeannie, as they made their way across the grass and onto the factory building, just in case someone else may be monitoring the live feed. Moving quickly, they made their way to a side door up some steps.

The door was alarmed but they had already pulled the fuses, which were located in a small room on the side of the building and using a jimmy, they prized open the door. The alarm had a battery backup but they cut the wires to the alarm. If it triggered a Wi-Fi connection to the local police, they would have to hope they were fast enough to exfil before the police arrived.

Once inside they knew no one was inside and both went in different directions laying the C4 explosives at the base of the tall steel roof supports that went upwards from the floor. Each C4 was hidden from view and they also placed several blocks under large machinery and also in the computer room, which was up some stairs. They made it look so easy but they had done this many times before. The explosives were on a remote detonator, connected to a phone which they would set off after they had taken care of Kwang.

They then exited the area through the hole in the fence they used to get in and moved the fence flap back into place using some ties they had with them so the hole was no longer visible unless someone was looking directly for it. Phase one was completed as they moved on to begin phase two at Kwang's residence.

They left the Kwangtech building and headed for Michael Kwang's large residence not far from his factory. He had a pair of Dobermans in a kennel around the back of his home and they were both asleep. They came prepared and left several pieces of meat that had been spiked with a tasteless odorless sleeping drug just in case they woke up. Once again, they disconnected the alarm and switched the power off to his home and since it was nighttime it didn't notice.

They quickly moved around the back where he had a swimming pool and broke in through the French windows on which they placed a laser cutter with a suction cup to cut a circular hole in the glass to avoid making any sound. They pulled the circular piece of glass out using the suction cup still making no sound. They reached in opened the door and quietly went inside.

They made their way up the stairs moving carefully, with weapons drawn. They both entered the bedroom of McGuire; he was asleep when they entered his room. Moving around the side of his bed they quickly, quietly, opened his bedside drawer looking inside in case he had a weapon there. There was a large Desert Eagle .44 caliber magnum inside the drawer and they removed his large weapon. They then quickly placed tape over his mouth which woke him up.

As he started to move, they already had ties on his wrists and he started to resist them. He was very strong but just being woken up he was a little groggy. But once again they moved in unison and were very fast and coordinated. They hit him hard on his head, with his own gun, knocking him out. They then gave him the deadly cocktail of Pufferfish and Curare following which, he was no trouble at all. He would be dead before they reached his bedroom door.

They moved on to Kwang's bedroom. It was a large room and taking the syringe out they quickly jabbed him with the deadly mix of curare and Pufferfish venom. The woman sleeping next to him was unaware that they were there and they left her alone. He didn't even wake up as the deadly mix did its work. We had discussed that he would be terminated to prevent him from ever doing this again and the method was decided by Bill. Phase two was successful.

The team then left Kwang's home and moved on to the most difficult part, which was phase three, heading for the SWIFT building. On their way, they triggered the explosives at Kwang's factory.

 We watched as the building collapsed when the explosives went off. It literally imploded with their carefully placed charges. But the computer room went up in flames because they used incendiary explosives and the room was burning fiercely.

We breathed a sigh of relief and I said to them both, "Good work guys all clear no one moving in your direction," Jake told them. We took a last look at the rapidly spreading fire and saw the entire factory in flames.

Pete had remained in the car with Big Nick as they didn't need him for phase 2 but they would for phase 3. The four of them headed for the SWIFT building and parked on the side street. We watched as they entered through the loading dock at the rear of the building.

Pete and the four-man SAS team who had now joined them on the side street, moved into the building. They headed for the power room to switch all the power off in the building. The SAS team knew exactly what they had to do and went ahead as planned to take out the guards. They cut the power and the emergency lights came on automatically. All the CCTV cameras were now turned off and were unable to be viewed there in the building but not to us.

The guards would assume, once again, that there was a power outage, not a breach. The team had done a trial run a week prior when they turned the power off while monitoring the guard's actions when the power went out at that time.

What they saw, on the trial run, was an untrained unit all walking around and no one headed for the basement where the power system was located. But we couldn't bank on that happening a second time. While the SAS team were now in the building, we were monitoring the CCTV cameras to advise them of any imminent danger.

They were to use tasers rather than weapons but if necessary, they would use their weapons with suppressors. The end game justified the means in this instance. Pete remained on the ground floor by their exit keeping an eye on the street ready for their exfil. The clock was ticking as Jack and Brian led by two SAS operatives, made their way up the stairway to the 6th floor.

We watched, with images from their body cams, as they went up the stairway. A door opened to the stairway on the 6th floor so they quickly moved to the wall remaining motionless. It was a guard coming down the stairs towards their location.

Jack readied his taser and before the guard realised there were two people on the stairs, Jack didn't hesitate, he shot the guard with his taser and the guard went down.

They quickly moved on to the 6th floor and carefully opened the door. There were two guards, as expected, one by the computer room door and the other close to the stairway.

"Two tangos ahead one is two yards from you and the other by the computer room, halfway down the corridor" he warned them.

They paused getting weapons ready as they waited for Jake to tell them the guard closest was looking the other way. As soon as Jake gave them the go-ahead, they opened the door silently and quickly grabbed the guard nearest them. One clamped his hand over the guard's mouth as they quickly pulled him back through the stairway door. The other guard was not looking at the stairwell so they were not seen.

They quickly tased the guard now held in the stairwell, rendering him unconscious. They tied his hands and feet with zip ties and propped him up next to the stairway wall out of sight from the hallway.

With him out of the way they had a twenty distance to the other guard who was directly outside the computer room door. He looked around and began to draw his weapon, so Brian dropped him with a double tap just making a very slight noise. Brian and Jack moved quickly into the computer room to download their software onto the mainframe.

Jeannie warned them there was another guard inside the computer room, who turned as the guard outside fell, he rushed towards them, but not fast enough, he was too late and was brought down with his weapon halfway drawn. Had he made a call or squelched his comms button a couple of times he could have warned the other guards but he didn't, instead he went for his weapon, a fatal mistake.

Now they were in the computer room placing the first thumb drive into the slot and started to enter the codes onto the keyboard. When that had cleared the computer of all traps, the second thumb drive was inserted. It would take four and a half minutes to load and could not be interrupted.

Meanwhile Jeannie and Jake were watching the screens checking if any guards were using the elevator or the hallways. So far so good but one guard was heading to Pete's location at the rear loading dock door.

Jeannie warned him, "Guard approaching your location," she said. "Roger that," Pete said as the guard opened the door to the loading dock.

He saw the huge door was open and immediately raised his phone to speak but Pete was already behind the door. Kicking it hard he sent the guard flying but as he went down he squelched his phone once. The two guards at the desk heard it and looked at their monitor which showed a freeze frame of the lobby and the loading area.

As Jake and Jeannie were watching the screens showing the lobby one of the guards in there raised his phone to speak, maybe to find out if it was an alarm. The big clock Jeannie had set still showed one and a half minutes to go to finish the download. The front desk guard called the other guard who had gone to check the loading dock door, just as Pete heard the call and spoke into the fallen guard's phone mouthpiece, "All ok here," he said.

We saw the guard place his phone back on its holder on his chest. He said something to the other guard who went over to the stairwell and headed up we assumed to the 6th floor and the computer room. Only the emergency lights were on at the time and the only light he had was his flashlight.

Jeannie warned Brian and Jack that a guard was heading up the stairway probably to their floor. One of the two SAS men rushed to the stairway door and dragged the tased guard back into the corridor pushing him into an office near the door.

They had moved the dropped guard in the computer room to the back behind the mainframe so he was out of sight. The other guard, who was heading up the stairs, reached the 6th floor and opened the stairway door. It opened towards him and as he was about to enter the corridor one of the SAS team was waiting for him by the door.

He pushed the opening door hard as he lunged at the guard but the guard had a damn fast reaction. A fight broke out and the guard put up one hell of a struggle. He could handle himself and was obviously trained in hand-to-hand combat, so the SAS operative had his hands full as the two were struggling.

The guard was reaching for his weapon as the SAS guy wrenched his arm up and outwards and jabbed him, with all his force, in his kidneys.

The fight was vicious as both were trying to kill each other. Then the guard grabbed his knife from a sheath in his belt and tried to slash the SAS guy's throat but it was parried away.

Finally, the SAS guy grabbed the wrist holding the knife and twisted it back towards the guard then putting his entire weight against the knife he pushed the knife into the guard's chest.

Just then Jack came out looked at the body lying in the corridor and looked at the dead guard, moving on past him, he announced that the program had, by then, completed the download and was operational.

"Jeannie, your program has been downloaded successfully and we're out of here." In the office, monitoring what was happening, we all breathed a sigh of relief. They were done with the hardest part of the takedown as they headed for the stairway and Brian told the office, "We're all leaving now."

Meanwhile Jeannie and Jake were now monitoring the streets and the lobby area watching to see if one of the lobby guards had called the police. They heard a squelch from Pete's phone and leapt down the emergency stairs two at a time.

They made it to the loading dock just before the front lobby guard arrived, weapon in hand, Jack was already there and having been warned by Jake who was monitoring the situation in real-time, had his gun drawn and took the guard down but not before the guard had gotten off three shots. The shots went wide and his weapon had no suppressor so the shot rang out echoing around the buildings and empty streets.

One bullet grazed Brian's arm, slicing through the black Nomex fabric of his jacket and cutting his arm but he just ignored it as they continued to leave the SWIFT building. They had no time to lose they fled the scene with Nick driving. The SAS team were now moving closely behind them in their own vehicle.

Two police cars were just pulling up to the front steps with four local cops inside. Someone must have tripped the alarm. The building was still in darkness and the front door was locked. Normally a guard would have unlocked the doors but because they had all been engaged and were, by that time, either unconscious or dead there was no one in the front lobby to let the cops in.

But by the time the cops arrived; the team had already left the scene and were hurtling down Pan Hoi one-way street heading to the waterfront; luckily, the cops had not seen them.

"Better slow down to normal speed," Pete told Nick as they were now a safe distance from the SWIFT building and there was only sporadic traffic now on the main King's Road as they were heading for their rendezvous point and the boat.

The job took only thirty minutes but had been well planned beforehand and like anything else, planning makes it seem easy. The guards never expected the SWIFT building to be attacked after all it was just an office building, housing a computer, not a bank.

Once they arrived at the boat, they announced to us in the office, "From Team Alpha, "Falcon has landed," and we all breathed a sigh of relief as their boat headed away from the scene. I told the team "Well done team alpha, mission accomplished," as they got in the boat.

Chapter 47

Bravo and Charlie

We gave the all-clear to Dave, and team Charlie, to take Sheri Dannetag quietly from her residence. He had already gone to the phone system box outside her home, disconnected it and cut the wires to the alarm in case there was a direct line she may have for her alarm system; he opened the alarm box there and cut the wires.

We watched as he made his way across her driveway, moving on the edge close to the bushes towards the back of the house. He went to a box at the back of her home where he knew the electric fuses were located and switched the power off, pulling the fuse that operated her alarm system just in case. He quickly, expertly, unlocked her back door with his lock-picking kit.

Then making no noise he entered her home, she had a dog, a large Bull Mastiff, who slept on the kitchen floor, so he carefully placed some doctored chunks of meat down where the dog would see them if he awoke. He then proceeded upstairs to her bedroom.

She had no guards at her home and he had a syringe ready with a fast-acting sleeping drug, the sort they used in mental hospitals when a patient is acting out. It would work before he had to lift her out of her bed to carry her down, fireman fashion, to the back door. He grabbed her robe from the hook on her bedroom door as he made his way over to her bed.

He took her arm and gave her the drug, which woke her up and still groggy she opened her mouth to scream, so Dave clamped his hand over her mouth so no sound came out. He then placed a gag in her mouth as she succumbed to the fast-acting drug.

He wrapped her in her robe tying the sash around her waist and began to leave her bedroom. He also took her mobile phone from the bedside table next to her and quickly moved down the stairs and left going out through the back door.

Her dog had awoken even though he made no sound at all. We hoped he would take the chunks of meat which he apparently did. We saw him get up, walk a few paces over to the meat and after gobbling up the meat he then laid down to sleep. Had that not happened Dave would have shot the dog, if he got in the way, which none of us wanted.

Once again, all the practice runs, research and work completed beforehand made the taking of Sheri Dannetag seem straightforward. He exited her home, closing the door with Dannetag slung over his shoulder. He made his way across her lawn to his car parked at the back of her home. He slung her onto the back seat and headed to the plane parked at a small airport nearby.

We didn't anticipate problems with her and Dave would be bringing her back to London, in Bill's private jet while she was still immobilised. She would meet Bill as he wanted to question her personally to find out why she was part of this deadly conspiracy.

Bill had arranged for her to have that plum job at The Hague many years before and was beyond angry with her now, but he intended to ascertain the extent of the damage she had caused. Dave already had flight plans and as he took off with a drugged Dannetag in the plane. Once he had taken off, he called in, "From team Charlie, Falcon has landed."

Two down, one to go, as we turned our attention to team Bravo, Mariah and Scott, in Bern, Switzerland who had been given the go-ahead by me to proceed with their carefully made plan. The Neumacher home, if we can call it that, was a castle on a hill outside Bern.

They parked out of view of the residence and both wearing black combat gear, they made their way up the hill to his dried-up moat. The camera feeds were inside the castle but we had already switched them off as part of Jeannie's work following the reccy Mariah had done a few weeks prior to the takedown. The two-person team would turn off his power in a box located in what may have been a guard house in the past.

It was located in the courtyard, protected once upon a time by the huge iron portcullis. Once the job was done, they would place a small charge on the reels holding the steel ropes to drop the heavy portcullis thus preventing any movement into or out of the castle. That was my idea, protecting the now empty home and was ironic as once again it would protect the residence but this time from the owner.

They had retrieved the plans of the castle from the local government planning office in the town of Bern a week prior, pretending to be builders and studying how to move around once they were inside. Planning this was everything and we would see now how it would go down.

I told Mariah and Scotty on their way to Neumacher's Castle, "Remember why you are heading to Neumacher's residence, He was the mastermind who planned the taking down of the world's financial system without any care for the massive damage it would do. He's also caused the murder of three innocent people, and that is only what we know about. His assassin is a cold-blooded killer who accepts money for killing anyone no matter who, so he will face the same as his boss. I didn't have to remind them what they were there for but I wanted them both to be under no illusion as to why they were taking down Boris Neumacher."

They reached the dried-up moat and proceeded to the underground tunnel they had planned to use. Silently, stealthily, they reached the tunnel entrance and entered unseen. Now they switched on their night vision the images of which were fed back to us in real time. We could see the curved tunnel walls as if we were moving right there with them.

There was a steel door to be opened from the tunnel leading into the castle. They brought with them a small cutting torch and cut around the door handle. Prior to the actual take-down, they believed there was a steel bar on the inside of the door. As they cut through the handle area, cutting a curve to remove the entire lock assembly, they pushed the door just enough to locate the steel bar on the inside of the door. Using a Jimmy, Scott carefully lifted the steel bar which was resting and held in place by two large iron supports on either side of the door frame.

He had to carefully open the door, just enough, to grab the heavy steel bar to avoid it crashing to the stone floor. Although it was heavy, he managed it, by moving through the door while holding the bar upwards and out of its locating hook on the doorframe. He carefully lowered it to the stone floor of the hallway making no sound as he carefully pushed it to one side so as not to block their exit.

They made their way to the guard room off to one side of the main hallway. Once they got into the room Mariah quickly loaded a program onto the CCTV computer in the guard room, to freeze each camera's feed. The cameras would only show a freeze frame view if they were accessed later and would not show who was there or any of the actions of Mariah or Scott.

Neumacher had a large staff, including his hit man Neil, who we had seen in Val d'Isere. Mariah found that he lived at Neumacher's castle as one of his bodyguards. Scott would use the Pufferfish cocktail on both him and Neumacher courtesy of Lord Bill who insisted they should face the same death as his son Richard.

They made their way up the servant's spiral stairway which curved around the inside of one of the outer curved corner walls. These were common in castles of the time that had circular walls at each corner so they could see any marauding armies and deal with them. But then again, Switzerland never bothered fighting in any of the wars, they left it to the rest of Europe!

Neumacher was on the 3rd floor and Neil was on the same floor a few rooms down the hall from Neumacher's bedroom. Pausing as they slowly entered the 3rd floor hallway they looked and listened for any signs of life but there was no one moving except themselves.

They proceeded with caution to Neil's room, his door was unlocked, probably in case he needed to act quickly. Neil was a pro, so as they entered, they looked for signs of a trip alarm. The plan to switch off the power meant the entire castle was in blackout except for emergency lights on the stairs.

Fortunately, his room was not alarmed and the camera outside in the hallway had been set, along with all the others, to a still image of an empty hallway. There was a guard room, with one guard inside, at the back of the castle. He would only see stills of empty halls.

They entered Neil's room and Mariah used her stun gun to immobilise him as he lay in bed. Unfortunately, it didn't work as it should have and he awoke with a start. Scott punched him hard on his throat, blocking his breathing, then as Mariah brought up the syringe into Neil's view, she told him, "Remember this? It's the same as you used in Brussels and London to kill the finance minister and Richard Whitehead."

He was still struggling to breathe with his eyes widened on hearing and seeing the syringe, held by Mariah, right in front of his face. But he could do nothing as Scott had him pinned down while he was still struggling to breathe with his larynx crushed. Mariah pushed the needle into his arm, holding it up so he could see what was happening.

She pushed it slowly in the same location as he had used on Richard. His frantic struggling stopped as he froze, with his eyes wide like a deer caught in the headlights, unable to move as the curare acted on his nervous system shutting his entire body down, paralyzing him from all movement. Poetic justice and I wished Bill and Lady W could have seen this for themselves. I was thinking, live by the sword and you will die by the sword and in his case, it was "Do as you would be done by!"

They moved away from him to deal with Neumacher, he was dead before they reached his bedroom door. For a cold-hearted hired killer, it gave us all satisfaction in knowing, that the last thoughts he had were knowing he was facing the same as he had administered to others.

We had no idea who else had crossed Neumacher, but his hired gun would never kill again and within minutes neither would the monster Boris Neumacher ever give his orders to kill anyone or bring down the world's banking system. They entered Neumacher's room as he lay in bed. He was a big man, who had chosen to use his billions for terrorism and the spread of socialism. He had, according to the experts who study elections, interfered with several European and South American elections. It was also said that he used his wealth to work behind the scenes to help socialism, or as it was called, the Democratic party in the US, using his wealth to promote a socialist regime.

He chose this path for evil rather than for a beneficial use for mankind. But he also used his wealth to give the impression of a wealthy, charitable, benefactor. He was the spider in the web who now faced the third part of what every person on this planet had to face, the consequence!

As I saw it there are three parts to everything we do, decisions we make, actions we take from those decisions and now for Neumacher that last part. He would face the consequences of his actions. It would be administered coldly and precisely as he had done in making his plans to use his wealth for evil not for good.

They went over to his bed and Mariah deliberately woke him up. He attempted to yell but Scott did the same as he had done to Neumacher's hitman, he punched him hard in the throat causing him to struggle for breath instead of trying to scream out a warning. Then as Scott held him down, he repeated the same words now to Neumacher as he had said to Neil.

"Remember when you told your man to kill the Belgian finance minister and to kill Richard Whitehead, on that station platform in London? He paused to let his words sink in. Well, this is a present from Richard Whitehead's father and mother Lord William and Lady Winnifred Whitehead." This is especially prepared for you Boris Neumacher, as Mariah held up the syringe for him to see. "In this syringe is the exact same poison you told Neil to use on them both and, just so you know,"

Dave told the still-struggling Neumacher, "We have destroyed your friend Kwang's operation in Hong Kong and removed Kwang permanently. We've also taken Sheri Dannetag who, as we speak, is on her way to London to meet Richard's father, Lord Whitehead for a little talk." He was shaking his head as if to say no, you've got it all wrong. But we knew everything about his plan.

Scott continued, "We also know all about your plan to destroy the world's banking by locking every bank from the SWIFT system." He looked shocked as Scott continued, "Yes we have it all and now you are about to pay for all you've done, we call it payback and you can call it what you will, but just so you know, this is your payback and you will be the richest man in the graveyard!"

"See this syringe," he said as Mariah held it for him to see, "It's the same little poisonous cocktail you used on the Belgian finance minister and on Richard Whitehead. It's now time for you to reap what you sew," he said as Neumacher realised what this meant. He started struggling frantically but Scott had his arms pinned and he was still struggling to breathe.

Mariah made sure he could see as the needle entered his arm and he looked on in horror at what was being administered. He was now facing the same outcome as he had instructed his pet killer to do and the irony was not lost in him. As Scott repeated, "Boris Neumacher you will definitely be the richest man in the graveyard." He repeated to let that sink in.

Like his assassin, Neil, he was dead before they reached his bedroom door. Their job done they left his castle through the same door and tunnel they had entered through. I smiled as Scott carefully lifted the steel bar and replaced it back into its hooks on the door frame. But this time with the door open behind it. I looked up at the mission clock, their part had taken just 40 minutes to accomplish. Once in their vehicle, Mariah announced, "From team bravo, "SWIFT has flown!"

 In the office we all breathed a sigh of relief on a job well done, Jake and Jeannie let out a yell with Jeannie jumping up and down that we had done it!

We relaxed for a brief while exhausted as we had been on adrenaline since we all arrived much earlier. It was now early Sunday morning and I sent Jeannie and Jake home. Come in on Tuesday I told them I'll attend things here at the office. I texted Bill telling him, "SWIFT has flown, repeat, SWIFT has flown."

There was still one thing left to do, find out who Claude Monserrat was. Mariah would continue to monitor his phone to see who he was contacting before we decided what to do with him. But as for Neumacher's plan, the SWIFT banking system was back in full operation and those responsible for attempting to use it for controlling the world banks are now all inoperative.

Our carefully made plans with all the work my team had done, had gone off like a well-oiled machine with no problems. No one would know what we had done, except those we had specifically told. A seemingly random set of events in three countries would in all probability, remain as just that, a random set of events.

That was, after all, my "Modus operandi," with only a few of the cases I had worked on, ever being made known publicly. I preferred it this way it left me clear to continue, and I would continue with my work behind the scenes, in the shadows.

Chapter 48

Closing the Loops

The team all headed back to "Blighty," Dave took a groggy Sheri Dannetag directly to Bill's home, he would join us all later. She was beyond angry at being taken in the middle of the night and drugged for the entire trip. Added to this Dave placed her wrists in nylon ties.

"What the hell do you think you are doing?" she yelled at Dave once they were in the car heading to Bill's home, "You'll see," he responded, "You'd better get some rest before I deliver you to someone who wants to meet you," he told her. At that, she went quiet as she knew where they were headed. "You've been here before," he said. "What the hell is this all about?" she asked again.

"You'll find out soon enough, I can't tell you more," he said and continued driving to Bill's mansion. They continued in silence which Dave preferred anyway. When they arrived, Bill came out to meet them. "Thanks Dave, any problems?" He asked. "Nope all went just fine, do you need me here anymore?" "No, we'll take it from here," meaning there was someone else in his home. Dave didn't need to know who.

Sheri was still in wrist ties but Bill didn't have them removed yet. "Do you have her phone with you?" Bill asked. Dave gave him the phone and left for London's debrief meeting at our office on Tuesday.

Bill took Sheri inside and waiting to see her was his wife Lady Winnifred. "You are a damn traitor to this country and to my husband who gave you your well-paid job at the International Criminal Court. Your traitorous act cost our son his life. Did you know that?" she asked a still groggy Dannetag. "What are you talking about, I never had anything to do with your son's death. Why am I here, take me home right now!"

Lady Winnifred, was having none of it and fixed her with a long cold stare, then gave a nod to Bill. She turned on her heel as if Sheri Dannetag was no longer important, she walked away.

Bill took her down to a room in his basement and sat her on a seat in a bare room furnished only with a table and two chairs. There was also a camera on the wall and on the table was a red folder. The basement room looked like it was once a medieval dungeon which it probably was when his castle was built back in the 16th century.

"So you're denying you know a man called Boris Neumacher?" He asked her. She looked angry as if to say, why is this happening to me as she shook her head saying, no she didn't know anyone with that name. "Then tell me why he has made several calls to your phone?" Bill went on.

He had plugged her mobile phone into a computer sitting on the large table. As the former head of MI6, he knew all about computers, software and the like and had a program to show calls made to and from her phone. There was a 10-digit number he highlighted, pressed a few keys and the highlighted number showed up more than a dozen times, along with dates and duration of each call.

"You see these numbers, highlighted in yellow? These are calls made to your phone from this number in Switzerland," he said using his pen to point to the screen. "Do you know who made those calls to your phone?" She remained silent, defiant. "The area code is Bern, in Switzerland does that ring a bell?" he said but she remained silent. "Well ok then, the location is from Boris Neumacher's home there. We know this from matching up the cell towers there, but you know all about that don't you because that was part of your job wasn't it? I gave you that job, remember?"

Bill was trying to remain calm but was seething inside. "Now look here at the duration of these calls, they are several minutes long proving you are lying!" he told her. "I'm going to ask you politely once again, what were you doing having any relationship with Boris Neumacher?" he said and waited for her response. She was trapped and she knew it, so he continued. "That was Boris asking me to set up protection for him at the next WEF meeting in Davos," she answered. "Really, twenty-six times?" Bill answered. "And look at this date here, this was the week before my son, Richard Whitehead, was due to leave for his trip to Val d'Isere, see how many calls you took, and here, this was you calling Neumacher?" he told her his voice remaining calm and here, this was you, on the Friday evening just before Richard left for his skiing trip the following day. "You were calling Neumacher to tell him something like, all is clear he will be at Val d'Isere, wasn't it?" "Your call was short, just enough time to set up our son's murder!" He looked coldly at her.

The once affable and jovial Lord William Whitehead was now gone, replaced by a cold, calculating former power behind MI6. This was Bill Whitehead who was adept at interrogation methods, as he had been as the MI6 leader behind the scenes all through the "Cold War." Now he was, once again, dealing with a traitor and he had all the time he needed to get the answers.

He waited for her response, but she had nothing to say, so he continued. "We were hoping we were wrong with you, especially since I had personally vouched for you and got you your job at the ICC. But the more calls we saw the more we knew what you were doing. There was no way on earth you had any reason for any conversation with this man, except to keep him informed of details that he could use for his acts of terrorism. Did you know what he and his conspirators were planning?"

Once again he awaited her response and once again, she remained silent. "I want an answer," he demanded as he slammed his fist on the table making her jump. "Well? Give me a reason why you and Boris Neumacher had so many conversations, were you dancing partners?" He asked. Again, no response.

"OK, let's move on, who else knew of your link with Neumacher?" he asked her. Still no response, so he paused before continuing, fixing her with a long cold stare. He removed his jacket and placed it over the back of his chair. He told her, "No one knows you are here so you will remain here until we get to the truth." Part of his training was to layer on the proof item by item blocking all the exits gradually Bill had been part of the team that uncovered the traitor Kim Philby, so he had plentyof experience. "Let me explain this to you in very clear terms what is about to happen to you. We have enough evidence proving you are a traitor not only to Britain but to all the countries across the world that use the SWIFT banking system as well as those who rely on the International Criminal Court for justice. What you have done, assisting this man Boris Neumacher, is one of the worst potential acts of terrorism since Adolf Hitler but this is far worse because it will affect everyone."

"You must have known what he was planning and with your help, he was planning to bring down the global SWIFT banking system. Have you any idea what would have happened if he had succeeded?" She said nothing. So, he explained the damage that would be done across the world in a detailed dialogue looking at her the whole time.

"Do you know what happens to traitors?" he asked, still no response. "Then let me tell you. You will be taken from here to a spot in my garden and you will face a firing squad that is already here waiting. You will be led to the wall and tied to a post. Then seven people will aim their rifles at you and on my wife's command, will fire, killing you instantly. My wife hates you with a vengeance that will be fulfilled when you are shot dead," he told her looking her in the face.

"Just to be clear no one knows you are here; you were taken in the night by one of my operatives, and your CCTV cameras were all switched off. Your guard knows nothing of where you are. We removed the battery in your mobile phone before you left The Hague, so you are not being tracked. You were flown in my private jet and brought here. No one saw you; no one is aware you will not be at work tomorrow. You are no more! Yes, it will cause a minor hiccup at the ICC but nothing compared to the damage you have done." He let this sink in so she knew this was her last trip on this Earth.

"So, now you know what is about to happen." I'm going upstairs to leave you with your thoughts and to tell you, the only way your life will continue, is to come clean now and tell me who else was in this or knew what you were doing." He left her and closed the barred door locking it behind him. He deliberately left her phone still plugged into the computer, at the side of the table as he left her, as if he had forgotten it was there.

The camera was still on as we watched her from our office as did Bill and his wife on a monitor in his office. "Do you think she'll break?" his wife asked, "Oh yes she'll break, it just may take some time, but now Neumacher has been stopped we have all the time we need."

Sheri looked over to her phone lying on the table at the side, plugged into the computer. She reached over and since it had no battery, she had to move over to use it to make a call plugged in the computer's USB drive.

 She had no idea both her phone and who she was calling were being recorded, she was still defiant, hoping against hope there was a way out. She made two calls, in quick succession, one to a number at the BIS Tower, to the number linked to Claude Monserrat, who managed the SWIFT application inside the BIS Tower. Her second call was to the unknown number that Neumacher had called at the location of the ICC.

Now we knew Monserrat was a foe, not a friend, I made a call to Mariah who was still in Switzerland and told her to move on Claude Monseratt immediately. He must be removed with maximum prejudice he told her. "Understood" she responded and the call was terminated as would Claude Monserrat very shortly after.

Bill and Lady W sat in the garden to have a cup of tea while Sheri was stewing downstairs in the basement. "I hope you're right," she said to Bill. He just looked at her and smiled. He had no intention to rush this and even if it took days, he would get her confession and also the names of anyone else involved.

Her call to Monserrat was just 5 seconds telling him he was exposed and to leave the BIS immediately. He would be leaving the BIS Tower where Mariah was waiting near his car in the underground parking lot. Her second call to the unknown number was longer.

"I'm caught she said you must leave immediately and good luck," was all she said "What, where are you," the recipient answered before she terminated the call. She obviously thought Bill had mistakenly left her phone there, but he did it deliberately. She replaced the phone exactly as she had found it and sat back, in deep thought. Bill then called our office where Jeannie, Jake and I were following the events at Bill's home streamed to us from the audio and video feed from his basement CCTV camera.

"We need to know where that other phone is and who is on the other end, in The Hague," he told Jeannie. "On it Bill, can you send me the audio so I can maybe match the voice" she said. Jeannie and Jake immediately went into action and downloaded the audio video feed from Sheri's phone.

Jeannie put the audio feed onto a voice-matching software program hoping to match the voice. But it was only as good as any voices loaded on the system, but at least it was a start. "Let me hear that phone call," I said. She played it over the speakers, it was very short but I could hear both sides of the conversation. I asked her to repeat it several times.

"Do you know what it is?" she asked. "Not from this, is it long enough to get a possible voice match?" I asked them both. "Four words are not usually enough unless we can get those words exactly matched," Jake answered. I thought about this to see what options I had to expose whoever it was on the other end of that short call. We only now had this last person who must be caught.

Bill went to the basement (dungeon) some 3 hours later to see Sheri and to bring her a bottle of water. "Have you come to your senses yet Sheri? Oh, and by the way thank you for getting us to Mr. Claude Monserrat, we were unsure what his role was, but you just confirmed it." She looked shocked. "You didn't honestly think I would leave your phone within reach unless I wanted to monitor who you would call." He told her.

"Look we have you banged to rights you are guilty of treason, both you and I know it. We have all the proof we need and you know what that means. You have only one chance to get life imprisonment rather than the death penalty. Who was the other person you called? If you tell us who else was involved, I'll see to it that you get a fair deal." But she declined to say anything.

"Sheri, we have all the proof, as things stand you will never leave this site, you committed treason and the penalty is death. Is this what you want? Surely, it's not? If you help me now, I will see to it that you get into the best place and I can do that as you know," he told her.

At this point, he went over to her mobile phone and made some keystrokes to make her last two calls come over the speakers. Bill was watching her reaction, as her voice came out warning the two recipients she had been caught. If she didn't believe him before, she would believe him now. "Sheri I'm trying to find a reason to save your life, give me that reason," he asked her. She was looking thoroughly dejected as she came to realise he was not making his story up.

"I'm removing the phone now and we have disconnected the computer so don't waste your time trying to send or receive any messages, they won't be possible. I'm going to leave you to think about all the information we have on you and what your future will be. Help me and you live, refuse and you don't, it's as simple as that" he told her.

"I'll send something down for you to eat, but rest assured, Sheri, you will stay here until we come to a decision and that lies entirely at your feet. But make no mistake, what you have done is deadly serious. Three murders are at your feet, including our son, and there are only two ways out of this. You know what your options are. I'll leave you to think about this," and with that, he turned and left her with her thoughts.

Lady W was waiting in the lounge and asked him if she had given up any names yet. "No, but I think the realisation of what is happening and the trouble she has gotten herself into now, is finally getting to her. I'll go down and see her later and perhaps you can take her some blankets, for the night."

It was a waiting game now and Bill had done this many, many, times before. There was no rush as the conspiracy had been stopped dead in its tracks, but it was important that they got the last link in the chain.

He called me at the office and updated me on the situation with Dannetag. "It's not finished yet until we get the last name she contacted. So, let's not leave this yet, I'll be back in touch when you have found the missing name," he said. As for Claude Monserrat over at the BIS Tower, Mariah will handle him you can add, "Foe" to his name. "We have one last name to find, chat soon," he hung up.

We were trying to get a hit on the voice signature, but no luck yet. I was concerned that with Dannetag missing from the office and the call made to whoever was her accomplice, their cover was blown. But knowing what Bill was capable of, he had found Claude Monserrat and we did have a new phone number.

Bill left Sheri to think about her options, while he made phone calls to the PM and to the Home Secretary informing them that "Falcon has Flown." He set up a meeting with both the Prime Minister and the Home Secretary, at 10 Downing Street, for the following Thursday.

Later he went down to see a thoroughly dejected Sheri wrapped in a blanket courtesy of his wife and began to question her again. "What have you decided?" has asked as he sat down opposite her.

She looked at him and asked, "You would really shoot me?" he answered, "That is the penalty for high crimes and treason. It has never been repealed. Kim Philby was also a spy and was caught as the leading member of the so-called "Cambridge Spy Ring," if you recall from your training. He was part of a group of young men who all joined the Soviet communist cause as far back as the 1930s.

Philby's case was in 1963 and he was working for the KGB and was also in charge of MI6 against the Soviet Union. Guy Burgess and Donald Maclean defected in 1951, but in Philby's case, he managed to defect to Russia. Otherwise, the order was out, that he would be dealt with using deadly force."

"I know this, it was part of our training," she said, "But I have not committed treason," she said. "Well, what do you call it, passing on details of an MI6 officer, Richard Whitehead, his whereabouts and when he would be in Switzerland, to the very man who had him murdered? If not for your call to Neumacher, my son may have lived."

"I had no idea what Neumacher would do," she said. "Sorry, but that is not damn well good enough. You were given the responsibility to manage communication for us and you swore an oath to protect your country, did you not?" His voice was cold as he placed her in the same trough as Km Philby. "So how do you explain passing on details of an MI6 officer to a foreign agent?" He demanded. "But I had no idea he would have Martin killed," she said. "OK how do you even know Neumacher, where did you first meet," Bill asked.

"We met at a function at The Hague, it was a party," she said. "He came over and introduced himself as working with the World Economic Forum which was true, I checked him out." "If you checked him out you would have also known he was a communist," Bill said. She had no answer to that. "So again, why did you tell him sensitive information related to our work at the ICC? You knew it was illegal? You were highly trained!" He said.

"Thinking back, to when you were placed at the ICC, it was you who approached me for the position, and now I'm thinking about it what happened to your predecessor. I seem to recall he was killed, on his way home. Was that your doing?" "He could tell by her look of guilt he was right. How had he missed that? You should be thinking of the only lifeline I am offering you now. Tell me everything and I mean everything, names places, everything," he said as he walked to the door.

Bill left her to stew for the day before going back down to see her again. When he went down to see her later, she was sitting with her head resting on the table. She looked asleep, so he went over to her to wake her up. She was dead, foaming at her mouth, she had used cyanide, maybe set into a tooth but whatever.

Bill was angry but there was nothing he could do now. He went upstairs to look at the CCTV monitor and scrolled it back to see what she had done, scrolling back to her last movements. He saw her reach into her mouth and pull something out then she bit down on it.

He noted the time of death, 4 pm. This part of the plan was now over, he was thinking "This Falcon has flown," then left her there. He would call the specialists to come and dispose of the body.

He went to his wife who was sitting outside in their garden, he sat next to her and took her hand in his. There was a deep sadness in her eyes as he looked at his beautiful wife. As he held her hands in his he told her that Sheri Dannetag was now dead. Lady Winnifred turned to look at her husband I didn't think you were going to dispose of her until you had everything she knew.

He paused looking out at their garden quietly before responding. "Even in death, she deceived us, by taking her own life before we could find out more than we already knew," he told her.

"Strange that now the person that orchestrated our son's murder, is now dead, I don't feel any different now than I did before I knew what part she played in this entire affair. There's only the emptiness of knowing that her death will never bring Richard back," she said.

They sat in silence, a deafening silence, only broken by the birds singing in their garden. "Life goes on," he said as they both held hands in the sadness of knowing their son's murder had not gone unpunished.

Bill knew time would heal the hurt they both felt sitting there surrounded by the beauty of life, as it must, but the hole left behind by their son's death would never be filled.

Chapter 49

The Missing Piece

I couldn't wait around doing nothing and called Dave to get the plane ready, we were going back to The Hague. It was early evening when we left London arriving at the small Rotterdam airport in the night.

My phone was tracking the unknown cell phone which was currently in use moving along the A4 heading north to either Schiphol or Amsterdam. We rented a fast Audi turbo and were racing after the car with the phone inside. We were catching up and I hoped to avoid getting caught by the police as we raced after the car.

When it came into view, we slowed down and remained a distance behind it and were now following the car which was now heading to Schiphol airport. Dave was an expert at tailing and kept back a few cars. I was looking to see who the driver was but with the reflections of all the streetlights, it was impossible. The car headed for one of the multi-story parking buildings and went up to the third floor.

If what I had begun to suspect after hearing the message from Sheri, turned out to be true, the person who exited the car was my friend Keith Davies. My phone indicated he was carrying both his and the other phone on him.

Dave and I had discussed how we would deal with whoever it was. We got out of our car and the parking area had only a few vehicles on it at this time of the evening. I walked over to the car we had been following.

I was totally bummed at seeing who the user of the unknown phone was. Keith saw us both and was surprised. But he knew he had been caught. "Fancy seeing you here," he said. "I think you know why we're here," I told him. "Are you coming on holiday with me?" he said, acting nonchalant." So, what brings you here, you're a long way from home," he said. "I think you know the answer to that question, we're here for the phone," I replied. "You could have called I would have sent it and saved you the journey," he said.

"Please give me the phone," I said. He went to reach inside his jacket and Dave drew his weapon at Keith. "Woah!" He said, "What the fuck are you doing the drawing on me and who's this bozo," he said. "He's with me, this is Dave," I said. "Keith, we traced calls made to and from your phone, not the one you and I use to communicate, but your other phone, so please hand it over."

I had instructed Dave that even if Keith was a longtime friend, he had to make his own judgment call if things became difficult. "Keith, you and I go way back but this?" "What business did you have with Boris Neumacher?" I asked him. "Oh Boris! he and I are old friends, we go way back he's just a mate, like you are," he answered lamely.

We had nothing on Keith except the phone Neumacher used to communicate with him, so we were on thin ice, but we both knew that as part of the ICC and as an experienced MI6 operative he must have known what Neumacher was up to, so why was he in communications with him.

"We have Sheri in custody and she's being charged with treason as we speak. We've also removed Neumacher and his henchman from ever operating again," I told him. "You have been busy," he responded cool as a cucumber. This wasn't going well but we needed his other phone, so I asked him again. "Keith you are going to give us the phone or we will have to take it from you," I said as Dave moved closer.

At this point, Keith was assessing his options, but he knew I was not messing around. I didn't want to have to take him down but if I had to, I knew I could. "OK, if I give you the phone you have to let me go because you have nothing on me except a few calls between a member of the WEF and me," he said. "You know that will not happen, you're part of Neumacher's team and you used our friendship to get information from me to help Neumacher. So, tell me, how did it feel, being a traitor and using me to help that fucking monster," I said my tone becoming more serious.

"You've got this completely wrong Max, I was never part of his operation, whatever it was. I was using him to see what he was up to," he said. "Sorry, but I'm not buying it. If as you say you were on our side, then you would have, at some point, told me, during the many meetings and calls we had. I briefed you, but you didn't give me anything in return and you had no reason not to as you knew we were on to Neumacher and his operation," I said

I looked over to Dave giving an imperceptible nod. Dave took his Taser out and used it on Keith, who wasn't expecting it. I didn't want to kill Keith but I had mixed feelings knowing he was lying but still seeing him as an old friend. I had to remain objective.

He went down and we moved fast, I took both phones from him along with his IDs as Dave placed ties on his hands and feet and immobilised him with a quick jab of a strong sleeping drug that would keep him quiet for hours. This time we didn't use the deadly cocktail as we needed answers from him.

We then bundled him into the trunk of our car to drive him back to our plane sitting at Rotterdam airport. As we were on our way, I opened the phone but they were both locked. I would be leaving that to Jeannie and Jake to do so we could track any calls he had made.

We passed the airfield security without any problems and headed to the plane. We got a still-immobilised Keith into the cargo hold and left heading for Stansted and home.

I was silent all the way back as I hated that my longtime friend, someone I trusted for years, was part of this conspiracy that would if allowed to continue, bring the world to the brink. I had to reframe my thoughts and focus on what the traitor Richard Davies had done.

Yes, I thought, he would now face the consequence for the part he played in relaying all I discussed with him back to the enemy, of that there was no doubt at all. He had his separate phone and had used it for his calls with Neumacher and had not told me about it creating layer upon layer of his deceit.

Did he know that I had gone silent for the past few weeks and never called him or messaged him? I wanted to know why he turned and I would know the answer to that when we started the interrogation. We would go through his bank accounts, his contacts everything he had been up to with a fine-toothed comb until we got to the truth.

Once we landed at Stansted, we switched to Bill's helicopter as we intended to take him, as planned, back to Bill's home for questioning. Dave gave him another jab, a smaller amount of the sleeping drug, just enough to get him back to Bill's and we bundled him into the back seat, slumped over and out cold.

We arrived landing on his lawn in front of his home and lifted a still groggy Keith half carrying half dragging him into Bill's home and down to his basement room. Bill followed us down as Dave used the ties to secure him to a chair.

Bill plugged Keith's phones into his computer where the details were forwarded to Jeannie and Jake. I had called them on the way to Bill's telling them we had Keith in custody and would be uploading both phones for them to get into and see what was on them. It was his secret phone we were most interested in.

It took them no time to break into his phone and to compare the calls made to and from Neumacher, there were many and some were directly after messages sent to him from me to him. It seemed his second phone was only used for contact with Neumacher as there were no other numbers called, which was another nail in his coffin. This proved the phone had been set up for that purpose only. We now had what we needed and he would be charged with treason there was no way out for him now.

Bill sat opposite and both Dave and I sat in to hear what he had to say. Strange how we see people, and friends, differently once we know, beyond doubt, they have betrayed us. I call it crossing the bridge when we come to realise what has happened and we then see a former friend as an enemy but now we are looking at them from the other side of the bridge not from the same side as they were as friends. I was seething inside that the person I thought was my friend was now part of this conspiracy.

Keith was silent as Bill received the information from my office which he put on the big screen in the room. "These are all the calls you received and made to Boris Neumacher who you knew was planning a conspiracy to take over the entire SWIFT inter-banking system," he said.

Why did you choose to be part of this instead of doing your sworn duty to protect and serve? He went on, "You Keith Davies are held to a higher standard than all others because you were placed in a position of trust. You have abused that trust and at the highest level." Bill said. Keith still remained silent.

"These highlighted calls were made directly following meetings with Max that he set up trusting you with information on the case he thought you were both trying to solve. You then betrayed both your friend and your country. You also knew that Sheri Dannetag was part of this conspiracy and you did nothing to stop her. Well, we did and she will never again be a threat to anyone," Bill said looking directly at Keith. "At that news, which was also news to me, Keith still made no sign of emotion,"

"We have also removed Neumacher, his assassin and others who we knew were also part of this. So I have only one question, why?" We waited for Richard to respond. He remained defiant even knowing the outcome was a certainty. In the world of espionage and counter-espionage, there is only one possible outcome when you are caught in your betrayal, death by firing squad.

"I have to inform you that if you refuse to answer it will be assumed you are guilty because, unlike the public courts, this is an intelligence breach court and I have been given the power to deal with you by the

Prime Minister and the Home Secretary. You are not subject to the usual counsel. You understand this well, it was part of your basic training. So, for the last and final time, we would like to know why you did it."

Keith, my long-time friend, said nothing in his own defence. He was caught, guilty as charged and he chose silence. All our conversations, our laughs, our experiences as cops over thirty years walking the beat in Ealing and Acton, all gone in less than a second; He was caught through one little phone. I was more sad than angry that my friend had chosen this dark path.

Bill nodded to Dave, standing behind Keith, who shot him twice with his suppressed weapon. I was shocked despite knowing we had all been betrayed but just like that, Bill had shown us he meant business and had ordered Keith Davies to be terminated right then and there on the orders of the Prime Minister and Home Secretary the former head of MI6 had closed the final loop, using deadly force.

The room was deafeningly silent as Bill nodded for me to follow him upstairs, I was in shock. He thanked me for the job my team and I had done in solving this case. We left for London this time by Dave's car. "Where to boss," he asked. To the office please Dave. I answered and we travelled in silence. I was devastated at where this case, all from one now-dead stranger, had taken us.

Chapter 50

The Dust Settles

When we arrived in London, I thanked Dave and headed to my office, feeling like shit. I called Pow Wow and sat down with a coffee not knowing where to begin, to tell them what had occurred over the past 24 hours.

They sat in shocked silence there was nothing more to say today. "This case is finally over with no loose ends and I thank you both for the incredible job you both did." It was now late in the afternoon so I told them to close the office and we would meet in two days' time.

Bill had arranged for the entire team to meet at his home three days later. What he didn't tell us was both the Prime Minister and the Home Secretary wanted to meet me and the team and as we were all there, they arrived in the Prime Minister's helicopter, complete with a detail of armed security officers. We were all in Bill's boardroom and stood as they both entered. The PM shook everyone's hand and stood at the front of the room.

"I wanted to personally thank you all for the outstanding job you achieved in defence of Great Britain and indeed the world," The Prime Minister said addressing us all. Bill informed us, of your progress so we were well aware of your activities, he said looking at each of us in turn.

"What you don't know is, through back channels, we had all those in the WEF under surveillance using our allies who were informed of the conspiracy. At any time, we could take necessary action if required. But we didn't need to. Your small group has stopped a plan to dismantle the entire banking system and you managed it with little help from outside. So again, thank you all for your dedicated service and I am sure we will need you in the not-too-distant future. The world has changed and we have to change with it," he said. "You were all outstanding and by the way, you were all funded by my office, through our "Discretionary fund," the Home Secretary told us and you can rest assured you may well be asked to help us again sometime in the not-too-distant future," he said.

"Turning to Jeannie the PM addressed her personally, we were intrigued, if not amazed, at Downing Street as to how you were able to break into so many systems with no one being aware. We could certainly use your skills," he said.

"Thank you, Mr. Prime Minister, but I love the job I have; we have fun doing what we do and I know my work is crucial to the success of our small company. But we are always at your service if you need us in the future," she said and that made me smile, with so much deception all around me, I had a gem of an assistant.

Now it's time for us all to celebrate your success the Prime Minister announced. Just then two of Bill's staff came in with a tray, champagne glasses and two bottles of Dom Perignon. I looked around at the team and was happy we had done exactly as we planned so carefully.

I looked at the group assembled as we all raised our glasses and I announced, "Jeannie is no longer my assistant, she is now my partner!" She rushed over and gave me a hug, as the team cheered. The PM and Home secretary shook her hand and congratulated her and me.

It was well earned and I was happy to have her as my business partner, not my assistant, she deserved it. I spent a little time with them all as did Jeannie. The PM and Home Secretary left us to our celebrations.

Later the team all went their separate ways and as Jeannie quietly told me, as we headed for my Jag, "We have several new cases waiting for us and one of them is a real doozie, "Partner!" She said. I smiled at my new handle as did she! We touched our champagne glasses and said Cheers, here's to the future!

THE END